PUMPKIN EATER

DAN SHARP MYSTERIES

Listed in suggested reading order

Lake on the Mountain

Pumpkin Eater

The Jade Butterfly

Shadow Puppet

After the Horses

Lion's Head Revisited

The God Game

JEFFREY ROUND

PUMPKIN EATER

A DAN SHARP MYSTERY

DUNDURN
TORONTO

Publisher: Scott Fraser
Cover designer: Laura Boyle
Cover image: istock.com/zbruch
Printer: Webcom, a division of Marquis Book Printing Inc.

Library and Archives Canada Cataloguing in Publication

Title: Pumpkin eater : a Dan Sharp mystery / Jeffrey Round.
Names: Round, Jeffrey, author.
Description: Reprint. Originally published: Toronto: Dundurn, 2014.
Identifiers: Canadiana 20190175605 | ISBN 9781459747043 (softcover)
Classification: LCC PS8585.O84929 P84 2019 | DDC C813/.54—dc23

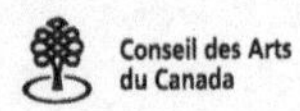

We acknowledge the support of the **Canada Council for the Arts**, which last year invested $153 million to bring the arts to Canadians throughout the country, and the **Ontario Arts Council** for our publishing program. We also acknowledge the financial support of the **Government of Ontario**, through the **Ontario Book Publishing Tax Credit** and the **Ontario Media Development Corporation**, and the **Government of Canada**.

Printed and bound in Canada.

VISIT US AT

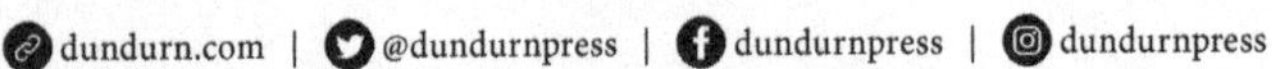
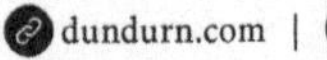

dundurn.com | @dundurnpress | dundurnpress | dundurnpress

Dundurn
3 Church Street, Suite 500
Toronto, Ontario, Canada
M5E 1M2

To same-sex parents everywhere

PROLOGUE: TORONTO 2008

This Little Piggy

DARKNESS GRIPPED HIM LIKE A VICE. The faint light filtering through from outside made everything black on black, broken here and there by minute variations in grey. Uniform, minimalist. Against a far wall the outline of a girder dipped down from the roof, warped and twisted like a giant DNA strand or a blackened starlit stairway to heaven. The shell of a processing unit stood off to one side, vaguely threatening like some obscure technology on a low-budget sci-fi set, impossible to say what it was if you didn't know which planet you were on or what series you'd landed in.

Dan sniffed the air. The scent of smoke lingered, a disquieting odour, though it was more than two years since the fire that gutted the slaughterhouse's interior. The hush inside the room was as soothing as a hand run over velvet.

An eerily hypnotic movie theme ran through his head: *The Exorcist*. He laughed silently and took a step forward. From off to the right came a curious grinding noise, like a pebble crushed underfoot. Maybe it was just his imagination.

He froze.

"Darryl Hillary?" he called out. "My name is Dan Sharp. I'm a missing persons investigator. I've been hired by your sister."

More silence.

It was just past 1 a.m. on a hot, humid August morning. Not the best weather for sleeping, though almost any bed would be better than this. Not the best weather for prowling around empty slaughterhouses in the dark, either. Dan's eyes searched for movement. He felt no fear at being there. It occurred to him that he was more at home in darkness than in light.

After fifteen years in the business, he was still surprised where he might end up looking for a client. During his first week on the job for a previous employer, a lifer with a big mouth informed him of the likelihood that a) he probably wouldn't last a month, and b) he would never be able to predict where the job might land him on any given day. He'd long since proven the first wrong, but the second prediction had shown itself right time and again.

As anonymous tips went, this one had seemed routine. A little past midnight, his cellphone buzzed, registering a phone booth. Dan heard what sounded like a fast food outlet in the background — orders being called out over the din of communal eating in a room echoing with restless diners. In the foreground, a voice of indeterminate sexuality — it could have been a young man, pitch notched up by nervousness, or a woman who'd smoked herself into a good baritone — puffed out the details of where he'd find his prey: a man named Darryl Hillary.

Dan knew better than to ask the caller for personal details. He'd long since learned that the bearer of these messages often had something to hide or to gain by passing along the intelligence. You seldom learned what it was, but the information was usually good, when it wasn't downright crazy or just implausible. But hey, it took all kinds.

"That guy you're looking for? Hillary? He's hiding out in the old slaughterhouse near Keele and St. Clair. He's there now."

Dan's mind went into overdrive: something about a suspicious fire, a big investigation into arson, allegations of insurance fraud involving unpaid government loans.

Play dumb, he told himself. "Didn't that burn down a couple years ago?"

"Yeah, North York Pork. That's the one. But the building's mostly still there."

"What's he hiding from?"

There was a pause. He shouldn't have pushed. That was all he'd get. He'd lost whoever was talking.

"Don't you know?"

"Maybe, but I wondered what you could tell me."

"Nothing. That's it."

The line went dead, the food court dying with it.

In his mind, Dan followed the trail backwards: fast food outlet, supermarket, meat distributor, slaughterhouse, and, finally, the farm. This little piggy goes to market. A curious connection, but ultimately meaningless. He recalled the newspaper photos of the fire engines, hoses turned skyward on a bleak winter day, as well as a humorous sidebar showing the char-blackened pork sides prepped for processing, now permanently overdone. If it was arson, then whoever set it at least had the good sense to do it after the slaughter, rather than get the animal activists riled at the thought of an abattoir of live pigs going up in flames.

Dan's connections with his sources were obscure almost to the point of being nonexistent. Sometimes the contact of a contact would phone or send him a message — for cash, of course. If there was news to be had, there was a price tag to go with it. What you learned after paying your snitch fee was anybody's guess, and where the tip came from was nobody's business. That wasn't Dan's concern. Finding his client was. As long as the information put him in touch with the right person it was all the same to him. With some, you could never tell. A tip leading to an abandoned slaughterhouse might be just the ticket or it could be a blind lead. The only way to know for sure was to follow it.

Dan waited in the darkness, conscious of the smell of burnt everything. Before entering the grounds he'd checked for guard dogs, tossing a few well-aimed rocks inside the fence. Nothing stirred, growled, or snarled. Nothing that he could see, at least. Burned-out building or not, he was technically trespassing, so better not to get caught by some rabid canine pulling your pants down around your ankles as you hoisted yourself over a fence.

Just inside the entrance, his nostrils curled at the smell of stale urine. Vagrants then, or at least a few ravers. Maybe even a couple of do-it-yourself journalist types. Cities abounded with the latter. Dan kept a couple on his payroll as occasional providers of obscure but useful information. Astonishing what someone living off the grid might turn up. There was nothing like a gung-ho would-be activist for sniffing out the dirt on your street that everyone else overlooked. One man's garbage was another's hot tip.

Darkness swallowed him again as he slid into a large open space. It was like being gradually submerged in different depths of water. As he moved farther into the room, his eyes grew accustomed to the negligible light. Here was where the meat would have been conveyed along assembly lines, waiting to be packaged and branded. He could just make out the curlicue of hooks overhead. Underfoot, the wire grills set in concrete would have kept the floor drained of blood and guts. He imagined freshly killed carcasses swinging from cutter to cutter, lurching down the line till what started out as a whole pig made the cut from pork loin through bacon on its way to becoming sliced baloney.

He stopped for a moment to consider the call that had sent him in search of his quarry. When he'd asked what his prey was hiding from, the voice had responded by turning it around on him: *Don't you know?* Hard to say what was hidden behind that question in answer to his question. People disappeared for a lot of reasons. Often money was behind it, but just as often you could find traces of fear, shame, desperation. It was hard to say.

The movie theme was running through his head now. That's when he heard the pebble.

"Darryl Hillary?" he called out. "My name is Dan Sharp. I'm a missing persons investigator. I've been hired by your sister."

Dan strained to see, but nothing distinguished itself in the blackness. He took another step and the ground gave way underfoot. He pitched backward. The misstep may have saved his life. Above him, the air parted with a swishing sound as though something hefty had been swung at his head, barely missing it. Senses heightened, Dan felt more than he saw the shadowy figure skipping nimbly away toward the entrance. Someone whose eyes were far better adjusted to the light.

The attack had come so quickly he barely registered the adrenaline surging in his veins. Now it set off panic alarms as he lay on the floor waiting to be sure he was alone and no longer in danger of having his head bashed in. Whoever it was wanted to get away more than finish him off.

"Darryl Hillary?" he called after the vanished figure.

There was no way of knowing whether his would-be attacker was Hillary, or even male, though he suspected it was. If it was Hillary then he'd probably thought whoever he was running from had finally caught up with him. Whatever horrors dwelled in his head waiting to spring out at any moment, he likely felt justified taking a swing at someone calling his name in a burned-out slaughterhouse.

Dan got to his feet and brushed himself off. It was plain stupid to be stumbling around without his flashlight. He'd been too busy congratulating himself on not being afraid of the dark, like some ten-year-old daring to walk through a haunted forest at midnight. Except in this case there'd be no one to brag to when he emerged, exhilarated, after not being eaten by goblins or ghouls or wicked stepmothers.

Steadying himself, he felt in his pocket for the Mini Mag that accompanied him everywhere he went, the way others were married to their Swiss Army knives. He twisted the knob and aimed it dead ahead. Obscure shapes sprang forward in a silvery gloom, as though he were underwater. Everything else stayed obstinately black just outside the range of the beam.

Something tickled his cheek. He put a hand up to brush it off, catching his fingers in the straying light.

Red.

Blood.

Not mine.

Dan swung the light overhead and a sense of revulsion overtook him. His stomach reeled. The body was trussed like a pig and hanging from a rusty meat hook.

A sound issued from his throat, half-gurgle and half-yell. Then silence rushed in to fill the vacuum that nature was said to abhor.

With his unbloodied hand he reached for his cell-phone, keeping the flashlight trained on the monster dangling above. He punched in the three numbers. The alert voice on the other end seemed to have been awaiting his call: *Ambulance, fire, or police?*

Only for what it was worth, this tip wasn't destined to be anonymous.

ONE

Tubular Bells

THE SIRENS SCREAMED LONG BEFORE Dan saw the stuttering lights and sleek cars arriving with their officers in fancy dress uniform. The first cruiser skidded to a stop just outside the fence — a little show of force, nothing too flashy. There wasn't much of an audience, after all. It was followed by a fire engine with a full crew and, finally, an ambulance to complete the set. Not that there was any chance the victim was still alive, Dan knew, but until that fact had been officially established, there would be no concession even to Death.

The second and third cruisers careened to a halt ten feet from the first, lights flashing crazily. The old police vehicles, since retired, had always reminded Dan of sharks: sleek, predatory things waiting to attack. The new twenty-first century design with its gleaming white, red, and blue motifs made him think of Crest toothpaste tubes more than anything. Slick and lean, with cavity fighting fluoride. A new breed of cop for the new millennium.

Two officers came warily toward him. Who knew, but he could be a crazy man on a killing spree. One cop was average build, youngish, probably a family man resenting the impositions of a night shift that kept him away from home. The other was oversized and fleshy, a teddy bear with a wheeze and buggy eyes. A heart attack in the making. Badges were flashed, names tossed at him. In return, Dan identified himself as the 911 caller. The three of them headed inside.

The other officers stayed outside, taping off the yard, diligent as prospectors mapping out a claim. Dan knew the rule of thumb was to cast your net large. You could always close down on an area later, but once the scene was under inspection it was too late to widen the scope. A final officer sat in his cruiser, probably writing up a request for the warrant that would allow them to make a thorough search of the premises.

With their larger and more penetrating flashlights, Dan got a better look at the slaughterhouse interior. Clearly, he'd been taking his chances wandering about in the dark. He ducked under a collapsed arch and headed into the main room where the body waited. The cops followed silently, playing their beams on the ground and over the walls, looking for who knew what. On seeing the body strung up, one of the officers made a sound of disgust; the other kept his feelings to himself, if he had any.

The corpse leered down at them. His quietus made and bare bodkin notwithstanding, the deceased's reticence stretched around them, matching the silence of the place. Death might have taken a holiday here and slept for a century or more without being disturbed.

"Hanging prisoners on meat hooks was a Nazi interrogation technique," Dan said as they stood gazing up.

Both officers turned to look at him as though he might have been directly responsible for any number of atrocities in the Second World War internment camps. For all they knew, he could have been Goebbels' right-hand man.

The fleshy officer scribbled something in a book then aimed his flashlight back up at the victim.

"Looks like somebody was trying to make a statement," he said to no one in particular, perhaps just tickling out a desire to become a murder profiler.

Footsteps approached. The medical officer arrived, grunted an acknowledgement to the others, then reached up and felt a limply hanging wrist for a pulse.

He shook his head: Death Acknowledged.

"Get your pictures then take it down," he said. "Not much I can do while it's up there."

A fourth officer entered and set up a tripod. As he fiddled with the knobs, Dan told the first two cops how he'd been hired to find someone who might or might not be the man hanging overhead at that moment, describing the anonymous call that had led him here. They listened with seeming indifference. In reality, Dan knew they were trying to decide whether to consider him a "person of interest," waiting to see if he'd say anything that might implicate himself. No one had cautioned him or advised him of his rights, so he wasn't under oath, but anything he said could be considered a "spontaneous confession." His profession would give his actions a modicum of credibility, but he was wary of saying anything that might flag him as suspicious. One wrong word could be the kiss of death. He was simply a missing persons investigator following the trail of a man to a burned-out slaughterhouse. Period. The fact that he was trespassing would be put aside for now. The more important fact — that he'd found a body rather than a living person — was another matter entirely. While it was unlikely that one man would kill another in such an elaborate fashion and then phone in the murder report, the police would assume nothing. At the very least, they'd let him prattle on to see if he contradicted himself or revealed anything beyond what he'd already told them. The rules of conduct in a police investigation could be as intricate as a Middle East diplomatic mission.

Camera flares lit up the walls, animating the corpse like a haunted-house zombie on the make. By now, the officer in the cruiser would have passed Dan's name back to the station to verify that he really was all he claimed. He would probably learn that Dan had helped solve other murders in the past, but it was up for grabs whether they would see him as an asset or as a guy who stuck his nose in police business when the chance presented itself. With luck someone would know him, maybe even back up his statements, then they'd all lighten up a bit. But it was nearly 2 a.m. on a Sunday morning and there was no telling who might be on the desk at that hour. Till then it was anybody's guess how things would turn out.

The forensics guys were fanning out, scouring the room for clues, the small details that might help identify the murderer. Dan's footsteps were their first concern. He'd done what every amateur sleuth did: contaminate the crime scene with his footprints but, fortunately, not with fingerprints or anything else. (*Such as?* he asked like some overeager junior detective. *Urine and feces,* he was told. *Sometimes blood and vomit.*) Thank god he hadn't had to take a leak, or worse. Also in his favour, he'd confined his trespassing to the concrete walk and wire grill, avoiding obliterating other tracks that might have formed in the ash-covered areas of the room. All by luck, of course; it wasn't as though he'd been expecting to find a corpse. If his steps had knocked anything into the troughs under the grills, they'd find it. He breathed a sigh of relief when they said that. At least his blundering wouldn't allow the killer to go free on the grounds that he'd compromised the evidence.

"Can you describe the person you saw, Mr. Sharp?"

"Not really. It was very dark and it happened very fast."

"But you're sure it was a man?"

"I'm not sure of anything. I made the usual assumption that if someone attacked me then it had to be a man. Not true, of course."

"So you were attacked then?"

Dan thought about it. "I can't even say that for sure ..."

One of the officers sighed, foreseeing the defence in court a few months hence: *So you agree, sir, that you didn't actually see or hear anything?*

"... though I'm inclined to believe I was. As I told you earlier, something whizzed past my head and I think whoever was in here took a swing at me with a bat or pipe."

Lights were splayed over the ground, offering several choice possibilities for weapons — a blackened pipe, some rebar with concrete chunks twisted onto the end, and a lengthy piece of wood that had somehow escaped the conflagration.

The officer turned to him. "But you weren't hurt?"

Dan shrugged. "Not really. I skinned my hands when I fell, but I wasn't struck because I fell down first."

"What made you fall?"

"I seem to remember something shifting underfoot and then suddenly I was on the floor."

"Where were you when you fell?"

"Right here," Dan said, without hesitation. "More or less beneath the body."

The fleshy officer shone his light on the floor. A piece of blackened grid jutted up, just the right size and angle to trip a man wandering about in the dark like a fool.

"I thought you said you had a flashlight."

Dan felt his face colour. "Yeah. I wasn't using it. I didn't want to alert anybody inside. I wanted to catch my misper by surprise, if he was here."

"Do you have permission to be in here, sir?"

"Afraid not."

"You were taking one hell of a risk wandering around in the dark." The admonishing note at last.

The officer shook his head in a fatherly fashion. He escorted Dan from the murder scene back to the entrance, where the flashing cruisers lit up the night like a blue and red bonfire.

"Sergeant Bryson will take your statement, sir."

The first officer left as another came up to them. This one was tall and jowly, his face grim and cadaverous from too many midnight shifts. Bryson looked gravely at his watch like an executioner about to start his work, jotting the time in a notebook. His questions were routine. He glanced up at Dan now and again, but otherwise noted his words in silence.

"Is there any chance of learning if this is the man I've been searching for?" Dan asked when he'd finished giving his report.

"Not at the moment," the officer said.

A voice called from inside the ruined building. Bryson turned to Dan. "Wait here, please, sir."

Dan slumped against the wall, easing down onto his heels. The evening had actually begun quite agreeably. He'd spent it with his teenage son, Ked, and his partner, Trevor. After a late dinner, they retreated to the rec room in the basement, hoping to beat an ongoing heat wave the city had endured for the past week.

Watching movies was a mutually agreed upon way of passing the time with little or no physical exertion. That night it was Ked's turn for choosing a title. He was spoiled for choice, but invariably picked something from the horror genre. Dan teased him for his selection, predicting the film would prove a snore of the first rank rather than the thrill its reputation presaged. Ked's eyes flashed a challenge at him.

Ked: "Dad, *Exorcist* was voted, like, the scariest movie of all time. Do you really think kajillions of people can be wrong?"

Dan: "Yes. Just look at Elvis. Or Madonna."

Ked: "Okay, never mind. Just watch it, all right?"

To Dan's surprise, the opening scene at an archaeological dig in Iraq piqued his interest. He found himself engrossed. In his experience, horror films seldom boasted cultural anecdotes let alone gifted actors in leading roles; this one promised both. Before long, the room was silent except for the film's dialogue and the eerie soundtrack that would accompany him to the slaughterhouse later that evening.

At the first sign of a break, a lump on the floor that appeared to be a lifeless bit of fur lifted its head and sniffed the air for signs of a walk or even just a few well-aimed kernels of popcorn. A thumping tail rewarded everything tossed in its direction.

"See? Even Ralph likes *Exorcist*," Ked proclaimed.

After a pee break and popcorn refill, the movie resumed. In the intermittent scenes between thrills and chills the threesome amused themselves by formulating a list of rules for surviving a horror film. By common consent, Rule Number One was, "Don't go into a room with the lights off." This sensible injunction — which Dan would recall with irony just a few hours later — was followed closely by Rule Number Two, "When you arrive at a deserted town, don't stick around to find out why it's deserted." Rule Number Three was, "Never go down to the basement alone."

As Ked passed the popcorn to Trevor, a sudden onscreen apparition made him jump, sending miniature white bombs flying through the air.

"Arggh!" he cried. "Ralph, treats!"

The dog leapt up instantly.

Dan glanced over at Trevor. "I'm particularly fond of Rule Number Four: If someone says your child is possessed by the devil and things start flying through the air, call in a priest immediately."

Ked's eyes widened into an approximation of demonic possession. "*Aaarggghhh!*" he cried, his expression more ludicrous than scary.

Ellen Burstyn had just had her second fit of overacting as the possessed girl's mother when Ked snorted in derision. The suggestion by a credulous doctor that Linda Blair's feats of levitation might be attributable to puberty and a brain lesion brought further scorn from Ked.

"Is that supposed to be scary?" he asked when a lugubrious face appeared onscreen and faded out again.

The game continued. Trevor held up a finger. "I know! Rule Number Five: Never run from monsters in high heels."

Dan looked over. "I've never seen a monster in high heels before."

"Your father's a funny guy," Trevor said, offering the popcorn bowl to Ked. "Lucky you're not warped too."

"I know!" Ked replied.

They watched the screen in silence for a while.

"Have you ever noticed how all these horror movies happen in quiet places like Amityville or Georgetown?" Dan asked.

"Which proves indisputably that the source of all evil is suburban USA," Trevor added.

"Hey, I know," Ked said. "Rule Number Six: If you're stuck in a small town in Maine or Texas and everyone has a chainsaw then just kill yourself and get it over with."

"Good one," Trevor agreed.

The movie theme unfolded eerily, its arpeggiated tendrils of sound and distinctive tone of the bells made demonic by the film. Those repetitive notes had been the sound of evil throughout Dan's teenage years.

"Rule Number Seven," he said, "always listen to the soundtrack to find out when the next attack is likely to occur."

The popcorn bowl changed hands again. Onscreen, Max von Sydow wiped green vomit from his glasses and held a crucifix over the inert form of the possessed girl, Regan.

Ked giggled. "Rule Number Eight: Never check to see if the monster is dead after you think you've killed it."

"Oh, yeah!" Dan and Trevor chimed in together.

By the time the credits rolled, Dan and Trevor agreed the film had been creepy, if not downright terrifying. Two more rules were posited to sum up the genre: Rule Number Nine, the villain is never who you think it is, and Rule Ten, the hero can never go home again.

"It's still pretty scary after all these years," Trevor said.

"It had its moments," Dan agreed. "How about you, maestro?" he said, turning to his son. "Happy with your choice?"

Ked rolled his eyes. "Guys, it was lame. Didn't you see that stupid make-up and overdone fake vomit? It looked like green porridge. It was totally goofy," he pronounced, the emperor turning thumbs down on the defeated gladiator. "I can't believe I even wanted to watch this crap."

"Better luck next time," Dan told his son.

Ked went off, trailed by the steadfast Ralph. "'Night, guys."

"'Night," they replied.

Dan looked over at Trevor and shrugged. "So what do we know about horror flicks?"

"That son of yours is a little too sophisticated for his own good. When I was his age, it scared the crap out of me," Trevor said.

They'd just undressed and were settling in upstairs when Dan's cell buzzed. He reached for it. The screen showed a pay phone number. *Not many of those left any more,* he thought.

Trevor glanced over at him. "Better answer it. You know you won't sleep until you do."

Dan sighed.

"Sharp." He listened for a while in silence then said, "Didn't that burn down a couple years ago?"

Trevor rolled over to watch him.

"What's he hiding from?" Then, after a pause, "Maybe, but I wondered what you could tell me."

The call ended abruptly.

"Damn."

Trevor looked over at Dan.

"Duty calls," Dan said, sitting up.

Trevor glanced at the bedside clock. "It's past midnight."

"I know, sorry. Don't wait up."

"I won't." Trevor pulled the covers up to his chin. "Have fun. Don't forget your crucifix."

It would have been good advice, if he'd followed it.

A voice crackled out of a walkie-talkie somewhere deep inside the slaughterhouse.

"Shit! Did you see this?"

"See what?" answered a second voice. Then "Holy crap! We gotta let the chief know right away."

Dan's imagination was running riot. What could be worse than a body strung up on a meat hook? Were there others he hadn't seen? He was alert as the officer returned and headed for the cruiser.

Bryson mumbled a few words into his cell, then, "Yeah, he's on a meat hook. Just like the guy said." He glanced at Dan. "But it gets weirder. Guy's missing an ear. It's sliced clean off." There was a pause. "Left, I think. Hang on." He picked up the walkie-talkie. "Harvey. Which ear?"

"The left one," came the reply.

"Yeah, left," Dan heard the first officer say.

This was followed by silence. Dan could hear the man's breathing quicken. "Yes, sir." His body stiffened. "Yes, sir. I understand fully."

Dan waited, curious, while the officer concluded his call.

The cop turned his grim face to Dan. "Anything else you can tell us?"

"Not that I can think of."

"All right. You need to leave now."

He brushed past Dan and headed back to the building. Dan followed.

"How can I find out if this is my guy or not?"

Officer Bryson halted. "Mr. Sharp, sir, you need to leave the site immediately."

"Sure, but who can I talk to once the identification is made?"

Bryson gave him a dismissive stare. "If you don't leave now, I'll have to charge you with trespassing. Or I could take you down to the station for a formal briefing. Do you want that, Mr. Sharp?"

"No."

The officer softened a bit. "There's no identification on the body. It could take a while. Maybe if you brought some dental records for your guy to the coroner's office tomorrow, you might get an answer."

He turned and entered the slaughterhouse. Dan didn't wait for a second invitation to leave.

TWO

The Vanishing Point

It was nearly three o'clock by the time Dan got back in his car. He'd been at the slaughterhouse almost two hours, most of that time with the officers. Now, heading east along St. Clair Avenue, he reviewed the facts in his mind. Three days earlier, he received a call from a woman claiming her brother had been missing since the previous afternoon. Was that too soon to declare him missing officially? No, Dan said. Not if she felt his disappearance was suspicious or unusual. In which case it was better to act sooner than later.

The woman, Darlene Hillary, had been frantic. Dan waited till she settled down before pressing her. Why did she think his disappearance was suspicious? That was easy: her brother, Darryl, almost never left the house and when he did he always left a note. *Agoraphobe*, Dan concluded. That morning, Darlene continued, when she was on her way to work, her brother hadn't said anything about going out. When she returned, he was gone. Could he be anywhere else? No, not that she could think of. Was it possible he got delayed somewhere and found himself unable to get in touch? That, too, was unlikely, she said. Nor had he taken any personal belongings, leaving out the possibility of an extended trip.

The answers were not encouraging. Worse, Darlene said her brother had received a threatening note and several disturbing anonymous calls over the past few months. He hadn't wanted to talk about them, but she wheedled it out of him when he began acting strangely, obsessing over locking doors and keeping the windows closed and the curtains drawn at all times. Clearly he believed the threats were real, though he hadn't told his sister what they were about. Dan listened with careful gravity. If someone was serious enough to make threats, then whoever it was might be serious enough to carry them out, though a final verdict was premature.

Almost all of Dan's questions hit dead ends. Darryl hadn't held a job in five years and therefore had no work colleagues, past or present, to question. He hadn't fraternized with neighbours, frequented pool halls or movie houses, so there was no one to ask about the last time they'd seen him socially. His sister worked at an old age home and was often gone for the better part of the day or night, depending on her shift. As far as she knew, her brother spent most of his free time watching TV in his bedroom or outside in their backyard. That habit ended suddenly when the calls started. The one possible lead that held out hope for Dan, as slim as it might seem, was that Darlene's brother was an occasional dope smoker. She'd admitted that after much hesitation, seeming to think it a grievous liability. "It's not that unusual," he reassured her.

Finding the drug dealers in any given neighbourhood was a shell game. Ask the right questions at the right time and you'd hit a mainline of information. The wrong questions asked of the wrong person on the wrong day, and you were almost guaranteed to see everybody's heads disappear, like a beach full of crabs at low tide. Lots of holes, but nothing showing aboveground. Once they got spooked, they could stay that way for months. Nobody forced these small-time dealers to sell their wares. For most of them, it was part-time work you did on top of your regular job as an underpaid garage mechanic or counter clerk at a late-night donut shop. A little *moolah* to ease the pain of whatever life didn't provide naturally. Selling crack to pay off the Mafia or to fund your own addiction was another matter, of course. There was often urgency there, but Dan doubted he was chasing that kind of animal.

"Darryl's a gentle man," his sister insisted.

A guitar player and a poet, as it turned out. In other words, the kind of guy who picked up a little weed in the neighbourhood then came home and smoked it in the solitude of his garage, with nobody the wiser. Only in this case it seemed he'd somehow got mixed up with the wrong crowd.

Darryl Hillary was beginning to sound a little weird. He was also one of the most reclusive, introverted young men in the city. According to his sister, almost no one knew of his existence. But even poets must have friends, Dan thought. And apparently an enemy or two, as well. Then again, weren't writers and journalists the first to be silenced? An uncensored poet could be a dangerous thing indeed. But in that case, if the body turned out to be his, why cut off an ear? Why not a tongue instead?

Dan sent in the usual requests for background checks. Nothing arrived on Friday and everything slowed down by the weekend. It was now going on sixty hours since the call with Hillary's sister. In that time, Dan had managed to find the local pusher, the one who supplied the neighbourhood weed. He repaired motors at a small appliance store. No glamour there. Clearly not a big-time dealer. The man was wary when Dan approached, no doubt worried about a bust. He loosened up when Dan flashed the picture and explained why he was looking for Darryl, while assuring him he wasn't a cop. The man admitted to knowing Darryl — Dan was careful not to ask in what context — but sounded convincing when he said he hadn't seen him in several months. Which likely meant that Hillary had scored big the last time they'd been in contact, though he wasn't about to ask for details of the transaction or to wonder if he was keeping proper sales tax records. Dan left his card and a request to be in touch if Darryl contacted him.

Heading downtown now, he wondered if it was this contact that had netted the call from the fast food outlet earlier in the evening. Dan was even reasonably sure which diner it was — there was only one open late in that neighbourhood, at the corner of Lansdowne and St. Clair, not far from the former abattoir. If he drove past now it would still be open, though his anonymous caller would long since have wolfed down an order of fries and a burger and bolted.

He turned south and headed east on College Street, past Yonge and over to Church. Despite the hour, the hookers were still on their corners, long-legged and ever optimistic that Daddy Warbucks would be cruising in their direction any minute. *Got the time? Your place or mine?* It was more than two decades since Dan had seen anything from that side of the fence, but there was a period in his teenage years when he'd needed to support himself. He'd done that by standing on a downtown corner until he met the man who would take him away from all that, briefly, before getting onto the straight-and-somewhat-narrow in his early twenties after finding himself the father of a young boy.

At seventeen, however, Dan had been desperate to escape his claustrophobic, dysfunctional background and his abusive, barely communicative father. He'd left the old man to drink himself to death, a task Stuart Sharp had accomplished quickly and efficiently once he got down to the business at hand, one of the few successes in his otherwise un-noteworthy life. Dan's mother's early death due to pneumonia was something he preferred not to dwell on, if he could avoid it.

In fact, when he considered his beginnings, Dan felt he'd been lucky overall. Life had its surprising twists and turns, but somehow his had turned out all right, where other people's hadn't. He was never more aware of this than when sitting down with clients to discuss the loved ones who'd disappeared — some after fights, some after disappointments, while others simply vanished without leaving a clue as to where they'd gone. Or why. He'd become expert at ferreting out the signs, following them like a trail of breadcrumbs to learn how and why people reinvented themselves. Assuming they were lucky enough to be given a choice and a second chance, that is. He became adept at sniffing the air, picking up the scent of one life and following it to where it morphed into another, the mismatched remnants of a shattered vessel pieced together into something that resembled a whole again. Those were the relatively lucky ones, Dan knew. Then there were the thousands who approached some kind of vanishing point and were never heard from again, donning a cloak of invisibility. Who knew, but some of them could be standing on a nearby street corner right now, having joined the ranks of the Girls of the Night.

Dan's stomach growled: it was payback time for staying up late. He swung south and headed down to the lake, following the concrete trail beneath the Gardiner Expressway, past the film studios and dockyard canals. A burger and fries combo from Wendy's was uppermost on his mind. He stopped at the Leslie Street outlet, the one with the friendly Jamaican woman who was there every night, no matter what time he turned up. He imagined she had kids to support, debts to pay off. Otherwise, why would she be there grinning like a madwoman at 3:18 in the morning?

He handed over his change and silently wished her a better future, whatever it might be, while wondering if Darryl Hillary liked Wendy's combos. Dan gratefully accepted the pungent-smelling bag of carbs and grease and a large Frosty before driving on. With one hand plunged into the paper to draw out a fistful of stringy fries, he passed the turn-off that would have led home. Instead, seemingly of its own accord, the car turned left on Queen Street, heading back over the Don Valley until it reached a cul-de-sac with a thicket of townhouses springing up like mushrooms. He stopped in front of a tall grey unit in a row of five. This place would soon have his name on it. His and Trevor's, if things turned out. Kedrick's, too, but that would be temporary now that Ked was nearing the end of high school and starting to think about university. And so the page turned, Dan mused.

His new neighbourhood was Corktown, a roughly triangular area bounded on the south and east by the Don River where it fed into Lake Ontario. To the north, Regent Park's housing projects were jammed together with the privileged gentrification of Cabbagetown, while poor, unfashionable Moss Park and its homeless shelters lay to the west. With Dan's rag-tag background, he could rightly claim to belong to all of these groups, and none.

Some declared that Corktown got its name from the wave of Irish immigrants arriving in the early-nineteenth century, though Dan preferred the local legend that it was due to the many breweries and a cork manufacturer that once employed a good number of the area's residents. In any case, it was a decidedly old world slice of Toronto's past containing the city's first Catholic parish. Somewhere beneath a current-day schoolyard, an unmarked graveyard held the remains of those parishioners, fleeing poverty and famine in the old world only to find death in the new one. Poor Protestants who couldn't afford the pew fees at nearby St. James Anglican Cathedral eventually erected their own place of worship, Little Trinity, the city's oldest surviving church. A Tudor Gothic structure built "for all people," it was set smack on King Street, the new arrivals seemingly unable to shake off the aristocratic shadows of the Dominion even here.

This would be Dan's second house in the city. Fifteen years earlier, he had bought his current home at the foot of Leslieville during a slump in the market. It had cost considerably less than expected, but he'd taken his good fortune in stride and made the best of it. Now, with the anticipated addition — meaning Trevor — his domestic arrangements needed expanding. He'd bid on the current property and paid dearly for it, gratefully accepting Trevor's offer to remake the interior and oversee the project's completion. It promised to be quietly spectacular when done. Dan was counting on that. It had to be right; this was probably the last place he'd buy before his retirement, if that day ever arrived.

He rolled down his window and gazed up at the structure. So far, things had gone according to schedule. The roof had been replaced and the interior gutted. Last week, the builders had installed new window casements on the upper floor. They gleamed in the dark. Once painted, however, they would blend in nicely. Trevor had worked hard to reassure the anxious community reps that no drastic changes would be made to the building's exterior. He promised to maintain the historic façade, matching it with those on either side. Dan liked being the townhouse in the middle, though he hoped for nicer neighbours than the current ones in newly trendified Leslieville, where the money had been flocking of late.

Grabbing his bag of fries and half-eaten hamburger, he stepped out of the car. He approached the house as though it were a nervous horse, touching the brick with his fingertips and feeling the city's restless pulse beneath his hands. *Home.* In his mind, he envisioned living here with Trevor and Ked, meeting the neighbours, learning the ins-and-outs of the community: which market had the best vegetables and fruits, which butcher to go to for the freshest cuts of meat, who the neighbourhood characters were.

Domesticity was growing on him daily. He couldn't wait to move in officially with Trevor. It would dispel the unease he felt waiting for their relationship to settle. At present, Trevor travelled back and forth from Toronto to the west coast, where he carried out occasional renovation projects. When the new house was finished, he'd move here for good. A new neighbourhood meant a new beginning, a new corner turned in life. It felt right.

Dan's mind went to the dark cloud on his horizon. Coaxing Trevor from his rustic British Columbia villa had been a protracted exercise. A self-proclaimed sociophobe, he'd lived in semi-retirement for the past half-dozen years on Mayne Island, a lesser-known cousin of Salt Springs in the Southern Gulf chains. One of the things Dan had enticed him with was the prospect of running the renovation project. Trevor had accepted, but on a no-promises, no-payment basis. If he stayed, the payment would be to live with Dan. He was unsure if he could fulfil that promise, however. Architectural design had been his occupation at one time, but he'd largely left it behind when he retreated to Mayne Island after the death of his lover. While living the life of a hermit had helped him regain his equilibrium, he wasn't sure that returning to urban life was on the agenda for him.

Dan monitored the progress anxiously. From the start, Trevor found Toronto challenging. Too much concrete. Too many buildings swaying overhead and blotting out the sky. Too many people. It was very different from his west coast Pleasantville existence, with its sweeping vistas of snow-capped mountains on one side and the endless ocean on the other. Dan had promised him Toronto wouldn't be all that different, but who was he fooling?

Meeting Trevor had transformed Dan's life. He now woke with a sense of excitement and purpose, a fervour he hadn't felt in years. Even Ked noticed it. "This guy does something for you, Dad. I hope he stays."

"So do I, Ked."

And so love came calling. Warm, funny, comfortable, just short of bearing tea and crumpets. A shimmering of light on the edge of the horizon. After all these years, it was looking like the real thing and standing in the shadow of the possible. Dan wasn't reluctant to accept the feelings, just slow to trust whether he could manage to love and be loved without losing his sense of self.

Purchasing the new home had taken a leap of faith. After leaving his former employer to work on his own, his reserves had dwindled. The housing market was sluggish; otherwise he'd simply have sold his current house and moved. Instinct told him to wait. While the country's neighbour to the south was mired in an economic recession, Canada had held its own for the most part, but he couldn't afford to sell just yet.

For the past decade, Dan had wanted to leave the city nearly every day. Toronto rubbed him raw in every possible way, but suddenly, ironically, just as he met someone who lived elsewhere he found he wanted to stay. For one thing, Ked needed him here. Ked's mother also lived in the city. Though she and Dan had never been a couple in the domestic sense — he joked that Ked was the result of his one slip into heterosexuality — their relationship was strong and central to Ked's life and well-being. In addition, Dan's best friend, Donny, lived here too. Until Dan met Trevor, that friendship had been the single most important relationship in his life, apart from Kedrick.

All this went through his mind as he sat on the stoop and finished his burger combo. He tucked the wrappers inside one another and stood, looking up. This was his future. Somehow, he'd intertwined the house's progress with the success of his new relationship. It was irrational, but the joy he felt on seeing the change was palpable. If one went smoothly, then it followed that the other would too.

A ragged light showed in the east as he parked his car. The streetlamps appeared as pools of blue against the thinning darkness overhead. He entered a silent house. Ralph wagged a tentative greeting from his bed in the kitchen, as if unsure whether to welcome Dan's late return. Surely there were rules about such things, even for humans?

Dan emptied his pockets, tossing keys and wallet onto the kitchen table, before running a glass of water. He took the glass into the living room and looked around. It was a welcoming home, one with signs of good taste, even in the dark. The floorboards were worn and the rugs faded, but the overall design said "solid." It wasn't exceptional as houses went, but it was a home and a well-loved one. Now he was about to leave it behind. Until this moment he hadn't thought how that would feel. Funny, he'd wanted to move for years, and now that he was about to do so he felt a sense of regret. It wouldn't stop him, though.

Light showed against the floor outside the bedroom. He pushed open the door and peered in. Trevor was sitting up reading by a bedside lamp. His features looked almost translucent, the skin pale with fatigue. His hair was matted from being pressed against the pillow. Dan guessed he'd simply given up fighting to get to sleep.

"Hi there."

Trevor put his book aside. "Welcome back."

Dan glanced over at the clock: 4:33 a.m. "Wow, it's late," he said, as though it had just occurred to him.

"Or very early, depending on your point of view," Trevor replied with a tired smile.

"I've just been to the new house," Dan said apologetically.

"How is it? Still there?"

"Pretty much. Looks good."

Trevor waited.

"I didn't want to call and chance waking you."

"I was up. I was a little worried."

"Sorry. It was inconsiderate." Dan held out his Frosty, melted down to a gelatinous sludge at the bottom.

Trevor accepted the cup. "A very bad habit, but thanks."

He sipped and returned it. Dan emptied it in a single gulp before dropping it into the garbage. He nestled in beside Trevor without taking off his clothes, as though another call might send him running off again.

Trevor ran a finger over his forearm. "Anything to report?"

Dan hesitated. He didn't want Trevor worrying he was risking his health or his life. Having already lost one partner, a second who purposely took risks might prove too difficult to bear.

Dan tried to make light of it. "I broke Rule Number One of surviving in a horror film: Don't go into a room with the lights off."

He gave a brief account of his find, without mentioning the state he'd found the body in. It might or might not make the newspapers over the next few days, but there was no need to force-feed Trevor the gruesome details.

"Is there more?"

Dan nodded slightly. "Whoever it was took a swing at me with a pipe, but he missed."

Trevor stiffened.

"I wasn't hurt," Dan quickly added.

"This time." Panic showed in Trevor's eyes, the fear of harm coming to someone he loved. The unspoken *What if?*

"This time, yes. Next time I'll be more careful."

Trevor shook his head. "You sound like a kid who just missed being hit by a car on his bike. How do you know you'll be more careful next time?"

Dan wanted to say that next time he wouldn't go tramping around the ruins of a burnt-out building without using his flashlight, or even that he wouldn't go at night, but it was just as likely that he would eventually find himself in some sort of danger. He couldn't avoid it forever.

"I know because I've got you and Ked to think about. I wouldn't want to lose you."

He reached for Trevor's hand and pressed it against his lips. Trevor gave him a slight smile: The Bogey Man Averted. For now, at least.

There was an intertwining of limbs as they sought each other. Before anything could be decided, fatigue took over and desire backed down. After a few minutes of cuddling and stroking, Trevor fell asleep. His grip loosened on Dan's biceps, the fingers straying across his chest.

Dan listened to Trevor's breathing. His mind was still in the grip of images gleaned earlier in the evening, pulling him back to the discovery at the slaughterhouse. None of it made sense without knowing why his client had been targeted. Assuming the dead man was Darryl Hillary, of course. He fell asleep with those thoughts in his head and Trevor snoring softly beside him. The alarm woke him three hours later.

THREE

The Rue Morgue

STILL WEARING HIS DRESSING GOWN, Dan stepped onto the back patio, coffee in one hand and newspaper in the other. The sun was bright; the air hung heavy with humidity. It already felt more like 35 Celsius than the mere 29 degrees the forecasters were predicting. Another hot one.

The paper carried an update about a sporadic series of garage fires in the city. They'd carried on through the summer. Just when you thought they were over, another popped up. Always garages, always in the middle of the night, but so far no injuries. Someone wanted to give the residents a good scare. Or maybe they simply wanted to add to the city's growing pains, tossing panic alongside transit confusion and the cacophony of languages as different cultures were set side by side. *Let the city go up in flames*, Dan thought. There were more pressing issues afoot.

He sipped from his mug and mulled over the events of the previous evening. The images presented themselves in chilling precision, from leaving his house to finally driving away from the slaughterhouse nearly two hours later, along with everything else that happened in between.

A knock interrupted his reveries. He opened the door to find an eager young courier beaming at him like there was no tomorrow and he loved his job delivering packages to strangers more than anything else on earth. *At least there's one happy person in the world this morning,* Dan thought. He signed the electronic pad and looked at the envelope. It was the file he'd ordered on Darryl Hillary.

He pulled open the tetra-pack and glanced quickly over the contents. It was a thin file. Was that all a man's life added up to when all was said and done? He set it on the hallway shelf to peruse later, if he still needed to — which he was beginning to doubt — and went back out to the porch.

He was holding off, but the call had to be made. The hardest part of his job was letting a client know of the death of a loved one. Dan's task was to locate people who had gone missing, not guarantee them safe passage home, especially if they were already dead before he came looking. He also knew the possibility of death must have occurred to most, if not all of the clients who hired him. There had to be long, dark nights when the knock never came at the door, when the phone failed to ring or the letter didn't fall into the post box. There had to be empty hours sitting and wondering: *What if…?* At some point you would have to sit back and ask yourself: *Was my missing mother, father, sister, brother, husband, wife or child still out there?* It had to occur to them.

There were plenty of times when Dan wondered how much of what his clients told him was the truth. All of it? Half? Or just the bare minimum they felt he needed to track someone down? What wasn't he being told by the obese, balding man covered in tattoos asking him to find his wife? What was the story behind the anorexic-looking mother wanting him to locate her teenage daughter? Often the tales were notably devoid of personal details. Darryl Hillary's severed ear, for instance. What did it signify? Had Hillary overheard something that cost him his life? Could the missing ear be a warning to future snitches to think twice before opening their mouths? What had he known? On the other hand, it might be the trademark of a gang slaying, a mutilation branding this as the work of a particular group anxious to leave their mark in more ways than one. Then again, the guy was hardly gang member material. His sister had said he was a pothead, but he was also a poet. That didn't spell anger and violence, unless his poetry turned in the realm of gangster rappers.

Behind all this, Dan's greatest fear was that he might inadvertently return someone to a scenario that would lead to further harm on the missing person's part. What if the reason for running away was to escape abuse? What if restoring someone to his or her family led to suicide or murder? What if, what if, and again what if? These were the questions that haunted him.

Dan knew he wasn't the only one with such thoughts weighing heavily on him. Similar doubts clouded the minds of some of the best police officers he'd met and worked with. They lived with the knowledge that locating a missing person in time could mean the difference between life and death. All too often the crucial hours slipped by because of negligence of one sort or another. Paperwork not done in time, messages not forwarded, subtler clues overlooked in favour of more obvious ones that led nowhere. Sometimes an outdated photograph meant a face wouldn't be recognized immediately. Or it might be the neighbour not questioned soon enough to prevent a twelve-year-old from being suffocated and stuffed into a green garbage bag inside a refrigerator in a rooming house on the street where she'd vanished a week earlier. It was the stuff of nightmares come alive: lions prowling in the streets, tanks rolling down hills into your village. There was always a fear that the one thing overlooked, the simplest effort not made, or the question left unasked meant someone would die or that a killer would escape. That was not far off the truth.

He'd talked to such cops. "There is no such thing as closure," they'd told him. "You can dehumanize things on the surface, but not deep down. You want to cut off the feelings, but you can't." They talked of *vics* and *perps*, not real people. They obsessed over physical details and tried to forget the names and faces, but their own faces marked them as haunted. Dan saw it. "You have to detach yourself," they told him. "You have to look at things objectively." But not one ever told him they'd been successful at it.

These bustling, over-exuberant tough guys and gals were all live-wired inside. Scarred by what they'd seen, their emotions caught in a precarious tightrope over an abyss, they walked and sometimes they fell. Like Constable Brian Lawrie, who left the force ten days after pulling the body of Sharin' Keenan Morningstar from the refrigerator of a rooming house in the Annex. For him it was "one crime scene too many," after being struck by how shiny her hair was when he found her stuffed in that garbage bag. Or his partner, Detective Mike Pedley, who followed the trail of her killer for years, always feeling himself just one step behind until he threw himself under the wheels of a subway train at Rosedale Station on an otherwise bright, upbeat sunny day.

Dan knew the men and women who worked on child murder cases were a breed apart, to use a cliché still deserved in many ways. "It's the living you have to worry about, not the dead," they said, if only to convince themselves. They referred to human remains as "trash" in an effort to make it less hurtful. "No offence intended to the deceased," they said. "We just can't take it personally." Dan understood. It was the language they used, but it was slight as far as armour went. He thought about the boy he'd been, the one who grew up tortured because he didn't know what to feel on hearing of his own mother's death, hating himself because at four he'd been calculating the advantages he might gain in sympathy from others rather than feeling sorry for her. There was always that particular brand of torture.

Dan's other great fear was of making the opposite kind of mistake. Of declaring the wrong person dead or, worse, speaking too soon and declaring the wrong person still alive. His gut instinct told him he'd found Darryl Hillary rather than some other unfortunate as he stared up at the body hanging from a meat hook, but logic told him not to jump to conclusions. In this case it might simply mean delaying the delivery of bad news another day, if bad news it turned out to be. One more day for Darryl Hillary's sister to live in hope. Was that such a bad thing? Sometimes *not* seeing was believing. Often, the relatives of victims preferred not to learn the truth, to go on believing their loved one was still in the land of the living even when all the evidence, forensic and otherwise, told a different story.

He took a last sip of coffee and looked down at his phone, his thumb rolling through the listings till he found the number for Darlene Hillary.

She picked up on the first ring.

"Ms. Hillary?"

"Darlene, yes."

"It's Dan Sharp."

He heard a sharp intake of breath. "You found Darryl?"

"I don't know yet. That's why I'm calling."

The voice turned hard. "What does that mean?"

"It means the man I found hasn't been identified yet."

"I don't understand. Oh, you mean he's …"

Dan felt the weariness overtake him. "A body has been found, but no identification has been made."

"He's dead then."

The voice sounded like a sack of wet cement hitting the ground. Dan sensed the instinctive clenching, the withdrawal that occurred when the news was bad. She was remarkably contained.

"I prefer not to jump to conclusions. We don't know for sure, so there's still reason to hope." He paused to let that sink in. "I was wondering if you would know the name of Darryl's dentist. I'd like to get his dental records to see if we can rule out the possibility that it is your brother."

There was a hesitation. "I'm sorry, I can't think straight. You want to know Darryl's dentist's name?"

"Yes, if you know it."

"I don't think he had one. Not in Toronto."

A total recluse, Dan thought.

"What about before that? A childhood dentist maybe?"

"There was a dentist in Timmins. We both went to him. But that was years ago."

"The records could still help us."

She was suddenly suspicious. "Who is 'us'?"

"The Toronto police." He pulled his dressing gown tighter.

Another pause. "I don't know if he's still alive. The dentist, I mean."

"It's worth a try," Dan said, shielding his face from the sun with his hand.

"Just a minute and I'll see if I can find my old address book."

He heard her shuffling off. He sipped his coffee and waited. She returned in less than a minute.

"I have it here," she said. "I keep everything."

As she relayed the information in a halting voice, Dan wrote down the particulars.

"I'm sorry I have to ask," he said, "but you mentioned that Darryl smoked drugs. As far as you know, does your brother have drug debts?"

"I don't think he has anything like that. I know he liked to smoke marijuana once in a while, but I don't think he was mixed up in anything like that."

He thanked her and hung up then called directory assistance in Timmins. The operator was unable to locate the dentist in question. She offered to look back several years till she found the name. Not much to do, Dan concluded, accepting her offer to help. The answer came quickly enough: the number had been delisted ten years previously.

He'd just clapped his cellphone closed when it rang again. He saw the name *Hillary* on his screen.

"He has a gold cap," she declared without preamble. "I just thought of it. It's on one of the lower front teeth. You can't really see it much except when he smiles. I hope that helps you."

"Yes, it's a great help," Dan said, trying to picture the dangling monster smiling at him. It was an eerie thought. Or maybe the gold tooth had been removed along with the left ear. Perhaps it was a psychopathic gold prospector the police should be looking for. "With any luck, it should tell us what we need to know. Thank you very much."

He finished his coffee without any further interruptions then went inside to dress.

The Centre of Forensic Sciences on Grosvenor Street was the largest laboratory of its kind in Canada. At any given moment, it employed more than two hundred and fifty personnel. Its slogan was *Scientia pro justicia*: "Science for justice." Working neither for the law nor against it, the centre was supposed to be as impartial as death. At any rate, that was its claim.

Dan closed his eyes and leaned his head against the coolness of a wall. His stomach, no longer grateful for the late-night Wendy's combo, had been rumbling for the past hour, demanding breakfast while the rest of him just wanted to go back to sleep. In the main-floor bathroom, he rinsed his face with cool water and surveyed the rugged landscape that constituted his features: jagged nose, brooding eyes under dark brows, broad cheekbones, and powerful chin. A red sickle ran from below the right eye up to his temple, arresting the viewer's gaze before granting permission to go further. It was a lasting gift from his father for coming home from school late when Dan was ten.

He pulled on the paper towels. At first they refused to give way before giving way far too easily and flooding the floor with brown sheets folded in half. He stooped to pick them up and left them on the counter for the next person who came along, presuming that person wouldn't be too picky about his drying towels. After all, you never knew where they'd been.

He came back out and sat in reception. A clock ticked at the far end of the hall. Somnolent, hypnotic, it was a reminder to the living of what no longer existed for the dead arrayed for viewing one floor below. He stared at it, his gaze blanking dully before the numbers registered.

Time.

Clock.

Morning.

He'd left the slaughterhouse seven hours ago. Three hours before that he'd been passing a quiet night with Trevor and Ked until it got interrupted. Was it not ironic to be sitting in the hallway of the Toronto morgue waiting to meet a corpse after spending the evening watching *The Exorcist*?

He stood and paced. Sitting was out of the question if he wanted to stay awake. A green brochure on a magazine stand caught his eye. He scanned the shiny chrome tables on the cover, turned the page and browsed the paragraphs outlining the manufacturer's specifications for modular mortuaries. He'd never heard of such things.

Fascinated, he read the jaunty, upbeat descriptions of "stand-alone, self-contained plant rooms" that would prove "ideal for any contemporary disaster situation." The rooms in the images were pristine. No bodies under sheets, no trails of blood or dismembered limbs lying on the floor. No doctors and nurses running around with worn expressions as the body count from the latest suicide bombing or train wreck piled up, proving just how far from ideal any contemporary disaster situation was likely to be.

Dan had visited dozens of morgues over his fifteen-year career. Like cemeteries, he found them to be lacklustre places, as opposed to the creepy television portrayals with their atmosphere of incipient doom. Hospitals were far more threatening to his peace of mind.

He'd once looked up the meaning of "morgue," intrigued by its similarity to the French *mort* or "dead." Surprisingly, the words were unrelated. It meant "to look at solemnly." Even more surprising were the associated synonyms of *condescension, disdain,* and *pride.* An unusual usage, Dan thought as he read on, only to learn that in its original form a morgue was a room in a prison where jailers studied the newly convicted to help identify them in future. It was only later, in the fifteenth century, that the word came to designate a room used for cold storage of bodies.

Not to be outdone, the ever-colourful Brits came up with their own euphemisms: "Rose Cottage" and

"Rainbow Room," which allowed doctors to discuss such matters freely in front of worried patients.

In one of the first detective stories, Edgar Allan Poe had written famously of "The Murders in the Rue Morgue." Since then, few had bettered his creative ingenuity. Without realizing it, he'd established a number of crime fiction conventions, including that of the eccentric but brilliant problem solver, an ineffectual police force, and what was to become known as the "locked room mystery." That single work changed the course of literary history, though its author thought little of it other than to say he felt its popularity stemmed from being "something in a new key." Novelty or not, it earned him a substantial fee of $56 on publication in 1841, adding a further brick in the wall of Poe's literary immortality. That, of course, was after a lifetime of financial hardship, but before being murdered at forty and defamed posthumously by his literary executor. Was his reputation as a great writer any consolation to him now?

Dan settled in for a long wait. Every once in a while someone in a uniform came through the hall and tossed him a sympathetic smile, telling him it would be just another few minutes, before disappearing down the corridor and around a corner that hid the aftermath of who knew what disasters, ideal or otherwise?

At ten thirty, a technician came by. He did a double take and turned back to Dan.

"Hey, sexy. Fancy meeting you here."

Dan looked up and smiled. "Howard. How are you?"

"Missing being in your loving arms, but otherwise doing very well. How are things? How is, um — Kedrick?"

"Good memory. We're both well, thanks. It's been a while."

"It has, hasn't it?" A spurt of embarrassment showed on Howard's face. "Sorry about that last time we were together. I guess I was a little jealous or something."

Dan shook his head. "Don't mention it."

"Did the beer stains come out of your jacket?"

Dan smiled. "Pretty much. So how did you come to be working in the city morgue? Didn't you use to work in film?"

Howard made a face. "Precisely. I used to do hair and make-up, but I find this far less stressful."

"Are you kidding?"

Howard gave him a rueful look. "Have you ever worked with actors?"

"Thankfully, no."

Howard checked his clipboard. "Say, you're not waiting for unit three, are you? The murder vic from the slaughterhouse?"

Dan nodded, suddenly alert. "That's me."

"Come on down the hall. They're nearly finished," Howard told him. "I can probably sneak you in if we're quiet."

"I think you said something like that the last time we saw each other," Dan said with a wink.

"Still a cheeky boy."

Dan followed him to a set of double doors with a red light blinking overhead. Howard turned the knob and peered through the crack. He waved Dan in after him.

The body lay on a table, covered by a sheet up to the shoulders, leaving the head exposed. From across the room, Dan could make out the severed ear base, the dried blood turned black and grimy.

There were three men in the room. The first, clearly a morgue attendant, carried a clipboard loosely under his arm. The second was the fleshy cop from the slaughterhouse last night. Probably continuity, Dan decided. He would have stayed with the body until the autopsy was completed to provide a continuity of evidence. In other words, so that no one could sneak in and fiddle about with the remains. Once that was done, the body would be sealed in a bag and left undisturbed till it was released to family. The other officer was new. He was smooth-faced and boyish, almost pretty. He'd have had a hard time in the training academy, Dan thought. Probably needed to prove himself at all times. His longish hair was slicked back Latino-style. Definitely not a regulation haircut.

Both cops were consulting sheets, making marks as the coroner told them his findings. They were as unlikely a pair as Jack Spratt and his lean-hating wife, the one small-framed and tidy, the other oversized and as unkempt as they came. The lumpy officer looked as though he'd never learned to tuck in his shirttails or iron his trousers. Even his boots were scuffed, the laces loosely tied.

"We're almost finished," said the morgue attendant, glancing over at Dan and Howard. "You can come in."

The two cops glanced over with disdain, reminding Dan of the original meaning of the word "morgue." Toronto cops had a reputation for being arrogant. To a degree it was deserved, but not by all. Dan had heard that small town cops resented them for making them all look bad. He'd met his share of cops. For the most part, he could take or leave them. Many were just ordinary folks off the beat, but some had a hardened attitude, as though they felt hard done by and ready to take it out on anybody who gave them cause. As if somebody had forced them to enter the ranks.

Apart from his size, the larger cop was nondescript. If he had the nerve for it, he'd probably be successful working undercover. He could take on any disguise with that doughboy face, potbelly, and stooped shoulders. With minimal effort, he might easily be mistaken for a truck driver, construction worker, or even a biker.

The other barely looked old enough to be a cop. He was chewing gum, making loud smacking noises. His small stature emphasized his cocky attitude, as though he needed to make up in presence what he lacked in size. His eyes were green. Envy, zealotry, hard to tell. He had a girl's nose and pouting lips. His hair, thick and honey-blonde, was the kind that seldom made it to middle age without receding, usually along with a sagging middle.

The larger cop said something to his partner, who turned to regard Dan with greater interest.

"You the one that found him?" he threw out.

"Yes, I am."

"Missing persons investigator, I understand?"

"Correct," Dan said. He could almost hear him thinking, *Wannabe cop.*

The officer turned away as though he couldn't possibly be of further interest.

"I have some information that might help identify the victim," Dan offered.

Both officers turned to him.

"What would that be, sir?" asked the larger one.

"I spoke with my client this morning. The man I'm searching for — Darryl Hillary — has a gold-capped lower incisor."

"Well, you're too late. We already know who this guy is," replied the younger officer with more than a hint of surliness. "We got his fingerprints on file."

Dan was aware of the competitiveness police officers felt around him. He wasn't a cop, yet he often found himself working in their presumed territory.

"Might I ask if this is the person I'm searching for then?"

The blonde cop smirked in a humourless way. "Ask all you want, but it's none of your business, sir."

Dan felt his anger igniting. There was more than one way to say "fuck you" to an arrogant prick who took his authority too seriously. As far as Dan was concerned, cops were just one more form of civil servant. They could stand to be a lot more civil to the taxpayers who hired them.

He turned to the coroner and held out his hand.

"Dan Sharp."

"Tim Johnson."

"Good to meet you, Tim. Did you notice a gold-capped incisor?"

"Yes, I did."

The attendant smiled and turned up the dead man's lip with a gloved hand. There for all the world to see was the gold cap. Dan got the feeling that Tim was relieved to be talking to someone who didn't look down on him. He also seemed more than happy to upstage this little martinet.

Howard stood looking down at the body with its missing ear and badly beaten face.

"Holy shit!" he exclaimed. "Who did this? It'll take more than a little lipstick and mascara to make this one presentable."

The younger officer eyed him then turned back to his partner. "Fucking queers," he muttered under his breath.

"Yeah, we're everywhere," Dan said, scowling.

The cop looked him over, taking note of his boxer's physique. "You're kidding me," he said, with a look of surprise. "You one of them too?"

"Spare me your hang-ups," Dan said.

The cop shook his head in disgust then turned to his partner. He nodded at the corpse. "First this perv and now queers. I think we're done here."

Dan's ears twigged at the word: *perv*. What did they know about Hillary that he didn't?

Once the officers left, the coroner nodded ruefully. "Not the most pleasant of chaps. They're not all like that, mind, but some of the younger ones need to be taken down a peg or two."

"You're welcome to try," Dan said. "I won't tackle them. They get away with far too much now, from what I hear."

Tim smiled. "And by the way, they mentioned the name, so yes, I'm happy to confirm that this is your man. Or perhaps I should say I'm sorry to confirm this is your man, depending on your outlook."

He pointed to the form on his clipboard where the name Darryl Hillary was printed next to the line identifying the deceased. They all looked down at the body, as though it might contradict them.

"Cause of death was strangling," said the coroner, pointing out purple ligature marks around the neck that Dan hadn't seen in the darkened slaughterhouse interior.

"So someone strong then," Dan noted.

"I'd say so. Or possibly more than one person. He was killed after being beaten. He was tormented first, quite methodically. I can assure you that considerable pain was inflicted before he died." He pointed to the face. "He suffered a broken nose and a bashed-in left cheekbone, both probably the result of being hit with a metal pipe or bar of some sort. It would have to have been exceptionally painful. The missing ear may have been sliced off while he was alive." He looked at Dan. "It's hard to say. If it was, then he died soon after. Strangling was the *coup de grâce*. I'd say this man knew he was going to die. And he probably welcomed it."

"So cruelty was part of the killer's intention," Dan said.

"Undoubtedly. But as to its purpose, I can't say. Someone may have been trying to extract information or maybe they just wanted him to suffer."

"Was the ear retrieved?"

"I gather it wasn't found on the premises, so whoever killed him may be a souvenir collector."

"That's a gruesome thought," Dan said.

The coroner nodded. "Howard was correct in saying he's going to have a hard time making Mr. Hillary presentable for the family." He looked over at Howard. "But Howard is one of the best. I have absolute faith in his work."

The coroner pulled the cover over Darryl Hillary's chest and face, reducing him to a lump beneath a sheet.

Dan shook the man's hand. "Thank you for your time and your candour."

"You're welcome."

Howard followed Dan out into the hallway. “Catch a coffee with me?” he asked. “I promise not to throw it at you.”

Dan smiled. “Why not?”

FOUR

Romeo and Juliet in Love

DARLENE HILLARY'S ADDRESS LAY NESTLED in Dan's cellphone beneath her home number. Though he dreaded it, Dan knew he had to give her the news as soon as possible. The most humane as well as the most difficult way to convey news of a loved one's death was to tell the relatives in person. The people who hired him to find their family members pinned a certain amount of hope on him. Usually, that hope was that he would find them alive and well, somehow and somewhere. Of course, the alternative was always an ever-present if unspoken possibility. No one realized this more than Dan. When he had bad news to deliver, most of the clients still expressed gratitude for the knowledge that would allow them to grieve and, when possible, get on with their lives. Some feared or hated him for the pain he brought. A few, however irrational it was, blamed him. No matter how Dan delivered the news, no matter under what circumstances, he felt like a monster.

He turned right onto the Gardiner Expressway and joined a queue of cars heading west out of the city. Twenty minutes later he reached Etobicoke, one of Toronto's "postal villages." This was where Darlene Hillary had lived with her brother. Dan nosed onto Daisy Avenue, a short street north of Lakeshore Boulevard. In this neighbourhood, the houses were minuscule, almost of dollhouse proportions. He found the number and pulled up at the curb. In the front yard, an apple tree offered up small red globes for viewing. Children on bikes screamed at one another and threw balls in a replica of an idyllic existence. The improbable dream that was the promise of suburbia.

The woman who came to the door was not much larger than a doll herself, but one that had aged badly. Raggedy Anne on the downlow. The planes of her face were hard, the skin dry, suggesting illness or possibly that she'd been living under great strain for some time. The eyes glinted, but not with joy. There was no mirth there, no trust. People who lived with grief or fear long enough ended up wearing it on their faces, Dan knew. A permanently down-turned mouth was one of the signs of a pessimistic personality. Darlene Hillary looked like someone who had long since accepted that life was going to be hard and there was no use bringing it up to management, because Heaven was deaf to all complaints. A bartender would have proved a more sympathetic listener to someone like her.

"You don't have to tell me," she said before he could introduce himself. "The police were here ten minutes ago."

Dan took the news in stride, remembering the dismissive Mr. and Mrs. Spratt. He felt both resentful and grateful they'd beat him to it.

"I'm sorry for your loss," he said, offering the obligatory catchall that cut through the awkwardness of emotion. "I wish I could have done more."

She nodded her acceptance of his admission that he'd been unable to find her brother in time, but letting him know there was no blame.

"If only he hadn't run. You might've been able to protect him."

Dan doubted that. "In my experience, people run when they believe the threats against them are real. Did your brother have any enemies?"

"Not that I knew of." A rueful shrug. "But then, how much do we really know about other people, even the ones we live with?"

A philosophical turn of mind then, Dan noted. Apparently she didn't expect an answer.

Normally, he would have left it there. He'd offer his condolences and make an exit. But something felt incomplete.

"Do you mind if I ask a few questions about your brother?"

He wasn't entirely sure why he needed to ask her anything. Unfinished business, perhaps. That and a feeling of wanting to do more for a man who'd died an undeservedly cruel and monstrous death.

Darlene Hillary ushered him into a tiny matchbox of a living room filled with unexceptional furniture. It was, Dan thought, the sort of furniture people bought when they had no idea what they wanted other than to have something to sit on or to invite guests in for a drink and offer them a footstool and a surface to put their glasses on. Dan glanced over a shelf crammed with knick-knacks and framed portraits. He caught a laughing face with a ready smile, limbs over- and under-twined in a row of teenage boys. This was a much younger Darryl Hillary. Not long out of high school, Dan imagined. Exuberant, even hopeful, as he and his pals faced the future and all it might bring. He hadn't always been friendless, then.

Darlene brought him his third cup of coffee that morning. He poured cream, stirred it into turbulent clouds and sat back in a worn brown armchair. It was comfortable, at least.

"Please, go ahead and ask me anything you like," Darlene said, her gaze fixed on his face.

"I asked earlier if your brother owed someone a substantial sum of money," Dan said, thinking of Darryl's drug habit. He recalled the cop's comment that Darryl Hillary's fingerprints had been on file. It would have been for some past offence. "I was wondering if anything came to mind since then."

"No. I'm pretty sure of that."

"Apart from occasional marijuana usage, did he ever indulge in drugs of the harder sort?"

She shook her head. "If he did, he didn't tell me. I'd find it hard to believe, in any case. He wasn't really an extremist in that way."

Dan nodded. What he found hard to believe was that her brother had received death threats because he smoked marijuana. Thousands of ordinary Canadians had been busted for possession of cannabis and worse. Dan doubted any of them had been threatened with death because of it. In any case, the crime was long overdue for a scrubbing off the books, and probably would have been but for the righteous heave-ho of so-called moralists to the south, whose policies overarched and affected Canada's own far more than most Canadians liked to acknowledge. But other than his predilection for an adolescent indulgence, Darryl Hillary seemed to have had little contact with the outside world.

Dan recalled Darlene's voice on the phone the first time they spoke. She'd sounded frantic. Instinct told him there had to be something else.

"The threatening calls you mentioned — did you overhear any of them? Do you have any idea what your brother was being threatened over? What he might have been running from?"

She looked resigned. "I didn't overhear anything directly. He said it was about his past. About … about the time he'd spent in prison."

Dan's eyebrows shot up. She'd lied to him. This was the first he'd heard anything about prison. Too late, he thought of the ardent courier and the file he'd left unread on the shelf in the hallway.

"For marijuana possession?"

"No." It was a whisper.

Dan waited.

She looked up. A sigh escaped her. "The charge was 'corruption of a minor.'"

Bells were clanging as Dan flashed back to one of the cop's referring to Darryl as a "perv."

"Your brother was convicted of having sex with an underage partner?"

She nodded. "That was a long time ago."

Dan looked over at the younger Darryl's photograph again. His ready smile now seemed to be a warning against over-optimism about everything life held in store for you.

"Please don't judge us," Darlene said.

"I won't. Can you tell me about it?"

Her fingers played with the nubbly fabric on the arm of the chair while she filled in the gaps in her story. She and Darryl were ten years apart in age, so she often felt more like a mother than an older sister. They'd grown up together in Northern Ontario. A poor existence, but not an unbearable one, she told him, like so much stage dressing for the story to come. The parents had been religious but the kids maintained their sanity despite their father's constant preaching and his dire warnings of an impending apocalypse that he seemed to welcome and felt his children should as well. It hadn't kept his son away from temptation, however. After his conviction, Darryl spent two years in prison. Following his release, he and Darlene moved to Toronto, hoping he'd be more anonymous in a larger urban centre. He'd stayed within the bounds of his parole and hadn't strayed from the court order forbidding contact with his former victim. The girl, fourteen at the time, would now be twenty-five. Darryl had been thirty when he died.

Sometime over the last year, Darlene said, her brother had been targeted by hate mail and death threats. When pressed, he'd admitted that it was in connection with "the old business."

"He hid it from me for some time," Darlene said. "But eventually he had to tell me. I'm just not sure how long it was going on."

"How did you find out about it?" Dan asked.

"Darryl's behaviour changed drastically. He was afraid of going outside. He even stopped sitting out back in the garden. Until the letters and calls came, he spent most of his time out there, even in the winter. He loved the garden. It was his place of refuge. Then suddenly he just stopped. He used to peer through the curtains when he had to go out for anything. I could tell something was up."

"And he believed the threats were real?"

She nodded. "How did these people even find him?" she asked, wiping away a stray tear. "The property was in my name. The address shouldn't have been listed in connection with him."

"They have their ways," Dan said. "Your brother would likely have been listed on the Sex Offenders Registry."

Darlene shook her head at the suggestion. "He shouldn't have been on it any more."

Under the new rules, Darryl's lawyers had applied to have his name and record removed, citing his case as an unlikely repeat offender. As far as anyone knew he had been taken off the list, but sometime over the last year her brother had been targeted by hate mail and death threats referring to his conviction.

"You said the girl was fourteen at the time?"

She nodded.

"Making your brother nineteen."

Brown eyes turned to him. "Not a very mature nineteen, not that it makes much difference." She looked away. "I'm not making excuses for him."

Dan nodded. "Their ages weren't that far apart. Am I right in thinking she was Darryl's girlfriend?"

Darlene nodded. "They were quite serious about each other. It wasn't just a casual thing for them. He once told me they planned to be married when she turned sixteen." She looked off wistfully. "You never saw two people so in love. He was devoted to her and she to him."

"The problem is they were more than four years apart in age," Dan said. "So what is called a 'Romeo and Juliet' clause would not have helped out here. Even if they declared themselves in a serious relationship, he would still be perceived by the court as an older aggressor."

She shrugged. "That's more or less what happened. Just before his trial, another young girl was raped and murdered by her older boyfriend. It was in all the papers. It didn't help Darryl one bit either."

"No, I'm sure it didn't." Dan thought for a moment. "If you don't mind, can you tell me how your brother ended up being charged?"

A spasm of anger crossed Darlene's face. "Our father turned him in. He caught them together one afternoon."

Leaving a trail of broken hearts and broken lives, Dan thought. He put down his cup and waited a moment. "Do you want me to come with you to the morgue?"

She shook her head. Finally, the tears started.

"Thank you, but no. They said I couldn't see him yet. It won't be for another day at least."

Dan thought of Darryl's badly beaten face, the severed ear. He had a flash of the body hanging overhead, like a hideous goblin in a child's horror story. He thought of the blood dripping onto his face as he lay on the floor after being swiped at with the pipe. It was common for the police to prevent the next of kin from seeing a badly damaged corpse. He wondered how much to tell her.

"They're probably trying to make sure he looks presentable before you see him. You don't want your last image of him to upset you."

She was watching him closely. "He must have been badly beaten."

Dan reached out a hand and put it on her shoulder. "I'm very sorry, Darlene."

She nodded, blubbering and unable to speak for almost a minute. Then the fury died out and she looked up again.

"I wish I'd told you about his past earlier," she said. "He never wanted anyone to know. He made me promise never to tell anyone."

Dan shook his head. "Believe me, it wouldn't have made any difference. I put out a number of calls, but my sources found where your brother was staying too late. I don't see how we could have found him any earlier, even if we'd known more about him. He was just too well hidden."

She nodded in recognition of his generosity in saying this. Even if she believed him, it wouldn't help her live with herself.

"Not well enough, I guess."

Dan hesitated, but he needed to ask. "Is it possible your brother might have had contact with his former girlfriend since his release from prison?"

Her eyes shifted. For a moment he saw her as a younger woman, watching her brother's life fall apart in a court of law for something she'd known but done nothing about.

"If he did, he didn't tell me about it. I doubt Darryl even knew where to find her. The girl's father moved the family away right after the trial."

Dan looked at this short, thin woman with the worn face. In another few years, he might pass her on the street and not recognize her. She was so unexceptional looking that he likely wouldn't take a second glance. She'd disappear into the crowd and lose herself forever. Just one more lost soul with a burden too huge to bear.

She walked him to the door. Dan stood on the porch, ready to leave her to mourn privately. He felt her hand on his arm.

"Wait, please."

He turned back to her.

Her dark eyes stared at him. "Will you help find this monster? Whoever killed Darryl?"

"I'll do whatever I can to help, but I'm not a cop."

"No. But you're a good man. I can see that. That's why I know you will help." She let go of his arm, but her eyes held him. "Please?"

He nodded. "I'll do what I can."

He knew he shouldn't have promised. His mind was already on the other files on his desk upstairs in the calm study, the living who still needed him. His interest wasn't in the dead, however sad their story.

Dan got in his car. He glanced in the mirror, watching the house move away in reverse. All he saw was a beige bungalow, as small and unexceptional as its owner.

Darryl Hillary's savaged features stayed with him all the way back to town, racing toward the cityscape with its sweeping waterfront high rises, the Rogers sports dome, the CN Tower dominating everything. He wondered if Darryl had begged for his life in his final moments and whether the killer had enjoyed watching him grovel in the ash-filled slaughterhouse. The location was as gruesome and ironic a place for a death as any he could imagine. It was in keeping with the cruel imagery of nursery rhymes and fairy tales: hideous witches, vicious wolves, poisoned apples, haunted castles, and all the terrible things lurking in the shadows and waiting for disobedient children.

What had gone through Darryl's mind when he learned his father had turned him in to the authorities for having sex with his underage girlfriend? Laws were meant to protect the weak and the unwilling. By the sounds of it, the girlfriend had been more than willing. Where was the crime in two people wanting pleasure from each other, even if one was younger than the law deemed acceptable? The real crime lay beneath a sheet in the Toronto morgue — a man beaten to death because he'd loved someone younger than himself.

Dan had wanted to ask Darlene if their father was still alive, but he stopped himself. What would the old man think now of his handiwork? Would he be pleased to know his son had had a final comeuppance for his youthful recklessness? How much in love did you have to be for it to be all right to have sex with someone younger? Darryl's sister had said the girlfriend hadn't been allowed to speak in Darryl's defence during the trial. The law dealt with technicalities, but it couldn't measure human emotion. Or the urge for revenge. But that was getting ahead of things a bit, assuming Darryl's death had anything to do with his criminal record.

He turned off the Gardiner and headed for home. Dan doubted there was much he could do for Darlene or Darryl at this point. He had his contacts and he could ask around to see if anyone knew anything, but the case was now in the hands of the police. Any overt activity on Dan's part could be construed as unlawful interference. That was a problem Dan didn't need or want.

What remained was to go back to the sort of humdrum tedium that marked most of his cases. He thought of the numerous Internet bookmarks he'd amassed over the past few years. The Help Us Find websites listing absconding debtors and child support payment defaulters. Much of it was dreary work and he detested it, but it was what he did best.

At four o'clock, he headed over to the downtown YMCA. He parked and waited for his son to emerge from his basketball game. Dan stayed in the car. The heat outside had swelled unbearably. Ked wasn't a great player, but he was dedicated and made up for his lack of skill in enthusiasm. He was one of the few kids Dan knew who played for the love of the sport, not out of any sort of bloodlust and competitive instinct. When he finally appeared, Dan was surprised to see a blonde girl hanging onto his arm as he came down the steps. Her hold was friendly, not possessive. Still, she could be twelve or thirteen, where Ked was about to turn fifteen in a month. What happened once he was sixteen and she was only thirteen?

Dan waited and watched. The pair exchanged a few words then the girl laughed and ran off to join two other girls by the bike rack. Ked waved at them and turned to look for his father's car.

As far as Dan knew, Ked hadn't started dating, but they'd had several talks about the topic. The previous month, Ked had surprised him by being forthright on the topic of his own sexuality.

"Would you be disappointed if I turned out to be straight?" he asked.

It was all Dan could do not to laugh. He mustered a serious expression before answering. "Not at all," he said. "I'm counting on you to give me grandchildren to look after me in my dotage."

He hadn't even thought of the possibility, but now that he said it he liked the thought of a continuance of his line.

"Seriously, Dad?"

Dan nodded. "Seriously. I just hope you're not disappointed that your father is gay."

Ked looked dismayed. "No, Dad. I don't care about that. I love you for whatever you are."

"And the same holds true for me. You wouldn't disappoint me by being yourself. In fact, I expect you to do just that."

Ked had seemed satisfied with that answer.

He ran over to the car now. Dan popped the lock and his son got in, looking relaxed and tanned. Just another handsome fourteen-year-old, happy to be alive and living in a land where certain freedoms were a given.

"Good game?" Dan asked.

"Awesome!" Ked said.

Fifteen minutes later, they were outside Ked's mother's house in the Annex. Dan gazed over the yard. Kendra eschewed flowers as being too fussy, but she had a neatly maintained lawn. Wide-leafed vines climbed the red brick, massing around the chimney. It always amazed Dan to think the mother of his child lived here, a woman who under other circumstances or in different times would have been his wife. They'd barely dated — nothing more than a casual affair in his second year at university. That little courtship had come about as a result of Dan's having a crush on her older brother. It was Arman who Dan had fantasized sleeping with. When Kendra showed up, she intrigued him enough to let her seduce him once.

She waved from the window. She'd been watching for Ked's arrival. Dan waved back.

"Say a big 'hello' to your mother for me."

"I will. You and Trevor are going to Uncle Donny's tonight for supper, right?"

"Right."

"Say 'hi' to Uncle Donny for me. Tell him to tell Lester he owes me a movie pass when he gets back."

Dan looked over. "Gets back from where?"

The look on Ked's face was priceless. He suddenly seemed to realize he'd said something he shouldn't have.

"Oh, that. Never mind. Maybe Uncle Donny will tell you."

He slipped out and closed the door with a quick wave.

Dan reversed the car and drove off. He checked his phone messages. Trevor had picked up "something special" for their evening out. Despite his misgivings about city living, Trevor seemed to be adapting to Dan's life fairly well. He'd charmed nearly everyone Dan introduced him to. He knew their favourite drinks, their favourite flowers. He had the right touch. Then again, Dan realized he shouldn't be surprised — the magic had worked on him from the start.

He left a message for Trevor to say he'd be by to pick him up. Donny had called as well. His message promised a "surprise guest" at dinner that evening but gave no clue who it might be. Dan drove on, intrigued.

FIVE

Molly Wood's Bush

CHURCH STREET RUNS THROUGH the heart of Toronto's gay community. Bounded by Jarvis on the east and Yonge to the west, with College at the south end and Bloor at its upper reaches, the gaybourhood contains four square city blocks of Prideful Living. The area was known as a cruising spot as far back as the early 1800s. Then it was owned by one Alexander Wood, merchant and magistrate, whose sexual proclivities landed him in hot water. Acting on behalf of an anonymous rape victim, Wood demanded to examine the genitals of several local men while in search of a supposed scratch the woman had imparted to her attacker. Some took exception to Wood's meticulous scrutiny of their privates, however, and griping gave way to suspicion. Eventually, it was alleged that Wood had invented the rape story to gain access to the men's particulars. He was nicknamed "Molly" and his estate dubbed Molly Wood's Bush. Nearly two centuries later, it was officially proclaimed Toronto's gay neighbourhood.

That night the heat wave was in full swing. The evening sun lit up the cafés where patrons were draped over patio chairs, limp as melted candles, waiting for a night in the ghetto to begin. Heads swivelled to regard the passing traffic before turning leisurely back to deliver the next *bon mot* to their companions. Here life was fun, relaxed. With a little luck and the price of a beer or six, no one needed to be alone for long.

It was just past eight when Dan and Trevor arrived at the Jarvis Street condo. Donny met them in the foyer dressed in impeccable summer wear: cool linens, muted colours set against deep earth tones. Donny was African-Canadian *haute couture*.

He brought them upstairs and ushered them inside. Cool air enveloped them as they entered the apartment. Soft jazz burbled in the background. It was something Dan thought he recognized, but couldn't name. A new piece of art adorned the hallway, frenzied colours merging in anarchic intensity, but with no discernible subject matter. Donny's *zeitgeist*, Dan knew, was 1950s New York, with its reams of Abstract Expressionist painters and the glory days of cool East Coast jazz. ("Before it made the mistake of going west," Donny always reminded him.) A golden glow met their eyes, emitted by dozens of candles, each smokeless and dripless, according to their host's exacting standards.

"Welcome to *Casa delle Candele*," he intoned with a bow.

Dan presented him with a bottle of Chartreuse. Donny took it with an expression of admiration and disbelief. He turned to Trevor.

"I'm sure I have your civilizing influence to thank for this. Before meeting you, the only thing he ever brought over was a two-four of beer and an occasional litre of Scotch when things weren't going so well. So, to you, I say a heartfelt thank-you."

"You're most welcome," Trevor replied.

Dan shook his head. "We can't all afford your standards," he said. "But just this once."

He looked past Donny's shoulder into the condo.

"I'm dying to know who the mystery guest is." He lowered his voice. "I hope it's not some old trick of yours."

Donny smiled mysteriously. "Speak friend and enter."

He led them down the hallway to the sitting room, where a woman bedecked in a sequined pantsuit and feather boa sat waiting. Her skin was burnished bronze, her lips pomegranate red and her hair a white Amazonian flag thrust straight up. On seeing Dan, she smiled and stood.

"Hello, Daniel." The voice was throaty, warm.

Dan's mouth fell open in a clichéd expression of surprise.

"Domingo Rhodes," he managed at last.

"You haven't forgotten."

"No, of course not." Dan turned apologetically to Trevor. "Domingo, this is my partner, Trevor James."

"Delighted." Domingo took Trevor's hand and held it, gazing coolly into his eyes.

"A pleasure to meet you, Domingo," Trevor said, sensing heightened emotion in the room but not recognizing the reason for it.

"Domingo's an old friend," Dan said after a moment.

"And former neighbour," she added with a laugh, finally releasing Trevor's hand. "We go back a long way. Way before your time." She glanced up at Donny. "Or his."

"Always proprietary," Donny chided. "Have a seat." He turned to Trevor. "What'll you have? Domingo's drinking a crantini. I've also got lychee and mango, if that's of interest. Gin or vodka. Otherwise, there are the usual pernicious concoctions."

"Summertime and the living's fine," Trevor said. "I'll try a lychee martini. Gin, please."

"Excellent," Donny replied, before turning to Dan. "*Et pour monsieur?*"

Dan's mouth twitched but nothing came out.

Donny rolled his eyes. "Right — you'll have a beer, as per usual. I'll see what I've got in the back of my fridge."

He left the room.

Domingo looked at Dan, sizing him up in a series of visual snapshots. "It's been a long time, Dan. It's really good to see you again."

"And you," Dan said, hoping he didn't sound as stilted as he felt. "It must be what … four, five years since you moved?"

"More than that. We last celebrated Ked's eighth birthday together."

"Seven, then. He turns fifteen next month."

"There you are then." Domingo's eyes sparkled, as though everything were a source of merriment for her.

"Are you still with…?"

"Adele, yes. We're still together. It'll be twenty years next summer."

"Congratulations. And the hair looks terrific, by the way," Dan added, gazing at her white ruff. "When did you start dyeing it?"

Domingo gave him a wistful smile. "Not dyed, but thanks anyway. It's the chemo, hon. It grew back like this."

Dan made a little noise of helpless acknowledgment. "I'm sorry," he said at last. "I hadn't heard."

"It's all right. I didn't tell anyone."

Donny returned with Trevor's martini and a beer bottle with a napkin tied deftly around its neck for Dan.

He picked up his own glass, raising it to the room with a nod. "To friends, old and new!"

Dinner was going well. The flames wavered and glowed brighter as evening came on. Donny leapt up from time to time to check on something or stir a pot, managing to perform both chef and host duties to perfection. A bocconcini and basil salad followed the *gnochetti in brodo*, a light, flavourful soup. They'd just started in on the *risotto ai funghi* — it was a decidedly Italian-themed evening — when Domingo asked about Lester.

"He's gone home," Donny said, matter-of-factly, though the forlorn look on his face told another side of the story.

Dan suddenly flashed back to Ked's comment. He sat up in his chair. "Wait a minute. By 'home' do you mean he went back to his family in Oshawa?"

"Yes, he left yesterday. I haven't told anyone yet." He turned to Domingo. "I keep secrets too."

Dan was floored by the news. "How did this happen? Because this" — he looked around him — "*this* is his real home. I thought he knew that by now."

Donny shrugged, avoiding eye contact with the others around the table. He would not betray his real feelings.

"Lester knows he's always welcome here, but he's turning sixteen next month and he misses his mother. Cow that she is."

"Children always miss their mothers," Domingo said sympathetically. "No matter who else we have in our lives, no matter how fortunate and blessed we may be, we have just one birth mother, and it's important to get that relationship right."

Donny's eyes flickered. "Lester said something like that, only not quite so articulately. It turns out he phoned her on Mother's Day. They've been in touch every other week." He shrugged. "He misses her and wants to reconnect. It's as simple as that."

"Are you saying he's gone back to live with them for good?" Dan asked, still struggling with the news.

Donny twirled his glass, looked away. "I am. He has."

"What about the stepfather?" Dan asked. "Won't he be a problem?"

Donny sighed and set the glass down. He gestured helplessly, as though to say there was nothing he could do. "I have no doubt you're right," he said, "but it's not up to me."

Dan recalled the garishly dressed, crudely spoken couple he'd met the previous year while working on a missing persons case involving a young man named Richard Philips. He hadn't been at all impressed with the mother or stepfather, but the real dilemma came when he located the fifteen-year-old, rechristened Lester and working in the city's porn industry with falsified ID. Dan was forced to choose between returning him to what was surely a terrifying and destructive life for a young gay man and finding a better place for him. Donny had stepped in to fill the breach, offering Lester temporary sanctuary, but ended up taking him in as a surrogate son, albeit covertly. The law was not on the side of runaways and their keepers, however well-meaning.

Dan looked at Donny. "What will he say about where he's been living for the past year? Aren't you afraid this might bring a lot of trouble for you?"

Donny shook his head. "He told her he's been living with friends, but he kept it vague. It could have legal ramifications for me for helping him hide, but on the other hand I know the kid well enough by now. He's not going to give them my name or address. He's anxious to get back to school and not miss another year. He knows he's falling behind. And in another month he'll be legal, so he can return here any time to visit."

"Your tutoring is probably far more valuable than anything he'll learn in high school," Dan snorted.

"Well, yes, I agree that everyone should know about Lennie Tristano and the history of jazz, but it's not exactly going to guarantee him a job when all is said and done, is it?"

Dan put down his drink. "I don't like it," he said. "I met those people. They were horrible. As much as I might feel for a mother and child who've been separated, it was doing him no good to be living with them. That stepfather was a homophobic monster. The way he talked about Lester made me cringe and I hadn't even met the boy then."

"I know, I know," Donny said. "I don't like it either, but I have no choice."

Trevor spoke up. "Maybe once he turns sixteen he can mention you. It might help his case with the parents if they know he has you standing behind him."

"Probably not," Donny said. "The truth is, they're having a hard enough time dealing with the fact their kid is gay. He's not going to back down on that one. I doubt it would improve matters by telling them he's been living with a 'person of colour.'"

Dan turned to Domingo. "What do you think?"

"I've met Lester a few times. He's a very nice boy. But like any kid, he has to make his own mistakes. Live and learn."

"That's right," Donny said. "I won't be the surrogate dad who kept him apart from his blood family. But as far as I'm concerned, I'm his chosen family. I told him he's welcome back here any time, even if it's just for a weekend stay-over."

They sat there silently contemplating this.

Donny stood. "Time for dessert," he said, heading for the kitchen.

"Seems kind of hard," Trevor ventured when Donny had gone. "Donny's looked after the boy for a year and now he just wants to leave."

"It's ingratitude," Dan said, colouring. "I don't like it."

Domingo looked at him sympathetically. "It's not ingratitude, Dan. It's a fifteen-year-old boy wanting to be a part of his family before it's too late. Don't judge him for it. Time will tell if it's the right thing or not."

Trevor put a hand on Dan's. "In any case, Donny has been both generous and courageous in having Lester here with him this past year. Let's hope it works out for the best."

"Oh, it will," Donny said, flouncing back into the room with a tray of tiramisu. "Anyway, that's me — social issues galore. But having that boy here has given me a new lease on life. No regrets — and I have you to thank for it, of course," he said, looking at Dan. "Anyway, I'd rather not talk about it any more, if you don't mind."

Domingo excused herself to use the bathroom. When she was gone, Dan turned and hissed at Donny. "What is she doing here?"

Donny gave him a baleful look. "She called me up last week and said she wanted to get in touch with you. I thought it was time you two talked, so I offered her your phone number. Then I remembered you were coming over this evening, so I invited her to join us. And here you both are."

Dan shook his head. "I didn't even know you'd kept in touch with her."

"I've kept in touch with all your cast-offs." He affected a mock-shiver. "There were so many of them I thought at one point I'd have to open a shelter."

Trevor grinned but turned away so Dan wouldn't see.

"There's nothing for you to worry about," Donny told Trevor. "You're one of the few he's met who were worth keeping. Apart from moi, of course."

Domingo returned. Donny refreshed everyone's drink.

Trevor looked over at Donny. "Dan said you'd started a new job."

Donny's face lit up. "Yes! You are looking at the official buyer for Mondo Beautique. It's a very upscale specialty chain where they purposely price things higher than necessary to discourage non-exclusive clientele. I fit right in."

Glasses were raised all around the table.

"Are you still in the private investigation business?" Domingo asked Dan.

"More or less. I've been on my own for the past year, though. It's been tough."

Donny looked over. "But not so tough that he would ever reconsider the offer to go back to his old firm."

Dan shook his head. "It was time for me to get out. As for the sort of cases I'm handling now, you don't want to know."

"Why is that?" Domingo asked.

Dan shrugged. "It's mostly a lot of chasing down child support evaders."

Trevor shot Dan a look to say he was being needlessly disingenuous, but he was not going to spill his secrets for him.

Donny caught the look passing between them. "Tell," he said. "You are doing something besides chasing dead-beats. What is it now? Chimney sweep? Rat catcher?"

"Nothing so innocuous," Dan said. "In fact, the opposite."

He told them briefly about his unsuccessful attempt at tracking down Darryl Hillary.

"He was sent to jail eleven years ago for dating a fourteen-year-old girl. He was nineteen at the time. They were serious about each other, apparently, till his father turned him in for statutory rape. He ended up doing two years in jail."

"And now he's dead," Domingo said.

Donny shook his head. "Seems a bit harsh when you consider Michael Jackson dated a fourteen-year-old boy and didn't do any time at all. But maybe boys don't count."

"I agree with you," Domingo said. "It's reverse discrimination. Had it been a fourteen-year-old girl sitting on Jackson's lap, he would have ended up in jail on charges sooner. But because boys are supposed to be tougher than girls, people weren't freaking out as much, especially not in the arts community, where homosexuality is taken as a matter of course."

"It's true," Dan said. "But the issue here is whether it's immoral for two people who want to have sex to do so no matter what their ages."

Donny nodded. "I always wonder if Liz Taylor knew. She defended Jackson to the ends of the earth. I can't believe she's naïve about such things. All those rumours about child molestation can't have passed her by."

"She's a smart woman and apparently they're very close," Trevor said. "Remember how she went to Singapore to bring him back to the States after the charges were laid?"

"I think she believed they were in love," Domingo said. "And that they were entitled to it."

The others turned to look at her.

She shrugged. "After all, the boy was an adolescent, not a child. Jackson might like 'em young, but that doesn't make him a child molester."

"I agree," Dan said. "I don't think he's a child molester. Not in the way we think of it. He was dating a younger man, not unlike what happened to my client and his girlfriend. If it were such a dirty secret, Jackson wouldn't have dated the boy in public. He even brought him to the music awards. He just misjudged the public's ability to tolerate such things."

Donny nodded. "Jerry Lee Lewis married his thirteen-year-old cousin, for god's sake!"

"What did that make him?" Dan asked.

"A pariah. It pretty much ended his recording career for nearly a decade. He also claims to have been fourteen when he married his first wife, who was seventeen. They just did it young down there."

Dan whistled. "Hey! How come you know so much about Lewis? He's not a jazz artist."

Donny raised a finger in warning. "Jerry Lee Lewis is a very cool guy and don't give me any grief over it."

"I was thirteen when I had sex with my first boyfriend," Domingo said. "He was in his twenties."

"It's an island thing," Donny said.

"That's right." Domingo smiled. "The women came later."

Donny turned to Dan. "How old were you when you first had sex with another man?"

"Twelve."

"And he was older, yes? I seem to recall something you told me about your youthful proclivities."

"Yes, he was probably in his thirties."

"And was it willing on your part?"

"Totally. I went after him."

"So who does that make a pervert, you or him?"

Dan shrugged. "Neither, in my estimation. I knew what I wanted and I knew where and how to get it."

"Exactly!" Donny exclaimed. "So why should Michael Jackson be treated any differently? Or Darryl Hillary or anyone else? If we lived in Holland, where the age of consent is twelve, none of this would matter. Your client's brother could have been ninety years old, and the worst he'd have to contend with would be societal opinion, which is often harsh, but seldom murderous. Why are we letting the wrong people set these legal parameters?"

"Well, the law is a set of conventions that changes over time," Domingo said. "But we shouldn't underestimate a young person's sexual urges."

"I draw the line at child prostitution, though," Trevor said.

"So do I," Donny agreed. "Money has no conscience. It's one of the reasons I agreed to rescue Lester when Dan brought him here last year. No kid should be forced to have sex with someone just to avoid his parents. End of story."

A moment of silence descended on the room. The conversation had circled back around to its beginning.

"Come on out here and see my view," Donny said to Trevor, who took the hint and followed him onto the balcony.

Dan and Domingo sat in silence for a moment.

"That poor man," Domingo said. "Your client, I mean."

"Yes, it's sad," Dan agreed.

She looked off in the distance, her eyes misty and diffuse. "It's not over yet," she said. "For you, I mean. But you know that already, don't you?"

Dan turned slowly to look at her. He shook his head. "No, I don't know anything like that. He's dead. What else is there to say? The police may have more questions to ask me, but as far as I'm concerned my part in it is over."

She smiled sadly, as though she knew him to be a pathetic liar. "No. It's got a long way to go and you're going to get wrapped up in it. You can feel it," she said then shook her head. "Sorry. I know you hate it when I do this. Let's not go there."

They soon heard Donny and Trevor returning. Domingo stood abruptly.

"Donny?"

"Yes, ma'am?"

"It's been a great pleasure, as always. Don't worry about the boy. Sunshine after rain, that sort of thing. He'll be fine. He's going to make you very proud of him." She shook her head as though she'd spoken out of turn. She leaned in and kissed him on the cheek. "Never mind my nonsense. I don't know what I'm saying half the time." She turned to Dan. "And Daniel, you are still a delight. One of the kind and caring folk who make this world a better place to live. Please — let's keep in touch. But remember, it's not over yet. You need to be prepared for it." Another kiss. "Say a very warm 'hello' to Ked for me. I hope he remembers his Auntie Domingo."

"I'm sure he does. I'll tell him you sent greetings."

She paused before taking Trevor's hands, staring into his eyes. "Dear, dear Trevor — thank you for bringing some peace to this man's heart," she said, nodding in Dan's direction. "Please be good to him."

Trevor nodded. "I intend to."

She smiled ambiguously then turned to Donny. He walked her to the door then returned to the sitting room. For a moment, no one spoke.

"Well, that was a blast from the past," Dan said at last. "She still makes the grandest exits this side of Buckingham Palace."

"She wanted to see you," Donny said with a hint of apology in his voice. "I'm sure you'll forgive me for inviting her in time."

Dan smiled slightly. "It's all right. It was overdue."

"She means well," Donny said, still in apology mode.

"I know."

"Another drink?"

Dan shook his head. "I'm good."

Trevor was looking from one to the other of them. "Will someone please let me in on the secret here?"

Dan shrugged. "Domingo interferes with things. She used to, anyway."

"'Interferes'?" Donny said ironically.

"What things?" Trevor asked.

Donny sighed. "She does this 'seeing' thing where she goes off in a sort of trance and says whatever comes into her mind. Sort of like a vision or a prophecy."

"It's creepy," Dan said.

Trevor looked at the two of them. "Is it real?"

"Real?" Donny repeated.

Trevor nodded. "Does it have validity? The things she says? There was someone on Mayne Island who could do that."

Dan just shook his head. "Who cares? It's creepy and invasive."

Donny nodded thoughtfully. "It often has an eerie sort of insight or validity, but not always at the time. More often with hindsight. The problem is — or Dan's problem with it is — she does it without being asked. She just holds your hand and looks into your eyes and lets fly."

Trevor turned to Dan. "Is that what she meant when she said 'it's not over yet'?"

Dan made an irritated noise. "Who knows? It just bugs me when she does it." He turned and went out onto the balcony.

Donny looked at Trevor. "The man doesn't like it. What can I say?"

Trevor smiled. "It's okay. I've seen his stubborn side. What do you think?"

Donny smirked. "About Domingo? I think that there are more things in heaven and earth, Horatio, than you can shake a damned stick at, so why get uptight about it?"

Trevor laughed. "I'm with you there!"

Dan returned to the room. "Want some help with cleaning up before we get out of your hair?"

Donny looked at him. "You're not in my hair, and no, I don't require any help. I have a built-in dishwasher and a robot for a vacuum cleaner. And I'm not referring to the boy, who always did a little bit of tidying here and there, but thank you for the offer. And thanks again for the Chartreuse. Now that you no longer drink twelve beer at a gulp, I can handle what you leave behind for me to tidy up."

Donny went down to the lobby, leaving them where he'd met them three hours earlier.

SIX

Heat

The night felt as though it might combust. The coolness of Donny's condo was just a memory. Each breath seemed a chore as they stepped into the car. Neither of them spoke till Dan flipped on the AC full blast and they sat back, shocked into inertia. Five minutes later they were heading east over the Don Valley, mulling over the news that Lester had left Donny and gone back to his family.

"There was more to it than that," Trevor said, looking down at the black glass of the river beneath them. "He told me about it when we went out onto the balcony together. He said he didn't want to bring it up in front of Domingo."

Dan turned to look, curious that Donny would have confided in Trevor. "Bring what up?"

"Donny thinks Lester got scared and decided he needed to get out of town."

"Scared of what?"

"Apparently he ran into someone from his past. A man he used to live with who abused him."

Dan thought this over for a moment. "I knew about the man. Donny never told me Lester had seen him since then."

They passed through Chinatown East, with its reams of fruit and vegetable stands over-ripening in the heat. Red and yellow lights winked and flashed, giving the impression the city was on fire. Pedestrians plodded with leaden footsteps, as though enduring a stronger gravity field than normal. No one was oblivious to the temperature.

"Lester didn't mention it till last week," Trevor told him. "That's when he decided to leave. Donny wants to talk to you about it when he can speak to you in private."

Dan mulled this over. Obviously it hadn't been a total secret, or Ked wouldn't have known about it. He wondered what explanation Lester had given Ked for wanting to return to his family.

They passed on into the heart of Leslieville. An overhang of branches held sway as the car turned onto their street and edged up to the house. A whiff of smoke hung in the air when they got out of the car. Dan thought of the garage arsonist and looked around. Nothing. Probably just a backyard fire burning somewhere.

They turned to the darkened house. A blast of stale heat hit them as they opened the door. The interior carried an air of quiet torpor. Ked's hoodie lay draped over the banister, as though he'd returned while they were out. Even in the heat, he was seldom without it. *He must have forgotten to take it when he left for his game earlier*, Dan thought.

Ralph thumped a greeting with his tail. Too hot to move, he was nonetheless alert for the possibility of a walk. Since Trevor's arrival, Ralph's behaviour had improved noticeably. His longstanding disagreements with Dan had diminished: fewer accidents on the front hall carpet, fewer items of clothing destroyed when he got frustrated at the long wait between walks.

"How's my favourite puppy?" Trevor intoned, giving Ralph a quick rub behind the ears.

"Is that how you get him to behave?" Dan asked.

"That and the occasional treat. Bribery and flattery work for most humans, so why not dogs?"

Everyone needed love, it seemed.

"Why not indeed?" Dan echoed, heading for the hall phone.

The first message was a goodnight call from Ked at his mother's house. His words were touching. "I miss you guys already," he said. His voice lowered confidentially. "But I'm not telling Mom that. Give Ralph a scratch behind the ears for me."

Done, Dan thought, bemused as the message ended and another began. The next voice was strange to his ears — curt, metallic. It sounded as though a very officious robot were talking.

"This is a message for Mr. Dan Sharp. Mr. Sharp, sir, this is Detective Karl Danes of the Toronto Police, 11 Division. We met last night at the North York Pork Slaughterhouse."

Dan pictured the fleshy police officer. The man's name had been something like Danes.

The voice continued. "Sir, something further has come to light in this regard and I would appreciate an hour or so of your time. If you could call the following number, day or night, and let me know when it would be convenient to meet with you, I would greatly appreciate it. My number is …"

Dan switched off the message. "Domingo," he said.

Trevor had followed him into the hall. He looked over.

Dan shook his head. "'It's not over yet.' She actually said that less than an hour ago."

Trevor watched Dan's face. "You don't sound surprised. Did you know you were going to get this message?"

Dan gave him an aggrieved look. "No. I didn't know anything about it. How could I? Anyway, what does 'not over yet' mean? Lots of things are not over. Darryl Hillary still needs to be accounted for, for one thing. His life may be over, but his story isn't finished till they catch his killer. Why is that significant?"

Trevor gave him a small smile. "I'm not trying to convince you of anything."

"I know."

Dan leaned in and kissed him. "Sorry, I don't mean to gripe at you. Thank you for understanding me better than I understand myself sometimes."

Trevor laughed. "Ah, there's the rub! It's not that I understand you better; it's just that I'm not in denial about who you are."

Ralph came over and gave Trevor an appealing look.

"I'll walk Ralph while you phone the good detective back. Then afterward let's share some body heat and say dirty things to one another."

"Deal."

They hadn't intended to have sex in that heat, but once they started it was too hard to stop. *No sleeping till this is over*, Dan told himself. He was surprised by the immediacy of his need, both physically and emotionally. His hunger for Trevor was ravenous, as though nothing could contain or hold it back. Some days he felt as if it would expand until he burst. His life was suddenly, unexpectedly beginning to make sense, a defining force bringing coherence to chaos.

Dan watched their bodies in the dresser mirror, his own hard and compact with a layering of hair, twinned against Trevor's smaller, smoother boyish frame. He felt like a twenty-year-old in lust again. The passion was real. They both felt it. Their desire kept them grappling over one another despite the sweat and the temperature inside, even hotter than outside.

As always, Dan dominated Trevor's lither body, overarching and urging till he felt himself entering, all the while wondering when the time would come that Trevor pushed him away and said, *Enough*. But not this time, not yet. He felt that initial resistance followed by the sudden surge inward, heard Trevor's softly sighing acceptance of the intrusion and his encouraging *Yes!*, as though this temporary joining might at last make them one. It was times like these, and no other, that Dan felt Trevor fully in accord with him, their mutual need an affirmation of their life together, far more than simply a brief respite from any thoughts of running back to his island sanctuary.

Afterward, exhausted and overcome with the heat and exertion, he lay with his head on Trevor's shoulder. Trevor absently reached up and traced the scar running along Dan's temple.

"I'm sorry if I seemed upset last night when you got home."

"Don't apologize for having feelings. You didn't know where I was. I would have been upset too."

Trevor shrugged. "Not for having feelings, but for subjecting you to them."

"That's part of partnership. Isn't it about sharing what's going on with one another? I once dated a guy who never asked how I was feeling in over two years. I'm not sure you can call it a relationship if you don't have a clue what's going on with your other half."

Trevor laughed. "I just don't want you to think I'm a nutcase. I've been honest with you about the past, but that's over and done with."

"Is it?"

Trevor gently tugged at Dan's hair. "What do you mean?"

"You can't just put what happened with you and Joe on a shelf and hope it will stay there. He's gone, but you've still got all those feelings to contend with. If you deny them, you'll explode."

Dan pictured the Japanese Garden on the west coast island where Trevor lived, and where the ashes of his ex-lover were scattered. To the casual eye, Trevor exuded confidence, a feeling inspired largely by his easygoing good looks. To those who knew him, however, the story was quite different. Part of him stayed on Mayne Island. There, he'd been protected, sheltered. Outside of his environment he was exposed and vulnerable, far more susceptible to currents of fear and self-doubt.

"How has it been these last few weeks?" Dan asked.

Trevor looked out the window. The CN Tower rose in the distance, a solitary inland lighthouse, immense, blinking out a warning to anyone straying too close to its realm. "I'm still adjusting to the city. After the island it feels crowded and chaotic. It's always noisy here. It's beautiful in its way, but it doesn't feel comforting."

Dan pulled him closer. "You know I'll do anything to fix whatever I can for you."

Trevor smiled. "Can you make four million people go away? Can you replace all the concrete with grass?"

"Not overnight, but I'll see what I can do about it in the long term."

Trevor kissed Dan's ear. "I don't expect you to fix my problems. I just need you to understand when I'm dealing with something that overwhelms me."

"I'll do my best."

"It's hard to explain. It's as though I wake up each morning with my mind already in fight-or-flight mode. I don't want to fear waking up every day. I know the city doesn't cause it, but being here exacerbates those feelings."

"That's a lot of anxiety for anyone to bear. I wouldn't want you to stay here if you really can't stand it."

Trevor twisted around to look at Dan directly. "Be patient with me. I really am trying."

"Don't worry. I can deal with whatever you throw at me."

Trevor looked chagrined. "That's just it. I don't want you to have to deal with me. Just accept me for what I am and let me do what I need to do. It will happen."

"All right."

"How about you? What do you want from me?"

Dan thought for a moment then said, "Companionship, more than anything. I want someone to share my concerns and make me laugh and feel better about my shortcomings. Sex is great, but there's no guarantee it will last till we're eighty. Intimacy is much better, when you come down to it. I want someone to rub my back when it aches and whisper in my ear when I'm sad and lonely."

Trevor ruffled Dan's hair and smiled.

"What? Is that too much to ask?" Dan said.

"Not at all. It's perfect. I just didn't know you were such a poet."

"All right. What do you want from me?"

"Much the same. I want someone to welcome me when I come home, someone who appreciates me just for coming in the door. Someone who makes me feel secure. I miss that."

Dan rolled over and propped his chin on his palm. "Why did you and Joe get involved? You knew he was HIV-positive when you met."

"The usual story: I fell in love when we met. Only I wasn't thinking about the dying part when I agreed to move in with him. I was only thinking about how I felt for him then."

"Did it last?"

"The love? Sure, but it wasn't always at a fever pitch. The daily routine of keeping Joseph healthy was demanding. I never thought it would become a full-time occupation, but at the end I had to choose between my career and looking after him. I cared too much about him to hire someone else to look after him, so I let the career slide. I wouldn't choose differently now, if that's what you're asking."

"You probably were a great caregiver."

He smiled sadly. "I think I was, but I couldn't detach. After Joe died, I lost my purpose in life. Even when I tried to bury myself in work it still seeped through. It felt like I had taken on this job no one else could do. So when …" He faltered.

"So when he killed himself, you felt you'd failed him."

Trevor nodded. "Yes."

"You took that on yourself too."

"I thought I could make a difference."

"You probably did. Chances are he would have killed himself sooner, if you hadn't been there."

Trevor shook his head. "That's what I'm not sure about. I live with the fear that he killed himself to free me from the relentlessness of his illness."

"A sacrifice …"

"When in reality he had become my reason for living. So when he died, in a way I died too."

The silence held. Dan didn't break it. This was Trevor's confession. He needed to bring it out in his own way, a little bit at a time. To examine the debris that remained after the blast, the annihilating heat that consumed everything, until one day the fears would be gone, the past would be remote and unable to threaten them. One day.

Dan reached up to stroke Trevor's face. This was where the richness of a relationship lay, he knew, in this sharing of themselves and sorting through the intimate details each would have to know in order to live with the other. The quirks and habits, the fears and desires. These were the things they needed to absorb carefully and slowly, sifting through the fragments of each other's life, one story and one emotion at a time, if they wanted to survive.

SEVEN

The Altar Boy and the Thief

To BYSTANDERS, THE POSTMODERN STRUCTURE overlooking Bay Street at College appears like some whimsical concoction spirited away from Las Vegas or Disneyland rather than the Metro Toronto Police headquarters. Outside, blue glass and pink marble glint in the sun. Inside, light streams generously down onto the atrium floor from ten stories above. Who says the police commission doesn't have good taste?

Dan arrived a few minutes before nine. The uniformed blonde at the desk smiled when he said his name.

"Constable Donna Blake," she said, reaching across the counter to shake his hand. "We've spoken on the phone many times."

Dan returned the smile. Although it was their first face-to-face encounter, he and Donna had had several heated though not entirely antagonistic exchanges over who he could and could not have access to by telephone after hours. What had started off as a minor irritation on both sides transformed over time to a form of passive-aggressive flirting, as though he'd been nibbling on her neck and she would occasionally slap him before letting him progress a little farther each time.

"A pleasure to meet you in person, Donna," he said cordially.

She looked at him appraisingly. "You too. You look kinda like you sound on the phone — rough and ready."

"Thanks, I think."

"Oh, don't worry," she said, giving him the once-over. "It's a compliment. What's your gym?"

"Extreme Fitness."

"Really? Mine too. See you there sometime?"

"You never know."

She checked her book. "Go up to the second floor and head down the left-hand corridor to the very end. There's a coffee machine and a bench. You can wait there till someone comes for you."

He felt her gaze on him as he turned and walked to the elevators.

Once upstairs, he didn't have long to wait. He'd been sitting less than a minute when a junior officer with a clipboard approached. *Another kid,* Dan thought. *Or am I just getting that much older than everyone else?* The officer flipped a page, inquired Dan's name in an aggressively efficient manner then indicated a door across the hall.

"In here, sir. They're expecting you."

Dan entered and was momentarily thrown off guard. Four faces looked up expectantly. There, seated with the two officers he'd encountered at the morgue, were the chief of police and Dan's former boss, Ed Burch. Ed was one of the few authority figures Dan respected wholeheartedly. He relaxed somewhat on seeing him, but was still aware he'd entered potentially hostile territory.

The room was designed to make newcomers feel less intimidated at being in the headquarters of one of the biggest power bases in the country outside of the military. Tall bay windows allowed in considerable light, as though the architect had been tasked with providing a police station that, while grand, in no way resembled a place of incarceration. It was a pleasant anteroom in Buckingham Palace, say, versus the dreaded Tower of London. Soft music gave it the aura of a spa, while ferns drooped lazily from ceiling hangers. Ironically, the hanging plants reminded Dan of the slaughterhouse, which, he knew, was what had brought him here today.

While Dan had already sized up the two younger officers, he knew the chief by reputation only. The man came forward, hand extended, a silver-haired bulldog with a disarming grin that settled back into a habitual frown as soon as it was no longer needed. Dan had been reluctantly impressed with the man's ability to present himself in public through various media appearances, as well as his efforts at building community relations with the force. Here was a man who worked hard to look and sound good. Still, Dan wasn't convinced they'd be on the same side of the barricades come the revolution. As chief of police, he believed in the unquestioned right of authority and had shown that, for good or bad, he would do anything to perpetuate and uphold it.

The chief indicated the officers Dan had met earlier. "Let me introduce you. Detective Danes and Constable First Class Pfeiffer, this is Mr. Dan Sharp."

Here, once again, were the force's bratty Jack Spratt and his awkward, shuffling wife. The missus — Detective Danes — was her usual hesitant self. This was the man who belonged to the voice on his answering machine, making the other one Constable Pfeiffer. The latter eyed him through barely raised lids. He was chewing gum again. Dan remembered the shorter officer's cockiness. There was something slightly restrained about him here in the presence of the chief. An invisible leash, perhaps. In the clear light of day, his uniform and the faint outline of a moustache were about the only things that differentiated him from an adolescent punk. That wasn't possible, of course. With his First Class officer designation, there would have to be at least four years between his entering the force and receiving First Class status. So maybe twenty-three or -four, at the very least. Still, he reminded Dan of a truculent teenager on the lookout for trouble.

Neither of the officers extended a hand. Dan nodded to the pair, who remained seated across the table. "We met at the morgue yesterday," he said simply.

"Both Detective Danes and Constable Pfeiffer are among the most highly regarded men on the force," the chief said then turned to Ed. "Now here's someone you know."

Dan greeted his former boss. "Hello, Ed. Fancy meeting you here."

"Good to see you again, Dan." A comforting smile and honest yet discerning eyes. Well built, with the self-confidence of a former pro hockey player.

Addressing his officers, the chief continued. "Mr. Sharp I know of by reputation only, but that reputation is an impeccable one corroborated by his former employer, Ed here, who was one of my best cops until the son-of-a-bitch went freelance on me."

Ed acknowledged the backhanded compliment with a smile.

"But I'm getting ahead of myself," the chief said. He turned directly to Dan. "Dan — may I call you Dan?"

Dan nodded. "Certainly."

"The reason we've asked you here today, as I'm sure you realize, is because of the body you discovered at the old slaughterhouse." His hands shuffled the papers on the desk before him, but his sharp blue eyes stayed on Dan's face.

"The man's name was Darryl Hillary," Dan said.

"Yes. I understand you had been hired to find him by his sister …" Here he looked down. "… Darlene Hillary."

"That's correct."

The chief looked back up at Dan again, taking his measure like any good tailor or undertaker. "None of what I'm saying here today is under overt censorship of any sort, but we would appreciate it if you would keep it to yourself for now. For reasons of discretion, we can't have the media finding out certain details I'm about to disclose just yet. Are you good with that?"

Dan inclined his head slightly: open to suggestion but not willing to be led down the garden path. "I'd have to know what it is first before agreeing to treat it confidentially, but if it's above board and nothing to do with me then I can give you a reasonable assurance I'll keep my mouth shut about it."

The chief looked to Ed. "You described him pretty well, Ed," he said.

"Dan's a straight shooter," Ed said, nodding.

Dan wasn't taken in by this surface dusting of comradely jousting. While he trusted his former boss, Ed had ties to the police that predated his relationship with Dan. Perhaps one loyalty outweighed the other. What lay behind this surprise meeting was impossible to say. He still needed to know why he'd been brought here. What more he could tell them that he hadn't already indicated in his statement the previous evening remained to be seen.

The chief gave him another shrewd look, as though trying to decide how much to confide in him: *Are you for us or against us?* As far as Dan was concerned, they'd invited him to this game of poker, so it was up to them to reveal their hand first.

"I won't mince words here, Dan. The reason we've asked you to come by today is because Ed suggested you might help us."

Dan's ears pricked up. This was the first he'd heard of being asked to help the police.

He turned to Ed, who took up the narrative briefly.

"That's right, Daniel. I've been asked to work as a special consultant on the case, in light of my capacity as a former police officer. When I heard what was being asked, I suggested you might have a part to play in it."

The chief's icy eyes travelled from Ed back to Dan. "We believe yesterday's murder is related to a larger investigation into a child prostitution ring, which has now taken on the proportions of a Canada-wide operation. Detective Danes was assigned to lead the operation in the GTA. With Hillary's murder, Constable Pfeiffer has just taken over as evidence officer. That's where Ed felt you might help us, Dan."

Dan noted how the chief liked to say his name, as though to bring him further into his confidence. He was struck by the suggestion that Hillary's death had to do with larger issues of child exploitation. Had his sister lied again about her brother's record? Was he in fact a more serious offender? Dan felt a tingle of repugnance to think that Darryl had done something worse than sleep with his underage girlfriend.

The chief continued. "With this recent death, we feel we may have the makings of a serial killer on our hands."

Dan stared at him. "You're saying it's not the first?"

The chief nodded. "This past spring, an ex-priest was murdered in Quebec. Although we're pretty sure we know who did it, his killer was never found."

"What makes you think the two murders are related?" Dan asked.

The chief gave a significant look to Constable Pfeiffer, who addressed Dan for the first time.

"Like the victim you found earlier this week," the young officer said, "the ex-priest was severely beaten and had his left ear cut off."

Dan recalled the change in attitude of the cop on duty at the slaughterhouse. Once the officer learned of the severed ear, Dan was suddenly no longer welcome on the site. Someone had murdered an ex-priest, and now a poet, cutting off their left ears. What did it signify? Perhaps more importantly, what did the two men have in common?

The chief cut in. "When Sergeant Danes phoned me with his report, I knew immediately what we were dealing with. You may recall that part of the National Sex Offender

Registry was dumped on the Internet last year. Both the ex-priest and Hillary were named on it."

Dan recalled reports of the incident, the inconclusive findings as to whether it had been deliberate or not. He held up a finger. "Excuse me. Was it proved to be an accident? The names being dumped on the Internet?"

The chief nodded in acknowledgement. "We still don't know how it got there, but the information was deliberately released by person or persons unknown."

Dan thought about Darlene Hillary's pleading question: *How did these people even find him?* she'd asked. *They have their ways*, he'd replied, thinking of the registry at the time. It gave cold comfort to know he'd been right.

The registry was created to compile information, including current addresses, phone numbers, and identifying markings, such as tattoos, that would enable police officers to finger possible suspects in sex-related crimes. Providing up-to-date personal information was mandatory on the part of the offenders. The public was never supposed to have access to the list, however. That the registry had been leaked on the Internet was cause for alarm for any number of reasons, including the possibility that someone might try to harm or kill anybody named in it, as seemed to have been the case here.

"So you think someone is targeting known sex offenders?"

The chief nodded. "That's my best guess at present. The only thing linking the two victims is that their names were on the Sex Offender Registry and they both had their left ear cut off." He scrutinized Dan's face. "Are you fine with everything we've told you so far?"

"Except for one thing. I understood from Hillary's sister that he had applied to have his name removed from the registry on the grounds that he was not likely to be a repeat offender."

A look passed between the chief and Danes, who shrugged.

"We don't know anything about that," the chief said, turning back to Dan.

"Okay." Dan nodded. "I still don't know why you're telling me this."

The chief opened a file and placed it in front of Dan. Clipped to the dossier was the photograph of a young man in jeans and a sweatshirt. His cherubic face and curly dark hair made him look like the junior member of a boy band.

"This is the chief suspect in the murder of the ex-priest, Guillaume Thierry. He was an altar boy at the church in Montreal where Thierry worked. Eventually, Thierry was convicted of sexual interference with a number of minors, all male. He went to jail for eight years and was released just two months before his murder." He put a finger on the photograph. "The young man's name is Gaetan Bélanger. He was a minor until a few days after Thierry was killed."

Dan had been listening intently. "Why do you think it was Bélanger instead of one of the other abuse victims?"

"Speculation, mostly, but he blogged his intentions to harm Thierry and was heard uttering death threats against him when he was released."

"He blogged it?" Dan asked, surprised.

"Yes. He put his intentions online. That doesn't make the threat more real, but it does constitute a clear motive."

"Physical evidence?"

"Nothing conclusive."

"Anything connecting him to Hillary?"

"Nothing yet. What we know of this kid since his molestation is that he's lived by thievery. He was caught twice over the past few years, both times before Thierry's murder. Nothing major, but the second instance earned him a term in juvenile detention. The first time he was caught stealing from a church — not the one where he was molested, but I'm sure there was a connection in his mind."

"But why kill Hillary?" Dan asked. "Why not murder another priest?"

"We're not sure why, but the missing ear tells us it's Bélanger. It seems to be his signature. That's why I've put two of my brightest officers on the case."

Dan looked over at Mr. and Mrs. Spratt. The missus, he felt sure, would not qualify as bright and probably had been put on the case for other reasons. As for young Mr. Spratt, Dan wasn't convinced, but his cockiness said he believed himself to be intellectually superior.

"Did the boy blog about his intentions to kill Darryl Hillary as well?" Dan asked.

Danes spoke up now. "Not specifically, but he has blogged a number of rants online directed at child molesters in general."

"Do you know if he had access to the leaked registry?"

Danes shook his head. "Nothing conclusive."

Dan looked back at the chief. "Presumably anyone on that registry stands to become a potential victim."

"That's what we're worried about."

Pfeiffer spoke up. "All our data indicates that Bélanger is holed up somewhere in Toronto. He may have been here for several months already. In fact, we believe he came to Ontario right after the murder. He probably blends in well. Young Quebeckers are far more likely to be bilingual than English kids."

Dan considered this. "Then why not put all your efforts into finding him?"

Pfeiffer's expression hardened. "Oh, we'll find him all right," he said with the sort of burning zeal Dan distrusted in authority figures. "But we'd prefer to find him before he kills again."

Ed spoke up. "That's why I thought of you, Daniel."

"Well, it's all very intriguing," Dan said. "But I still don't understand how I can be of help."

The chief smiled tersely. "You are here because of the swiftness and accuracy of your search for Darryl Hillary. We understand you located him in less than three days. That's impressive." He looked at Ed. "It was just coincidence that I mentioned your name to Ed yesterday in connection with the case."

Ed spoke again. "You're here, Daniel, because I said you were one of the best missing persons investigators I've come across, as well as being the number one person in the country for finding missing juveniles."

Dan shook his head. "Still, I'm not a police officer and as far as I know the police force doesn't hire outside. So, again, I ask why I'm here."

The chief looked at Burch then at Dan. "Ed said that you have some very good contacts on the street. I'm told they are contacts the police are not always privy to, for a variety of reasons. We would like access to those sources."

Dan sat back. At last it was clear. He shook his head.

"Even if I gave you the names of the people I use, I doubt any of them would help you. Many of them live on the fringes of society. They want nothing to do with the socio-economic systems of the city, or even of the world, for that matter." He shrugged. "I know it sounds kooky, but these people have as little to do with our government and political system as possible. Most of them would not willingly have anything to do with the police, if they could help it. You might say that money talks, but I'm sure you realize there are things even money can't buy. These people can be as fanatical in their devotion to their beliefs as any radical jihadists. And the upshot, if I just handed over my contacts to you, would be that I would lose their trust. Probably forever."

"They wouldn't need to know," the chief said with a calculating look.

Dan shook his head. He stood. "I'm sorry, but I don't think I can help you."

The chief looked grimly at him. "Will you at least think it over?"

Dan nodded. "I'll think it over. I'm not unreasonable. I'm just telling you what I'm dealing with."

He looked around at the faces watching him. Dan wondered if they resented his refusal. He thought about how audacious it was for them to have asked. He felt bad for Ed, who obviously thought he might have been willing to consider the offer seriously.

He stood.

"Gentlemen."

"Thank you for your time," the chief said.

Dan pushed open the big wooden doors and headed for the men's room. His early morning coffee was going right through him. He lined up at the nearest urinal. After a moment, he heard the door open. Pfeiffer came and stood next to him. The cop took time with his zipper. Out of the corner of his eye, Dan caught him looking over. If he hadn't known better he would swear he was being flirted with. After Pfeiffer's homophobic insults at the morgue, this pseudo-come-on was ludicrous.

Dan glanced down. Compared with his own endowment, Constable First Class Pfeiffer really was just a boy.

"You could be doing someone a big favour," the cop said.

Dan zipped himself up. "What kind of favour did you have in mind?"

Pfeiffer seemed unruffled by the innuendo. "A professional favour." He looked over. "You might be wondering why we would care so much about a bunch of perverts. Truth is, everyone's entitled to be protected from murder."

"Actually," said Dan, "I don't doubt that at all. Cops are hired to enforce the law, not to judge people. The man you referred to as a 'perv' in the morgue yesterday was actually the boyfriend of the girl he went to jail for. There wasn't that much difference in age between them."

Pfeiffer gave him a reproachful look. "Still, he broke the law."

"And he paid a penalty for it well beyond his so-called 'crime.' Some might say it was an unjust law in his situation. Personal philosophy aside, I don't think he deserved to die and so, yes, I would do what I could to help prevent another such death. In any case, the law protects us all equally, or so I've been led to believe."

Pfeiffer shrugged. "So they say."

Dan turned to look at him. "It wasn't so long ago that the law put guys like me in jail for our so-called sexual persuasion. Anyone caught looking down at another man's penis while standing at a urinal, even if out of envy and not desire, would definitely have been considered suspect in that regard."

Dan stepped over to the sink, rinsed his hands, and left. Pfeiffer was still standing at the urinal when the door closed on him.

Ed caught up with Dan at the elevators. His ex-boss looked sheepish.

"Sorry to get you down here for the wrong reasons," Ed said.

"I can't do it, Ed. As much as I'd like to help out, it won't work. My sources don't trust cops."

"I told them that. They insisted we get you in here anyway."

"So why don't they listen?"

"Because they're hoping I will change your mind. The truth is, your sources don't need to know that a particular request to find someone comes from the police."

"I suppose not."

"So, if I were to hire you to help me find someone, you could conceivably invoke the aid of your best sources with no one being the wiser."

Dan shrugged. "If I wanted to, that is."

"And because I respect you, I would not engage your services without full disclosure."

Dan looked at Ed. "I know that, Ed."

Ed smiled his comforting smile. "So please don't be offended if I come to you in future with a request and you happen not to like where it comes from. I hope you will at least consider it before you turn me down."

Dan gave him a rueful nod. "You know I'd take any request from you seriously."

Ed held out an envelope. "Then please take this one seriously."

"What is it?"

"It's the kid's photograph. If you come across anyone … if you hear anything."

Dan hesitated. He thought of Darlene Hillary's request then nodded and took the envelope. "All right. I can do that much for you."

"Appreciated, Daniel."

At that moment, the elevator dinged. The doors whooshed open and a tall figure in black strode past them.

Dan looked after the man's back as he disappeared down the hall.

"Wasn't that…?"

Ed looked over in surprise. "Someone you know?"

"Sort of. Someone famous, at least," Dan said. "I think that was Jags Rohmer. Big rock star from the eighties. Kind of faded now. Still, it's not everyday you see a celebrity in real life."

"I saw Woody Harrelson in a restaurant once. He was quite ordinary looking. You expect them to be bigger than life or lit up in neon or something, but nope — it was just Woody, bald as a billiard ball."

"What could Jags Rohmer be doing here?" Dan wondered.

Ed shrugged. "Your guess is as good as mine. Probably better in this case, since I don't know who he is."

They shook hands.

Dan got in the elevator and pushed the button for the ground floor. The doors closed. He wondered if Jags Rohmer would be made to sit on a bench in the hallway before being summoned to a meeting by some junior official with a clipboard.

EIGHT

Moles

Dan watched as the curly red-headed figure on the ledge lit a joint. He held the smoke in for five, ten, fifteen seconds before exhaling slowly. One foot on the radiator, shoulder against the wall, body in full recline mode. At five-eight, and easily two hundred and forty pounds, he could move like a ninja when he wanted to. Right now he was stationary.

He held out the roach to Dan, who shook his head.

"Look, dude. Don't even come here if you're thinking of chatting with the cops."

He glanced at a window high above where a finger of light pointed into his underground cavern from the Other World.

"How do I know you weren't followed?" The head tilted skyward. "They could be up there right now planning to raid my place."

He stood and headed to a console hosting a dozen miniature display screens, tapped in a few quick commands and scrutinized a monitor in the lower right-hand corner. Satisfied with what he saw, he swivelled in his seat and faced Dan.

"All good. Nothing moving out there. You weren't followed."

"You know me, Germ. I'm cool."

Dan was never sure if Germ was just paranoid or if he ran a sideline business that required him to keep watch on whoever or whatever approached his private underground preserve. Better safe than sorry, in either case.

Dan shook his head. "Besides, I never told them I was coming here to see you. As far as they know, I could be visiting my grandmother right now."

Germ gave him an ironic look. "Yeah, right. Your grandmother who lives in a derelict underground garage."

Dan smiled. "She probably did once. She was a very cool old lady in her day. Anyway, it's not like I mentioned your name or anything. They just wanted to know if I could put them in touch with my sources."

"And you said?" Another quick intake of spliff. No coughing. The guy was hardcore.

"I told them not a chance. I said that if I named you I'd lose you and that you were worth far too much to me to risk losing."

"Good man," Germ squeaked out.

Smoke dribbled from the edges of his mouth, hypnotic and swirling. The milky-blue strands gave a decorative embellishment to the graffiti covering the walls. Every inch of floor, walls and ceiling, even the pipes, was covered in a fabulous concoction of colours and shapes and grimacing creatures. It was life as a permanent acid trip, depicted with all the fervour of a manic cartoonist or an obsessive tattoo artist. Van Gogh or Toulouse-Lautrec as street artists, David Wojnarowicz at his transgressive heights, Keith Haring at his most radiant, and Jean-Michel Basquiat at his most manic-hallucinogenic. It was the sort of artwork found in unexpected places — subway lines, construction fences, the underside of bridges — like an alternate meaning superimposed on top of everyday reality. As though you could read into things only if you knew the secret code that allowed you to penetrate the city's inner core. *And people say the underground is dead*, Dan thought.

"Nice work, by the way. Yours?" he asked

"Nope. This is Velvet Blue's stuff. Cool, isn't it?"

Velvet Blue was the Japanese girlfriend of the man smoking pot. A female ninja in her own right, she was a whirlwind with the litheness of a pygmy gymnast. The pair was famous for their artwork-cum-industrial sabotage, collages of graffiti and photographs installed over commercial advertising campaigns, signed R.Y.M. *Reclaim Your Mind.* Art with a social message. The signature was Internet code for the curious to inquire who was behind the toothpaste ad featuring earthworms wriggling from the tube, the mad lyricism of Baudelaire superimposed over sunscreen bottles, or the skull-and-crossbones laid across Tylenol capsules. Germ and Velvet Blue were among the last few practitioners of civil disobedience in public spaces. They were adept at it. "That's highly valuable mindspace being exploited by these corporations with little or no public benefit," Germ told Dan the first time they met. "Also valuable in a financial sense, of course. They don't take well to having their little campaigns fucked with," he said jubilantly. Germ and Velvet Blue were also among the most knowledgeable people in the city in terms of what was happening on the ground level, dishing dirt with the hoi polloi.

Having accomplished what he'd set out to do in alerting people that their minds were under attack, Germ changed strategies and took up another target. His latest fascination was for abandoned buildings — the detritus of modern living — and thus Dan's great respect for his arcane knowledge. If you wanted to find someone living off the grid — the ones who didn't show up on CCTV feeds all over the city, the people who never ventured into banks and shopping malls and subways or entered their PINs in ATMs — then Germ was your man. A sophisticated urban guerrilla, he knew the terrain better than anyone Dan had ever met.

"Anyway, I just wanted to pass the idea by you. You could be doing something significant to help others escape harm."

The shaggy head nodded. "Which I have no problem with. Just that helping them means participating in the System. And I know you understand my position on that entirely."

Dan held up a hand. "No need for the lecture. I know the score."

Germ grinned and took another toke. "You probably know it by heart by now, right?"

"Nearly," Dan said. "Hey, I come from the dirt. I'm no fan of the System either. My father and his father both lived and died in the mines."

"Which makes us brothers under the skin. My old man? A sanitation engineer. That's garbage collector to the rest of us. So I come by my trade legit."

By "trade" he meant street art as much as picking up the cast-offs that people above ground considered waste. His underground bunker was outfitted with salvaged furniture and electronics.

While Germ thought of himself as a social critic, he was also a highly talented photographer. His online galleries of abandoned places and discarded objects had the aura of high art. Unmoved by ordinary beauty, only the lowest of the low received his loving adoration: peeling paint, mould-covered surfaces, rusting fixtures, broken furniture, shattered glass, rotting mattresses, dangling wires. Here was Jackson Pollock with a camera and a social vision. With the right agent, his work might have been showcased anywhere: New York's MoMA, London's Saatchi, or any prestigious gallery worth its name featuring the avant garde. Instead, he spilled his work online, where anyone could access it for free.

Dan had come across him by accident while tracking a young drug addict. His mother had warned him her son was suicidal. Dan put all his effort into finding the boy, who had a penchant for hiding out in abandoned buildings. He needed an expert on the city's abandoned sites and found one through a site called *Germ Warfare*.

Germ — short for Germaine — was its author and creator. Dan contacted him and asked for his help, explaining the urgency. Off the top of his head, Germ named ten buildings that had recently been vacated — meaning their interiors were up for habitation by anyone looking for a free place to sleep. He'd been correct in helping pinpoint the building in question, but not in time for Dan to prevent the young man's suicide.

The connection continued. Dan found reason to draw on Germ's specialized knowledge several times in the intervening months. Germ eventually trusted Dan enough to invite him to his secret hideout, introducing him to his girlfriend, Velvet Blue.

Germ and Velvet Blue inhabited their underground lair like a pair of happy moles, making their way to the surface only when necessary. A slight girl, Velvet Blue could take care of herself in a scrape. She was the martial arts expert in the family, where Germ handled the creative-espionage side of things. They lived in abandoned warehouses and underground tunnels, planning raids and industrial sabotage, taking the city's pulse from below ground level.

"So you said you're looking for someone," Germ said.

"*Was.* I was looking. He's dead. I think one of your contacts called to tell me where he was, but I got there too late. He was murdered."

Germ contemplated this with a grim expression. "Taking a life, man. That is definitely not cool."

"No, I think not. So tell me about your last visit to the slaughterhouse."

"Right. Like I said on the phone, it was a little weird. I was doing one of my photo essays on urban decay. Places like that usually you find, like, these kids. You know — the stoner type looking to get away from their parents." He glanced at the roach in his hand and laughed. "Been there, still doing that."

Dan waited patiently for Germ's thoughts to get back on track.

"Anyway. Saw this strange kid there. Something odd about him, something a little off. Not sure what."

"In what way 'odd'? Physically?"

Germ shook his head. "Just … something. Couldn't put my finger on it. You know when that little voice inside says something isn't right, but you can't always tell what it is? Something says, 'Be wary, stay alert.' New York subway style. Like that. Looked like he was waiting for someone. Only it felt odd somehow. Like he already knew whoever he was waiting for wasn't coming." He shook his head again. "But then why would he be waiting? You know what I mean?"

Dan shrugged. "Not exactly."

Germ seemed to lose focus for a moment. He ran his hand over a long blue outline on the wall behind him, following the minute convolutions of his mind.

"Wow, cool."

He left off with whatever had captivated him and looked back at Dan.

"Anyway. Like I said, I saw him twice. First time, I was making a preliminary run of the place for when I came back to take the photos. That's another thing." He looked meaningfully at Dan. "He seemed to freak a little when I took out my camera. You know? You could tell he was up to something, because he acted like he didn't want to be seen — you know the way kids do — though he didn't go to any great length to hide himself. He was just … there, but sort of removed at the same time."

He paused and seemed to get lost in his thoughts.

"You said you saw him twice…."

Germ waved the roach around, took one last toke, then stubbed it out on the floor.

"Yeah, right. Second time, when I came back to take the rest of the photos, he was there in almost the same spot. It was as if he hadn't moved from one week to the next. Like he was frozen in place. That was part of the weirdness, I guess. Everything about him registered as odd on some level. Even his clothes. He was all dressed up like a proper little British schoolboy. So what was he doing in a derelict old place like that?"

Dan nodded. "Maybe he was doing the same thing you were doing — getting stoned and exploring."

Germ laughed. "Yeah. So true."

He turned back to the console and typed in a command. A series of thumbnail images popped up onscreen. He scrutinized them for a moment then brought up three.

"Here, have a look. That's the kid."

Dan examined the photographs. All were shot from behind or in profile. Germ was right — the boy seemed purposefully to be avoiding his camera. Dan noted his slight figure, the navy blazer and hair poking out from under his cap. He might have been any kid wandering around a deserted spot. There was nothing to distinguish him in the photos, nothing particularly unusual except the setting.

"I can't see much of him," Dan said. He pulled out the photo of Gaetan Bélanger that Ed had given him. "Could it have been him?"

Germ focused on the snap, picked it up, and moved it around in the light. He scowled and scratched his head. Then he nodded.

"Could be. Wrong clothes, of course," he said, referring to the sweatshirt and jeans Gaetan had on. "About the same age, though. But if I place him in context, there is a similarity." He put the photo down. "Who is he?"

"A teenage boy wanted for the murder of a priest back in Quebec."

Germ picked up the photo again. "This kid? He looks too cute to be mean."

"Cute but strong, apparently. He garrotted his victim."

"No shit?" Germ looked down at the shot with greater respect, almost reverence, as though he might be considering changing his photographic interests from social decay to physical violence. "Yeah, it coulda been him now that I think of it. I'll take a closer look if I see him again. Guess I better be more careful running around these old places. Never know who you're going to run into."

"Better safe than sorry," Dan said.

Germ looked up at Dan. "Why'd he do it?"

"The priest molested him, but the boy felt he hadn't been punished enough after he got out of jail, so he tracked him down and finished him off, if what I've heard is correct."

"Wow! As lurid as they come. There's a headline for the *Sun*." He brushed aside a lock with his hand. "Velvet Blue was molested by some guy when she was, like, thirteen."

"What'd she do?"

"She kicked him in the balls and told him next time she'd break his neck for him. Never tried it again, apparently."

Dan tossed down the photo of Darryl Hillary.

"What about this guy? Ever see him at the slaughterhouse? This was the guy who was murdered a couple days ago."

Germ looked it over. "Nah. Not him. For sure I didn't see him there. I recognize him, though."

Dan's interest was piqued. If Darryl was such a recluse, it seemed odd that Germ would know him. "From where?"

"Scored our dope from the same source. He showed up at the guy's porch when I was there one day. Can't say why I remember him, but I just do. Something about how frightened he looked. Something in his eyes that reminded me of a beaten dog. Yeah, I guess that was it."

"Do you think he was afraid of the pusher?"

Germ laughed. "No, man. Not Dudley. He'd never hurt a fly. Guy's a nervous little wreck of a man. Kids rip him off all the time. Just cuts off their credit and puts them on his black list, but he never goes after them. Not the type, man. Not the type." He thought about this. "Killing's not his thing. That's more for the hardcore drug dealers."

"Do you think this guy might have had dealings with any of the hardcore types?"

Germ shrugged. "Impossible to say. As I said, I only saw him the once. Didn't say a word to him, just nodded and went about my business."

A phone rang. Germ reached into his shirt pocket and pulled out a cell. He flipped it open and listened without saying a word.

Dan looked around at the walls. The colours were lurid, mostly primaries with dull browns and greys splashed in between, the better to offset the subjects from their backgrounds.

He glanced over at the bank of screens. For the most part, they were static scenes he assumed had something to do with security. The watchful eye. Some were far too dark to give more than a glimpse of the terrain, providing blurry details of buildings and vacant lots. One showed the door Dan had entered, another gave a close-up of the interior of the freight elevator he'd come down on, a rickety contraption that always landed with a bump. The overall effect was of a vast security system designed to keep something in or out of the building. Most of the views were so uninteresting that Dan wondered why Germ bothered to keep tabs on them. A row of garbage bins, a grainy close-up of an entry phone. He presumed it was the one he used to gain access to the compound. For compound it was. Whatever Germ was avoiding, whatever required so much security, it wouldn't find him easily.

Dan looked over and saw the record player in a far corner. High-end, made for connoisseurs, sitting next to a rack of LPs. He fanned through them, mostly seventies with a few sixties records. Cult and collector's items, for the most part. The hard-to-score stuff that audiophiles went mad for.

He flipped through the covers until a face jumped out at him: Jags Rohmer early in his career. Boyish bangs, pouting lips, beret pitched rakishly on his head. Too serious looking to be misread as teen heartthrob material, for all the arty posing.

Germ grunted and said, "Okay." He snapped his cellphone shut and watched Dan sift through the records.

"Vinyl is final, man. They've never made a product to equal it for sound reproduction. Richest, deepest recording playback you will ever hear."

"I agree."

Germ was rolling another joint. The paper twitched expertly between his fingers.

"Live music's a different story, of course. But that ain't the one I'm telling at the moment. The day of the great performer is gone and whether it'll ever come back is anybody's guess. You don't need to learn how to play an instrument any more, just how to press buttons. The music industry fucked itself when it went digital. Instant copying for the masses. I don't mind ripping off the corporations, but that hits the artists. And as we all know, it's fucking hard to live on art in this world."

Dan thought he'd like to put Donny and Germ together for an audiophile chat. It would be one to remember. He held up the Jags Rohmer album.

"I've never seen this before."

Germ came over to him. "Collector's item, my man. Not many of those around. Record company went bankrupt. Guy was fantastic. One of the best in his day."

"Probably still is."

Germ tipped his head. "Who knows? No one's heard a thing from him for years. He could be dead."

Dan looked over. "I saw him this morning."

"No way!"

"Way. He was at the station when I went in for my chat with the brass. I bumped into him in the hallway when I left."

Germ's face was incredulous. "Jags Rohmer was at a police station? What did he do?"

Dan laughed. "Nothing, so far as I know. He was roaming the hallway on his own, but it was him for sure."

Germ sat back on the ledge and lit the joint. He crooned softly to himself: "*Sell me your dreams, tell me your pleasures. Open your heart, I want your treasures …*"

Dan waited while Germ was off in his other dimension. *Just let me know when you land, dude*, he thought.

Germ nodded. He spoke again. "Saw him once in '94 or '95. Back when I was a kid. Guy was in his prime then. Left a lasting impression, I can say that. All dressed up in black leather, S&M accoutrements. Had a reputation for being a hardcore rocker, but he always had an intellectual bent."

His expression went all whimsical for a moment, looking off into the past again.

"Wouldn't mind hearing a little more from him before he hangs up his spurs for good."

Dan handed over the album. "Write him a fan letter. I'm sure he'd appreciate it." He winked.

Germ looked at him. "Funny guy."

"Hey — even hardcore rockers like to be told they're appreciated."

"Yeah, but I'd have to buy a stamp, which means fraternizing with the post office, which means …"

"… supporting the government," Dan chimed in. "I know."

"And we all know the bastard in power now is just one throw away from the Third Reich. You mark my words, that son of a bitch is going to leave a lasting legacy we will take years to dig out from."

"'That son of a bitch'? Do you even know our current prime minister's name?"

Germ held up a warning finger. "Not mine, man. I don't vote. And not to be uttered within these hallowed halls, my friend. Spare me the negative vibes. You want to talk about him, take it outside."

"All right. I'm going anyway. I've got to get back."

At the elevator, Dan turned for one last look. "If you change your mind about helping find the kid ..."

"You'll be the first to know about it." Germ indicated the upstairs world with a quick nod. "Look around when you get up there. Make sure you weren't followed. I don't want any messes to clean up."

"Got it."

The elevator doors closed on a mass of purple and red swirls that made Dan think of an underground river of fire.

NINE

Whoosh!

Dan left the underground garage feeling slightly nauseated from the second-hand smoke. While some enjoyed the buzz, he recoiled from it like a pastor finding smut left behind in the men's room. Outside, the afternoon light rushed at him as he headed to the parking lot. The sky tingled with that brilliant luminescence it carries right before or after a storm. Darkness hovered over the west end of the city. No doubt they were in for a drenching. It would be a welcome relief from all the heat and humidity.

Dan was intrigued by Germ's description of the boy he'd seen in the deserted warehouse. He hoped Germ might happen upon him again, though the chances of that were small unless he was actively seeking him out.

He'd just got in the car when his phone buzzed. It was Donny.

"Finally I hear from you in person," Dan said. "Do I get the real story of Lester's defection now?"

Donny chuckled. A match struck on the other end of the phone.

"The real story," Donny murmured. "That's a good one."

Dan waited for him to settle into his cigarette like a comfy sofa.

"You remember Lester telling us he got raped a few months before you rescued him last summer?"

"I sure do."

"Well, he ran into the bastard not long ago. Twice, in fact. He wasn't going to tell me, but he started having anxiety attacks and I knew something was up. I asked him, but he said it was nothing. I waited a while and asked again. He started crying and finally broke down and said he'd seen the guy. The first time was on Church Street. The second time was right outside our condo. He was scared to death. He was getting paranoid thinking the guy knew where he lived and might be looking for him."

"Does Lester owe him money?"

"He says not, but the guy looked after him for a while. I gather he was something like a pimp to some of the street kids, only not quite. A go-between might be more like it. He provides party favours for some wealthy clients. I'm sure he gets a kick-back of some sort. Maybe he thinks Lester owes him."

"Do you think he was coming after Lester?"

Donny hesitated. "My guess? It was a coincidence."

"All right, but two times in a row?

"Yeah, I know. That's why the kid got scared." Donny exhaled, deep in thought. "The guy's a real bastard. Violent, creepy. Anyway. Lester was afraid I might not be able to protect him if this bastard comes after him. Lester heard a rumour he was protected by the police. He says no one will touch the guy."

"So he decided to take his chances with his evil mother and very unpleasant stepfather."

"Not much of a choice, is it?"

"I'll say."

"Anyway, that's the official story. For the record."

"Have you heard from him yet?"

"No, not since he left."

"Well, I'm sure he hasn't forgotten you. Hang in there. He'll call."

"Oh, I'm sure he will. I just don't know what to tell him when he does. If this guy really is after him, maybe it's better if he stays away for a while."

Dan heard him hemming over this one. "Let me know if there's anything I can do to help."

"Find the guy and put him away."

"If I had a name, I might be able to do something about it."

There was a silence.

"I'll ask Lester when I hear from him," Donny said.

"Okay, let me know. Thanks for dinner the other night. Trev and I both enjoyed it."

"My pleasure. And for the record? I highly approve of the new boyfriend. You'd better not screw this one up."

"I don't intend to."

"Good to hear it. Ciao."

Dan swung by Corktown, but there were no signs of life at the house. It was better that way, because whenever he dropped in he seemed to interrupt work for the duration of his visit. He checked his watch. Trevor had promised to cook tonight, but there was still time to pick up dessert. He got back in the car and headed south. In his search for a new home, he'd considered the nearby historic Distillery District but found it too chi-chi for his tastes. Corktown had the right balance of down-at-heels charm buried in a solid neighbourhood sensibility. The Distillery would serve as his neighbourhood market. Despite how it attracted the moneyed demimonde, with their insatiable appetites and imperious tastes, Dan loved its cobblestone walkways and stone buildings.

The storm broke as he parked. Rain scattered the pedestrians, sluicing down the windows of bars and trendy cafés and the chocolate factory, forming a river along the cobblestone. Whatever Trevor had planned for supper, there was always room for chocolate. It gave Dan a warm feeling to buy him things, to show that he hardly stopped thinking about him all day long. He didn't want to consider whether this was a healthy expression of love or a subliminal form of bribery or merely an infatuation bordering on obsession, but somehow Trevor was never far from his mind.

Chocolate in hand, he made it back in time for dinner. A yeasty odour permeated the house with its warm-smelling goodness.

"Do I smell bread?" he called out.

"You do," came the reply.

"You were out working all day and you come home and bake?"

Trevor grinned as he entered the kitchen. "You can thank my compulsive behaviour."

"You don't have to do this," Dan said, "though I appreciate it."

"I can't just sit around waiting for you to come home like some bored housewife."

Dan handed him the box of dessert. Trevor looked inside and beamed.

"Mmmm … tarts. This will go nicely with what we're having."

"That's what I thought."

Trevor wrapped a dishtowel around his hands and removed a tray of rolls from the oven. He offered one to Dan.

"Good day?" he asked.

Dan pulled the roll open and savoured the steamy release of air.

"Actually, yes. I finally talked to Donny and got the story about Lester. I'm not sure it's anything to worry about." He took a bite. "*Mmmm!* Apart from that, I mostly played hooky after meeting with the police. Unlike you, I haven't done much of anything."

"Lucky you."

Dan took another bite. "These are fantastic."

"I do my best. So you were saying about the police? Did they ask more questions?"

"They asked me to hand over my sources. I gather they were impressed that I was able to find Darryl Hillary so fast, even if I found him too late to save him."

Trevor set the tray down and turned off the oven. "And?"

"I can't do it. If I give them names, those people will never speak to me again and they certainly won't help the police out. I went over to talk to one of my sources about it afterward, but I already knew the answer. It's like asking someone to climb the Berlin Wall. It's *verboten* with that set."

"Maybe it's better that way. To leave you out of it, I mean ..."

The phone rang.

"I'll get it upstairs," Dan said.

"Dinner's in forty-five minutes," Trevor called after him in an admonitory tone. "So don't go anywhere."

"Got it," Dan said.

He bounded up the stairs to his office. He grabbed the phone and listened to the deep voice asking for Dan Sharp. Gravel-tinged, enigmatic. Like its owner was used to keeping people guessing.

"That's me," Dan replied.

"You come highly recommended."

"That could mean a lot of things."

Dan heard a begrudging laugh.

"Well, what it means at this moment is that I would like to hire you. If possible, I would very much like to meet with you to discuss my concerns."

Dan paused. Nothing further was forthcoming from the voice on the other end.

"Are you still there?"

"Yes," Dan said. "Before we go any further, who am I speaking to?"

There was a long pause. Dan thought for a moment the caller was considering giving him a false name. Finally, he spoke.

"My name is Jags Rohmer."

Now it was Dan's turn to be tongue-tied.

"*The* Jags Rohmer?"

Sarcasm crept into the voice. "How many do you know?"

"Okay, I will meet you, Mr. Rohmer."

The voice turned coy. "Because I'm famous?"

"No, because now I believe you're serious."

"Good. May I come by in ten minutes?"

Dan hesitated. "I'm free for another forty-five minutes. After that I've got a family commitment."

"This won't take long."

"Okay. My address is —"

"I have your address. I'll see you in ten minutes."

He hung up and sat back in his seat.

Jags Rohmer was Canada's answer to David Bowie, at least if you thought Canada couldn't afford stars who weren't copycats of somebody else. As far as Dan was concerned, Rohmer was a far more wide-ranging musician than the average pop star. He was a singer, songwriter, keyboard player, and performer on any number of obscure, indigenous instruments that gave his music its unusual tones. He'd emerged from the ruins of the punk scene in the late seventies. His career had been on the ascendant through the eighties, but he went silent in the mid-nineties, all but disappearing after that. A final, cryptic album emerged in the wake of 9/11, coming like a eulogy on the world and vanishing in the aftermath of the disaster. For many, it had seemed his epitaph. Most of his diehard fans hated it, but a few lauded it as a masterpiece of nuance and newfound maturity. They waited impatiently for more, but nothing had been forthcoming since. Many thought he'd died.

And now he'd just been resurrected on the other end of the phone.

Dan went downstairs where Ked had just returned from his mother's.

"Hey, Dad!"

"Hey, sonny boy!"

Ked gave him a funny look. "What is this? An episode of *Father Knows Best*?"

Dan snorted. "Maybe. It sounds like something they ought to consider making a national holiday."

"Yeah, as if."

A few minutes later, Ked was helping Trevor set the table when the doorbell rang.

"I'll get it!" Ked yelled, as he dashed to the front door.

They heard a mumbled conversation then Ked returned to the kitchen.

Ked: "Dad, um, Jags Rohmer is at the door?"

Dan: "Thanks, son. Please tell him I'll be right there."

Ked: "Uh, yeah. I will."

He turned to Trevor. "Did you know about this?"

Trevor shook his head.

Ked took a big breath and headed for the hall. Before he reached it, he turned back and looked at Dan. "Is this for real?"

"Yes, son."

"Whoa!" they heard him say as he rounded the corner and headed for the door.

Dan's first impression was how tall Jags Rohmer really was, though his presence defied logic and seemed to suggest he was even taller than his six foot three.

"Come in," Dan said.

"Thanks, but ..." Rohmer peered over Dan's shoulder and waved at Trevor in the next room. "If you don't mind, I'd prefer to conduct business in my car."

Dan looked at him blankly.

"If that's all right with you. Just a preference."

Dan shrugged. "Sure." He turned to the dining room. "I won't be long," he called to Trevor, closing the door behind him.

A Porsche Carrera GT was parked outside the house. Dan had only a hazy idea of the vehicle's cost, but he was pretty sure it easily equalled the price of his new house.

"Nice car," Dan said. "But if you ever come back, park it around the side so my neighbours won't start getting strange ideas."

Jags smirked. They got in the car.

"Shall we take a little ride?"

"Sounds good to me."

He turned the key and the car drifted away from the curb. Jags manoeuvred a corner and headed south. The car felt airborne as the towers of the city approached. The ride was smooth, like a razor on glass.

"Do you know anything about Porsches, Dan?"

"Not a lot. Other than that I will never be able to buy one. That's all I need to know."

"Fair enough. Let me tell you a few facts then. Just because I like to do that." Jags looked over at him and winked. "Manufactured in Germany, as you probably know, this car has a 5.7 litre V10 engine. Six-twelve horsepower."

"Sounds very impressive."

"It is. The Porsche people claim you can accelerate from zero to a hundred kilometres in less than four seconds, with a maximum speed of 330 kliks. Fast, huh?"

"Scary fast," Dan agreed.

"Personally, I've never managed to get from zero to a hundred in less than eight seconds, give or take a few nanos. On the other hand, I've had it up to 340 kliks, going full-out on a deserted stretch of highway in Joshua Tree National Park."

The city drifted by, soundless, outside the windows. Dan waited for Jags to tell him the reason for his visit, but he concentrated on driving. Traffic was thinning. They drifted lazily from lane to lane. Jags kept a light foot. The car moved along effortlessly.

"As I said on the phone, you come highly recommended."

"Glad to hear it. What exactly have I been recommended to do?"

Jags looked over. "I want to hire you to look out for me."

Dan was puzzled. "To look out for you?"

"Watch my ass and keep me out of trouble."

"I think you've been misinformed. That's not my field. I find missing people."

"Yes, that's what I was told. What I want is something more proactive. I want you to prevent me from going missing."

Dan laughed. "I'm not a hard-ass. I'm not trained to fight to prevent anyone from being kidnapped, if that's what you're saying."

Jags turned in his seat and made a face. "Ach, it doesn't have to be so intense and noirish. Nothing sinister in the wings. Mostly I want a babysitter — someone to keep on his toes when I can't. I don't want a SWAT team. I just need someone to watch my back."

"Fair enough. Why?"

"Among other reasons, I've got a book coming out."

Dan was perplexed. "Fiction?"

"No. Memoirs. It's a tell-all about my sordid little life."

"Are you expecting some trouble from disgruntled former band members?"

Jags laughed. "Yeah, you could say that. Former whatevers, in fact. Girlfriends, wives, songwriting partners. Just … whatever. I need someone to watch my back right now."

Dan made a face.

"C'mon," Jags told him. "I'm not expecting trouble, but I'm sure you could take out a few guys at once, if you wanted to. You're built like a prize-fighter. Me? I'm turning into the Pillsbury Doughboy."

"Mr. Rohmer …"

"Jags."

"Jags, I'm sure it would be an honour to work for you, but …"

"But what?"

"But it's not my thing."

"That's no reason. Look, I'll pay you triple whatever you charge."

They were on the ramp running directly over Corktown. Dan glanced off to the right. One of those adjoining roofs was his. He thought of his diminishing reserves and the mounting costs for the new home. From missing persons investigator to bodyguard. Maybe it was time to expand his skill set.

Jags turned off at the bottom of the ramp, heading up to Queen Street and then east again. They were soon back on Dan's street. The car turned right and slid into place in front of Dan's house.

Jags turned to regard him. He looked at his dash. "You said forty-five minutes. We've got ten minutes left. So what do you think?"

"Jags, I don't think so ..."

Dan reached for the door handle. Jags snapped the lock down.

"Do I have to kidnap you?"

"That won't help." Something occurred to Dan. "You were at the police station today."

"Right. And you were at the elevator when I got off on the third floor. Green striped V-neck T-shirt and jeans. With the older man in the checked shirt and beige pants."

"Good recall," Dan said. "Is that where you got my name?"

Jags nodded. "I met with some police officers there. A dumpy one and a short one who thinks he's Cock of the Walk."

An image of Detective Danes and Constable Pfeiffer came to Dan's mind. "Yeah, I think I know the ones you mean."

"They recommended you to me. The older guy told them you were cool."

Dan wondered what Ed had said to Detective Danes and Constable Pfeiffer to make them recommend him.

"Did they tell you my last client was murdered?"

"Is that a joke?"

"I never joke."

"I like you even better then. Did your last client hire you to be his bodyguard?"

"No. I never met him. His sister hired me to find him. He disappeared a few days before I found him. I got there too late."

"That's different. Not your fault."

Dan sized him up. "Did they tell you I was gay?"

"I don't mind queers."

Dan held up a warning finger. "I can use that word. You can't."

Jags' mouth twitched into a smile. "Ooh, discrimination."

"You betcha. That's our word now."

"Better tell the boys at Metro HQ. I don't think they got the memo."

Dan smiled. "I hear you."

He looked off across the street at a couple passing by with a baby in a stroller. How had his life become so different from everyone else's?

Jags placed a hand on Dan's shoulder. "Look, Dan — I checked you out. You come highly recommended from a number of sources, not just the cops. Plus I like you — you talk straight. Well, for a gay guy." He smiled again. "I'd trust you before I'd trust one of those muscle-bound lunks you meet at the gym and whatnot."

"I'm not sure that's a compliment."

"Sure it is." Jags seemed to be running out of arguments. "Look, do you have anything pressing at the moment? Apart from your murdered client, I mean."

Dan inclined his head. "Actually, no."

"Then why not try it for a week? It won't be an everyday thing. Every other day, at best. Mostly when I do public appearances."

He released the lock and waited.

Dan's hand moved to the handle. He turned to Jags. "Okay. I'll try it."

"Good. Any questions?"

"Just one. Where'd you get your name?"

Jags smiled. "I'm very fond of cars, as you can see. By the time my first record came out, I'd already smashed up three Jaguars."

"Ouch. You ought to be ashamed of yourself. That's a very cool car."

"Tell me about it."

Dan got out of the car. It turned sleekly and drove off with a *whoosh!* leaving him standing on the sidewalk outside his home.

TEN

Fame

TREVOR AND KED WERE IN THE LIVING ROOM when Dan entered. They reminded him of a pair of devious teenagers who minutes before had been smoking and playing cards, but were now trying to simulate innocence while noxious fumes hung in the air.

"Well?" Trevor ventured.

"I've got Jags Rohmer as a client," he told them.

"Dad, that's so cool!" Ked exclaimed.

"But you're not to tell anyone," Dan quickly added.

"What? No fair!"

"You heard me. This is a confidential arrangement. You can talk about it when the job is done."

Ked glowered. "Then why did you have to tell me now?"

"Because I need to keep you in the loop. It's going to change a few things around here. And by the way, your dog needs walking. He told me so at the door when I came in."

Ked rolled his eyes then stomped out of the room.

"Congratulations, I guess?" Trevor said.

Dan shrugged. "I took the job because I need the money, not because he's famous."

"Good money?"

"Very good." He stopped to consider. "And I think I might like the guy."

"That's always a plus. So what will you be doing for him? Did he lose someone?"

Dan looked at him. "Actually, no. He didn't lose anyone. He needs a bodyguard so he doesn't lose himself."

Trevor shook his head. "Since when are you a bodyguard?"

"Since today. Are you shocked?"

Trevor hesitated. "A little, I guess. What brought this on? For him, I mean."

"His autobiography is coming out and he wants back-up for his public appearances. And I need the cash flow right now."

Consternation showed on Trevor's face. "Wish I could be more help in that department."

Dan held up his hand. "We agreed that's not your part here. Not for now, anyway. I don't want you to start worrying about it. Not about the house or about money or about anything."

"Well, good. I'll just put all that worry on hold. Let me know when you think it's time to start, because I'm sure I'll be primed for it." Trevor screwed up his mouth. Too much to say and no good way to say it. "Will you have to carry a gun?"

Dan shook his head. "This isn't going to be dangerous."

"Still, I mean … a bodyguard? It sounds a bit ominous, Dan."

Dan hesitated. He hadn't really considered Trevor's reaction when he agreed to take the job. "I'm sorry, I should have discussed it with you first. I don't want to give you anything to worry about."

Trevor shook his head. "That's not it. I know you'll be sensible."

"What is it then?"

Trevor shrugged. "I just wish you had a risk-free job."

"Like what, an accountant?"

Trevor grinned. "Yeah, something like that. You'd make a super-sexy accountant in your pinstripe three-piece. Anyway, supper is nearly ready. Be a good boy and go wash your hands and get ready to eat. Afterward, you can be my dishwasher. That's relatively safe, I think."

"Give me five minutes. I've got a few phone calls to make first."

"Don't be long," Trevor said with mock-gruffness.

His office felt like a tomb. Lights down low, the rumble of traffic outside on the street, the air nicely chill from the AC. Death might be a pleasant lull, if this was any indication. All that peace and nothing to disturb you. He had Ed on the phone. His ex-boss sounded happily surprised to hear from him. He was probably hoping Dan had changed his mind about offering his sources. Dan nipped that possibility in the bud. He didn't want it to become an issue, especially as he'd cultivated a number of those sources while working for Ed's firm. He mentioned Jags Rohmer. Ed remembered the name from their conversation outside the elevator but still had only a vague idea who he was.

"I could hum a few bars of his songs if you think it would help."

"No, thanks, Daniel. I seem to recall that you're a worse singer than I am. My ex-wife said something to that effect in her divorce suit. Anyway, what about him?"

"He showed up on my doorstep this evening. He wants to hire me as a bodyguard."

"A bodyguard?" Ed snorted.

"Yes. I was wondering if you had anything to do with it."

"Not intentionally. Does this have something to do with our meeting at the police station?"

"He seemed to think you recommended me to them. I wondered if you said anything to make them think I did personal bodyguard work."

"Not me," Ed said.

"Okay, no problem."

"My turn. I know it's none of my business, but don't tell me that. One of your last cases with us, right before you deserted us ..."

"Before I retired from the firm," Dan corrected.

"Whatever you want to call it. And I'm still trying to find a replacement, by the way, so the offer to return is still there. Anyway, right before you left me without the best investigator I ever had, there was a case involving a teenager who went missing after being picked up by the police for soliciting at a gay cruising area in Oshawa."

A pot clanked downstairs in the kitchen.

Ed was referring to Lester before he changed his name from Richard and before he had the good fortune to move in with Donny.

"I vaguely remember it."

"Vaguely? Like hell, Danny. You've got a mind like a steel trap."

"As I said, I *vaguely* remember it, but go on."

"No need. You just answered my question."

"What question?"

"Whether you solved the case or not."

Dan hesitated. "I never found Richard Philips."

Ed was silent for a while. Then he burst out laughing. "You 'vaguely' remember it yet you have the boy's name on the tip of your tongue."

"I remember some things better than others."

"But you didn't find him?"

"I didn't find Richard Philips, no."

"I wondered. Because that was the only case where you ever showed a 'no return' on a file. No clues, no possible leads. It just didn't add up. Not for the unshakable Dan Sharp."

"You can't win 'em all, Ed."

"I guess not. Okay, I just wondered."

"Should I ask why?"

Ed sighed. "I'm not supposed to say anything, but there is a possibility that somehow that boy's case is connected to the current investigation."

Dan felt a tingle. "In what way?"

"That's all I can say for now, Daniel. You're not the only one who keeps secrets."

"Point taken."

Dan was beginning to feel bad for not telling Ed the truth. He thought about it while the line hummed between them. Downstairs, the front door opened. Ked had returned with Ralph. A leash tinkled, claws scampered across the floor.

"Do you remember how old that kid was, Ed?"

"No. I don't have that kind of memory. How old was he?"

"He turned fifteen just after the case came to us. His birthday is the day before Ked's."

"Interesting coincidence. So?"

"So … Ked's birthday is next month. Ask me in a month and I might remember the case a little more clearly."

Ed guffawed. "Meaning when the boy is sixteen and legal. You *do* know where he is!"

"Gotta go, Ed. Supper's on the table."

He put down the phone then picked it up again immediately. *What are the chances?* he asked himself, pulling out the card for the chief of police. He stared at the small white rectangle with its neat blue lines. All that law and order nestled in the palm of his hand. He started dialling.

When Dan came back downstairs he found Trevor seated at the table with a knowing look on his face. Ked drummed his fingers on the tabletop and looked off in the distance. Dan glanced up at the clock: he'd been considerably more than five minutes.

"You're incorrigible," Trevor said, shaking his head.

"Yeah, and he's late, too," Ked added.

Dan tried to look chagrined. "That's pretty much the same conclusion Ed Burch just drew about me. Sorry, I was a bit longer than I'd expected."

Trevor indicated the empty place. "Sit. Nothing got burned, but the pasta's going to be soggy."

"Does working for Jags Rohmer mean you're going to become completely unreliable from now on, Dad?" Ked asked.

Dan turned to him. "Just remember: *Father Knows Best*. If you can do that, all will be well."

Ked harrumphed.

Trevor set their plates on the table. Ked dug in, all but wolfing down his food. Dan picked up his fork then looked away. A streetcar went by on Queen, making the walls tremble.

Trevor waited for him to begin. Dan was lost in thought. "Want to talk about it?"

Dan looked over. "What?"

"I'm not prying, but you seem preoccupied."

"Yeah, it's all right." He speared a piece of rigatoni and gulped it down. "I called Ed. My former boss. Ed didn't know about Jags. In fact, if you can believe it, Ed doesn't even know who he is apart from 'some old rocker.' Personally, I find it hard to believe that anyone over the age of ten cannot have an idea who Jags Rohmer is, but that's beside the point. Ed lives in his own world anyway, so I'll leave him to it."

Trevor held up a carafe. Ruby red. "Wine?"

"Yes, please," Ked piped up. "It will make up for the unconscionable wait."

Dan looked over at his son. "'Unconscionable'?"

Ked shrugged. "Incorrigible, unconscionable — what's the difference?"

"About the same difference as between wine and root beer. Your drink's in the fridge, by the way. Help yourself, buddy."

Ked got up and went to the fridge.

Trevor filled his glass. Dan took a gulp of wine without tasting it.

"Where was I? Oh, yes — Jags Rohmer and Ed Burch. So there's that. Then I …"

Trevor put up a hand. "Wait a minute. There's what?"

Dan shook his head, clearing the cobwebs. "He didn't know anything about my being hired by Jags. But Jags told me Ed had recommended me to two of the cops I met this morning. Ed didn't feel he'd said anything to that effect."

"Meaning?"

"I don't know. It's just odd, isn't it? The person who hires you says you've been recommended by a friend and the friend says nothing of the sort happened."

"Yes, it's odd."

"So then I phoned the chief of police …"

Trevor and Ked caught each other's glance.

"What?" Dan asked.

Trevor shook his head. "First Jags Rohmer and now the chief of police? Where have you been hanging out lately?"

"Yeah. Take us with you next time, Dad," Ked said then bent his head and began shovelling pasta into his mouth.

"Anyway," Dan continued, spearing a stalk of asparagus with his fork. He brought it to his mouth then put it down again. "I was shocked when I was actually put through to his private line. It's like I had a magic pass or something. All he could tell me is that he and his crew had a meeting with Jags and somehow my name came up as a possible bodyguard for hire."

"So it should be all right then. Shouldn't it?"

"I guess. I gather Jags was insistent on wanting some sort of protection and they weren't about to provide it for him, so they eased him off on me. At least that's the sense I got. I know Ed Burch provided some impeccable references for me, but he wouldn't recommend me as a bodyguard. It's just not something I've ever done before."

Trevor took stock of this. "When do you start?"

Dan thought back to his conversation with Jags. "I don't know. He never said." He finally tucked a bite of pasta into his mouth.

Trevor cocked an eyebrow at him. "It all sounds a bit sketchy to me."

Ked sat back, regarding Dan over a frothy glass of root beer. "To me, too." He shrugged. "But *Father Knows Best*, right?"

"That's right," Dan told him. "You just keep telling yourself that."

Trevor passed the basket of rolls.

"Anyway, as long as I get paid, it doesn't matter," Dan said, reaching for a roll and never thinking for a moment how much he might regret having said that in the days to come.

A week went by. Dan heard nothing further from the police department about the murder investigation. He called Darlene Hillary one morning, murmuring vague reassurances that things were pending. They both knew it meant nothing. Dan wished he hadn't said he'd try to help. A lover's promise whispered in the heat of passion, gone forever afterward.

Jags, on the other hand, was true to his word. He wasn't overly demanding of Dan's time or resources. They met mid-week to discuss Dan's salary and his duties. None of what Jags proposed sounded pressing, so Dan began to relax. The most worrying thing was Jags' confession about his behaviour.

"I apologize in advance," he told Dan. The voice was gravelly, like he'd been up singing dirges all night. "But you may from time to time have to put up with my whims."

"'Whims'?"

"Moods. Hissy fits. Don't take offence. I piss everyone off, sooner or later."

"Ah, you mean that bitchy rock star stuff. Are you saying you want me to put you in your place from time to time?"

Jags cocked a shaggy eyebrow at him. "Something like that."

"No problem."

He handed Dan a complicated-looking set of keys, like something a medieval monk might remove from his cassock as he went about taking last confessions from dying prisoners. "For my penthouse," he said, reciting the address of a well-known luxury condominium. "It'll save you having to get past security. And believe me, you'd rather not deal with them if you don't have to."

"Man-eaters?"

"Eastern European ex-Stasi. Very efficient. Very deadly. Just like a pack of Rottweilers." He nodded to the ring. "There's an additional key on there. It's for my house on Algonquin Island."

"Nice."

Dan pictured the reclusive slip of land fronting the harbour, one in a chain of islands protecting the city from offshore squalls in this century and from marauding Americans in earlier times.

"You probably won't need to use it," Jags continued, "but you have it anyway. I'll write the address down for you with a map, because otherwise you'd never find it."

For the most part, Jags seemed to want Dan around for public appearances. To date, that had consisted of accompanying him on a shopping spree at Holt Renfrew. Despite the warnings about his temperament, Jags didn't treat Dan as an underling so much as a companion. He even deferred to Dan's taste in clothes, wanting his opinion on a Zegna blazer and a silk Armani shirt, along with a pair of six-hundred-dollar Ferragamo loafers. Dan okayed the purchases then directed him to Farley Chatto, one of his favourite designers. (*Hey! Everyone needs a little Farley in their life* ran the designer's slogan.) Donny had recently turned him onto the Regina native, who had designed for Elton John among others. Not that Dan could afford a Farley any more than he could the Italian designers. Nor did he have much to dress up for apart from the occasional funeral, but he still enjoyed wearing homegrown chic. For his part, Jags was suitably impressed with the whimsical, sexy designs. He held up a jacket with silk-satin detailing. A mere $3000.

"I like it," he said.

After that, he routinely asked for Dan's opinion.

"I draw the line at underwear," Dan warned.

He was beginning to feel as if he'd been brought on a shopping spree by his best friend. His very rich best friend. No one approached Jags directly, not even to ask for an autograph, though he was recognized several times that afternoon. The crowd seemed intimidated by him. *Of course*, Dan thought. *Torontonians don't approach celebrities. We stand and gawk from afar*. He was amused by their reticence, knowing that in LA or New York, Jags would be deluged with requests for autographs and photographs, even donations to improbable causes. The dreary side of being rich and recognizable.

The only difficult moment came when Dan tried to stop a young woman from taking Jags' photograph with her cellphone. He got a sense of how celebrities must feel like animals in a zoo, with people turning to stare at the exotica, never leaving you alone for a moment. Always feeling you needed to be on guard, to look your best. Always being *on*. You would hate it, he realized.

The woman looked terrified the instant Dan turned to her. Though he wasn't acting in an official capacity, and nothing about his dress suggested security, his body language said he was in charge.

He wagged a finger, blocking her view of the singer, who was buried up to the elbows in a sale table of cashmere sweaters like a kid bent on finding free candy. The woman's eyes widened, darting nervously around as though she might need to escape if he became dangerous.

"No photographs, please," Dan said calmly.

"I'm sorry," she said, pocketing the phone. "It's really him, isn't it?"

Her face was pink, her breathing shallow and quick. She had all the symptoms of love at first sight.

Dan nodded. "It really is."

"Please tell him I love him," she gushed. "I always have."

"Right."

"Tell him we're all waiting for his next album."

She continued to stare, as though he were the doorway to the universe where all the fabulous people like Jags Rohmer lived.

"Tell him he should do a duet with Prince ..."

"Will do. Thanks. Let's let the man have some peace."

"Sorry. Yeah, sure."

He watched her slink away in the direction of ladies lingerie, an overgrown teenager stalking her heartthrob. Maybe her next purchase would reflect her true desires: a discreet pair of black undies that she would willingly discard for him and him alone. Who knew, but she might return in five minutes asking for an address, somewhere to mail them to him, only slightly used.

Throughout all of this, Jags ignored the scene, acting as though none of it concerned him. Only later did it occur to Dan that Jags had almost no contact with other people. Zilch. He never spoke of family or friends; no one called his cellphone. How was it that someone so well-known could be so isolated from the world?

They left the store, exiting into gloom and merging with a stream of traffic under a nighttime sky that compressed the heat and held the city hostage in its relentless grip.

ELEVEN

Blue Mountains

THE HEAT WAVE LASTED two full weeks before breaking over the course of several spectacular storms that trooped through the city, leaving considerable damage behind. The garage fires subsided. No one thought of them. The Canadian National Exhibition had started: Ferris wheels, trade shows, cotton candy, and a licence to get silly. Toronto turned its collective mind to fun.

Mornings were cooler now, which meant for Dan that the day started on an easier footing. Life began to feel more under control. The renovations were going well and the pay for celebrity babysitting Jags was helping him relax.

On Saturday, he drove Trevor to the airport to catch an early flight to BC where he hoped to tackle some unfinished business and put his house up for sale. If all went well, Dan reasoned, Trevor would be ready to step into his new life entirely when he returned.

Ked had gone to spend the weekend at his mother's. Dan returned to an empty house, apart from one ginger-coloured dog with a questioning look on its face.

"I know what you're thinking," Dan told him. "You're wondering why the fun people always leave while the Grinch stays home? Is that it, boy?"

Ralph silently wagged his tail.

Dan had just crawled back into bed, hoping for one more hour of oblivion, when the phone rang. He rolled over and checked the clock: 8:57. He considered not answering but weakened on the fourth ring.

It was Jags.

"How are you tied in this weekend?" his employer asked, sounding like an aggressive trader keen on liquidating his entire portfolio.

Dan frowned. "Hello and how are you?"

"Yeah, all of that. So how are things sitting with you?"

Dan propped himself up on an elbow. "I've got a few things to do. Nothing pressing. What did you have in mind?"

"I need to get out of town."

"Any particular reason?"

"Pre-launch jitters. I need to get away from myself."

An interesting way of putting it, Dan mused, without pursuing the thought any further. He assumed this was one of Jags' whims. If so, there was no use questioning it. He'd already said they came and went without warning.

"I'm thinking a couple hours north of here," Jags continued. "I've got a little cottage up Collingwood way."

"That's a nice area. How long are we talking?"

There was a pause. "I don't know. A couple days at most, nothing more than that."

Dan tried to recall what Trevor had said about his return flight. Was it Tuesday or Wednesday? He'd written it down somewhere, but in his pre-caffeinated state he couldn't think where. *Oh, right — the calendar!* He glanced over at the circled date: *Wednesday*. Dan had promised to pick him up at the airport. Ked would be back from his mother's on Sunday evening, but he'd be fine on his own for one night or else he could stay with Kendra if he preferred.

"So what do you think? I don't mean to pressure you, but I've gotta get the fuck out of here."

An urgent whim then.

The voice was edgy, bordering on anxious. Dan wondered what he might be faced with if he and Jags spent the weekend confined in a remote cottage. Did zoo keepers separate the bears come closing time or did they all sleep in one happy little enclosure?

"I'm good till Wednesday," he said, even as he regretted giving Jags such wide latitude.

"We'll be back by then," Jags declared. "I need to be back for some press stuff on Tuesday afternoon. Anyway, that gives us three days. So we're cool, yeah?"

"Good with me," Dan said. He had a sudden thought. "Oh, shit! The dog."

"Bring him," Jags said immediately. "I like dogs."

"Are you sure? What about your car? He's not really Porsche-trained."

Jags thought this over. "I'll use a different car. Something that's less noticeable."

Again it was a strange way of putting things, but Dan let it pass.

"I'll swing by in half an hour and pick you up. Don't pack anything but a change of clothes," Jags said. "I have everything you need up there."

Two hours passed. Dan was beginning to think Jags had changed his mind when he drove up in a beat-up station wagon, apparently the reason for the delay. He greeted Dan curtly, paying no attention to Ralph. For a man who claimed to like dogs, he seemed at a loss on how to deal with one. Ralph came up to him and waited for the obligatory pat on the head. Jags looked at him twice then walked away. Undaunted, Ralph followed.

"Why is he doing that?" Jags asked.

"It means he likes you."

"Oh. Kind of like a fan following me around."

"Something like that. Give him a pat and he'll stop."

Jags touched the top of Ralph's head. Satisfied, Ralph trotted back to Dan, who ordered him into the back seat, where he settled with a grunt and a look of satisfaction, knowing he was going on an adventure.

They set off. Jags seemed distant as he navigated the maze of one-way streets leading to the expressway. Presumably this was one of those moods he'd warned Dan about. *Don't take offence. I piss everyone off, sooner or later.* Sooner rather than later then, was what it looked like.

"Is something wrong?" Dan asked when they'd been in the car ten minutes and Jags had hardly spoken.

"No, nothing."

"You seem preoccupied."

Jags shrugged it off. "Just watching the traffic. It's a weekend. You know how all the shitty drivers come out then."

"That's normal."

"It's just ..."

"Just what?" Dan prompted.

There was a pause. Jags glanced down at his phone. "I've been getting these weird calls. Hangups and whatnot."

"Crazed fans?" Dan asked, trying to make light of it.

Jags grunted. "Maybe. It's just that no one has this number." He brightened. "It's probably nothing."

"'Nothing' is good," Dan said.

Jags slipped a CD into the player. If Dan thought he was going to be serenaded with a full-tilt Jags Rohmer soundtrack on the way up, he was mistaken. Jags' preference for travelling was light classical music: Telemann's *Paris Quartets*, to be exact.

Once past the city limits, Jags relaxed. His driving was every bit as expert in the wagon as it had been in the Porsche. His preference for speed was obvious, although Dan never felt unsafe. Dan caught him checking the rearview mirror every few minutes. He saw Dan watching him and laughed.

"Just keeping an eye out for cops," he said. "I've got a heavy accelerator foot."

He slowed and pulled over to the outside lane.

Dan was beginning to wonder if Jags was on something when his mood finally broke and he started chatting. His publisher had been in touch; they'd had a favourable notice in the *Globe and Mail*. A good sign, Jags said. As far as reviews went, it was the more literary of the newspapers. If they liked his style — colourful, breezy, and straight-up — then others would be receptive to the book.

Once he started talking, he didn't seem to want to stop. Dan found his observations engaging. Nor did he dominate the talk, relegating Dan to the role of prisoner-listener. He was equally interested in Dan's side of the conversation. For his part, Dan resisted asking the obvious questions about his life and his colourful career. He talked with him as he would with a new acquaintance about whom he knew a little, but presumed nothing. Jags seemed grateful to be treated as just another guy.

The drive was quiet and uneventful. Jags made good time, even in his unassuming old carrier. Two hours north of Toronto, long before they closed in on Collingwood, the famous hills appeared in the distance like a smudge on the horizon. Blue and smoky. Dan had always been intrigued by their colour, how they managed to look that same cool shade of cobalt every time he approached. He'd heard various theories: the colour was caused by the atmosphere over the mountains or how light from the clouds diffracted as it hit the range or even that the blue pine forest with its billions of needles gave the mountains their unique appearance. In fact, it was none of the above. The mountains were composed of an unusual form of blue clay. It wasn't an illusion. They really were blue.

Dan was pleasantly surprised to discover that Jags' cottage was unpretentious and humble. He thought the rock-and-roll crowd was all about ostentation and a primal scream approach to life, but then Jags Rohmer had always been a cut above the rest. He could growl out a raunchy blues number with the best of them, but his voice took on a quiet yearning when he needed to embellish an emotion. He had an innate feel for dramatic phrasing, not unlike an opera singer's. His voice was authoritative yet soothing, as though urging you to do your best while consoling you for whatever trials you might be enduring. He appealed to both heart and mind, without condescending to either, and with more than a little soul to back it up.

Dan stood back and watched Jags unlock the door then toss their bags inside. With Ralph leading the way, they took a quick tour. The property lay nestled in a small basin at the foot of the mountains, engulfed by the surrounding forest.

"Nice place," Dan said.

"Thanks. I use it as an occasional retreat. A few days is usually enough for me. I can't stay here long or I get antsy."

"Why's that?"

Jags shrugged. "When I bought the place, I had dreams of resurrecting my childhood. Lots and lots of solitude. The only problem is I've been a city dweller for my entire adult life, so coming here is always a bit of a shock. It hits me the way the chaos of the city hits people who aren't used to that."

They wandered around the cottage and emerged on the far side. Jags looked ruefully at the building, as though reluctant to go in. He retrieved a couple of beers and they settled side by side on the porch. After a thorough sniff around the yard to make the acquaintance of the neighbours, both seen and unseen, Ralph settled at their feet and fell asleep. Apparently he'd found the drive taxing.

Jags was relaxed now. He scanned the bush at the edge of the property line, as though measuring how far it had encroached in his absence. Despite his ambivalence for rural life, he seemed to be in his element. Dan felt he was seeing the real man at last. He ventured a question that had been on his mind since they'd met.

"Where'd you go for the last ten years? What drove you away?"

Jags swatted at a fly. He lifted his bottle and took a swig, his eyes searching the horizon again. "From the pop music circus, you mean?"

Dan nodded. "Yeah, that."

"I got tired of it. You know John Lennon's 'Watching the Wheels'?"

Dan nodded.

"He wrote that song just as he was coming out of a five-year hiatus from recording. He wanted the world to know he'd stepped off the merry-go-round and was just living his life."

"Right before he was shot dead."

"Yeah — thanks for that little reminder. Anyway, that was me. I was a burnout. I just wanted to sit on the sidelines and watch it all going by. I had what everybody thought they wanted: fame, money, power. But they all had something I wanted."

"What's that?"

"A normal life."

Dan laughed. "You're kidding me, right?"

Jags scowled. "No, I'm not fucking kidding you. What are you laughing at?"

"Jags, there's no such thing as a normal life."

"Well, try living the kind of life I lived, where everybody has a claim on you, where everybody has expectations of you, and then you'll know what I mean. I have no sense of what reality is."

Dan shook his head. "While you're feeling sorry for yourself, stop to think about what everybody else has: kids who need things from you, spouses who want things from you, and — worst of all — demanding, insensitive employers who expect things from you. There's no such thing as normal, Jags."

Jags seemed perturbed by this, like an astronaut returning from an extended voyage in outer space and confronting G-forces for the first time in years. "Well, anyway, I'm tired of people wanting things from me. I just want to be left alone."

"Yeah, you and Greta Garbo. Good luck with that."

Jags looked at him from the corner of an eye. "Asshole," he said.

Dan shrugged. "Pretentious twat."

They both laughed at the same time. Jags grabbed him by the wrists and shook his arms.

"See, this is what I've been dying for. Someone to treat me like the idiot I am. Someone to tell it to me like it is."

"You should have had kids," Dan reflected. "They do it for free."

"Fuck. Do you think maybe I've just taken myself too seriously for too many years?"

Dan shrugged. "Could be."

Jags let go of his wrists. "Thanks, buddy. For telling it to me like it is."

"Any time."

†

Half an hour later, they headed inside. A stone chimney dominated the centre of the room. Jags took a bottle of bourbon off a shelf and poured two glasses, sliding one across to Dan.

Dan shook his head. His mind was buzzing with half-remembered sensations of all-night drinking sessions long past. He didn't want them to return.

"Can't do it. I'm on the wagon," he said. "Besides, I won't be much good to you as a bodyguard if I'm drinking."

Jags didn't appear to be listening. He downed his glass then stood and kicked an empty firewood cradle.

"We'll need to get a few logs in, in case we feel like a fire later," he said. "Not that it'll get cold, but it's always nice for atmosphere."

The cottage was open-concept, apart from a bathroom and a single bedroom furnished with double bunk beds. Dan wondered for a moment if Jags did have kids after all, but then remembered it was his own childhood he said he'd been trying to recreate. The other sleeping spaces included elevated lofts at either end, open to the rest of the cottage. Dan worried how comfortable he was going to be without privacy, but then they weren't planning on a long stay.

"Where will I sleep?"

"Wherever. Pick a bed or a couch and make yourself comfy when the time comes. There are blankets and pillows in the closet. You can sleep on that couch there" — he pointed out a long grey sofa that resembled a giant cigar with back support and end flaps — "if you want something really snazzy. Big designer number. It cost me ten thousand dollars."

Jags pulled something from a satchel and tossed it at Dan. "Here," he said. "In case you get bored."

Dan looked down at a copy of Jags' autobiography with a happy-looking Jags beaming at the world from the cover.

"Nice shot," he said.

"Yeah. It's not the real me, though." Jags shrugged and looked around the space. "It's too fucking quiet in here."

He flicked on the stereo. Something loud and punk filled the room. Dan found it irritating. He preferred the Telemann. He followed Jags into a bedroom that doubled as an office. A skull sat on a bookshelf, face turned to the wall. Dan picked it up. The thing leered at him. It looked real, though it might have been a monkey skull, he reasoned. Wasn't it illegal to own human remains?

He looked at Jags. "What's this for?"

"Gift from an obsessive fan. *Memento mori*. You know what that means?"

"Sure. 'Remember you will die.'"

"That's right. Not something we can afford to forget. Death comes to us all."

Dan set the skull back on the shelf, aiming the eye sockets at the room like twin camera lenses. "A bit maudlin, isn't it?"

Jags looked up and grimaced. "Yeah. Could you just turn it back around?"

Dan angled the sepulchral leer to the wall. Over in a far corner, a noose dangled from an exposed ceiling beam.

"And that?"

Jags sipped his bourbon. "Just a prop. From one of my tours."

"Nice. Adds to the décor."

"That's why I like you. You don't stand there and pretend it's raining when someone's pissing on your head."

Dan laughed. "I've heard it said in much less flattering terms. Thanks for the literary spin on it."

Jags lifted his glass and drank. "Any time."

The music got raunchier as Jags got drunker. He shifted his focus to a pile of papers, riffling through them — who knew what lay there, maybe a year's worth of laundry lists or a brilliant set of song lyrics never heard by the public — leaving Dan on his own.

Jags' agent called. Jags answered but left the music turned up loud while they talked. They seemed to be quarrelling over something, though it might simply have been his way of conversing over loud music. Dan went outside, letting the screen door bang. If Jags wanted noise then he could provide a reasonable soundtrack without much difficulty.

Jags' voice followed him out of the house and into the yard. The surrounding brush was dense and led to an even denser forest not far off. The tree line was broken occasionally by barren rock that cropped up here and there. A crescent moon hung in the sky. Dan could never remember when it was on the wane and when newly reborn. Waning, he guessed.

Ralph got up and followed Dan around the back of the cottage. It was nearly dusk. A bat flitted through the air, hungry for its first taste of insect. Dan liked bats, even if other people feared them. On the other hand, he disliked bugs. Bats ate a third of their weight in insects each night. If bats went extinct, he reasoned, the world would be overrun with creepy-crawlies. Therefore it was better to like bats.

He returned with a few pieces of firewood in hand and dropped them beside the fireplace. Jags finished his call and began to make supper. The meal wasn't particularly memorable as far as Dan was concerned, having been spoiled by Trevor's gourmet skills the past few months. During dinner, Jags kept the bottle of bourbon beside his plate. He refilled his glass as soon as it went down a bit. He drank much faster than Dan had even in his heavy-drinking days. His speech soon got a little rough around the edges.

After supper he egged Dan into a game of chess. Dan hadn't played in years and knew his game was rotten. Even drunk, Jags beat him after a half-dozen moves. Jags sneered and put the board away. He went out on the porch and lit a cigarette, staring off into the darkness outlining the trees.

Eventually, he came back in. He sat with his glass and tilted the bottle toward him, sending an amber rivulet across the table. He didn't bother to clean it up. It ran over the edge and onto the floor. Dan had seen this sort of drunken behaviour before. He wasn't going to start pandering to an overgrown slob. Besides, it wasn't his cabin.

As Jags got sloppier, Dan was reminded of how his father used to drink himself to sleep. Or to oblivion, whichever came first. The drinking went on till Dan left home at seventeen. Presumably it continued till his father's death ended the long, sad saga.

Dan looked over where Jags lay with his head on the table. As far as he was concerned, his bodyguard duties didn't include putting drunken rock stars to bed. He could stay there till morning and wake with a crick in his neck or maybe he'd be lucky and have to get up to puke in the middle of the night and crawl off to the bedroom. Either way, Dan was prepared to leave him at the table to fend for himself, invoking the self-righteousness of an ex-drinker.

It felt late. There'd be no fire tonight. Dan turned off the stereo. He went around the room closing the shutters, before putting out the lights and settling on the ten-thousand-dollar sofa. It didn't feel any more comfortable than a regular sofa. Jags could have bought something for five hundred dollars and put the rest of the money to better use.

He picked up Jags' book. It was an engaging read, but his depiction of childhood sounded almost too ideal. It included everything but the gingerbread house and the devoted mother wearing an apron day and night, at least until Jags ran away as a teenager and found himself in Toronto's Queen West punk scene. What could have been more normal than that?

Jags was harder on no one more than himself. He was candid about his drug abuse and his relationship problems. The whiffs of scandal felt more like true confessions from a friend with a problem to confide, rather than a plea for sympathy. When it involved others, Jags was credible and kind in his reportage. Dan had read more than half the book by the time he put out the light and lay on the pillow, wondering how long it would take to fall asleep.

He stirred and lifted his head in darkness. Something had woken him: a ghostly hand on his throat, a spirit visiting his dreams. His watch glowed: 1:33. He'd been asleep for two hours. Ralph lay on the rug beside the couch, alert.

Jags was no longer at the table. The bedroom door was closed. An unearthly sound spread through the room. It was Ralph, growling long and low. He was up now and staring at the door. The fur on his back bristled. Inside, they were safe from prowling animals, Dan knew. Not even a bear could get in, unless it happened to be able to pick locks. Still, knowing how isolated they were from the world and how complete the darkness was outside left him feeling vulnerable. He wondered what sort of people might be in the area looking for uninhabited cabins to rob. The alternative could be worse. What if someone had spotted Jags' car and thought they were easy marks out there in the middle of nowhere?

Ralph continued the low, sustained growl deep in his throat. Dan pulled on his jeans and crept over to the window. He stood looking out on total blackness. If there was anything out there, he couldn't see it. He thought he heard Jags snoring in the other room. A sleeping drunk was a happy drunk.

The wind blew around the cabin, a low drone that died to a whisper before picking up again. It worried Dan. If there were anything prowling outside, he wouldn't hear it.

Ralph's growling rose to an eerie falsetto whine. Clearly he too was worried by the possibilities. Dan turned to him.

"What is it, buddy? Do you smell something?"

Encouraged by Dan's words, Ralph went to the door, sniffing and scratching at the sill.

"I don't think it's a good idea for me to let you out," Dan told him. "Whatever's out there could be a lot bigger than you. And it might like to eat dogs."

Ralph looked questioningly at him. Dan's hand crept over his head and patted his neck.

"Glad you're here, Ralphie," he said. "When we get home, you get an extra bone."

A light rain began to fall. It grew steadily stronger as the wind increased. Dan continued to watch out the window. Shapes defined themselves in the darkness, the black outline of trees shivering in the gusts, the shed with the car farther off. He didn't check his watch again till he felt his legs tire. He was shocked to see the time: 3:46 a.m. He'd been standing and staring out the window for more than two hours. It seemed like he'd been there for about twenty-five minutes. Time had slipped past while he was focused on the darkness outside. Somehow, it had contracted and pulled him in with it. Maybe he was being absorbed into a black hole. Maybe it would seem like that in the tomb.

He stood there a while longer, reluctant to give up his vigil. Finally, the weariness in his legs told him to stop. Nothing more would happen tonight. He lay down again, trying to remain alert and conscious. He was asleep again in minutes.

Morning, a shaft of light bisected the gloom, lighting up Dan's torso and the blankets that clung to the supple musculature of his frame. He looked up at the opening overhead. It made him think of a bus stop ad featuring a teary-eyed, dirty-faced child holding out an empty bowl. "Honey, do we really need another skylight?" the ad asked all those yuppies intent on bettering their homes. *Do we really need another anything?* Dan wondered. Whenever the rich got into trouble, Dan's conclusion was invariably that they had too much time and money on their hands. Otherwise they'd be too busy earning a living like everyone else to get in hot water. Kennedy curse? What Kennedy curse?

Dan looked out the window. Whatever had been out there a few hours previously, there was no sign of it now. He picked up Jags' book and resumed where he'd left off. Jags was well into his career successes and excesses by now. The celebrity gossip was a bit more salacious, but nothing that would make an enemy of its author. The tone grew darker as the price of fame left its mark: anxiety, depression, drugs, and broken relationships. Perhaps he hadn't been exaggerating when he'd said he just wanted a normal life, or some semblance of it.

Jags still hadn't stirred by the time he finished. Dan clanked around in the kitchen, made some scrambled eggs and toast and put them on a platter in the middle of the table. He was just pouring the coffee when Jags' head appeared through the crack.

"Help yourself to breakfast," Dan told him.

"I'll do that." Jags looked distractedly around. "What happened to the party?"

"You're what's left of it."

Jags didn't say another word till he'd poured himself a cup of java and downed half of it. He looked over at the coffee table where Dan had left the book.

"Did you read it?"

"Yes. It kept me up most of the night."

"Any good?"

"It's well-written. Extremely visual. You've got a good writing style."

"You sound like a connoisseur. What kind of books do you read?"

"I like a lot of things: Proust, Cormac McCarthy, Richard Ford. But it's not that kind of book. This is just nice, clean prose with a straightforward outlook and some very convincing opinions about music and art that do you justice. I enjoyed every word, and that's rare with me and books."

"A critic, huh?"

Dan pushed the platter of eggs toward him. "No, just a discerning reader. You can fit in only so much reading time in this life, so it's important to make every book count."

"A good way of looking at it."

"Anyway, that's my take, for what it's worth. Maybe in another twenty years you'll be ready to write Part Two."

Jags smiled ruefully. "Let's see if I live that long."

Dan opened the front door and stood on the porch. "Ralph thought he heard something in the night," he remarked, looking across at the tree line.

Jags came toward him. His expression was dark. "Like what?"

"Hard to say. He got quite worked up. He was growling a lot. I thought there might have been a bear prowling around."

Jags snagged a pair of binoculars hanging from the wall. He scanned the trees anxiously then stared at the ground leading up the path to the porch. "We'll go," he said after a moment.

"What?"

"We'll go back to town. It's probably not safe here."

"If it was just a bear, it'll be gone by now," Dan protested.

Jags shook his head. "They come back sometimes. They're drawn to things. Smells, dead animals. Something always brings them back."

"Up to you," Dan said, bewildered. "But we're probably safe here."

Jags shook his head. "It was a bad idea. I shouldn't have asked you to come."

Dan watched him, wondering what was going on in his head. Jags continued to look around, as though trying to convince himself of something. He seemed spooked.

"Yeah, we'll go. It's too fucking quiet out here anyway."

Jags dropped Dan off at home. The house was still and silent when he entered. Ralph scampered in, looked around for Ked and Trevor, then resigned himself to a boring afternoon lying on his kitchen bed. Dan checked his messages. There was one from Ed, apologizing for disturbing him and saying the police were pressuring him to ask Dan again about his sources. Dan didn't feel up to returning the call. Donny had left a message asking him to phone. He sounded anxious. Dan guessed it had to do with Lester.

Sure enough, when he called, Donny told him Lester had left a message on his machine, saying he was being kept in the house against his will.

He sounded agitated. "I could kick myself for not being here when he called."

"You can't stay in the house forever. He'll call back."

"He said they watch him every minute and lock him in his room at night. Apparently they took away his cellphone, so he had to sneak his mother's phone from her purse when she was in the bathroom, otherwise he wouldn't have been able to call me."

"Have they hurt him or mistreated him physically?"

"I don't know. His message didn't say anything like that."

"We could call social services, but chances are they'd be on the parents' side, since we're dealing with a runaway. As long as there's no physical abuse, they can take away his roaming privileges without being considered to be abusing him."

Donny sighed. "I don't know what to do."

"Unless we know for sure that they're hurting him, it's probably better to do nothing."

There was a noticeable pause on Donny's end. "He threatened to torch the house if they won't let him out."

"Oh, boy."

"Exactly. I feel like I have to rescue him. I can't stand it. I know I'm not his father, but I feel as though I am and that makes it imperative for me to do something."

Dan had never heard him sound so at his wit's end. Donny the Imperturbable was in a flap, and it wasn't an amusing thought.

"Do you know where their house is?"

"No."

"Then you're just going to have to wait till he calls again and find out what, if anything, you can do to help. But I'm warning you — don't get involved in some kind of kidnapping scheme. You have no legal hold over that boy."

"I know, I know. I just feel so useless."

Dan sensed his frustration. "Lester's a bright kid. He'll think of something."

"Preferably something that doesn't include torching his family home."

"Preferably, yes. Let's not go there, all right?"

Dan hung up, feeling he hadn't done much to console his friend, but knowing that he would feel much the same in Donny's shoes. There could be no words to console him right now.

The machine's final message was from Domingo. Would Dan be free for lunch any time in the next couple days?

Yes, he thought. *I would.*

TWELVE

The Maharajah's Plate

TUCKED AWAY ON THE NORTHEAST CORNER of Hayden Street, just south of Bloor, The Bishop and the Belcher was Domingo's favourite downtown hangout. In winter it was a cosy, curl-up-by-the-fire-and-indulge sort of place; in summer it had the regulation outdoor patio, replete with loud straights who thought coming to the edge of the gay ghetto was a lark. The joke was on them because the place was gay-owned and -operated. *Just look for the inverted rainbow triangle on the front door*, Dan wanted to tell them. *Better than a smear of lamb's blood to the ancient Hebrews.* The B & B was *vrai gay*, just not as gauche as its way-downtown sister and brother hangouts like Slack's and Woody's. With fewer drag queens and no hustlers to speak of, it boasted the best pub menu on the strip, including some of the tastiest curries this side of Sri Lanka.

By the time Dan arrived, Domingo was on her third fancy drink, replete with paper umbrellas and fruit chachka. She looked up, smacked her blood red lips and flashed a dazzling smile.

"Hello, gorgeous, how are you?"

Dan sat, bathing in the glow of her vibrancy. It was hard to believe she'd undergone chemotherapy recently.

"Great, thanks. It's great to see you. How are you?"

She lifted her glass in salute. "As you see. Alive and well and enjoying every minute of life."

"As it should be."

A waiter swooped down on the table. After a quick perusal of the specials, Dan settled on the Maharajah's Plate while Domingo ordered the Pulled Pork Lettuce Wrap. They handed their menus over to the waiter. Domingo took another sip through her twisty straw.

"How's the new man?"

"Perfect in every way."

"Except?"

Dan felt himself falter. She was watching him, doing that thing he hated.

"Why do you ask? Is your intuition telling you something?"

She smiled and shook her head. "No. I can see it in your eyes. Perfect in every way, but?"

Dan shrugged. "Except he's not sure he likes it here. He's not a city boy."

She put down her glass. "You certainly seemed content together. He adores you, I can tell. I'm glad to see you with someone who appreciates you."

"Thank you."

She looked at the high-rise condos around them. Well detailed, handsomely constructed. This was a city of clean lines and easy propriety. A genteel people lived here. "Besides, what's not to like? I always forget what an attractive city this is. Clean. Safe."

"We could do more."

She leaned her chin on her hand and smiled indulgently. "It's not for everybody, but on the whole I think we're a good people."

Dan shrugged. "Is that enough? Shouldn't we be good *for* something?"

She looked at him in surprise. "Why so down on the hometown?"

"Just a hang-up I have about complacency. What's the use of being polite, if all we can do is feel smug about it?"

"I know other countries look down on us. We're not cool. They think we're naïve and lacking in culture. I'd say the world is conflicted — they look down on us, but they envy our freedom, our natural beauty, our spacious living, our racial integration. And the great thing about it, if you've noticed, is that we don't care what they think."

Dan laughed. "How true."

"Plus, it keeps out the riff-raff. That's what I love about Canada. So what if we're a weird combination of naïve and smug? At least we don't go around invading other nations and lying about our reasons for doing it, like some countries I could name."

She made a coy face and Dan laughed.

"Americans aren't so worldly, either. They lived in their isolationist bubble for so long, insulated by television and dreaming that life was a theme park designed by Walt

Disney, till they had a rude awakening a while back. Now they're tearing themselves apart, half of them fighting to keep their delusions while the other half wants to point out the warts on the witch's nose. Both sides blame the other for all their problems."

Domingo ran a hand through that shock of white hair. She was right, Dan thought. There were worse things than a naïve populace.

"I didn't get much of a chance to talk to you the other night. I'm sorry to hear what you went through."

"Thanks, but I try not to dwell on it. There's nothing so humbling as looking at a shadow on an X-ray, knowing something is growing inside you. Women's bodies are funny. We grow babies who grow up and die and we grow lumps in our breasts that feed those babies, and they kill us. I had such beautiful breasts, round and firm, like polished melons. They gleamed in the moonlight, Adi used to tell me."

She picked up her drink then set it back down.

"But there's no sense in dwelling on that, either." She nodded. "Adi's been a pillar. A true rock. I couldn't ask for more from her. I really couldn't."

She waved her arms in the air, as if to make the topic vanish. Their server returned and set their plates nimbly on the table. Cutlery followed, wrapped in paper napkins as though they'd been embalmed.

Domingo took a bite, sighed, and looked up. "I swear someone's been stealing my mother's recipes. It doesn't get much better than this."

Dan speared a shrimp with his fork. He tasted and nodded. "I hope they keep this cook a long, long time. A good curry chef is hard to find."

Domingo looked across the table at him. "So what else is new in your life?"

Dan nodded. "Well, apart from the boyfriend, who you'll be glad to know is putting me through my paces, we also have a housing project on the go."

Domingo looked impressed. "Do tell."

"Not much to tell yet. It's a townhouse in Corktown."

"Ooh, Corktown! How swank."

"Trevor's designing the interior. It's costing a fortune, apart from the architecture plans, which are his contribution. It's not going to be ready for another month. I just wish he'd commit to living here."

"What's stopping him?"

"He's had a hard time. His ex-lover killed himself. It took Trevor a long time to get over it. The city makes him edgy. He prefers solitude. He lived on an island in BC for the last ten years."

"That's rough." Domingo nodded. "It's so easy to get lost in life, and so hard to get found again." She smiled. "Not you, though. You go on your straightforward route, dead ahead, for good or for bad, just as if there was no other way."

"I don't really think about it. It's not as though we have a choice."

She shook her head. "But the rest of us aren't like that, Daniel. The rest of us live life without a road map, for the most part. It's not as easy for us."

"You think it's easy for me?"

"Not really. But you just seem so sure of yourself. It's part of your charm. I'm just not sure you realize that others don't find the choices in life so easy to make."

Dan shrugged. "Anyway, I just wish he could decide."

"He will. Just be patient. Otherwise, if you rush it, you will regret it, thinking you never gave him the time to figure things out for himself."

"But what will he decide?"

"You don't need me to tell you." She smiled. "You already know how it will go."

"I guess I'll have to wait and see then." Dan wiped his mouth with his napkin. "I wanted to tell you that you were right about what you said the other night. The case, I mean. It isn't over yet and I am getting involved. Exactly as you said I would."

"So are you a believer now?"

Dan shrugged, not ready to commit to one side or the other. "I'm not sure. I'm trying to be open-minded. I already did some investigating into this in the past."

"Really? You surprise me. You were so against it when I lived beside you."

"It's not that I doubted you. It's just that I've never heard of a crime being stopped by a psychic premonition."

"Oh, Dan." She looked sadly at him. "I thought you understood. It's not about stopping things. Sometimes you can gain insight, but you can't change the course of events. Not if it's meant to be. What you can change is your reaction to what is to come. Be a better person, that sort of thing. Don't worry, though, you don't need improving. I think your positives are all in the right place. For a non-believer."

"It's not that I don't believe, it's that I don't understand. And that makes me a tad suspicious of any claims."

"I don't like claims either. Just take what comes and be the best person you can. That way there are no regrets, no matter what happens."

She smiled and took another drink through the plastic curlicue protruding from her glass.

"Oh, by the way. I have a new client," he said.

"Who is it?"

"Well, before I tell you, I was kind of hoping you might take a look and tell me what you come up with."

She smiled. "Really? You're actually asking me to look into something for you on the other side?"

"Not some*thing*. Some*one*. I'm just curious to know what you see."

She smiled. "Well, you have changed."

"Are you up to it?"

"I'm always up to it, baby."

She put down her fork, took a big sip from her glass then closed her eyes.

"I see a bright light. It's like a star or something. Your client must be very important, whoever it is."

Dan let out a whoop. "Domingo, I now believe in you forever."

She opened her eyes. "Did I say something right?"

"Bang on. Can you tell me if he's a good person?"

She looked quizzically at him. "Good?"

"Trustworthy, I guess I mean."

She closed her eyes and got silent again for a moment. "Well, he's complex, that's for sure. The only thing is, the light goes out if I watch it too long."

"As in?"

"Extinction."

Dan studied her face. “That doesn’t sound good. What’s the source of the extinction?”

There was a long pause. “It comes from the self. It’s some sort of auto-extinction.”

Dan frowned. “As in suicide?”

Her eyes were still closed. Domingo seemed to be concentrating harder. “I don’t think so. It seems to be some form of *indulgence*, I want to call it.”

Dan thought of Jags’ tendency to drink till he passed out. “Like drugs or alcohol?”

There was a pause while she consulted some inner realm. “I don’t know. It seems to come and go. It’s there then it’s out then it’s there again. The light, I mean.”

She opened her eyes.

Dan was staring at her. “Any idea what that means?”

“None at all. Except that your client needs to take care it doesn’t become permanent.”

“Okay, thanks.”

“So who is this client? I’m curious.”

“Jags Rohmer.”

“You’re kidding!”

“Domingo, you know me well enough by now to know that I never kid.”

She laughed. “True enough. What’s he like?”

“He doesn’t have a clue what reality is. He says he just wants a normal life.”

Domingo almost choked. “Well, here’s to rock star clients.” She took another drink then looked over at Dan. “Shall we have a more mundane conversation now?”

Dan smiled. “Sure, and thanks for the input.”

"No problem." She paused. "I'm worried about Donny. Or, more precisely, I'm worried about how Donny is reacting to Lester's departure. Is there anything we can do, do you think?"

Dan looked across the road at a cyclist weaving in and out among the cars, a handful of pedestrians talking on cellphones, gesticulating and looking as though they had no idea where they were.

His gaze returned to Domingo's face. "I'm concerned about Donny and Lester too. As you know, I introduced them. I thought I was doing Lester a favour at the time, but I soon learned it was just as big a deal to Donny, which was why he agreed to keep the boy. Who knew he saw himself as a father?"

She smiled. "I knew."

"The kid spent time on the streets. He had it worse than some, but not as bad as others. He told me a story of being raped by an older man he lived with, though he has since tested HIV-negative. He was on the streets for a relatively short time and I think he's been thoroughly rehabilitated, to use the clinical term, largely due to Donny's influence and care."

"Amen to that," Domingo interjected.

"He's very protective of the boy and also strict with him, in a good way. The difference between what Donny does and what Lester's mother does is that Donny does it for Lester's own good. My guess is that his mother is just trying to mould him for her own ends."

"She sounds like a rotten parent."

Dan set down his fork. "They both are. I was his caseworker and I met with them just once."

Dan recalled a mohair sweater, fuchsia pink fingernails filed down to a point and tapping incessantly on his desktop as she demanded he find her son. Lester's stepfather was clearly uncomfortable with the idea of having a gay son in the house and wanted nothing to do with the boy.

"I found him and dragged him out of the gutter. At the time he was involved in making porn videos and selling himself on the street. It didn't take me long to realize he didn't want to be there, either. He just didn't want to be sent home to a manipulative mother and an abusive stepfather. I guess those memories must have faded a bit, if he thought he would be okay to go home. Nevertheless, he made his choice."

"Everyone is allowed a change of mind."

"Oh, I agree wholeheartedly. What I don't agree with is the idea that Donny might become implicated in separating a minor from his family, however horrible they may be. So, to return to your original question, yes, I do think something can be done. I just haven't had the time to figure out what."

"Who was the man who raped him? Was he caught?"

"No. And he's resurfaced, making matters worse. It's one of the reasons Lester wanted to leave the city. Lester told me they lived together for a short while. He provided for the kid. Everyone thought they were father and son. They even went to church together, apparently."

"So, a fairly normal looking and acting individual outwardly?"

"So it would seem."

Domingo smiled ruefully.

"What is it?"

"You'd think a child molester would be a hideous looking person, someone you would instinctively be repelled by."

"No. Often they're quite ordinary looking. Normal. Not a monster at all. It's why they can get so close to children, disarm their families into thinking they can be trusted."

"Our kids make us vulnerable," she said. "I'm sure I don't have to tell you that."

She shaded her eyes with her hand and turned her head. Her own son had been on a missing persons list for more than seven years, Dan knew. He'd disappeared without a word one summer morning. Dan had searched but found no trace of him.

"I'm ..." Dan began.

"No, don't say anything. It was stupid of me. Please forget I brought it up."

After a moment she looked up, eyes misty but her smile in place.

The rest of the meal passed quietly, as though there was little left to be said. Domingo pushed aside her plate and looked at her watch, declaring an imminent appointment.

"I'll get the cheque," Dan told her. "You can get the next one, as long as it's in this calendar year."

She smiled and leaned down to kiss his cheek. "You're sweet, thanks. I'll hold you to the next date."

Dan's gaze followed her down the street and around the corner to the rest of her life. A missing child, a bout of chemotherapy. But here they both were, as Donny had said. Life certainly held its surprises.

Dan was in no rush. He finished his meal and sat there watching the clean, safe city with its unworldly citizens going by.

THIRTEEN

Little Jack Horny

DAN LEFT THE PUB and made his way back to his car. The headline in a newspaper box stopped him dead: *Child Victim or Cunning Killer?* There on the front page of the *Star* was a photograph of Gaetan Bélanger. Dan's mind was running in circles. So much for keeping the info quiet "for reasons of discretion." He wondered what the chief of police was thinking right at that moment.

He fished in his pockets for change and cursed his luck at having emptied them back at the pub for a tip. He watched as a woman came up and tipped in two quarters, opened the door, and removed a copy of the paper. He was considering how to distract her to keep the door from slamming when she looked over, extracted a second paper, and handed it to him.

"Two-for-one day," she said gleefully before walking away, her heels clicking against the sidewalk like knitting needles.

He went around the corner and sat on a bench beneath a locust tree. The article outlined the discovery of a third victim, whose death was being blamed on the Quebec teenager now hiding out in Toronto.

> Police are seeking a child abuse survivor in what they now suspect may be a serial killing spree. Gaetan Bélanger, 16, of Lévis, QC, is sought in connection with the murder of Donald Perry, 42, of Scarborough.
>
> Perry was third to die in what is believed to be a co-ordinated series of attacks on sex offenders whose names were released on the Internet last year.
>
> Guillaume Thierry, a former priest convicted of abusing Bélanger and nearly a dozen other boys at several churches he was associated with in Montreal, was found dead on May 23.
>
> Darryl Hillary of Etobicoke was murdered on August 11. Neither Perry nor Hillary had any known connection with Bélanger.
>
> An unnamed source in the police force said the names appear to have been taken at random from the leaked registry that left the identities of several hundred convicted sex offenders on public view for more than a week.

Photos of Thierry, Hillary, and Perry were inset below. A sidebar mentioned severe mutilation to all three victims, but gave no further details. Dan wondered what constituted "severe." Had Thierry and Perry been left in worse shape than Hillary? Perhaps Dan's unexpected arrival at the slaughterhouse had prevented Bélanger from inflicting more grievous physical harm on Darryl. If so, there was that to be thankful for at least.

His cellphone buzzed: *Unknown Number* showed on the display. He flipped open the phone and put it to his ear.

"Sharp."

A shrill treble sounded in his ear. "Greetings, Dan. Constable Pfeiffer here."

The cop's timing was uncanny. Dan looked around, scanning the street where a sea of sunglasses stared out from neighbourhood patios. He was half-convinced that Pfeiffer was sitting watching him from some nearby café.

"Not sure if you heard the news, Dan."

Dan snapped the paper open and held it out to full view. "If you're referring to the exposé in the *Star*, then yes. I have it in hand."

"So our Little Jack Horny has struck again."

"Excuse me?" Dan said, thinking he had heard wrong.

"Little Jack Horny. It's our unofficial nickname for the case down at HQ."

"Classy. But I thought you guys were keeping this under wraps for now."

"Yeah. Funny that. Wonder how it happened." Pfeiffer's voice went from mocking to accusatory. "A shame about that third death," he said. "Especially when you could have prevented it."

Dan was momentarily stunned. "You really believe that? I know even less about the whereabouts of Gaetan Bélanger than you do."

"I'd like to believe that, Dan, but your movements tell me otherwise."

Dan shook his head. "What are you saying?"

"I know you've got Jags Rohmer for a client. Shouldn't you be trying to find Bélanger before he gets him too?"

Ice went down Dan's spine. "What's Rohmer got to do with any of this?"

He heard Pfeiffer laugh. "You better ask him, I guess."

"Ask him what?"

"Just ask him, Dan."

The call ended. Dan pocketed the phone and finished the article. By the time he was done, he wished he'd never heard of Darryl Hillary or Jags Rohmer.

Yorkville was three blocks away. He hoofed it over. Once the preserve of beatniks, hippies, and soon-to-be-famous musicians like Joni Mitchell, Gordon Lightfoot, and Neil Young, the neighbourhood had upped its ante in the ensuing decades and was now the private preserve of the financial elite, ensconced in a few square blocks where bidding wars for condos reached into the millions.

Dan remembered Jags' warning that the building's security was formidable. He entered, gave them a cursory glance and turned aside before he could register on their radar. They looked like the sort of team you might see in a James Bond film, where the hero has to use all of his wits and a beautiful, scantily clad woman to get past them. Using a key was easier.

Upstairs, he stepped out of the elevator and quickly found the door. Jags answered wearing only a dressing gown. He looked surprised to see Dan but nodded at him to come in.

"Oh, right. I gave you the key, didn't I?"

The room was cluttered. Art on the walls, statues on the side tables. Shelves crammed with books, records, CDs. Expensive-looking rugs on the floors. Dan tossed the *Star* on the coffee table. Jags gave him a quizzical look.

"A review of my book?"

"Hardly," Dan said. "Look at the headline."

Jags glanced at the paper then back at Dan. "So?"

"You don't know what this is about?"

Jags shook his head. "Enlighten me, good sir."

"I'd prefer if you would enlighten *me*. Constable Pfeiffer suggested I ask you about your involvement."

"My involvement?" Now Jags looked uneasy. "I'm not sure what you're trying to tell me."

"Why did you hire me as a bodyguard? The real reason, please. And don't give me a load of crap about needing protection from someone you've libelled in your book, because those people are all dead from drug overdoses or such has-beens that they would probably be thrilled to have the publicity."

"Nice way to talk about former stars."

Dan felt himself losing it. "I don't give a fuck about former anything. What connection do you have with this murder?"

Jags sat on the couch and gestured for Dan to do the same. When he didn't, Jags looked up at him.

"Sit," he said, and indicated the chair opposite.

Dan sat slowly, keeping his eyes on Jags. "You led me to believe I was recommended to you by my former boss, Ed Burch. I called Ed. He knew nothing about it. He doesn't even know who you are."

"How unkind." Jags wiped his brow with a kerchief then looked at Dan. "I went to the police because I thought I might have a problem. What I told you was true, however. There are people from my past who were upset thinking I might expose something incriminating about them. I've got too much good sense — not to mention legal counsel — to do that, but until they read the book they won't know for sure."

Dan was getting impatient. "As I said, there's nothing in your book that anyone would get upset over or take exception to. Does the world not know that Keith Richards was a junkie or that John Lennon was a first-class jackass behind his Saint of the Peace Movement routine?"

Dan waited.

Jags shrugged. "You're right. It's old news. On the other hand, I could have said that John Lennon once had a boyfriend named Stuart Sutcliffe …"

He watched Dan's face for a reaction, but found none.

"… and that poor Stuart died of a brain haemorrhage two months after John kicked the shit out of him. This was back in Hamburg in the days before the Beatles went viral. And afterward, of course, John would only ever talk about Stuart when he was in his cups. No charges were ever laid, but that *would* have been news."

Jags eyed him. Dan's face was impassive.

"Why do you really need a bodyguard?"

Jags sighed. "Okay."

He stood and went over to a desk. He fished around in a small silver bowl on a bookshelf and brought out an antique key. It fit neatly into the desk's lock. The drawer slid open. He retrieved a slim envelope and passed it to Dan.

Dan lifted the flap and a Polaroid dovetailed into his hand. At first glance he couldn't figure out what he was seeing. It appeared to be a close-up of a dried, curled leaf lying on a dirt background. Then the colours jumped out at him. He was looking at a severed human ear. He fought the nausea.

Jags' voice was soft, almost taunting. "Takes a while, but it kind of gets to you once you figure it out, doesn't it?"

Dan slid the photo back in the envelope and handed it back with a nod.

"Now that's a real *memento mori*," Jags said.

Dan nodded. "You should have told me about this from the beginning."

Jags was watching him. "They warned me not to. Said you might not take me on if I did."

"Who?"

"The cops. The cocky one — Pfeiffer — seemed particularly adamant about it. He said you were more than just a gun for hire and that you probably wouldn't go for it if you didn't like it."

"He doesn't know me in the least, but he was right on that score."

Jags put the envelope back in the drawer and locked it again. He turned to look at Dan seated on the couch.

"I'm sorry I didn't tell you. I was desperate. I wanted you to take me on and I didn't want to jeopardize that. I needed someone who was more than just a hunk of muscle. Someone who was savvy. They assured me you had a reputation for doing whatever you had to do to make things happen right."

Dan glanced away. On the wall were three framed platinum records. He wondered which ones they were. Probably from early on in Jags' career. His later records tended to confuse and polarize his fans. They weren't sure if his experimenting was just a joke, maybe on them. An image came to mind of a melting face — Jags' face — on some cover. A disturbing image. The man dealt in the bizarre.

"You're right," he said. "If you'd shown me this photo I wouldn't have taken the job. I've got a son and a partner. I wouldn't do anything that might endanger them."

He looked down at the paper. Darryl Hillary's eyes burned up at him.

"Did you read it? Do you know what any of this is about?"

Jags nodded. "Yeah. They're looking for some kid who kills sex abusers."

Dan looked over at him. "Are you a sex abuser?"

Jags tensed. His expression darkened. He looked as though he might tear Dan limb from limb.

"What the fuck are you asking me? What are you saying?"

Dan picked up the paper and tossed it at Jags. "I'm asking you why the guy who killed three men would be sending you photographs."

Jags looked genuinely confused. "What?"

"That picture you just showed me was of a severed ear."

"I know that! Why the fuck do you think I freaked out?"

He pointed to the paper. "Severed ears. The kid cuts off his victims' ears."

Jags suddenly paled. "He does what?"

"So I ask you again, are you a sex abuser?"

"No!"

"Has your name ever appeared on the Sex Offenders Registry?"

"Fuck no! I … I …"

"Then why was that photograph sent to you?"

"I have no fucking idea. And I had no idea it had anything to do with this … this crazy business."

Jags strode across the room and stood face to face with Dan. He waited till they were eye to eye.

"I swear on my life that I have never abused a kid, sexually or otherwise."

Dan waited a beat. "What about all those groupies you slept with? Can you say for sure whether any of them weren't under the age of consent?"

A look of fear came over Jags' face. "Are you telling me that…? But they were all willing!"

"They were all willing?"

"Yes."

"Surely you can't be naïve enough to think that that makes it legal."

Jags' mouth seemed to be doing some sort of mastication exercise. "But it was years ago … decades." His voice trailed off. He sat and cradled his head in his hands.

"Have you had other warnings?" Dan asked. "Abusive phone calls? Emails?"

Jags looked up. "No, it can't be." He nodded. "The day I asked you to go to the cottage with me, someone called and threatened to kill me."

"And that's why you wanted to go out of the city so suddenly?"

Jags nodded. "Yes."

Dan waited.

"Have you any idea," Jags said slowly, "how many musicians have slept with any number of groupies without knowing whether they were legal or not?"

"I couldn't begin to guess," Dan said.

"Think about it. It was the punk era. Everybody fucked everything. This was pre-AIDS, even. We'd never heard of the shit. If it had a pulse, you fucked it. And sometimes even if it didn't. Nobody cared. No one would even remember what happened between 1977 and 1987 because we were all too wasted to recall. One moment you were shagging someone in the back room of some rancid little club then the next you were shooting up heroin with water you drew out of a toilet. Soiled? Used? Maybe. Who the fuck cared? Those were crazy days. Off-the-map crazy. Total zonkers."

Dan held out the paper. "You think that's an excuse?"

Jags took it from him and shook his head. "I'm telling you, that universe had no rules and no way is anyone going to come after me now and say, 'Excuse me, but you boffed me when I was fifteen years old and some murdering sod wants to talk to you about it.' Ain't gonna happen." He slammed down the paper. "Ain't gonna happen!"

"Okay. So who sent you the photograph?"

"Why would someone even care about what I did then?"

He looked so distraught Dan almost felt sorry for him.

"The motive for these murders seems to be because their names were on a list of registered sex offenders —"

"I'm telling you, I'm not!"

Dan cut him off. "I heard you. So if your name wasn't on the list then it's something else. Or it's a mistake. I suggest you take that photograph back into the headquarters and tell them you require round-the-clock police protection."

Jags turned to him with a pleading look. "In the meantime, what are we going to do about it?"

"We?" Dan shook his head slowly. "Hiring me to keep rowdy fans from pinching your ass at a book signing is one thing, but getting me involved in a serial killer's fantasies are quite another. Consider me no longer in your employ, Mr. Rohmer."

"No, wait. Dan, please! There's someone out there who wants me dead. I need you to protect me. You're the only one I trust!"

"I can't do this."

Jags watched as Dan went out the door. "If I die, it'll be your fault!" was the last thing Dan heard from him.

FOURTEEN

Cold as Ashes

Dan felt restless as dusk came on. He couldn't remember the last time he'd been on his own for more than a few hours at a time. Trevor was in BC till Wednesday. Ked had stayed at his mother's for another night. On the other hand, there was Ralph. Dan walked and fed him then, having done his duties, he left the house and headed for the Danforth. Nobody knew why it was called *the* Danforth. It just was. The Danforth was the closest thing Toronto came to having a European cultural ethos, its restaurants and bars reflecting the touristy cafés of Paris or Athens.

As he reached the busy thoroughfare that split the city's east end, Dan looked around. Distant strains of music promised soft distractions, fun company. He found himself outside The Only Cafe, where a local band was putting on a set of funk-and-roll. So then. It was decided. This would be a test. He set himself a limit of two pints. If he could go into a bar alone and contain his thirst then he was doing well.

After years of unrestrained drinking, his son had finally confronted Dan's alcoholic tendencies. Happily, that had coincided with Trevor's appearance in his life. Sweet distraction. Since then, in private, he'd been able to keep his drinking to a minimum. With the noise and bustle of the world at his shoulder, however, it might prove a different story. When he left, he'd know whether he had any willpower to speak of or if he was truly a spectre in the purgatory inhabited by alcoholics. *There but for the grace of Trevor go I*, Dan told himself.

The Only was a hangout for would-be Rastafarians and a hip young crowd — stylish clothes, self-conscious hair — with the occasional middle-aged yuppie drifting in for a taste of remembered cool, before careers and mortgages and kids and stock portfolios interfered with all that fun and living.

An ambiguous sexual tone hung in the air, in keeping with the imported beer and gourmet sandwiches. The city had been taken over by an amorphous generation, unperturbed by definitions of any sort. The men looked at Dan with interest, if not outright desire. There was no telling in here. If nothing else, he probably looked as though he might prove a good dope deal. The women were coyer, glancing sideways at him before deciding he wasn't their cup of joy, that he didn't have the right moves after all. At least not for them. These kids had their own brand of gaydar.

Dan downed his requisite pint, teasing it out a full twenty minutes before deciding this wasn't really his scene. Grabbing a souvlaki from a street vendor, he headed west toward the Don Valley and drifted into the Old Nick, an Empire Freehouse with a less trendy clientele who had fewer concerns about their hair. It might have been the sort of establishment Samuel Pepys had in mind when he declared pubs the heart of England. He was greeted by an insistent bass beat of raised voices, the clatter of cutlery, and the clinking of many glasses against the bar top. Tin ceilings, oak-planked floors. It was a good place to waste an hour, but the faded good humour of the staff was cut shorter with each successive demanding customer. *If it wasn't for the money, I'd tell them all to…!* Here no one flirted with him but the bartender, a genuine troll of sixty or more. Whether or not the man was gay wasn't at issue here. Dan suspected he'd flirt with anyone for an extra loonie tossed ringside at the end of the bout. Whether you lost or won at the game of love wasn't his concern, so long as he saw you off with a laugh and a friendly wave inviting you to try your luck again tomorrow. *All the sad young men …*

He sat and ordered.

Posters loomed overhead. Every bar had its dead heroes. This one was no exception. Janis Joplin, Jimi Hendrix, and John Lennon topped the list. Farther down, Billie Holiday, Jim Morrison, Kurt Cobain, Al Wilson, Bob Marley, and Sid Vicious all weighed in on the count. Dan had nothing against maudlin memories of the dead, but he had reservations about Vicious. What was there to mourn about a sadistic, anti-social murderer? Nothing. Sid had had no talent, so nothing wasted there. He'd done nothing in his short life to redeem his time on Earth. Just another self-styled Nazi who did the world a favour by topping himself before he killed again.

The list of the dead — many of them members of the notorious 27 Club — was long, but this one had an unusual variation: jazz guitarist Lenny Breau. A soft-spoken Canadian, Breau had been a real talent, unlike Vicious and his mates, who went looking for trouble. Strangled and thrown into an LA swimming pool, the crime was still officially unsolved, though Dan recalled that the wife loomed large on the list of suspects. It made no difference. Breau's talent had burned out on drugs and bad company well before his time. A true waste, in other words.

Despite the morgue on the walls, this was more Dan's scene. Overhead, CNN flashed across his retinas, a grab bag of arbitrary information crammed onscreen. There was the TSE index flirting with the weather girl, car accidents taking down prime ministers, floods and movie premieres all rolled into one flashing, twitching mosaic of *Here and Now!* All the while Father Time was ticking, reminding you the world was passing as you gawked and ate and gossiped. *What's the hour? A quarter past eternity. Do you know where your life has gone?*

Dan's eyes flickered, taking in the panorama of life across the globe. All the news, angst and fashion that money could buy. There was the usual celeb-fest as the city prepared to host the annual film festival. Dan yawned. He didn't care what Brad and Angelina were up to. Not that they weren't nice people with good causes when they wanted to be. He just had more pressing concerns. Next, a police officer subpoenaed for breach of confidence had failed to surrender his laptop. *No doubt protecting his stash of lap-dance pictures or some such*, Dan thought. *Rotten luck buddy*. A photographic highlight contrasting Japanese and Canadian fashion trends failed to catch Dan's interest.

His eyes flickered away. Across the room, a woman caught his glance. Attractive in the shadows, she might not prove so enticing close up, he realized. Such was life. But then he wasn't wanting a closer look. Dan tried to guess what or who she was: a failed actor on the lookout for a private drama, a rewarding part she could cast herself in, no need for the director to glance her way and like her legs. Or maybe she was a single mom having second thoughts in mid-life, wondering again why she'd put her dreams permanently on hold for those ungrateful brats who had no idea that she'd once been young and carefree like them, while her deadbeat ex-husband still hung out at parties and ogled younger women as though he was still in his twenties. A real life version of *Jeopardy! I'll take* Failed Lives *for a hundred, Alex*. The stories repeated themselves up and down the bar.

She gave up after Dan failed to respond on her fifth try, turning her attention to a heavyset man on the other side of the room. He seemed to appreciate the attention, downing his pint for a bit of extra courage. *Your luck, fellow*, Dan thought.

This wasn't how he wanted to spend his night, single and desperate for company, whether in a gay bar or a straight one. If he wanted to, he knew he'd find oblivion in the bottle here. In a gay bar, after one drink too many it would almost certainly end with another man's body beside his before the night was over. Given the choice, which would he choose: a sweaty, naked romp or a perspiring glass of gold and white froth? Both had their immediate appeal, but he was a one-man dog, when it came down to it. He'd far prefer to bed down with a cup of hot cocoa and a delicious man who was currently on an island somewhere off the coast of BC.

He was about to leave when a hard-looking pair of eyes flashed at him from the glare of a spotlight. He stopped to focus on the patina of glass overhead. There was the chief of police, staring down the barrel end of a TV camera. The tickertape below promised full updates on the city's latest murder. Dan sat glued to the set as the chief glowered at him. The man was intense but clearly comfortable in front of a camera delivering his news, and equally comfortable if a bit more aggressive when fielding questions. He was a quarterback making a run in the world of sound bites, a soldier of fortune with the instincts of a stage actor. A media-savvy cop. And so the world turned.

Dan finished his requisite second pint and left without ordering a third, as he'd promised himself. It felt like a victory, however small. Heading home, he calculated how many hours till Trevor's return. One more night alone with Ralph wouldn't be so terrible. The dog couldn't help that he wasn't Dan's choice of company. Oblivion couldn't come too soon, though.

The curtains blew freely back and forth. Dan was stuck in a small, cramped space, waiting for someone. Outside, the rain ran down the window in slow, steady streams. Burgundy drapes reflected the colour of blood. The walls were every shade of black.

A candle flame appeared in the doorway, making his heart leap. Terror gripped him. Had he been bad again? He hid behind the altar to let whoever it was go by. Footsteps approached and stopped. Someone sniffed the air, as though sensing a presence. He peeked around the corner, surprised to see Jags Rohmer in a priest's robe.

Jags moved past without seeing him. He was about to leave when a second figure appeared. It was Darryl Hillary. So he wasn't dead after all. Dan sensed something stirring in his consciousness. He guessed he was dreaming, but he couldn't wake himself.

He started at a noise behind him just as someone grabbed his arms and pinned him against the wall. He struggled to resist the offending lips on his face, the fingers on his body tearing at his clothes. He was thrown onto the floor of the altar, the marble cold against his face. The attacker lowered himself onto Dan's body, forcing his legs open. Dan felt the searing pain, the agony of violation. The more he protested, the more urgent the other's actions became as a hot poker raked his insides.

Dan twisted his torso around to get a glimpse of his abuser, but the man's face was obscured by a hood. He opened his mouth to scream and his attacker forced something between his teeth. A wafer. Dan was choking on the body of Christ.

The man pounded into him, crushing him with his weight and forcing himself deep inside. Dan could barely stand the pain. An arm slipped free. His hand groped in a pocket and pulled out a Swiss Army knife. He reached up and deftly sliced off the man's left ear.

His attacker screamed and leapt up. Dan watched the chief of police lurch frenziedly from the room. He struggled to his feet, squeezing himself into the darkness behind the altar while wiping saliva from his lips. He felt blood dripping, dripping on his hand.

He opened his eyes. He was sprawled on the living room couch. Ralph was licking his fingers and watching him with concern. Dan felt a wave of nausea and raced to the bathroom. He heaved and flushed, but it was only getting worse. He'd just managed to sit when a stream of burning liquid shot from his bowels. Hot poker indeed. That was the last time he'd buy souvlaki from a street vendor.

When the deluge was over, Dan got up and washed his face. He was grateful he was alone. Trevor would be compassionate, but Ked might worry he was drinking again. He groped his way downstairs. Coffee would help clear the cobwebs from his mind, but the cupboard was bare. He'd run out yesterday. Of course Trevor would have replaced it by now.

It was just past 3:00 a.m. He roused himself and went out to the back patio, staring up at the blackness. It was nearly as dark as the inside of the slaughterhouse. Had Darryl seen his killer coming? Had he recognized him? Dan stood there, imagining Hillary's last moments. What was he thinking after the first blow, the first spilling of blood? Had he felt anger, fear, disbelief? Probably all three.

Dan imagined his blood as the darkest thing in the shadows, his life essence glowing and luminous and black all at once. Something so macabre and strange it would be shown like a science exhibition, some phosphorous essence, impossible and wondrous, put on display for centuries. Had he been expiating the sins of love for human kind? He'd dared to love what was forbidden. In his mind, Dan watched as Darryl knelt before his killer, like a martyr arriving at Golgotha. Was Death something horrible in that moment or was it a thing to be embraced? Did he cling, in the last few seconds, to his dreams of what could have been or willingly place himself in Death's hands, like a baby waiting to be taken up in arms stronger than his? How did you give it all up? How did you age into that state of mind? Was there gratitude that he'd fulfilled his earthly obligations or was it doom and terror right to the final moment of consciousness, the last fleeting images dying on the retinas, haunted and tormented, before they closed forever?

An hour later, coffee in hand, Dan was parked across from the slaughterhouse. The remnants of yellow police tape flapped around the yard like a warning. The place was deserted.

He let Ralph out of the car first. If anyone confronted him, he'd simply say he was walking his dog. No matter that he'd driven half an hour across town in the middle of the night to do so.

As if by instinct, Ralph headed for the door where Dan had entered the nightmare realms of Darryl Hillary's tomb two weeks earlier.

"Good boy!" he called softly.

Dan followed silently, shaking his head like a reluctant dog owner chasing his disobedient dog, all the while knowing the dog was taking him where he wanted to go.

The silence hit him as he stepped over the threshold, a hush as smooth as velvet. No horror theme played in his head tonight. After a few moments, his eyes adjusted. It was just light enough to make out the debris and retrace his route.

He followed Ralph to the centre of the space, saw the hooks grappling with the open air. The one Darryl had been hanging from was gone. A gap-toothed space took up its place in line.

Ralph sniffed the ground beneath the missing hook and looked anxiously back at Dan.

"Good boy, Ralph."

Ralph moved on, squeezing through into another passageway Dan hadn't noticed on that other night. He followed cautiously. It took him to a small cubby space with a hole in the roof directly overhead. It was brighter here. He flicked on his Maglight. The floor held the remnants of a fire, its ashes piled in a heap, empty food tins dropped onto the fire pit.

Dan squatted and stared into the ash, glimpsing a teenaged boy huddled over an open flame trying to make sense of his existence. An existence that no longer mattered in the everyday world.

Gaetan Bélanger ate a meal here, he thought. *Maybe he slept here, possibly more than once.*

Bélanger was an orphan who had legally become his own person on his sixteenth birthday. Dan had left home at seventeen, though he'd felt orphaned long before. Six years later, he had his own son. *Our kids make us vulnerable*, Domingo had said.

Dan lay on the floor and hugged Ralph when the dog came over to him. He felt vulnerable all over again.

He thought of Ked. His son was tall and broad-shouldered for a fourteen-year-old. Did grown men and women find him sexually appealing? Maybe mistake him for an adult? Some must, he knew. Ked was good-looking, his features sharper and more refined than Dan's. Thanks to Kendra. Her genes had mellowed Dan's harsher aspects. Ked might even grow to be bigger than Dan one day, though he'd be softer, less muscular unless he trained for long hours in a gym.

Would someone try to steal the last of his childhood from him before his time? Child abuse. It was the most heinous of sexual crimes, the compulsion to tangle the hidden mysteries of innocence and desire. To take from a child what it didn't even know it had. Because you can never know you are innocent. You only realize it once you've lost it. And once lost, you can never get it back.

FIFTEEN

Gasper

The plane was late. Dan fidgeted. Read the newspaper. Fidgeted some more. Hung out at Starbucks till he couldn't force himself to ingest any more caffeine. Every few minutes, he glanced at the arrivals board. DELAYED. No change. DELAYED. No change. DELAYED. No change. He felt his anxiety growing. Plane crashes happened all the time.

He checked his messages. Three calls registered Jags' cell number. The first was a hang-up. The second was a drunken Jags trying to sound coherent. He made what barely passed for an apology, as far as Dan was concerned, and pleaded with Dan to call him. There was a long pause then Jags said he'd been getting weird hang-up calls again. *No one has this number, so how the fuck could...?* The call ended mid-sentence.

The final call came an hour later. Jags sounded agitated and even less coherent. He mumbled something about feeling claustrophobic in the condo, declared he was going out to the island. His words trailed off. *I don't even have a fucking friend to talk to.*

Pay somebody, Dan thought.

Last on the caller's list was Donny. He said he had something important to discuss and suggested a get-together later in the day. Dan left a message agreeing to meet him at the suggested time and place.

Finally, the flight board registered the arrival of Trevor's plane, the status giving way from DELAYED to ARRIVED. He was on the ground. Safe.

Dan's anxiety turned to relief. He knew the fear he endured when someone he loved went away was nothing rational. It was a holdover dating back to his mother's early death from pneumonia one Christmas after being locked out in the snow by his father. The experience had scarred him. Rationality didn't enter the picture. Fear was primal and irrational, but you couldn't stop living because you were afraid. Bad things happened to people all the time.

Dan's heart swelled as he caught sight of Trevor emerging from the crowd. *You are beautiful*, Dan thought. *So heart-achingly beautiful.* The feelings came at him in a rush and nearly knocked him off his feet. It was the sort of impossible beauty you glimpsed passing a store window, like catching sight of a stranger in a line-up, before vanishing again. Only with Trevor it didn't vanish. It stayed and stayed, replenishing every time Dan looked at him. Impossible to touch or hold, but knowing it was there and that it was his to bask in. Being loved by someone beautiful had to be better than being beautiful yourself.

To find the mortal world enough, Dan thought. *Please let me.*

Then Trevor was beside him, reaching out to him. "How's it going? Enjoying the bodyguard work?"

Eyes flickered over the two men hugging and kissing. But this was Toronto in the twenty-first century. Despite what anybody might think, nobody dared speak a word against them.

"I quit," Dan said, when Trevor released his grip on Dan's shoulder.

"What? Already?" Trevor laughed. "Jags too much for you?"

Dan grabbed Trevor's bag and they headed for the parking lot.

Dan told him about the photograph of the severed ear and how Pfeiffer had advised Jags not to tell Dan about it.

They were in the car, driving down the ramp inside the parking garage. Dan put a credit card in the machine and waited as the arm rose like a starting gate at a horse race. The car shot ahead. Dan's anger had passed since his confrontation with Jags. If Jags was telling the truth, he hadn't known the full implications of his decision to conceal the truth. On the other hand, the police had been correct in assuming Dan wouldn't have taken on the job if he'd known the facts. Dan was beginning to think Danes and Pfeiffer were really to blame. *Jags wasn't such a bad guy*, Dan thought. His pathetic admission that he had no one to talk to was getting to him.

He was still grim by the time they returned home. He'd hoped Trevor would have greeted him on his return with an exultant declaration that he was there to stay, but so far he'd said nothing about his decision. He pulled Trevor's bag from the trunk.

"I think you're being too hard on yourself about this," Trevor told him.

Dan turned to him. "Three men have already been killed. It won't help if someone else dies."

"Do you honestly think someone is going to kill Jags Rohmer?"

Dan shrugged. "I don't know. It's possible. He practically begged me not to leave him."

Trevor shook his head. "You don't owe him anything."

"I realize that, but I can't help feeling I've abandoned him."

"Dan, everyone has problems. You can't rescue everybody."

"Is that what you think I'm doing with you?"

The words were out before he could think what he was saying or try to stop himself. All the pleasure and anticipation of Trevor's return were suddenly stripped away.

"I'm sorry," Dan said quietly. "I didn't mean that."

They were standing on the front step. Dan reached for Trevor's hand and was glad he felt no resistance when he took it.

"I'm really sorry."

"I understand your frustration. I wasn't suggesting you should leave him hanging, but there are limits to what you can do."

"I don't abandon people, Trevor. I don't drop cases because they're difficult. And I always finish what I start." He shrugged. "There's an old Jewish saying: 'In a place where there are no good men, be a good man.'"

Trevor said, "You are a good man. You don't have to prove it. But you do have to live with your conscience, so you need to do what you think is right."

The front door swung open. Dan placed Trevor's bag on the inside step.

"My conscience is not always the easiest thing to live with."

Trevor laughed. "Don't I know it!"

"What do you think I should do?"

"Why not swing around and talk to him? See how you feel then. Maybe you're right — maybe he needs you. On the other hand, he may have found someone else to hold his hand already."

Dan phoned Jags' cell. There was no answer. Jags had said he was going to his island hideaway. Dan waited till Trevor was settled then headed for the waterfront, trying Jags' number every ten minutes. His anxiety began to mount, though he reminded himself there was nothing ominous in not getting an answer.

The terminal was crowded. He eyed the Centre Island ferry as it filled with families and screaming kids. The hot weather always brought them out. He gave it a pass. Though it was smaller and slower, Dan waited for the Ward's Island ferry. He'd have an easier trip and it would get him to Jags' house almost as fast. He could see it heading in now, a tortoise crawling across desert sands, avoiding the fleet, impatient sailboats that zigzagged around it. Once the boat docked, Dan waited impatiently for it to unload. Finally, the operator swung the gate open to the waiting crowd. The ride over seemed interminable.

Algonquin is one of several small islands that comprises North America's largest car-free urban centre. The five-hundred-and-seventy-acre alluvial deposit had slowly formed from eroding sand bluffs farther to the east. The isolation was nearly complete. To be in the city, yet cut off from it at the same time was an almost magical illusion. Yet it wasn't an illusion. All in all, this was as remote as Toronto could get.

Dan disembarked and followed the trail to Algonquin. A wide wooden bridge spanned the estuary dividing the islands. Dan crossed over and vanished beneath an overhang of trees. Little more than an overgrown footpath, Dacotah Avenue cut the island in half. Dan's unease grew as he counted down the numbers, the feeling of remoteness increasing the farther he went. The island had always seemed a haven, made idyllic by soft evergreens and marshland backing onto the canals lined with boats. Now it felt ominous and threatening.

The houses were separated from one another by forest. Jags' was near the middle, a deep blue chalet engulfed in lush garden beds. Dreamy and distant, it was another world entirely.

Wind blew through the branches high overhead. All was silent, not a soul in sight. Dan recalled the second rule of horror film survival: *When you arrive at a deserted town, don't stick around to find out why it's empty.*

The upstairs curtains were drawn. At the far end of the path, under an overhang of trees, a sailboat scudded by, sudden and unexpected, like a deer leaping across a road.

Dan knocked; there was no answer. Maybe Jags was passed out in an alcoholic stupor. If he'd even made it over here. Dan took out the key ring — there was no sense turning back now. He let himself in, looking warily around. Music was playing softly, nothing he recognized, certainly nothing of Jags'. He heard a *clunk*. Someone was in the house.

"Jags? It's Dan. Are you here?"

No answer. He walked cautiously around the main floor. Empty. Island homes had no basements, being barely above sea level. He headed upstairs, looking first into one room then another. Two doors stood open; the last was closed. He was aware of his heart's erratic rhythm as he approached and pushed open the final door.

The room was dim, the blinds turned down. Dan's eyes took a second to adjust. When they did, he felt the bone-white shock of fear, the mind's artful reluctance as it tried to sidestep what it was seeing. A shadowy figure lay prone on the carpet, a coil of rope twined around the neck like an oversized necklace.

Before Dan could react, Jags stirred. His eyes opened. He sat up and looked around groggily.

"What the fuck are you doing here?" he asked hoarsely.

He loosened the rope, pulling the ligature over his head, and took a few deep breaths.

"Satisfied?" Jags asked, rubbing his throat.

Dan knelt and yanked the rope from his hands. "What is this?" he demanded.

"What does it look like?"

"It looks like some kind of pathetic suicide attempt. Are you that desperate for publicity? You want me to tell everyone I saved your life so your book will sell even more copies?"

Jags actually laughed. "Is that what you think?"

Dan wanted to slap him, but he resisted. Was there a law against beating celebrities for doing the same stupid things that other people did?

"I may have gone a little too far this time," Jags said.

"A little too far at pretending to kill yourself?"

"Stop saying that," Jags growled, waving him off. "Get out of here."

Dan stood and took a step back.

"And shut the door behind you. I'd like a little privacy. I'll be out in a minute."

"All right, but I'm taking this with me."

Dan brandished the rope as though it were some kind of prize. He went back downstairs and sat on the couch in the main room, wondering what kind of stupidity he'd got himself into this time and how long before he could get out of it. He looked at the rope, the bristling fibres. He laid it lengthwise on the coffee table as if it were an ornament.

After a few minutes, Jags came down. He went over to the counter and poured himself a cup of coffee.

"I thought I fired you," he said.

"No, I fired you."

"You want some coffee?"

Dan shook his head. "No."

Jags watched him for a moment then laughed. "You still don't know, do you?"

Dan gave him a sharp look, but said nothing.

"Auto-erotic asphyxiation," Jags said at last. "I just need to be careful not to take it too far."

Dan felt his anger quickly replaced with bewilderment. "You what?"

Jags scowled. "No judgements, please. I'm not interested in hearing from the self-righteously inexperienced."

Dan said nothing. He felt like an exasperated parent

on hearing the latest admission of reckless stupidity from his most inconsiderate child.

"Anyway, thanks for ..." Jags shrugged. "For saving me. Or whatever."

"You're welcome. Maybe."

Jags laughed again. "You look pathetic."

"*I* look pathetic? Really?"

Jags scowled. "Look, if you haven't tried it, don't knock it. I've used a lot of drugs in my time and I can say without doubt that this is the best high you'll ever have. Clean, too. Better than coke by a long shot."

"Weren't you better off making records? How the hell did you get into this?"

Jags sipped his coffee. "I got into it when life took a dark turn, for want of a better phrase. And I'm known as a phrasemaker, so believe me when I say I have no words to describe what I went through. I spent an entire decade where I started my day with Prozac and ended it with bourbon, in case you missed the gossip rags. I'm mostly down to bourbon and a twisted rope."

"Well, thank God for small mercies."

Jags looked at him with amusement. "Aren't you a lyrics reader?"

Dan stared dumbly at him.

"I thought you said you knew my work."

"Somewhat."

"So the album titled *Gasper*. What do you think that's about?"

"I haven't a fucking clue."

"Think about it. First song: *Oxygen-Free*. Did you think that was about clean air?"

"Well, yes, frankly."

"Third song, *Rope*?" Jags began singing in that clear, famous voice of his Dan had heard on the radio so many times: "*So glad to be alive, my friend; just keep me dangling from your end ...*"

Dan shook his head. "I never really thought about it."

"Well, think about it. That's what guys like me are for. To open your mind and drag you kicking and screaming to places you've never been before."

Dan rolled his eyes. "You fucking, fucking twat."

"I never claimed to be the boy next door, Danny. Get over yourself." He shrugged. "Auto-erotic asphyxiation. Breath-control play. It's nothing new. We're talking about restricting the flow of oxygen to the brain for sexual arousal, to put it bluntly."

"I've heard of it," Dan told him.

"The carotid arteries" — Jags indicated either side of his neck — "these babies right here. That's the mainline of oxygen to your brain. When you cut it off ..." He pressed his fingers tightly against the sides of his throat till his face turned red. "It produces a semi-hallucinogenic state, but one that's completely lucid. You know what's going on, but you're out of it at the same time. Add an orgasm to that, and you've got a pure high. Total cool. Exquisite pleasure. And, might I add, highly addictive in its way."

"Who the hell would come up with something like that?"

"Hangings," Jags replied.

Dan turned to him. "What?"

"Think about it. What happens to men when they're hanged? They get erections. It's not a myth. It's like they get off one last time as they're heading out permanently. I guess someone got the idea that if you could induce that state temporarily, it might be a rush. And it is." Jags watched him intently. "You should try it sometime."

Dan shook his head. "Not for me."

Jags shrugged. "You don't have an adventurous personality?"

"Not in that sense, I don't."

"Of course, it can be dangerous when done alone. But then so can swimming. Deaths are not uncommon. At least, if you don't know what you're doing. Better to share the fun." He looked around. "As long as you can trust the other person, of course. They say Michael Hutchence was one."

Dan looked blankly at him.

"The singer from INXS?"

Dan shrugged. "I thought he was a suicide."

"The verdict's still out on that one. I think they made him a suicide to clean him up a bit. Funny when suicide's a better alternative to dying from your sexual highs."

"Right."

"One of the most famous cases was from Japan in the 1930s. Another of my songs: *Sada*." He hummed a tune Dan recognized. "Sada Abe was the lover of a man named Kichizo …"

"That song's true?"

"Oh, yeah. She worked for Kichizo in his eel restaurant. Kichizo wasn't attracted to his wife, but Sada turned his crank. The story goes that the first time he jumped her in the kitchen, she stabbed him with a cutting knife. Apparently he enjoyed it. So did she. Eventually they went on to mutual strangulation sessions that could go on for hours. That was the *little death* I wrote about in the chorus."

He hummed another phrase, his voice as hypnotic as a snake charmer's.

"Eventually, Sada strangled Kichizo while he was unconscious from sleeping pills. She put her scarf around his neck and tightened it till he died. She testified later in court that he asked her to do it."

"But no one believed her."

"Not really. You see, after he died she cut off his penis and testicles and carried them around in her purse."

"Stop, you're making me sick."

Jags stared like a wolf eyeing a rabbit. "There's a curious photo of her just after her arrest. She's smiling. But not only that, so are the officers who arrested her. It's like they're all sharing this very private joke together."

Dan put up a hand. "Spare me. If you want my opinion —"

"I don't."

"Nevertheless, you should know that what you're doing —"

"— is illegal?"

Dan made a face. "Just shut up and listen for once."

Jags made an exasperated sound.

"My teenage son listens better than you do."

"Glad to hear it. What was the sermon you were about to deliver?"

Dan held up a menacing finger. "No sermon. I was simply going to say that if you wanted an easier, less dangerous version of this, try poppers."

"What?"

"Amyl nitrate. It's the gay man's version of auto-asphyxiation. Cheaper, non-life threatening, but I'd bet my right ball it works just as well."

Jags appeared to be considering this. "Any side effects?"

"Yeah, it rots your brain cells with continued use — or so I'm told — but that's still better than dying and letting your loved ones find you like that."

"There'd be no one to find me."

"Is that self-pity?"

"No." Jags drew the string tighter on his dressing gown and threw Dan a sharp look. "Anyway, what the fuck are you doing here? I thought I fired you."

"Whatever. Anyway, I thought I'd give you one more chance to redeem yourself. The offer's on the table for this moment only. If you want me to work with you — not *for* you, but *with* you — if you want me to help save your degenerate carcass then now's the time to say so." He stopped and looked at Jags. "Besides, it wouldn't sit well with my conscience if you ended up dead because I refused to help out."

Jags smiled and made a small bow. "Welcome back, brother. I accept your offer. The book launch is this Saturday at seven."

Dan nodded. "I'll be there."

Jags slipped an envelope out of his pocket. He proffered it to Dan. "Here, take this."

Dan looked at it.

"It's the photograph of the ear."

Dan held out his hand and accepted the envelope. "Why?"

"In case anything happens to me, I want you to have it." Jags looked pleased with himself. "With any luck it'll remind you that you don't want another dead client on your hands."

SIXTEEN

Crime Busters

THE CITY SKYLINE APPROACHED as the ferry pushed its way homeward. Dan stood alone near the back of the boat while the other passengers huddled at the bow and pointed out landmarks made less familiar by perspective and distance. He pulled out his cellphone and dialled. Germ picked up on the first ring.

"Dan my man."

"Hi, Germ. Glad you're answering."

"Truth to tell, you're getting to be a habit with me. Thought my life was interesting till I met you. Kicks, you know?"

Dan laughed. *Kicks*. Right. Smoking dope seemed so passé at that moment. "As long as they're the healthy kind, I guess."

Now it was Germ's turn to laugh. "What can I do for you today?"

"How would you like to help one of your all-time heroes?"

Curiosity crept into his voice. "Who's that?"

"You tell me."

A snort. "Huh?"

"Who did you say was one of your all-time heroes?"

"Jags Rohmer?"

"You got it, baby."

"What's he got to do with the price of milk?"

"He's now my client."

"No way!"

"Way, dude."

There was a palpable silence.

"Okay. So what can I possibly do for a guy like Jags Rohmer? He need artwork for a new CD or something? That would be way cool."

"Not exactly."

"So spill."

"Okay," Dan said slowly. "But everything I tell you here is off the record, probably for all time. You good with that?"

"Sure. I trust you, man."

"All right. That issue I brought up recently …"

"The missing kid who garrots his victims?"

Dan looked over as a sailboat breezed past with three blonde women lounging in the sun. Dan disliked being on the water. Why be stuck on a boat when you could be on solid land? He hated the torpor, hated the confinement. *You can keep the water. Give me a mountain and I'll climb it any day*, he thought. Same with tanning. What was wrong with being your natural colour, whatever it was?

"That's the one."

"Waaaaaaait a minute. Are you telling me that Jags has something to do with the shit we talked about the other day?"

"Germ, I am not at liberty to say much. All I will tell you is that Jags Rohmer is my client and any information you give me would be going to help him out of a tight spot."

"I'd have to think about it. What's he need the help for?"

"He's being threatened. I can't go into it in any more detail than that."

"No shit!"

"Shit. Are you in?"

A heavy exhalation. "Okay. I'm in. I'd do anything to help that guy."

"Cool. We'll talk about fees and what I need from you when I have a chance to assess the situation a little better."

"Sure. Just one thing ..."

"Yes?"

"Gonna need an autograph from the dude. Just to be sure this is on the level."

Dan smiled. "I'm sure that can be arranged. In the meantime, I've got some artwork to show you. I can be there in half an hour."

"Come on over."

Dan hung up. The ferry was just pulling into the dock. His car was five minutes away.

†

The curly head of hair was bent down over the photo. Dan waited. Germ said nothing for a while then looked up with a grim expression.

"Why would someone send him this? Who would cut off a guy's ear? I mean, van Gogh cut off an ear, but it was *his* ear, you know?" He thought this over. "Jags Rohmer can't be a child molester. I mean, I've heard some weird things, but that one's hard for me to believe."

"If you help me find Gaetan Bélanger, we'll know for sure."

"Ah, I had a feeling you were working your way around to that."

Germ sat back with his arms splayed over the back of the couch. His mouth was making little twitching movements. "If I help you find this kid, you've got to guarantee me that he won't be hurt."

Dan said nothing.

"I don't want this shit on my karma, dude. Guy gets hurt and it'll be my fault for leading you to him. Well?"

Dan shrugged. "I won't be the one arresting him, Germ. I can't say anything for sure."

Germ started to protest, but Dan cut him off.

"Let's just say this is a very high-profile case and the police are not going to risk a public assassination when they catch him. I can guarantee that much."

Germ smirked. "Ever hear of Lee Harvey Oswald?"

"That was the U.S. In fact, it was Texas, which is a whole different universe."

"Yeah, maybe you're right."

Germ looked away. He seemed to be mulling this over. "Yeah, I guess that makes sense," he said after a while.

He shook his head again. "The fuck could Jags Rohmer have to do with this shit?"

"I honestly have no idea, but he swore to me he never molested any children. I believe him, for what it's worth ..."

"Yeah, but he's a rock star, right?"

"Exactly. Who knows what he got up to with some groupie way back when he was barely in his twenties. He could have diddled some fifteen-year-old without knowing her real age. That's likely, of course. But I don't think it counts as child molestation. Strictly speaking it would be statutory rape, which is illegal, but I think you and I are on the same side of the fence on that one. A teenager's right to do with her body what she pleases, etc."

"Yeah, yeah. I hear you. Don't start feeding me my own lingo."

His eyes flashed around the room. They stopped at the console.

"Okay, so what I gotta do is get a few cameras set up in the likeliest places." His mind was kicking into gear. "Velvet Blue will help. We've already had a few sightings of a possible match for the kid I saw at the slaughterhouse. Can't say for sure it's Bélanger yet, but if it is then that newspaper article is going to drive him further underground. If I were him, I'd stay so far underground even the rats couldn't find me."

"He still has to come out to eat now and then," Dan ventured.

Germ shook his head. "Not necessarily. Maybe he's got a friend bringing him food."

Dan nodded. "Yeah, there's that, but let's not get lost in maybes. We need to concentrate on the best possible scenario, deal?"

"I'm cool with that."

Germ looked down at the photo again, an expression of disgust on his face. "But if some fucker is capable of doing shit like this then our involvement's got to be at a distance. I can't have him finding me and Velvet Blue. He'd be worse than the cops for retribution." He grinned. "Besides, she might kill him if he tries anything."

He took Dan over to the console and pointed to a screen in the lower right-hand corner. Dan saw a perimeter fence with a gravel road leading off to the right.

"This is the old dairy in the west end, just off Dundas West. You know it?"

Dan shrugged. "I don't think so."

"It's not far from the slaughterhouse where your last guy was done." Germ tapped the screen. "I've got a couple kids there who said they might have seen your guy. Emphasis on *might*."

"What were they doing there?"

Germ looked up. "They live there. Same as you live at your address."

"And that's where they saw him?"

"No. They saw him at an abandoned storage site not far from there. They could tell he was a newbie. Everyone living underground knows when someone else comes on the scene. The network is small and tight. Even if you avoid the others, someone's bound to notice you before too long."

Dan thought a moment. "Okay, so what do we do? I don't want anyone getting too close to him in case he tries anything."

"Velvet Blue and I can take care of ourselves. I think Mohawk's got a black belt."

"Mohawk?"

"First Nations. Real good guy. One of the kids who lives at the dairy. He can take a look around — from a distance, of course. Is there a reward on the guy's head?"

"Besides what I pay? So far just the usual Crime Busters fee."

"Oh, yeah. That snitch line thing. Well, better than nothing, I suppose."

Dan took stock of this. "I thought you said your guys wouldn't touch money from the System."

"Well, sometimes you gotta take what's out there. Me, I'm a bit choosier. In this case, I feel I'm helping Mr. Jags Rohmer. It's not about the money; it's about love."

"He's that important to you?"

"Yeah, in a way. Guy turned my life around when I was a fucked-up, suicidal teenager. His music, man? It's got more soul and more meaning than all the crap out there today. Fucking JT and Beyoncé, man. Useless little prats. What do they know?"

Dan smiled. "I hear you."

"So, I'm doing it for him."

"Well, I'm sure he thanks you."

"But I still want that autograph."

Germ assured him the cameras would be up and operational within two days. Dan left him to his work. Pulling the elevator doors open on the ground floor, he looked around to make sure he wasn't being watched. Outside the warehouse, the street was empty.

SEVENTEEN

When Children Kill

THE HOUSE LOOKED DESERTED when Dan arrived. The lights were off. No Trevor. No Ked. And strangest of all, no Ralph. In the kitchen he found the remnants of a meal in the sink. At least they'd been there. Then he heard the scream from the basement.

A woman's scream. The paint-peeling, blood curdling type.

It wasn't just supper he'd missed. He'd forgotten their Fright Night movie date. Forgot even what day it was. He trouped downstairs to find Trevor and Ked glued to the TV. Ralph's tail wagged at his arrival, but he stayed put, unwilling to abandon his seat to greet the latecomer. Or else he found the movie that absorbing.

Ked pressed pause on the remote. Onscreen, a boat careened over a waterfall, stopped and held.

Trevor and Ked turned and stared at him.

"What?" Dan asked.

"That's what we'd like to know," Trevor said.

"You forgot our movie," Ked said.

"Sorry."

"And supper," Trevor added, "but we'll forgive you for that."

"You've been acting awfully strange, Dad," Ked added.

"More than normal, you mean?"

Ked nodded. "Oh, yeah. Way more."

Dan sat on the couch and looked at the TV. "Okay. I'll try to act normal. If I can remember what that is."

Ked pressed the play button and sent the boat into freefall. As flies to wanton boys are we to the gods.

"Dad, you're missing a great movie. It's awesome! This giant anaconda takes over the Amazon and attacks a boat full of filmmakers."

"So far," Trevor said, "they've broken just about every rule for surviving in a horror film we could think of and then some. But the monkey's cute as hell."

Dan settled in for the adventure. When the movie finally ended, they waited while the credits flickered and died. Ked said goodnight and went up to bed with Ralph trailing behind.

Dan turned to Trevor. "Sorry for missing supper."

"You've got a lot going on."

Dan nodded. The week had passed in a blur.

"Donny called earlier. . . ."

Dan clapped his forehead with his palm. "Shit! I forgot I was supposed to meet him this afternoon."

"He'll forgive you."

Dan reached for his cellphone.

"Don't bother. I told him you were pressed for time and just forgot. He said he'd talk to you tomorrow."

Dan looked over. "Is it about Lester?"

Trevor nodded. "Yes. He called again."

"How is he?"

"Physically okay, I guess. But all is not well."

"The parents are still at it?"

"More than ever. Donny's afraid he's going to do something rash. Worse, I'm afraid Donny is going to do something rash. Lester gave him the family address in Oshawa."

"Oh, no."

Trevor eyed him. "Oh, yes. Don't be surprised to hear he has some cockamamie scheme to get the kid back to Toronto."

"I don't like it," Dan said.

"Nor I. I told him to talk to you before he does anything."

"Thanks."

Dan leaned in and they kissed tentatively. Not having Trevor near these past few days, he'd felt as though he were missing a part of himself.

"Let's go upstairs," Dan said, reaching for Trevor's hand.

Dan undressed and lay watching Trevor. He loved the lean silkiness of him, as though he were both boy and man. His face was one Michelangelo might have sculpted, like a model whose beauty would be celebrated for centuries. But he was not only beautiful. He was also kind, Dan knew. It didn't matter if they'd known one another less than a year. You couldn't fake goodness or decency.

Trevor came to him and made love dutifully, but Dan sensed his distraction.

“Everything okay?” he asked.

“I know this is still supposed to be our honeymoon period. Sorry.”

“No apologies necessary,” Dan said. “Tell me what’s going on.”

There was a long silence.

“It was difficult coming back here,” Trevor said. “I had a panic attack putting the house up for sale. Then I had another one getting on the plane. The only thing that made me do it was the thought of losing you if I didn’t.”

Dan looked chagrined. “I’m sorry … I don’t know what to say.”

“You don’t have to say anything,” Trevor said. “I just want you to know what’s going on with me.”

“Do you want to talk about it?”

“No, not yet. Just hold me, please.”

They clung to one another in silence until Dan felt Trevor’s body relax. He tried to twin their breathing and found he could do it for a while, but somehow Trevor’s always galloped ahead, as though even in sleep he was anxious to get away. As if under the skin lay something that could not be smoothed away with a kiss or a caress.

Dan got up and went down the hall to his office. The desk lamp focused a bright beam within a narrow radius, leaving the rest of the room in shadow. Peace and calm reigned here. It was his sanctuary.

Jags’ world had taken over his own lately. Shamefully, he’d neglected both Trevor and Ked. He’d also neglected his cases of deadbeat dads skipping out on childcare payments. A little overtime was required so he could spend more family time over the weekend.

He turned on his laptop and pulled the keyboard close. How anyone could not care enough about their child's welfare to do whatever it took to support them was beyond his understanding. He'd taken full responsibility for Ked when Kendra told him she was pregnant. Her family would have disowned her — or worse — had she revealed her pregnancy. An extended stay in California during the final months resolved that problem. The rest was up to Dan on Kendra's return with their newborn son. He hadn't regretted it once in all the years since. In fact, raising Ked had given him purpose and helped ease some of the burdens of his own childhood. In many ways, Ked had been his redemption.

He logged on to a website for non-payment of child support and felt ironically gratified to see a few women cropping up among the deadbeat dads. Nice to know it wasn't endemic to the male of the species. Most of the absconders were ordinary looking. It wasn't as if you expected a leer on the deadbeat's face and a left arm that ended in a hook, but the assumption was that a certain mentality must be betrayed by its features. Not so. They also had a vast array of trades at their disposal: waiters and carpenters, accountants and IT workers. No stock brokers, Dan noted. Presumably, if you had money and didn't care about your kid, you just paid off your spouse and were shot of it. Others seemed comically geared to get a laugh when you read the sections on LAST KNOWN EMPLOYER: Chicken-on-the-Run, Getaway Travel, East-West Carnivals Ltd. *I'm outta here and good luck finding me, Mary Jo!* As for aliases, the deadbeat moms had the drop on the deadbeat dads by a long shot. One woman was known by thirteen individual names, not counting her real one. Under OTHER TRAITS were listed a bird tattoo ("species unknown") on her left breast and a sword and shield over her belly button. No doubt the latter would be viewed as an enticement in some circles, Dan mused. Or maybe the sword and shield were to deter any further children from springing from her womb, while the bird could be read as an ironic comment on her flighty tendencies.

Dan found nothing helpful to his current cases on any of the sites. He'd combed through them many times. Boredom crept in. Without thinking, he found himself typing in the words: *whenchildrenkill.com*. The photos and stories were both fascinating and utterly grotesque. Children who killed other children, children who killed adults and strangers, children who killed their own parents.

His eye ran down the page. The site was a repository for some of the most gruesome murders he'd ever come across. Of course, he wasn't surprised that children might have murderous intentions — youthful emotion tended to the extreme. What surprised him was the ferocity with which some of the murders had been carried out. Here were children who killed siblings out of jealousy or murdered their parents for seemingly innocuous reasons: friendships disapproved of, dates not allowed, scoldings over sloppy schoolwork. He thought of his own father and how much he'd hated the man's drunken brutality. But in all the years his father had abused him, Dan never once thought of doing away with him. It was the nature of the beast, he knew. He'd eventually found the courage to leave the situation behind, but not before his father had inflicted a permanent reminder of where he came from in the red line that ran down the side of his face.

After an hour on the site, his eyes began to give out. He crept down to the kitchen to share a late-night snack with Ralph, who seemed happy for the company and sloppy leftovers. Finally, when there was nothing else to kill time with, Dan went back up to bed and snuggled in beside Trevor without waking him.

The store on Queen Street West was ablaze with lights and chock-a-block with customers. It looked like a Boxing Day sale. A guaranteed sell-out. Dan found himself perusing a shelf of children's books. He was surprised how many of the titles boasted some form of violent interaction between children and their antagonists. The latest Harry Potter was prominent, of course. The series famously portrayed adolescents who battled dark forces in a universe where good and evil clashed in ways far more ingeniously than in the real one. There was also a selection of classics describing dark happenings to even younger children. A chicly coutured Little Red Riding Hood faced her nemesis, the Big Bad Wolf, alongside a volume entitled *Bearskinner* by the Brothers Grimm. (*How aptly named they were*, Dan told himself). The list of atrocities mounted. Was it any wonder kids grew up violent or fearful or sometimes both? Dan had never exposed Ked to anything of that nature, but neither had his son been drawn to violence on television. Then again, Ked was different from most kids. Or so Dan prided himself.

He turned his attention to the gathering. He was supposed to be watching out for his boss, not fantasizing about children's literature. He put aside a copy of Jags' book for Germ. He'd have to remember to get him to sign it.

Dan stood on the sidelines watching the hopeful fans approach their idol, hands holding out copies of the book. Jags had dressed impeccably. Dan couldn't help noticing he'd worn his Farley Chatto jacket, with flannel trousers and a linen shirt open at the neck.

When he smiled, there was something almost feminine in his face. Androgynous, amorphous. He would exchange a few words with a fan, look down and turn the pages before signing his name. Broad hands smoothed his inky hair into place behind his ears. The man was nearing sixty, but his sex appeal was undeniable. He could easily have passed for forty.

Dan noticed a stir over by the door as a woman entered to join the gathering. It was Joni Mitchell, dropping in to visit a ghost of her past. She was the only visitor Jags stood to greet during the course of the evening. Dan recognized a few other faces from somewhere, though if pressed he couldn't have said exactly where. An alternate universe where famous people lived their curious lives and cavorted with one another.

Jags signed for nearly two hours. He looked happy. He was back in his element. As much as he claimed to disdain celebrityhood, it suited him. He wouldn't know what to do if he moved to his Collingwood cabin in the woods with little or no human interaction. *Once a star, always a star*, Dan thought. And Jags Rohmer would always be that.

Joni Mitchell left after a brief chat with some of the other famous faces. By nine o'clock, almost everyone had gone. Dan was glad when the storeowner flipped the *Closed* sign on his door and turned the lock. Day was done.

They were just about to leave when Dan remembered the copy he'd picked up for Germ. Jags flipped open the cover, scratched out his printed name with two bold strokes, and signed with a flamboyance stretching across the page.

As he waited, Dan looked down at a pile of books on a sale table. There, on one side, was a book with a curious title. He picked it up: *An Incredibly Ordinary Life* by Anonymous. Perhaps it was what Jags might aspire to write next.

EIGHTEEN

Word on the Street

JAGS DROPPED HIM OFF in his Porsche. Dan emerged with the signed book under his arm. In the kitchen, a note said Trevor and Ked had gone to the Ex. At least they had each other for company while he was busy, Dan thought. He tossed his coat over the banister railing and poured himself a beer. The hallway answering machine yielded a single message.

"Hey there, mister man." It was Germ. "Drop by when you get a mo. I got some of that nice black tea you like." Followed by a cackle.

The man really was cracked, Dan mused. At least he'd be pleased with the book.

Dan called back immediately. They had just got through their opening preamble when Germ went silent. Dan waited.

"Uh-oh, we got some static on the line."

Dan paused and listened for it. "I don't hear it."

"Trust me, dude. Call me back from another line."

“What?”

“Just do it. Find another phone and call me.”

Five minutes later, he had Ked’s cellphone. The voice that answered sounded suspicious.

“It’s Dan.”

“One minute.”

He heard a hum as the line went quiet. Eventually, Germ came back on.

“Okay, this line’s all right for now. Where are you?”

“At home. I borrowed my son’s cell.”

Germ laughed. “Well, I’m sure your son’s a good kid, but don’t let them start tapping his line too. Kids have got all kinds of secrets.”

“Tapping?”

“Dude, I’m telling you. That other line was being listened in on. I was monitoring the interference. I can’t tell you who was on the other end, but it was there.”

“Fuck!”

Dan looked out the window toward the street, as though whoever was spying on him might be skulking under bushes and hiding behind parked cars. As if.

“From now on, use a payphone when you call, but even payphones are liable to be tapped, depending on your ’hood, right? I mean, a lot of guys selling dope use public phones thinking they’re safe. Wrong ’hood, wrong phone, and you got a tap. Next thing you know, you’re busted. So how are things?”

“Things were fine till just this last thirty seconds.”

“Don’t sweat it, dude. You could always get a new cell phone with a calling card from a corner store. Much harder for them to trace.”

"All right."

"Like you to meet me."

"When?"

"Now."

"Okay. Where?"

"Don't come to the usual place. Remember that place where I shot the video for you last year?"

Dan recalled an earlier instance when Germ's capabilities came in handy.

"Yeah."

"Go there. Bring your kid's phone with you. Here's what we're gonna do ..."

Half an hour later Dan arrived at a deserted warehouse in the city's west end. He parked on the street and sat waiting. There were no other vehicles in sight. Outside, the sky was glowering. Ten minutes went by. A car passed, slowed, then moved on.

Ked's phone rang.

"Sharp."

"I'm here. Come in, man."

He walked up to the building and saw the camera pointing at him like an accusing finger. A door clicked open. Dan entered and felt his way carefully down a darkened staircase. At the far end of the corridor he saw a tiny red light. It blinked and he walked toward it. He smelled dope.

Follow the trail, he thought.

A shadow moved and Germ greeted him.

"This is *so-o-o* not my usual place," he said. "Nowhere to sit, and I can't even offer you tea. Toke?"

He held out the glowing wand.

"No, thanks."

"One of these days then."

"We'll see."

"I won't lecture you, but you need to relax a little. Believe me, you'll live longer."

"Great, but for what it's worth I wasn't planning a long stay on the planet this time around."

"Cool. I hear you." Germ took a gargantuan toke and dropped the roach, grinding it into red splinters underfoot till it stopped smoking. "So, what I wanted to tell you is this. Your guy? This Gaetan kid? He's in town. He's been spotted, but since the *Star* exposé he's hiding extra low. If he was invisible before, he's super-invisible now. Like, nonexistent."

"Do you know where he is?"

"Sorta."

"Meaning?"

"Meaning, where does the wind blow? I know the general area, sure. Whether or not I can pinpoint it to one particular building, I can't say yet. Kid's been moving around a lot. But dude."

He stopped. Dan waited.

"Are you sure he's the one?"

"I'm not at all sure," Dan said. "I've never seen him. All I know is he blogged a death threat against an ex-priest who ended up murdered. He may also have dumped a file of names from the Sex Offenders Registry on-line. At least three people on that list are now dead."

"Okay, but everything I hear about him says he's all talk, no walk. Big pussycat type."

"Meaning?"

"Meaning I'm reluctant to expose him. Meaning if I turn him over to you and the cops get hold of him, I think I'm gonna feel bad before too long. Et cetera. Don't think he's your guy, is all I'm saying."

"Okay," Dan said. "So what then?"

"Let me see if I can track him down. Then we'll talk. Give me a few more days."

Germ's voice lowered. The conversation continued *sotto voce* for a while then concluded quickly.

"By the way," Dan said, "I've got something for you from Mr. Jags Rohmer himself."

He held out the book. Germ all but snatched it from his hands.

"No way!"

"Way."

"Cool! Thanks, man."

Germ slipped away to the far end of the building, disappearing into blackness. He really was a mole, Dan thought in amazement.

When he emerged, sheets of rain were falling. They'd been so far underground he hadn't heard it begin. He turned the corner in time to see a tow-truck driving away with his car. He yelled and waved his hands, but the truck continued on heedlessly. Cursing, he turned up his collar and started to walk.

He made it half a block before he heard the siren. Blue and red lights flashed over his shoulder, phantom hands grabbing him from behind. His gut clenched like a kid caught stealing from a corner store. Germ's nonsense about phone taps had hard-wired him into paranoia. He stepped over to the side of the road to let the car pass. Instead, it swooped up beside him. The vehicle was unmarked.

The light went off. Dan waited as the window lowered. Constable Pfeiffer leered up at him.

"Evening, Dan." He nodded to the inside of the car. "It's a bit wet out. Care to join me?"

"Is this an official invitation?"

"Absolutely not. I just don't like to leave a guy standing out in the rain. Especially after his car's been towed." He grinned.

"Actually, there were no parking restrictions in that lane. I'm inclined to think it was stolen."

"Always a possibility. I could look into that for you."

Pfeiffer was chewing his trademark gum. He waited as the rain dripped down Dan's cheeks.

"You're getting wet."

The automatic locks clicked open. Dan shrugged and went around the front of the car. He slid into the passenger seat and looked over at Pfeiffer. It was the first time they'd been face to face since the meeting at headquarters, and the first they'd spoken since Pfeiffer had told him Jags was mixed up in the case.

He'd shaved his moustache, Dan noted. Dressed in jeans and a sweatshirt, he really did look like a street punk. Dan thought of the pissing contest they'd had in the bathroom of the police station. A literal pissing contest, with Pfeiffer trying to impress him. Dan wanted to laugh. He was an overgrown boy playing at being a man.

A rap tune beat insistently in the background, too low to make out the words. The music was punctuated every few bars by what sounded like gunshots. *Very ghetto*, Dan thought.

“I thought you’d prefer this to standing in the rain,” Pfeiffer said.

Dan didn’t say anything.

“How are things going with your new client?” Pfeiffer asked in a jovial tone.

“I’m not at leisure to talk about my clients.”

“No problem,” Pfeiffer told him. “I wouldn’t want you to break client confidentiality.”

Dan waited. He had no idea what game they were playing, so he hadn’t a clue how to proceed. If this were a sexual pick-up, he’d have a better sense of the banter expected of him, but he doubted this macho little prig would ever admit to being gay or even bisexual.

Pfeiffer put the car in gear and drove. “Where to?” he asked.

“It’s your move,” Dan said.

Pfeiffer looked out the window at the warehouse. “Quite an interesting neighbourhood. What brings you out to the middle of nowhere at this time of night?”

“Heard there was a good smoke-damage sale.”

“Smoke damage. That’s good.”

Pfeiffer laughed a high, clear laugh. *Doesn’t get out enough*, Dan concluded.

“You’re funny.”

“I’m a lot of things,” Dan said.

“So is this where your friends live?”

“What friends?”

Dan had no doubt Pfeiffer knew why he was here. He wondered if somehow Ked’s cellphone had been monitored too. If so, how much did Pfeiffer already know about Germ and Velvet Blue?

"Security cameras?" Pfeiffer asked, looking over at the building.

"Is that a question?" Dan said, thinking of the rows of monitors in Germ's underground sanctuary. "Because I couldn't tell you."

Pfeiffer shrugged. "I could always tell your friends that you brought me here and showed me their set-up."

They still wouldn't help you, Dan thought.

Pfeiffer shrugged off his silence. "No matter. I can see a few good places where I'd hide them if it were my place. 'Course, my place is smaller, so they're harder to conceal. I've got nearly a dozen inside and out."

He waited a beat for Dan to pick up on this.

"Your place has a dozen security cameras?" Dan asked. "Why?"

"For security," Pfeiffer said, laughing at his own joke. He shrugged. "You never know."

"Wouldn't one at the front and another in the back be sufficient?"

"Yeah, but this way I have a better chance of catching a facial if anyone tries anything. I've got some high up, some low, some head on. I learned it from a couple of guys who specialize in this sort of thing. They did that house on Carlton for Zundel after the pipe bomb blew a hole through his garage door."

"Ernst Zundel?" Dan asked. "The Holocaust denier who claims that Nazis are behind UFOs?" He shook his head. "You're kidding, right?"

Pfeiffer's expression turned serious. "He's a very bright guy. People don't give him enough credit."

"Yeah, well, I can't say I blame them. He says some pretty crazy things."

Pfeiffer put the car in gear and drove for a while.

"You should know about security. It's important. You've got a family to protect, right? Couple of kids?"

Dan felt the fear creep into his gut. Was this a threat? The guy was a maniac.

"Actually, just one. But you're right, I do my best to protect him. Whatever it takes."

"Yeah, sure. Doesn't matter if you're gay or not. You people have kids these days. You can get married even. The whole nine yards."

Dan waited, reluctant to antagonize him but knowing that was how threats worked. A word was spoken, a name mentioned, then the victim did the rest out of fear. It didn't matter whether the threat was real, the effect was the same. Protection money didn't protect you from anything, it simply guaranteed you didn't need to be protected.

"Whether or not you help me, I will get this Bélanger kid." Pfeiffer looked over at him meaningfully. "But I will remember afterward whether you helped me or not."

"And here I was starting to think maybe you liked me, just showing up out of the blue and all."

"Hey, you never know," Pfeiffer said.

They were stopped on a red. The light went green and the car jolted forward.

"What's Jags Rohmer got to do with any of this?" Dan asked to change the subject.

Pfeiffer looked him over. "Did you ask him?"

"Yes, and he denied having his name on the Sex Offenders Registry. Do you know something I don't?"

Pfeiffer shrugged. "Maybe I was wrong. Maybe he doesn't have anything to do with it."

"You know what I mean," Dan said, bristling. "Why did he receive a photograph with a severed ear? He said he showed it to you. That's Bélanger's signature. So why is he targeting Rohmer?"

Pfeiffer concentrated on driving. They were getting into traffic now, the streets less deserted. He pursed his lips at the question. Either he knew something and didn't want to say what, or else he knew nothing and wanted Dan to think he did.

"I guess that's something you'll have to find out for yourself."

"Rohmer swears he's not into kids," Dan said. "I believe him."

"Well, there you are," Pfeiffer said.

They were on Bloor Street near Clinton. The rain was still coming down, leaving shivery little trails of light on the pavement.

"Isn't this city amazing?" Pfeiffer asked. "Here we are in the centre of Toronto and you look out the window and what do you see? Korean writing! We're in Little Korea. A bit south of here we'd be in Little Italy."

The wipers beat a tattoo rhythm in time with the music. The effect was hypnotic.

"What's your background?" Pfeiffer asked.

"White trash," Dan said. "Or is that politically incorrect?"

Pfeiffer laughed. "Yeah. I guess it is. Me, too."

Amazing, Dan thought. *I get picked up for a lesson in ethnicity*.

"This case I'm working on," Pfeiffer began. "It didn't begin with the murder of that priest in Quebec last year. It started a long time before that. It actually started with the perpetrators. The real perpetrators."

"Meaning?"

"The abusers." Pfeiffer nodded, as though confirming something to himself. "We've been trying to clean up a group of molesters. There are some very big names in that file."

Dan looked over.

"I can't tell you," Pfeiffer said. "So don't ask."

"I doubt I'd want to know."

"Still, a few of them are real well known. I guarantee you'd be surprised if I named names." He looked meaningfully at Dan.

"No doubt," Dan said. "Despite my profession, I still have some faith in the human race, which is why I can occasionally be shocked and disillusioned when people do bad things. I always hope for better."

Pfeiffer looked over at him and sneered. "Whatever."

"So if you've got the goods on these guys, then why are they out walking around?"

"Not all of them are. Some got put away." Pfeiffer nodded to himself. "But some of them were given clemency."

"A deal?"

"Yeah, that's right. They turned in a few others. There was a list of kids they shared. Boys and girls. We eventually got the pimp and broke up the ring, but it still operates on a smaller scale."

"Not surprising, if there's money to be made."

"Then the first murder happened. We saw the blog. We all knew it was Bélanger, but no one expected him to come after anybody else. Especially not here. That was his mistake."

Pfeiffer turned south on Yonge Street. The rain had stopped. He rolled the windows down and looked out. Bookshops, once a hub of the city's cultural activity, hunkered like dinosaurs on the strip, their displays overcrowded with second-hand covers. They were flanked with pizza-by-the-slice outlets, XXX porn shops, money marts, cheap cafés, and running-shoe retailers. Even these were looking ratty and on the downlow. Was there anything not being sold for less online now?

South of Gerrard, they passed the Evergreen Centre, a halfway house for street kids. Pfeiffer slowed to look at the crowd gathered outside, a dozen teenagers bantering and smoking. Several of them had dogs, but no place to go, apparently.

"Lotta kids out there," Dan said.

He thought of Lester. Farther back in time, he saw himself in the glare of a car's headlights reflected on a homeless boy's face.

Pfeiffer interrupted his thoughts. "The RCMP missing child statistics over the last decade lists more than sixty thousand kids. Some of them end up here. At a guess, I'd say at least three quarters have tried drugs. Maybe half have sold themselves for sex. What do you think?"

Dan shrugged. He wasn't being drawn into this game. How far did this maniac's knowledge reach into his past? He shuddered to think about it.

Pfeiffer swerved over to the curb and switched off the engine. They sat in silence for a moment. At the end of an alley, a boy of about thirteen or fourteen appeared to be waiting for someone.

"That's one of the kids we're keeping an eye on. He sells drugs now. Ecstasy, meth. Whatever he can get his hands on."

They watched as a car stopped, rolled down its window, and a head leaned out. The kid went over, looked furtively around then handed something to the driver. The driver handed back a bill and rolled his window up before driving off again.

"How do you know so much about Jags Rohmer?" Dan asked.

"Actually, through a personal connection. He dated my mother once."

A surprise answer.

Dan turned to him. "Dated?"

"Yeah. She wasn't just one of his groupies, if that's what you're saying. He actually dated her."

"Okay."

The boy skipped off down the alley, disappearing into the night.

"You see these kids from time to time," Pfeiffer said. "The hustlers. No one keeps track of them. I helped fish one out of the water on Toronto Island last year. He was twelve."

Dan gave him a sharp look. "Are you saying there was an underage gay murder on Toronto Island? I never heard about it, if there was."

Pfeiffer shrugged. "You never heard about it for two reasons. First, the papers weren't informed it was a 'gay' murder. Second, they don't usually report deaths that get chalked up to suicide."

Dan reflected on this. "I assume you know that Rohmer lives on the island. Are you suggesting it was him, because I'm pretty sure he's not gay."

Pfeiffer shook his head. "We don't think it was him. This kid was strung out on crystal meth. There's no evidence anyone pushed him into the water. He was a casualty of his lifestyle, which included living with a very rich man who is immune to prosecution under the law. Nice system, eh?"

"Yeah," Dan murmured. "Money has its privileges."

"In this case, privilege has its privileges. This guy is well connected."

He said a name that sounded familiar, partly because the family was a prominent one, but also because the man was a former cabinet minister under the Mulroney regime. Dan thought of the Mulroney era as the moment of no return in Canadian politics, when Canadian politicians went American-style, lying to voters and defaming their opponents. Dirty politics. Then again, was there any other kind? When the Conservative party folded, the man in question disappeared. His career had been on the upswing till then. After the bloodbath that saw the party reduced from 151 seats to two — the Canadian voters' punishment for being lied to — he never made it back.

"I know who you mean," Dan said. "Rumour had it his personal habits were overlooked by Mulroney, but when Mulroney retired he was pretty much told not to look for re-election if he wanted to keep out of the papers. I gather he did as he was told."

"Probably a smart move. For some reason, those people always feel an urge to become prominent in public affairs. Must be the ego. The end result is inevitably bad for everyone."

"Should you be telling me this?"

"Why not? Playing by the rules only slows things down. It means a lot of wasted time and more corpses. Touch the right nerve and you can even make a dead man dance."

"What are you telling me?"

Pfeiffer smiled a coy smile. For a moment Dan thought he wasn't going to answer.

"Sometimes you have to make things happen any way you can. The press, for instance. Personally, I'd like to nuke them all. The way they portray us, the things they write about the chief. He's a good man, though they'd never say that."

Dan wasn't so sure he'd concur on that, but he let it ride. Pfeiffer's conversation was getting a little too interesting to interrupt.

"I've got contacts, though."

"At the *Star*?" Dan asked, wondering about the recent article. It didn't take much to put two and two together, if that's what Pfeiffer was telling him.

"There and other places. You want those bastards on your side. Sometimes it helps to do them a favour or two. Where'd they get certain little details from? The press talks things up, we talk them down again. All moves on the chessboard. Look busy and keep out of trouble till you bag someone for the crime. Done. Game over. If you don't tell them what they want to hear, they'll make something up. Better to tell them what you want them to know."

Pfeiffer reached into his chest pocket and retrieved an envelope. With one hand, he flipped open the flap and handed it to Dan.

"Tell me what you think this is."

Dan took the envelope and let a Xeroxed sheet fall into his hands. Frankly, he was getting tired of men handing him envelopes and asking him to guess their contents.

It appeared to be some sort of surveillance camera set-up. The shot had been taken through glass, possibly a car window or maybe even from a street café. The man standing on the corner in the photo appeared to be waiting for someone. The next three shots showed him greeting what looked like an adolescent, then the pair in conversation, followed by a shot of the two walking away together.

"Looks like a pick-up," Dan said. "Possibly a drug deal going on or maybe a sexual transaction."

"Both, as it turned out. This was our 'known heavy' on the downtown streets for quite a few years. He operated a slick business. He picked 'em up and beat 'em up. Famous for it, really. His game was to take the kids in and feed them at first. The abuse started soon after, but by then they were trapped. He drugged them, made them dependent on him, and scared the shit out of them. We've never been able to get any of them to name him — they're all afraid of him."

"What was his appeal?"

"Lost, lonely kid on the street. He played big brother to them. Promised them things: fancy lifestyle, splashy parties. Made them feel special. The kid starts dreaming of glamour, life off the streets, and they'd fall for anything. He also took photos of them, which he used to sell the kids on the Internet. A password-protected site."

"How does he get away with it?"

"He's smart. His clients look online then let him know what they're interested in. As far as he's concerned, he's sending the kids out for entertainment purposes. Just a guy passing along a phone number to a kid who calls and gets an invitation to a party. The clients are respectable, wealthy. Above suspicion as far as the law is concerned. They're careful, don't get their hands dirty. No one knows their names. If there's any hint of scandal, they fade into the woodwork. Who's a kid going to complain to if anything happens? They know they're operating outside the law. And they need the work, so they won't say a thing. There's always a next time."

"I can understand that," Dan said.

"And then there are the other kind. Guys who put their lives on the line trying to stop stuff like this from happening. Some of them are fucking heroes," Pfeiffer said vehemently.

"You're talking about undercover cops?"

"Sure. Cops who pretend to be outside the law so that the criminals will trust them. We got our own on both sides, you know what I mean? Some of ours are working undercover but acting as though they're guilty."

Dan was about to reply when he heard a buzzing. Pfeiffer grabbed at his shirt pocket and pulled out a cellphone. He stared at it.

"Shit."

He flicked it open.

"Yeah?" Pause. "What do you expect me to do about it now? Okay, okay." he grumbled. Another pause. "I said okay. I'm coming."

He flicked the cell closed then muttered under his breath. He turned to Dan.

"I have a problem. I can either drop you here or you can come with me for the ride and I'll take you to your car when I'm done."

Dan looked out at the bleak streets. The rain was coming down again, lashing the windows like some wilful dominatrix. The chance of catching a cab was about nil.

"I'll take Door Number Two."

"Hold on."

Pfeiffer flicked his emergency flashers back on and they rushed forward through the rainy streets.

NINETEEN

A Wicked Witch

THEY HEADED EAST ON DUNDAS, past Jarvis and over to Parliament. Pfeiffer shot through the intersection on a red.

"That was your neighbourhood back there, wasn't it?" he asked, still chewing his gum. "The gay neighbourhood?"

"Actually, I'm in Leslieville. They let some of us out of the ghetto for good behaviour."

"Ha-ha. You're a funny guy."

"We established that already."

Pfeiffer reached a hand out the window and retrieved the overhead light, setting it on the console between them.

"Handy little thing," Dan said. "I should get one."

Pfeiffer glanced over with a smirk. "Yeah, right. Just you try using it and see what happens."

"Nobody seems to be bothering you."

They turned down Winchester and pulled into a darkened laneway. Tall trees overhung a large, empty yard. The building was stone, more mausoleum than house, and set back from the street. Even in the dark Dan could see it was run-down, the grounds neglected.

"Who lives here?" Dan asked.

Pfeiffer looked over at him. "Come in and find out."

They headed up the walk. The outside light was off, but illumination streamed through a crack where the door had been left open. They entered and Pfeiffer closed it behind them.

A high ceiling did nothing to dispel the gloom. Neglect had crept into the place like a stain that wouldn't wash out. The wallpaper, crimson-and-cream candy stripes with fluted edges, looked as though it had been chosen for some period movie long since filmed and forgotten, its stars now has-beens or in the grave. A burgundy carpet threading along the hallway and up the stairs had seen better days, and those days circa 1870 Weimar. The ghost of Versailles lingered here and there amid gilt-framed mirrors and paintings of dour-faced forebears. A few of the ceramic pieces would still fetch a price, Dan thought, but only because of their vintage.

"I'm here," Pfeiffer called out.

A dog barked. Dan heard it snuffling under a door leading from the hall.

"In here, darling."

It was a woman's voice, its provenance indeterminate. It might have belonged to a disembodied spirit, hovering in the hallways and floating through the house.

Pfeiffer pushed the door open. A white puffball the size of a large rat came scurrying up to the two men. Pfeiffer pushed it aside with his foot. It gave a shriek and ran back into the room.

Across the floor, Dan spied a woman in a caftan seated on a tall-backed chair. He wondered how long she'd been sitting waiting for them to find her in that pose.

"Dan Sharp, this is my mother."

"None of that 'mother' stuff," she commanded in a throaty growl. "It's Marilyn, thank you."

Dan recalled Pfeiffer's remark that his mother had dated Jags Rohmer. He guessed her to be in her late fifties. He knew the type. She was part of a breed of women who came of age in the 1970s, caught between the sexual revolution of the sixties and the feminist movement that followed in its wake, women with gloomy eyes and smoky voices who had had a brief fling with a rock star or been discovered by some now-forgotten fashion designer while standing on a street corner and photographed in chic outfits during a modelling career that spanned approximately one week. The same women who ever after embodied a sense of entitlement that took them places they didn't really belong other than through the sheer force of their personalities. Pfeiffer's mother was one of those.

Then she leaned forward. Dan caught a glimpse of her in the light, the planes of her face shifting into focus for a moment before she backed into the shadows again. *Marilyn Pfeiffer*. Suddenly the name rang out in a brilliant cacophony. She'd been famous once, he recalled. A leading role in an iconic Canadian film thirty years or more ago.

"*Chance Encounter*," Dan said.

Marilyn seemed suddenly animated. "All that was a long time ago," she said. "But really? You remember?"

"You're a Canadian icon."

She demurred. "Yes, always a pity about that adjective *Canadian*."

"Dan's client is Jags Rohmer," Pfeiffer told her.

She regarded him with greater interest now, her attention focused on his face, as though scanning for headline news.

"What do you do for Jags? Are you his agent?"

"No, I'm his personal bodyguard."

She stiffened, as if the answer had somehow made her wary. "Well, tell him Marilyn says 'hello.'"

Pfeiffer fidgeted in Dan's line of vision. "Show him the record."

"Show him yourself. It's over there somewhere."

Dan turned to see a cabinet stuffed with magazines, books, and knick-knacks. Here and there, the spines of record albums jutted out at irregular angles, as though an eccentric librarian had made a half-hearted attempt at organizing them by some arcane system of reference: colour coding, perhaps, or thematically by mood. Who knew what treasures it held? Donny and Germ would have a field day here, he suspected.

"Mother's got an album autographed by Jags. One of his first."

"*The* first."

Pfeiffer held something out to his mother.

"Here are your cigarettes. Don't you keep a spare pack around here somewhere? It might save me from having to drop by at midnight."

She gave him a sour look. "What difference does it make? I knew you weren't working."

"I could have been."

She accepted the cigarettes and waved her arms wearily, with an affectation of disdain. "I'm sure I have some somewhere, but could you find anything in here? I dare you to try."

She turned to Dan. "And he calls himself a policeman."

She pulled off the cellophane and slid a cigarette between her lips. Pfeiffer leaned in and lit it for her. The gesture was oddly intimate. She inhaled and sat back, then exhaling slowly as she regarded Dan. She seemed more than a little drunk.

"It was his choice, you know. I would never have wanted him to take on such a career. He could have been anything. Anything at all. But he chose law enforcement."

Pfeiffer scowled. "What's wrong with law enforcement?"

She sighed heavily. "Just like your father. I suppose I shouldn't be surprised. You were always happiest bossing people around and telling everyone what to do."

Pfeiffer beamed. "That's because I'm good at it."

"Did you get that promotion yet?" she demanded.

He frowned. "I told you I got it last year."

"Ah, yes. You did. I forgot." She stared at him. "Offer your friend a drink."

"We're not staying."

She gave Dan the kind of look he was used to getting from desperate men in bars at closing time. "I would hate for him to go back to Mr. Jags Rohmer and say he didn't receive adequate hospitality from me on his arrival."

Dan smiled. "I won't say anything of the kind."

"Have whatever you like," she said, waving imperiously at a bar in the far corner. "We have the best of everything. My son can vouch for that."

Pfeiffer shook his head at Dan.

Marilyn looked over at her son. "I left something for you in the dining room on the table."

"What?"

"Go and see." She shooed him with her hand.

When he was gone, she turned to Dan, focusing on him with careful gravity.

She gestured in the direction her son had gone. "I sent him to UCC, you know. He was a good student. Not the best, but still, he could have been anything he wanted."

Dan wondered if that last comment were true. Pfeiffer hadn't struck him as the intellectual type. He was familiar with the boys at Upper Canada College. He'd even dated a couple. Snotty and privileged, they kept to their own when they weren't slumming it. He had no time for that set.

"I understand your son is highly regarded in the force, Marilyn. I'm sure he'll make something of himself."

She rolled her eyes. "Yes, but is he happy?"

"Reasonably, I'm sure," Dan said, not wanting to give her grounds for an argument, either way.

"'Reasonably,'" she repeated with a look of disdain. "I guess that's all any of us are entitled to, a *reasonable* amount of happiness."

She stared off into the distance. Dan was beginning to think she'd forgotten him or perhaps had dismissed him. That was when he saw it: the amphetamine glare behind the eyes. The dreamy distance on a long, empty road.

She spoke again. "I was a bad mother. I suppose I can't expect much in return."

Dan said nothing.

She looked over at him. "What has Jags said?"

Dan looked confusedly at her. "I'm sorry?"

She stared. "About me. What has he said about me?"

"Ah." He took his cue. "I never discuss his private life with him."

"Then you don't know him." She looked scornfully away. "Well, he will talk to you about me eventually. Don't listen to a word he says. I'm warning you now, it's all bullshit."

The word seemed oddly harsh coming from her.

"I'm sure he won't be unkind," Dan said, wishing Pfeiffer would hurry so they could leave. "He never speaks ill of anyone, to tell the truth."

"Really?" She seemed disappointed. "How shocking."

Pfeiffer came suddenly back into the room. "There's nothing on the table," he said.

"No?" Marilyn didn't bother to look surprised. "Well, never mind. I just needed to talk to your friend for a moment." She turned her gaze on Dan again. "And we had such a nice conversation, didn't we?"

Dan bowed his head slightly. "Yes, indeed we did."

"'Yes, indeed we did,'" she repeated in a mocking tone.

Pfeiffer looked at her sharply. "We've got to go, Mother."

"Well, thank you for stopping by. I won't get up."

"Good to meet you, Marilyn," Dan said, turning.

"Goodbye then."

Pfeiffer kissed her on the cheek. He followed Dan to the door. The dog kept its distance, watching warily as they left.

Outside in the car, Pfeiffer turned to him. "What did you think of her?" he asked like an overeager child.

"She's a very attractive woman," Dan replied, hoping it would suffice for an answer.

"People always say that," Pfeiffer said in a way that suggested he expected everyone to be impressed.

"I'm not surprised," Dan said.

"What did she say to you while I was out of the room?"

"She asked if you were happy."

"She always asks if I'm happy."

"She's your mother, so she would be concerned."

"I'm very good to her," Pfeiffer said petulantly, as though someone had suggested otherwise.

"I'm sure she appreciates what you do for her," Dan said. "After all, you came running to bring her cigarettes at midnight ..."

"I didn't *run*," Pfeiffer cut in tersely. "I never run. And I asked if you would mind going with me first."

"Yes, no argument about that."

"She didn't show you the album cover?"

"Jags' album? No. Did she date him long?"

Pfeiffer turned to him. He seemed to be studying Dan's face. "Long enough. We were kind of family for a while. We used to go to church sometimes. We'd take the host together." He looked over. "Are you Catholic? Do you know what the host is?"

"I'm not Catholic. I know what the host is." He thought about it for a moment, recalling his odd dream. "Jags was religious?"

"Sure." Pfeiffer shrugged. "What's wrong with that?"

"Nothing. It just doesn't jive with the Jags I know. People change, of course."

Pfeiffer turned the key and backed out of the drive. "I'll take you to your car."

"You know where it is?"

Pfeiffer smirked. "Sure. I had it towed just a few streets over from where I picked you up."

With the lights flashing, it took fifteen minutes to get back across town. As they approached the empty warehouse, Pfeiffer swerved down a narrow back alley, emerging onto a street hosting a handful of forlorn houses and a drab row of container buildings. Dan's car sat beneath a streetlamp.

As Dan got out, Pfeiffer rolled down his window.

"Thanks for coming with me."

"We'll have to do it again some time."

Pfeiffer laughed again. Dan felt as though he'd just made friends with a wild animal. Feral. Instinctive. He just wasn't sure what to do about it.

"Tell your friends I'm hoping to hear something from them about Gaetan Bélanger very soon," Pfeiffer said.

The car roared off.

TWENTY

Fries with That

DAN GOT INTO HIS CAR and watched as Pfeiffer's taillights disappeared around a corner, leaving two red streaks on the wet pavement. He checked the time. He'd been gone more than an hour and a half.

He sat and waited another five minutes then drove slowly around the block, circling the warehouse twice till he was sure he was alone. He turned into an abandoned garage and shut off the engine. From there, he had a full view of the street. Not a single car went by. The rain had stopped. A silvery moon hung in the sky, obscured by a wisp of cloud that made it glow with a jazzy veil.

Finally, convinced no one was watching, he stepped out of the car and walked back to the warehouse where he'd met Germ earlier. The camera whirred overhead, focusing on his face.

A speakerphone crackled. "Of all the gin joints in all the world, and he walks into mine."

Dan smiled. "All clear. Sorry it took a while."

"So we caught the rat in our little trap?"

"We did. It was the one I thought it would be."

"Cool. What did you tell him?"

"Exactly as we agreed. The police think this is your little hideout. No doubt they'll be back to talk shop soon."

Germ laughed.

"Well, let them. I won't be there. I'll lose this camera after tonight. We'll have to devise another method of contact in future."

There was a pause and the speaker crackled again.

"Do you think they'll be angry with you?" Germ asked.

"No doubt, once they realize I fooled them. I'll deal with that when the time comes."

"Very good. I'll be in touch."

"Until we meet again, Agent Germ."

"*Auf wiedersehen*, dude."

The line went dead. The camera's movements stopped. Dan was left standing alone in the middle of a desolate neighbourhood.

The excitement had left him hungry. He headed over to the burger place on Lansdowne. No one was following. He went in and ordered a killer meal — double cheeseburger, fries with gravy — but forwent the shake. He was nearing forty, after all. One day it would all catch up. Until then, he still had a thirty-three-inch waist and there were a few more indulgences to be had.

Making his way to a free booth, he skirted the rowdy teenagers looking for a place to belong. Most of them were underage. It was an unlicensed establishment. The ones who were alone chatted on cellphones; the ones with friends chatted with each other between cellphone conversations. Dan found them all annoying, but not unbearable. He'd had worse company in his day.

It seemed like a night to get comfy with the phone, but first he set his tray on the table and popped a gravy-covered fry in his mouth. They were the wide-cut fries, chunky and fresh, never frozen. He could practically hear the advertising jingle. His taste buds were geared for ecstasy. He quickly unwrapped his burger and bit into it, devouring a quarter of it in a single bite. The lettuce stayed firm under the bun, rather than spilling out the sides the way it did at fast food places. This was a good burger. He sighed and chewed contentedly. Life had its gratifying little moments.

He licked his fingers clean then pulled out his cell. It was his own this time, not Ked's. He didn't care who intercepted this particular call. In fact, he'd be glad if the news got around about what had happened to him that evening.

"Ed Burch."

"Hi, Ed. Dan Sharp here."

He could imagine his ex-boss's inquisitive mind digging for the reason for his call. *Whenever someone calls it's always for a reason, even if they just say "hi." Remember that, Daniel,* Ed used to say. A stater of the obvious Ed was, but sometimes the obvious was precisely what got overlooked.

"Hey, Daniel. Good to hear from you. A little late for a social call, isn't it?"

"Apologies. This is something I'd rather not leave till tomorrow."

"Not a problem. Hit me."

"I'm calling about your friends at the police."

"Oh?"

"They're getting a bit invasive for my liking."

There was an uncomfortable silence on the other end. Dan managed to get two more fries into his mouth before Ed spoke.

"How so?"

"They've been tapping my phone line."

Dan heard a breath drawn between clenched teeth.

"I'm sorry ..."

"I got picked up tonight by one of the officers on the Bélanger case. It was an unofficial visit in an unmarked car as I was leaving one of my sources."

"Good God! Any trouble?"

"Depends how you define 'trouble.'"

He reached for the ketchup bottle. The fries were just begging to be turned into poutine. He aimed and squirted. The ketchup cut a bright red swath across his tray, barely missing his sleeve. Sometimes he suspected he just bought the hamburgers as an excuse to eat the fries. All right, admit it — he *did* buy the burgers as an excuse to eat the fries.

"I was parked legally, but when I came out my car had been towed. Next thing I knew, Constable Pfeiffer pulled up beside me and invited me for a ride. All very Mafia-like, except the ride didn't end with me being outfitted in a pair of cement shoes."

Ed groaned. "Danny, I'm sorry. If I'd known they were going to do this, I'd never have brought up your name."

Dan believed him. His former boss wouldn't have set him up.

"Actually," Ed continued, "I'm not surprised to hear it was Pfeiffer. I don't think anyone else would have the nerve to do something like that."

"Not Danes?"

"Danes is mostly a bubble-head in my books. The chief likes him because he's stupid and loyal. I doubt he could be that devious unless prompted."

"So you think that this was likely unsanctioned by the force?"

"Hard to say what's unsanctioned and what's unofficially sanctioned but just overlooked, if you catch my meaning. This case is number one on the chief's agenda since the *Star* article appeared. That made him squirm a bit, as I'm sure you can imagine."

"No doubt," Dan said. "And I wouldn't be surprised if Pfeiffer had something to do with that piece of journalism."

"Really?"

"He was hinting at it, though he didn't come out and say anything directly."

Ed paused. "The word on the street is that Pfeiffer gets his best results from being a rogue cop. Even though he's a junior, nobody wants to stop him from doing his thing as long as he gets results. That way, it's not on the chief's head and no one complains publicly."

"Where does he get his balls? Actually, never mind. I met his mother tonight, so I think I know."

Ed guffawed. "You what?"

"In the middle of our little talk, his cellphone rang and he had to go deliver cigarettes to Cabbagetown."

"Unbelievable."

"I'll say."

There was a pause.

"Be careful with him, Dan."

"You know me, Ed. I'm naturally wary."

Ed was silent again. "No, I mean be especially careful. He's got a reputation for being a troublemaker. He's a hard-nose. He was involved in a brutality lawsuit, but it didn't stick. Rumour has it his last promotion came about because of some evidence he got from a suspect that no one else could crack. Officially, the chief didn't know about it. Unofficially, who's to say? Pfeiffer was left alone with the guy for fifteen minutes and came out of the room with what he needed to know. My guess is he's not above resorting to threats or even violence to get what he wants."

Dan thought of Pfeiffer's prying questions about his family. "I'm not surprised," he said.

"For what it's worth, I can let it slip that I heard about this from you and see if he gets his knuckles rapped."

Dan thought this over. "Leave it for now. Thanks for the warning. I'll talk to you soon though."

"Be good."

Dan closed his phone and hunkered down on his fries.

TWENTY-ONE

Early Retirement

THERE WERE NO FURTHER BREAKS in the case. The furor seemed to have died down a little. The Ex ended and school started, marking an official end to summer. There were no further garage fires reported. The city seemed unnaturally calm for once.

It was another week before Dan heard from Germ. It took a moment before his subconscious registered the ring and another before he could tell which of his cellphones it came from. The room was as dark as the inside of a coffin. His fingers groped till they found the new one. Dan rolled out of bed, clutching the phone and trying not to wake Trevor.

Germ's calls often came in the middle of the night, so it was no surprise to know the intrepid mole was still up and doing his thing at 6:00 a.m.

"Late night?" Dan asked with a yawn, expecting to hear something about an all-night rave.

"No, dude." He surprised Dan by saying he was just getting up and about to have breakfast.

"Hang on. I'm just checking the line … okay, we're good." He heard a laugh. "This cheap technology, man, I love how it outsmarts the fucking System every time."

"Gotta love those corner store cellphones."

"Fucking Taiwan, eh?" Germ was practically gloating. "Hey, got something I need you to see."

"What is it?"

"Think we caught something on tape. Come over. The real place this time. Just make sure you're not followed."

He hung up before Dan could ask what they'd caught.

He made it across town in less than half an hour. If he'd had Pfeiffer's flashers he might have shaved off a bit of time, but he still made the lights all the way from Rosedale Valley and along Dupont to Casa Loma, that misplaced bit of Scottish royalty on the hill. Sunday morning traffic wasn't formidable. Dan's car fairly flew along. He kept one eye on the mirror, but nothing seemed to be following him. By the time he passed the old slaughterhouse, he was sure no one was on his tail.

Germ buzzed him in. He jumped on the elevator and braced himself as it bumped and jerked its way down.

Below, the space was in its usual state of chaos-in-transition. Someone — probably Velvet Blue — had added to the interior mural. A fiery-eyed Amazon with a bow and arrow stared down wrathfully from the middle of the ceiling like some biblical angel hell bent on retribution. A Sistine ceiling for the new revolution. Dan was pretty sure he wouldn't want to wake up lying on the floor beneath it stoned and hung over. Still, it was impressive.

Germ directed him to a chair. Dan sat across from the console and watched as he exercised his technological genius.

"We covered every major derelict building in the neighbourhood — well, except the ones where we got friends living. They can be our eyes for us. Tell us if anybody new comes on the scene. I emailed copies of the kid's photo to all of them."

He passed over a printed copy of the photograph. Dan picked it up, studied it silently, then tucked it into his shirt pocket.

"Hope you don't mind?" Germ asked.

"No, good idea."

"Anyway, I was just fast-forwarding through the tapes at one of the sites we put up last week when I found this …"

He stopped and pointed to something blurry. Dan could barely make out a human shape in a darkened interior.

"It was Velvet Blue's idea, actually. I was just going to cover the main entrances." He shrugged. "People gotta come and go, right? Anyway, I hadn't thought of using a camera in the stairwell. Makes sense, though. You can get into a building a million ways, but of course once you're inside you're going to use the stairs when you need to go up and down."

Dan looked over Germ's shoulder at the monitor.

"It was a stroke of genius," Germ enthused.

"What are we looking at?"

"It's an old retirement home. But it's not exactly empty." Germ tapped in a command and the image came into focus: a boy's shoulders and the back of his cap-covered head. He wore the same blazer and flannel trousers he'd had on in Germ's earlier shots.

"Is this the same kid you saw at the slaughterhouse?" Dan asked.

"That's him."

He tapped the console again. The same figure appeared in profile. Dan tried to superimpose the image he had in his mind of Gaetan Bélanger over this face. There were similarities, but nothing conclusive.

"What do you think?" Germ asked.

"Could be," Dan said. "I'm not convinced. The hair looks different, but with the cap on it's hard to say."

"Whether it's your guy or not, I can't say. But I can tell you he didn't come through the yard and up to the front door, like you'd expect. He arrived from the far side, over a fence, and got in some other way I can't figure out. I think maybe he climbed through a second-floor window." He turned to Dan. "Why? Why would you do that?"

Dan shrugged.

Germ held up a professorial finger: *Listen and learn, my friend.*

"Because he was expecting cameras. Or at least avoiding any obvious placement of them. CCTV is easy to avoid apart from the counters in 7-Elevens and whatnot so long as you stay away from main entrances. No one expects you to come in through the bathroom window, to borrow a phrase."

Germ turned back to the console. He hit another key and the figure began to dance in jerky little movements up the stairs.

"So here we have him going up to the second floor and into a room at the far end. What does he do there? Can't say. If it's not him, then maybe that's where this Gaetan guy is holed up."

Dan looked at the camera feed. A thought occurred to him. "Unless that is Gaetan Bélanger in disguise. Did we get a shot of anyone else?"

"No, really sorry, man." Germ looked chagrined. "The camera's just out of range for where he's heading."

After all the work it had taken Dan to convince Germ to help, now he was reacting with genuine enthusiasm as much as disappointment at the challenges they faced in getting results.

"Don't worry, this is good work," Dan told him.

"Oh, by the way!" Germ looked excited again. "I found something else. Let me show you. I've been researching your boy."

He turned back to the console, fiddling with the keys, his fingers flying faster than Dan could think. He snapped the ENTER key and a website swirled onscreen. It was Gaetan Bélanger's blog, recently updated. Dan wondered where he kept his computer. How could a teenager on the run have access to the Internet? He wouldn't get that in an abandoned building unless he had a wireless account.

"WiFi hotspots," Germ explained. "Lotta people use other people's accounts when they're not password protected. I do it all the time. That way, no one can tell where it comes from, because you don't pay any bills. No addresses, no names."

Dan focused on the blog entry. French dominated the text, except for the occasional curse word. English seemed to be the universal language when it came to swearing.

"My French isn't so good," Dan lamented.

"Mine either. Hey, Velvet Blue?" he called out.

"Yeah, baby?"

"Could you come here a minute?"

A diminutive figure stole into the room. She nodded at Dan then trained her eyes on the screen.

Germ smiled at her. "Could we ask you to avail yourself of your translating skills?"

"Sure, baby."

Germ looked over at Dan. "Vietnam, eh? The French were there once upon a time."

Velvet Blue frowned at the screen. "Something about a rocker," she said at last.

Dan's ears were on fire. She looked over at him.

"You know that old-style music from the sixties?"

"Yes." He nodded. She could call it what she wanted. He wasn't about to give her a lecture on music history. His eyes went down the screen, searching for a name. "There." He pointed. "What does it say about Jags Rohmer?"

She looked at his finger on the screen then back at Dan. "You need to move your hand."

"Sorry."

They waited while she read in silence, a bibliophile sphinx. She looked up at him. "The guy says he knows things about Jags Rohmer. Something about how he corrupts people."

"In what way?"

She read down. "It says he corrupts people's minds."

She turned and gave Dan an appraising look. "What do they want from him? Aren't rockers supposed to corrupt people's minds?"

"That's exactly what Jags would say," Dan told her. "Thanks for this and for the footage of the other place. It's great work."

Germ nodded vigorously. “We’re going to go back to the retirement home tonight and string up two more cameras. We’ll get it right.”

“Actually,” Dan said, “I think there’s a more direct way to deal with this. This is really all I need. Well, except for the street address.”

Germ looked crestfallen. “But we can get it right, man. We can cover this place from end to end. You’ll be amazed by what we can do.”

Dan squinted at the figure on the first monitor, frozen mid-step. “Cameras can tell us only so much. There’s no way of knowing for sure whether this is Gaetan Bélanger or not. I need to go there in person and have a look around.”

Germ looked incredulous. “In person? I thought you said this guy’s a killer.”

Dan nodded. “Best way is the direct way.”

Germ sighed. “Yeah, I guess maybe you’re right.” He began writing an address on a piece of paper. “This baby’s not far from here.”

Dan looked back at the monitor. “I think we need a code word for this kid, in case we have anyone listening in on our conversations in future.”

Germ looked at the image onscreen.

“How about Little Boy Blue?” he said. “On account of that blue blazer he’s always wearing.”

“Good one.”

The place looked dismal. Dan always wondered how buildings came to be abandoned. The obvious cause was through the death of the owner, but why was no one motivated enough to sell a piece of property after the owner had died? Of course, there could be any number of reasons — keeping the land in the family, waiting for the right time. Still, it gave him a haunted feeling to see an abandoned house with no explanation why it had been left empty.

The retirement home was a deserted, L-shaped configuration. In the parking lot, the pavement curled and wore away in pieces; weeds grew through it. The welcome sign was grey and weathered, strips of plastic backing falling off. The curtains had been drawn on most of the windows. A few were pulled back here and there as though invisible inhabitants were peeking out without wishing to be seen.

Dan parked a block away. He slipped into the yard during a lull in traffic. No use getting reported as suspicious by some overzealous commuter. One Crime Busters tip on a cellphone and he'd have the police on his back in minutes.

Someone had done him a favour by forcing the front door. A remedial padlock had met a similar fate. Surprisingly, the home's glass was intact. In Dan's youth, windows would have been the first things to go. Sudbury boys were amazingly adept at destruction. A grade school friend, Rex, had taught him first how to aim and throw and then how to break windows. The two went hand in hand. Windows on empty houses were for breaking — that was the rule. Construction sites were for getting into and undoing all the hard work the builders had done by day. A freshly plastered wall just invited a can of pop to be spilled over it, causing the surface to bubble and slide off. Mayhem and madness. Looking back, Dan thought with shame of his own renovation project, hoping Toronto kids had better things to do with their time.

His nostrils caught the tang of urine. Every abandoned building smelled of it. Inside, things were in a desperate state. What the owners hadn't stripped before leaving had been attacked with vigour by trespassers once the home closed. The day room looked like a club for the insane and disreputable. The walls had been tagged and sprayed by a number of hands in a Gallery of the Anonymous. Mauves and golds predominated. Faded Doric columns floated to the ceiling, while acanthus leaves littered the bases. A legion of naked gladiators tussled in erotic frenzy, dragging the local population of nymphs and cherubs into the X-rated arena. A dominatrix sporting black knickers and a see-through brassiere towered on foot-high stilettos. Madness gleamed in her eyes; lightning bolts blazed from her nipples. An erotic nightmare giving you the come on. It was as though Ilsa the SS officer had swallowed the Roman coliseum and vomited all over the walls.

Paint struggled to free itself from the walls in every room. A bathtub had been ripped from its moorings and set sail in the middle of a hallway. The place was a proto-punk funhouse, an Iggy Pop nightmare. Dan followed the long dark corridor to a door at the far end. Inside, a half-drained swimming pool was filled with detritus, its plastic covering peeled back and pushed under. Chairs and side tables lay drowning in the swampy water. Here, the smell of urine was supplanted by a kingdom of mould.

Emerging from the room, Dan heard voices coming down the stairs. He froze, wondering if he was about to encounter Gaetan Bélanger. He tucked into a darkened alcove. Two youngish looking men were descending:

1st man: "I got fifteen bucks last night just from begging on the corner."

2nd man: "Really?"

1st man: "Yeah, man. I got to the LCBO by nine thirty, drank till eleven thirty, and passed out by twelve."

2nd man: "Good night?"

1st man: "Oh, yeah!"

They moved out of sight. Dan heard them leaving by the front door. He kept his ears primed for additional voices. There was no other sound apart from his footsteps as he went from room to room. On the second floor, the rows of doorways beckoned him into the abandoned quarters of former residents. All open except for one. Whoever was using the place as a hotel probably lived here.

Dan felt absurd knocking on a door in an empty building. He was tempted to claim he was a police officer but doubted whether anyone inside would care. He called out. Nothing stirred within.

Well, then. That made things easier. Locks were simple to pick — a tension wrench and a paperclip were all it took for the most common variety. No need for messy break-ins. This one was about as basic as it got. Obviously, the staff didn't want granny barricading herself in the room with her powders and pills. Dan inserted the wrench and twisted. He jabbed the paperclip, feeling the up-thrust till the tumblers fell in place. He was inside in less than a minute.

It was surprisingly clean. A mattress lay on the floor, empty pop cans scattered around it. Someone had swept a pile of litter into a corner. A single window looked onto a wooden fence and the wrecking yard on the other side.

Not the most inspiring view to comfort you in your final days, but not a total disaster either. Anyone hiding out here would be safe from prying eyes.

A blue blazer hung in the closet. Little Boy Blue's room then.

In the bathroom Dan found sample-sized containers of soap and shampoo, alongside a canister of shaving cream and a pack of disposable razors. A can of Nair sat on the edge of a tub beside an empty packet of hair dye and a used towel. A canister of hairspray lay overturned in a corner. Whoever lived here was obsessed with hair products. Change your hair colour, change your life. Little Boy Blue seemed to be a practitioner of disguises.

Apart from the empty pop cans and a few candy bar wrappers, there was no sign of food. A bottle of contact lens cleaner sat perched on a pile of sci-fi paperbacks. Dan picked up the top one. It was in French.

He snapped a few photos with his cellphone and left, locking the door behind him. As he crept down the stairs, he saw the camera Velvet Blue had rigged at the entryway. If he hadn't been looking, he might never have noticed it.

Outside, he placed a small flat stone up against the base of the door to tell him if anyone entered between now and when he returned. He looked at the sky. A storm hovered on the horizon like some sort of omen.

TWENTY-TWO

No One Can Be Nowhere

"It's important to Donny," Trevor told him. "You already stood him up once. He's getting frantic. He kept saying how much he needs you now."

Dan sat across the table from Trevor. He'd just come in, beating the storm by minutes. His gut was telling him the other thing needed his attention more than Donny and his cockamamie scheme to bring a wayward boy back to the fold.

Trevor continued. "He requested a pow-wow tonight. He wants us to help him brainstorm how we can help Lester."

Dan envisioned a SWAT team in vests, armed with Kalishnikovs and battering down the door of a dreary Oshawa bungalow, wide-eyed neighbours on the lawn wondering why the television cameras were there as Donny led the others in a vain attempt at liberating a boy who, as far as Dan was concerned, had gone willingly into captivity.

Trevor's expression softened. "Then again, you look pretty tired. I can make excuses for you, if you prefer."

Dan shook his head. "No, it's all right. You don't need to play secretary for me."

"Hey! You are my life's purpose at this moment."

Dan smiled. "Lord and master?"

"Just about."

Dan's gaze drifted off. What had that witch of a mother said to make Lester come home? No doubt she'd put on the charm the same way she'd put on her mohair sweaters and bubblegum pink nails before crooking a cruel finger at the son who'd escaped her evil claws once, only to be seduced into returning. Dan wondered how much distance lay between a boy like Lester and someone like Gaetan Bélanger. Probably not much.

Trevor was watching him. "Where are you, Dan?"

Dan shook his head. "Just thinking."

"Really? What a surprise. About anything in particular?"

Dan nodded. "I'd like to meet this kid."

"What kid?"

Dan pulled the photograph of Bélanger from his breast pocket and laid it on the table.

"You're not serious?" Trevor stared at him. "He's already killed three people. Were you thinking he might consent to a quiet little interview with you?"

Dan shrugged. "I think we'd have things in common. He comes from the same kind of background as me."

Outside the wind blew wildly. Rain slashed at the windows. The storm was coming on full tilt.

"I might remind you it's a background you've spent a lot of time distancing yourself from," Trevor said.

Dan shrugged. "I have a messy past. I don't deny it. In the end it made me stronger, less afraid. But this kid's only sixteen. I'm more than twice his age and I can see these things now. I need to talk to him and let him know it gets better. That it *can* get better."

"Not with three murders on his conscience. He's likely to be desperate."

"I know this kid, Trevor. He thinks no one understands what he went through. And maybe it's true, but it doesn't matter. Not really."

"You think it would help him to try to relate to you?"

Dan studied the picture on the table. The wary eyes and dark circles beneath them that spoke of inner torture, things that haunted him, real or otherwise.

"Who are you, my friend? Just another lost boy? Where are you right now?"

Trevor put a hand on Dan's arm, pulling him back to the real world. "If he's living in abandoned warehouses and hiding from the police, you can't even begin to imagine the state of mind he must be in."

"Yes, I can. I slept in parks. I sold my body to survive."

"But no one was hunting you down for murder." Trevor studied Dan's face. "You're worrying me."

Dan came around the table and hugged him so tightly that Trevor had to make him stop.

"I won't endanger myself," Dan said. "Not so long as I've got you and Ked in my life."

Trevor rubbed his arm. "Okay. So what do we do now?"

Dan looked up. "We bring things from the darkness into the light."

Trevor gave him a blank look. "I was referring specifically to Donny's invitation."

"Oh, that. I guess we better get over there."

It was time for the posse party. Donny had invited Domingo as well. They all bumped into one another in the lobby. Domingo's hair was slicked to her skull like a Hollywood-styled mercenary-for-hire, as though she'd come groomed for the part.

To Dan, it seemed as if the lobby in Donny's building was perpetually filled with twenty-somethings in search of the next party. Their ringing hilarity was at odds with the small, silent cabal gathered to help form a plan to spring Lester from his prison-home.

The concierge nodded to the twenty-somethings while casting gloomy glances at Dan, Trevor, and Domingo, as though they'd come to storm the walls of the Bastille. Donny came down to meet them, hugging them solemnly one by one.

"Hi, and thank you very much for coming," he intoned like some novice diplomat addressing a committee convened to discuss nuclear disarmament between hostile nations.

He looked worn and haggard. Dan wondered if he'd been sleeping erratically the past few weeks while thinking of ways to rescue Lester. No one spoke as they rode up in the elevator, while the fidgety twenty-somethings checked their cellphones for nonexistent messages.

"I've spent a long time thinking about things," Donny began as they exited into his hallway.

They waited till he closed his condo door and put the lock on the chain, cloistering them like a party of counter-revolutionaries planning an assassination. Gavrilo Princip and his cronies hunting the Archduke Ferdinand.

"My first thought was to offer them money for Lester, but I realized that was not a very practical solution. Not to mention that I don't have much to offer."

Dan shook his head. "That would be tantamount to buying a child. Besides being impractical, it's illegal. I won't support anything against the law."

Donny made a face. "Well, that leaves out just about every plan I've come up with."

"Then we'll have to come up with something different," Domingo said.

Donny ushered them into the sitting room. In place of his usual impeccable hosting, he had put out bowls of nuts and finger snacks with a tall bottle of Grey Goose beside several shot glasses and a bucket of ice. Dispensing with the frivolities was how he put it.

"Help yourselves," he told them.

It was a solemn gathering. Donny stood with his back to the fireplace. His condo was built for maximum light exposure, leaving everyone perfectly lit as they stared at one another.

"When did you last hear from Lester?" Dan asked, thinking someone had better direct this meeting.

"A couple days ago. He called in the evening. I spoke to him briefly before he had to get off the phone. He says they monitor him night and day. It's making him crazy.

They keep him locked in his room and won't let him leave the house without one of them by his side."

From its position in the hall, Donny's newest art acquisition, with its swirling twilight colours, seemed an apt rendering of his internal state. Dan wondered if he paced back and forth in front of it when he was alone.

"Not surprising," Dan said. "He was a runaway for more than a year. They also have a good idea what sort of things he got involved in to make money while he was on the street. It's in his best interest not to go back to that."

"He won't," Donny said vehemently. "I've talked to him about that. It's in the past. We need to let it rest."

"It may be in Lester's past," Dan reminded him. "But it's no doubt very much in his parents' minds at present. They know he was involved with prostitution when he disappeared for a year. I'd be wary of his movements, too."

Donny started to speak, but Dan held him off.

"I know what you're going to say. Lester needs to get away from them regardless. I agree, so long as he *wants* to get away from them."

"He does. I asked him."

"Okay. So what options do we have? Kidnapping is out. I won't support anything illegal, as I've said."

Domingo used the tongs to fish an ice cube from the bucket. She splashed a little vodka into the glass after it. "What about luring him to a shopping mall or public space?" she suggested, swirling her drink. "He could just sneak away while their attention is distracted."

"You mean some kind of vigilante rescue operation?" Dan asked. "No way. That's still kidnapping. He's underage."

"For another three weeks," Donny said, a look of resolve clinging to his features.

Dan put a hand on his forearm. "Another three weeks is not forever."

"I won't forgive myself if anything happens to him in the meantime."

Dan shook his head. "Nothing's going to happen to him that hasn't already happened. The parents may try to brainwash him into thinking he's straight, but they are not going to kill him." Dan looked around the table. "The facts are simple: on his sixteenth birthday, he can voluntarily leave home and go where he wants. If they try to hold him, they can be charged with forcible confinement."

"I told him that already. But what if he gets desperate and tries something that ends up getting him hurt?"

"That would be unfortunate," Dan said. "Can't you convince him to hang on till then?"

Donny shook his head. "I tried. He wouldn't listen."

"Okay." Dan looked around the table. "Suggestions?"

They were all talked out. The vodka bottle was down by half. A heavy pall hung over the room. No conclusive plan of action had been reached. Donny had calmed down, though he looked more depressed than hopeful. He was now inclined to leave things till he heard from Lester again and try to convince him to bide his confinement until the day he turned sixteen.

Dan looked at his watch. "I'm sorry, but I've got to leave. I've got minority problems of my own I need to attend to."

"You're not telling me Ked is acting up?" Donny said, a surprised look on his face.

"Not Ked, no."

Trevor nodded to Domingo. "Why don't you ask Domingo?"

Dan stared at him. "Ask her what?"

"You know. Ask her what she can tell you about this Bélanger kid."

They all turned to Domingo. "What's the deal?" she asked.

Dan looked down at the welter of glasses on the coffee table then back up at Domingo. "I've got a kid I'm trying to track down. Is there any way to look into that with your … you know?"

"What specifically do you want to know?"

Dan shrugged. "Are we dealing with a serial killer?"

Her eyebrows rose, rakish, wary. "Wow. I don't know if I want to grapple with that. Certainly not with a head full of vodka."

"No problem." Dan turned away with a look of relief.

"But I could try," she said. "If you want me to."

Dan shrugged. "If you're not comfortable with it …"

Domingo smiled. "Let me try. What's his name?"

"Gaetan Bélanger. He's sixteen years old … from Quebec."

"Where is he now?"

"As far as we know, he's somewhere in the west end of Toronto."

"Okay, that's enough for me to go on. If there's anything there, it will come to me. It always does."

She sat back on the sofa. They waited as she pressed her palms against her eyes. Donny went out onto the balcony and lit a cigarette.

Domingo sighed and breathed heavily. “There’s some darkness in his past. Some ghost he can’t let go of,” she said at last. “Some childhood trauma.”

Dan and Trevor exchanged looks. “Makes sense,” Dan said. “He was sexually molested by a priest.”

Domingo opened her eyes. “That’s awful. But I’m not sure it makes him a killer.” She returned to her inner visions. “He’s very frustrated. He’s searching for something. Maybe a place to live?”

“That makes perfect sense.”

She looked up. “Anything else?”

Dan nodded. “Try another kid. See if you can get anything on him.”

“Name?”

Dan’s mouth opened, but nothing came out. “I don’t know.”

Domingo waited. “I don’t think I can zero in on nobody.”

Dan nodded. “Okay. Try Little Boy Blue. That’s our code name for him.”

They waited again as she pressed her palms into her eyes. A full minute passed. Outside, six floors below, someone warbled out a Supremes song, the wonder of love still alive after all these years. Traffic spluttered past. Pigeons flapped their way against the skyline. The world ground on. Life was a noisy affair.

At last, she said, “He’s not there.”

“How so?” Dan asked.

She shook her head, hands still glued to her eyes. "It's like he doesn't really exist. There's an empty space if you reach out to touch him. This kid is nowhere."

"No one can be nowhere," Dan said.

Domingo giggled and opened her eyes. "That's what the Buddha said."

Dan thought over her observations. "What do you think it means?"

She cocked her head, an inquisitive parrot. "I feel a pull when I try to picture him. I start to see him then it's like he just disappears into thin air. But how do you vanish into thin air?"

"Actually, it makes sense in a way," Trevor said. "Dan doesn't think he exists."

Dan nodded. "I think it's a disguise. I think they're the same person. I think Little Boy Blue is actually Gaetan Bélanger. But only when he's out in public."

Domingo gave him a curious look. "It really is a mystery," she said. "I'd like to know the solution, when you figure it out."

Dan bent down and kissed her cheek. "Thanks."

He turned to Donny, returned from the balcony. His face was still a portrait of despair.

"I've got to go. Try not to drive yourself crazy about Lester. We'll get him back. I promise.

TWENTY-THREE

Little Boy Blue

DAN PULLED UP IN HIS CAR and sat watching the retirement home. The same boarded-up doors and miraculously intact windows. It was just past eight in the morning, a little on the cool side. Nothing stirred. At eight thirty, he got out and stretched. A quick check showed the stone was still in place at the front door. In back, everything looked intact. He tried the door. Locked. A gash of red graffiti rolled around one corner of the building, a delicate curl leading to who knew where. A surrealist surfer riding a wave to nowhere. Dan couldn't remember seeing it before. He got back in the car and settled in for the wait. He'd brought a *New York Times* and a Wendy's combo — super-size everything. While he didn't relish cold fries, he knew he'd want to nibble something — anything — to keep his mind off the time.

This part of the job hearkened back to his beginnings as an insurance fraud investigator, when he would disguise himself and sit invisibly back as claimants for accident insurance went about their lives, waiting to see if their actions contradicted the statements about their injuries. It was a job he'd quickly come to despise. He left as soon as he realized he was implicating innocent people just trying to get along as best they could. No sin in living, he told himself the day he quit. Let others figure out who was doing the dirty.

He finished the combo and picked up the paper. It didn't hold his attention. He never brought books. He became too engrossed in them and forgot to keep his eye on things. The radio was annoying — *light* jazz, *light* classical, *heavy* rock — where was the mainstream these days? He switched over to 1010 Talk Radio and listened to the babble of people trying to express themselves, dying to be heard. So much to say, so few to listen. All the lonely people. The Beatles had it right all those years ago.

At one o'clock he told himself to leave. Nothing was happening. At two thirty he was sure he was wasting his time. Four o'clock came and went. *The unshakeable Dan Sharp*, Ed called him. Something to that doggedness then.

It was ten minutes to five when the figure scurried into sight at the far end of the property. Blue blazer, cap pulled well down. If Dan had had his head buried in a book he would have missed the slight movement. It was Little Boy Blue. Or rather it was Gaetan Bélanger as Little Boy Blue, so Dan believed.

The boy headed for the back, carrying a paper sack. Another fan of fast food. Dan waited a beat before he got out of the car. He walked casually up to the building then turned the corner and stealthily approached the front door, slipping inside the crepuscular interior.

He crept past the day room with its coliseum touch-up, skirting the drowned pool. He stopped and strained his ears. A faint murmuring came from upstairs. Gregorian chant, a monotonous line without harmony of any sort. Someone was talking softly, as though even here in this inner sanctum he was afraid of being overheard. From time to time the pitch shifted, an antiphonal response in the liturgy before reverting to the original tone. A second voice then. An answer song. Was someone with Little Boy Blue?

He crept softly up the stairs till he could see along the hallway. The door to the room where he had found the blazer and hair products was standing open, daylight shining a clear path on the floor. Dan made his way along, thankful the stripping crew had left the hall carpet intact. Nothing like footsteps to advertise your presence. He paused and waited for the sound to resume. There it was again. He was about to fathom the answer to at least one mystery.

He reached the door and stopped. The sound was less distinct now. He peered inside. The room was empty. He looked cautiously around. He could have sworn the voices had come from this room. They resumed suddenly from a baseboard register, the talk carrying from somewhere below.

He crept back down the stairs, scanning for a basement entrance. He found the stairwell near the joint in the L-shaped corridors and descended one cautious step at a time, mindful not to let his tread give him away. There he was, breaking Horror Film Survival Rule Number Three: *Never go down to the basement alone.*

Someone spoke, paused, spoke again. The response came in a different pitch. All talking suddenly ceased as Dan reached the landing. He braced for an assault. Nothing happened; no one emerged to challenge him.

A soft, childlike laugh came from a door at the far end. As Dan edged his way along he heard a stealthy sound, as though something was being dragged across the floor. The smell of fries hung in the air.

He inched forward and peered through a crack. In the semi-darkness, he could make out a bag set on the floor beside a blazer and cap. A slim young man in black T-shirt, tight jeans, and worn runners sat cross-legged on the floor. Gaetan Bélanger. There was no one else there. Where was Little Boy Blue?

This kid is nowhere, Domingo had said.

Dan watched the boy pick through the bag. His mutterings resumed. He seemed to be talking to his food, speaking in French mostly, but now and then a word or two in English. He pulled out a hamburger, tore it open, and ate ravenously. With his lean build, he no doubt came by his hunger honestly.

Dan had confronted missing people in the flesh many times before. Sometimes he'd been able to talk them into going back to their lives or at least give him a credible explanation why they had disappeared, at least enough that would satisfy the people who hired him, before agreeing to leave them alone and not reveal their whereabouts, if they chose. But he'd never knowingly confronted a murderer before. He'd have to ad lib this one.

He stepped into the room and said, "You shouldn't be here. You're trespassing."

The boy froze, his eyes frantically scanning the hallway behind Dan to see if he'd come alone. Even in the gloom, Dan could see his face was prematurely worn and weighed down with things no kid at that age should have to feel.

"I'm alone," Dan said. "I'm not going to hurt you."

The boy put the unfinished hamburger down on the wrapper and reached into his pocket. Dan could just make out the knife.

"I'm not armed," Dan said, holding up his hands.

"Fuck off."

"I just want to talk to you."

"You came here before."

Dan was shaken. The kid must have been hiding somewhere when he picked the lock and entered.

"You're with the police."

He had only the slightest of accents. Pfeiffer had been right in saying that kids from Quebec were ahead of the bilingual game when it came to their English counterparts.

"I'm not with the police," Dan said. "Are you afraid of them?"

"They're going to kill me!" he screamed. "You came here to kill me!"

"That's not true," Dan told him. "I just want to talk."

Dan watched the hand wielding the knife, saw how it waved erratically when he spoke.

"What do you want?"

"All right. I'll be honest with you. I know who you are."

The boy made a whimpering noise.

"It's Gaetan. Am I right?"

The boy's body tensed.

"I know what happened to you at the church. I'm on your side."

The knife slashed the air.

"Get the fuck out or I'm going to kill you."

"I know this sounds crazy, but there are people who want to help you, Gaetan."

He shook his head. "Why would they?"

"Because they believe what happened to you was wrong. They want to help you get your life back."

"My life back? I died in that church!"

He lunged. Dan backed off. The knife tore at empty air.

"You didn't die. You survived. Whatever they did to you, you survived."

The kid shook his head. "Bullshit!"

"You survived. And you're still here to talk about it."

"What the fuck do you care?"

"You can tell people what happened to you so it won't happen to someone else."

The boy sneered. "I don't believe that."

"It's true."

"Why should I care?"

His breathing was erratic. Dan saw there'd soon be no reasoning with him. He was approaching a state where people did inexplicable things. They lunged at armed police officers, challenged authority, doubted everything. And when they got shot or stabbed or jumped off the edge of a building twenty stories up, everyone said they had it coming. Dan wasn't going to have any of that here.

He recalled Trevor's question when he'd accepted the bodyguard job: *Will you carry a gun?* The outcome today would determine whether his choice had been a wise or a foolish one.

He tried for a casual tone. "Who were you talking to just now? Was there another boy here?"

Gaetan advanced with the knife held forward. "Fuck you. You don't know anything!"

Dan put his hands in the air. "I'm not going to hurt you," he said.

The blade slashed and Dan jumped.

"Get out or I'll kill you."

Dan's mind flashed quicksilver, his synapses working at the speed of light. What were the chances he could wrest the knife from the kid without hurting either of them? *Flash!* In his state, the boy was capable of doing a lot of damage. *Flash!* Better to leave it for the police. *Flash!* On the other hand, if he could stop Bélanger here and now, he might prevent other deaths. *Flash! Flash!* He thought of Trevor's admonition. He thought of Ked growing up without a father. *Why be a hero?* he wondered, even as he tried to think of a way to outsmart a desperate teenager with a knife.

Flash!

The boy lunged. He was quicker on his feet than Dan expected. Dan felt the jab as he stumbled back into the hallway. The door slammed shut.

Dan waited a beat then called out, "I just want to help you."

No response. He placed his hand against the rib where he'd been cut. He thought of Darryl Hillary's bashed-in face and missing ear. He thought of tomorrow's sensational headline featuring his picture: *Missing Persons Investigator Becomes Fourth Mutilation Victim.* A scrabbling sound came from inside the room. Before it could register, Dan heard a crash followed by a trickling noise. Nothing further reached his ears. He opened the door and peered in. The air was dense and musty.

It's like he just disappears into thin air, Domingo had said.

If nature abhorred a vacuum, how did a boy simply disappear?

Then he saw it. A cloud of dirt belched from a closet doorway. Debris covered the floor. Dan had his Mini Mag out as he reached in and began to dig. The dust filled his lungs and made him cough. He pulled his T-shirt over his nose till he could breathe freely again then turned back to the hole. The beam picked out a tunnel leading upward. Gaetan wasn't trapped. He'd triggered a collapse of bricks and drywall. Obviously, he'd been prepared for an ambush.

Dan looked around. The blazer and cap were gone. His disguise. He raced up the stairs and around to the back, searching for the end of the tunnel. He spotted it across the yard: a shed with a door flapping gently.

Dan glanced at the fence that led to the wrecking yard. Beyond it lay a maze of urban streets and back alleys. By the time he hoisted himself over, there'd be no telling which way Gaetan had gone. He suddenly felt exhausted. He crouched to catch his breath, spitting out dust and dirt.

Back in his car, he leaned his head on the steering wheel. The cut wasn't as bad as he'd expected. He pulled the first aid kit from his glove compartment, unwrapped a bandage, poured antiseptic on it, and applied it gently to the wound.

He'd been foolish to come alone. Still, nothing terrible had happened. Or had it? He'd just alerted a murder suspect that someone knew where he'd been hiding out. You could strike that shelter off the list. Which left about five or six hundred other possibilities, unless he scrammed out of the city for good. For that, however, he'd need a car or a bus ticket. Buying a ticket meant risking public exposure. If so, the police would need to cover the bus and train stations. But would they be looking for Gaetan Bélanger or Little Boy Blue?

Dan parked his car down the street from Germ's bunker and walked over to the entrance. When Germ didn't respond to the buzzer, Dan got out and waved at the camera. No blinking lights, no crackling speakers. Odd. Then again, even underground activist geeks had to sleep and eat and use the bathroom sometime.

He took out his cell and dialled Germ's number. Germ picked up in seconds.

"I'm outside," Dan said.

Germ mumbled something Dan didn't catch. The latch clicked and the door unlocked. Dan entered and pulled it closed behind him. The elevator rumbled down like a bumpy spaceship, banged to a landing and reopened onto a jumble of misplaced objects, smashed and broken. Glass and DVD shards covered the floor. Germ glowered from across the room like an angry charwoman, a push broom in his hand to complete the portrait.

"No way," was all Dan said.

"Way," Germ contradicted.

"Who?"

Germ shrugged and kicked at the load of debris by his feet.

"Guy in a mask."

"No ID?"

"No, dude. You think he's gonna come in here and make a mess like this and identify himself so I can hang him out to dry afterward?"

Dan glanced over at the console. All its screens had been bashed in. Dan felt his stomach clutch.

"He smashed all the fucking monitors."

Germ nodded.

"Why?"

"So I couldn't track something, is my guess. He made me show him the tapes. I think he recognized some of the sites."

"Wait a second. You mean he wanted to see footage from your hidden cameras?"

Germ nodded. "He even knew which locations. He was furious when he saw Little Boy Blue on screen. Guess he figured we'd been holding out on him."

Ed's warning about Pfeiffer's rogue ways came to mind. "Describe him for me. Big? Small?"

Germ looked up from his broom. "On the short side. Not big. Coulda taken him out with one arm, if he hadn't been holding a crowbar."

"Did you catch his eye colour?"

"Yeah, green, I think. I wasn't exactly gazing into them with love or anything, but they struck me as being green."

"That sounds like Pfeiffer."

"Who's that?"

"The cop who followed me the other night. It's got to be him."

Germ gestured around at the studio. "Why would he do this?"

Dan looked at the destruction and shook his head. "Clearly, whoever it was came here to destroy something."

Germ nodded. "What I wanna know is how the fuck he found me. I'm as off the map as it gets. Plus you've been using a different cellphone, so we know he can't have hacked into it."

"I don't know," Dan said softly. "Maybe he already knew everything before I switched phones."

"No one is safe from the System," Germ proclaimed gloomily.

Dan saw his smashed laptop lying off to one side. "He destroyed the master copies of the files?"

"'Fraid so."

Dan suddenly remembered why he'd come. "That's a problem. I wanted to ask you to keep a close eye on the camera feeds in the next little while."

Germ set his broom aside and came over. "Fill me in, dude."

Dan updated Germ on his encounter at the retirement home. When Germ saw the blood on Dan's T-shirt, he rolled a joint and insisted Dan take a toke. Dan relented.

"But just this once, okay?"

"Fair enough," Germ told him. "Better than the Red Cross any day."

Dan continued his account of his meeting with Gaetan, pointing out the existential question: were there two boys or just one? "When I got there, I thought I heard two people talking. It sounded like a conversation, but when I found Gaetan he was alone."

"Talking to himself?"

"Could be. As far as I could tell, Gaetan arrived alone.

Maybe the other person was already inside the building and left before I saw him. In any case, he's not going back there. I hoped you could tell me where he ends up."

Germ grinned. "No problem with that. The cameras are still in place. The only problem is displaying them. I need to get a few new screens first."

"Get what you need and send me the bill," Dan said.

Germ shrugged. "Not a biggie. I'll put in a call to a friend. I use second-hand monitors, so they're cheap. I should be able to grab some by tomorrow."

Dan looked around and shook his head, thinking how deep he was getting in and wondering who else might get dragged down with him.

"I'm sorry, Germ. I never meant to put you or Velvet Blue in range of these people."

"Yeah, good thing Velvet wasn't here," Germ said ruefully. "Or maybe too bad. She would have taken him out before he knew what was happening."

Dan checked his watch. He was going to be late for dinner. Worse, he'd have to explain to Trevor where he'd been. It wasn't going to be an easy talk. So far he'd managed not to sabotage this relationship, but lately he'd been pushing it to the limits.

"Gotta go," Dan said. "You want to report the break-in to the police?"

He saw Germ's face and laughed.

"Yeah, right. What an idea. Report the System to the System."

"Then I'll leave you with it," Dan told him.

He strode back to the elevator. It had stayed waiting for him with its doors open.

TWENTY-FOUR

Keeping Mum

TREVOR WAS UP AND GONE before the dawn light. Something about a special order cabinetry installation and busy tradesmen coming to the house early. Dan got up an hour later, exhausted and unsettled by his confrontation with Gaetan Bélanger and the break-in at Germ's underground fortress the night before. No sense going back to bed, he could tell it wouldn't help.

The bandage on his right side had seeped through in the night, leaving pinpricks of blood on the sheets. He rinsed the sheets and left them to soak in the basement sink. The night before, he'd managed to get to the bathroom and clean himself up before Trevor noticed. If he wondered why Dan had come to bed wearing a T-shirt, he hadn't said anything. Sex was going to be tricky for the next few days, however.

He was just trying to decide between having coffee and reading the newspaper at home or going out for a bite when his phone rang.

"It's Jags. I'm on the island." He sounded unusually subdued. "Can you come over?"

Dan hesitated. "I'm just getting going here. Do you mind if I grab a shower and a bit of breakfast before I head out?"

"This can't wait."

"Something happened?"

"You could say that. Someone just tried to kill me."

Dan's mind leapt at the possibilities. "Are you all right?"

"For now. Just come over."

"I'm on my way."

Dan put down the phone, cursing the man for living in the one spot in the city that was inaccessible by car.

He swung down to the water. The ferry would take too long. He caught a water taxi directly to Algonquin Island then headed over to Jags' place. The sun was just climbing over the branches. The air felt hushed and expectant.

He knocked. Jags furtively opened the door and beckoned him in.

"You need to get an airlift service over to this place," Dan told him.

His eyes travelled around the room, searching for signs of a problem. He didn't see anything unusual. At least nothing unusual for a rock star's island retreat.

"Did you see it?" Jags asked, closing the door behind him.

Dan gave him a blank look. "See what?"

Jags sighed and shook his head. "Come here."

Dan followed him to the nearest window. Jags pointed off to the right.

"Right there."

Dan's eyes followed his hand. He found it: an arrow embedded in the wall of the porch.

"I take it that's not a decoration? Not one of your 'props'?"

Jags' eyes darted warily from cottage to trees and back again. His voice was strained. "No, Dan. It's not a prop."

"When did you find it?"

"I didn't find it. It nearly found me. It whizzed past when I was out watering my garden this morning. Let's just say it came very close to hitting me."

"Did you see anyone?"

"I saw a kid running away."

Dan's eyebrows shot up. "What did he look like?"

"Nondescript. A schoolboy. He had on a cap and —"

"A blue blazer?"

Jags nodded. "Does this have anything to do with that ear photograph I got last month?"

"I think so," Dan said. "In fact, I'm afraid it probably does."

He turned to the window and looked up and down the street. The nearest house was set off through the trees at the end of Jags' lot.

"Pretty isolated here. Did anyone else witness this?"

Annoyance spread across Jags' face. "Are you fucking kidding me? Look at this place." He shook his head. "It's like this all day long," he said, a little more subdued.

Dan looked around the room. With all the windows, it was possible to see right through the cottage from outside. Hard to hide in an aquarium like that. The glass might prove a deterrent against an arrow, but sooner or later Bélanger would come up with a gun.

"Are you sure you didn't recognize the kid?"

Jags shook his head impatiently. "No, I'm telling you —"

"And you're sure there's nothing you're leaving out? Some detail you need to tell me?"

"Fucking hell, Dan! Do you think I'd be holding out on you with someone shooting arrows at me?"

"Okay, okay. But if anything comes to mind, you need to let me know immediately."

Jags was exasperated. "What kind of things? What are you thinking?"

"I'm thinking that Gaetan Bélanger just tried to kill you."

"This kid they're all looking for?" Jags' mouth hung open.

"Yeah," Dan said. "The same one who sent you the ear photo. Just that." He looked around again. "Ok. I think it's time to go."

Jags stared after him. "You're leaving me again?"

"No, you're coming with me. You need to get off this isolated island and stay in your penthouse where you have professional door staff to weed out unwanted visitors. Either that or you should leave town for a while."

Jags nodded. "Okay. Give me a minute to grab a few things."

Dan opened the door and looked around before stepping out. He scrutinized the scenery, wondering if Gaetan Bélanger was hiding in the shrubbery.

Jags returned with a small bag.

Dan said, "We'll have to tell the police about this."

Jags shook his head. "I don't want anyone to know."

"You have to be kidding me."

"I don't want the publicity. It's not a good time for it."

"For fuck's sakes," Dan said. "This was a murder attempt. You have to let someone know."

Jags sighed. "Okay, okay. Just give me an hour. I need to let my publicist know what's going on. She made me promise to pass everything by her first."

Dan rolled his eyes and looked at his watch. "An hour," he said. "Now let's get back to the city."

Dan dropped Jags off at his condo and watched him go inside, after making him promise to report the incident to the police.

He sat in his car, thinking over what he'd encountered. So far, all roads seemed to lead straight back to Jags Rohmer. Jags with his fame and his fancy cars. Jags with his auto-erotic asphyxiation. Jags with his mysterious, isolated cottage on Algonquin Island and his Blue Mountain sanctuary. And, most of all, Jags with his sexually amorphous past and his taste for extremes. While Dan didn't believe the reclusive star was out murdering pedophiles and cutting off their ears, he knew instinctively the picture he had was incomplete. For one thing, Jags could have sent himself the ear photograph. But why would he? Except for showing it to Dan and the police, he'd kept quiet about it. Even the obvious explanation that he wanted publicity for his book rang false.

There were other things that worried him. Jags had been written up in Gaetan Bélanger's blog. But what was the connection? And what about the mysterious intruder at the Blue Mountain retreat? When Dan got up to investigate, he thought Jags had been in his bedroom, when in fact he could have been outside the cottage rather than asleep in his room. But, again, what purpose would that serve? The only one Dan could think of was that Jags was trying to convince him that someone was after him. And now here was a crossbow attack, once again conveniently without witnesses.

Dan thought of Constable Pfeiffer's admonition that he'd personally pulled a dead boy out of the water off Toronto Island. He hadn't said which of the dozen islands it had been. But then he hadn't had to. They were all connected, each within a short walk of any other. At night, the island was darker than anywhere in the city. You could easily kill somebody and not be seen. The number of island residents had to be in the low hundreds, at best. If you kept your own secrets, who was there to spread them?

There was one person who might be able to shed light on Dan's enigmatic employer. He'd thought about her over the past few days, ever since meeting her, but suddenly found himself decided. He would pay a visit to Marilyn Pfeiffer and see if she had anything relevant to say.

It was drizzling when he rolled up in front of her Cabbagetown address. He sat and watched the house. Neglect was its salient feature. It stood there — withdrawn, lonely. Those were the words that came to mind as he stared at the façade, rundown and overgrown with vines. Like Jags Rohmer, she too was a recluse, he realized. He thought briefly of Darryl Hillary, yet another recluse who had hidden behind a less wealthy façade. He thought of the jumbled contents inside Marilyn's home, the disparate objects marshalled together like the favourite belongings of a dead pharaoh and placed inside a sarcophagus to accompany her into eternity.

He got out of his car and walked with a heavy tread up to the door. She answered his knock almost immediately. She didn't look surprised to see him.

"You're my son's friend," she said.

Dan didn't bother to correct her. "Dan Sharp."

"Yes, I remember. The one who works for Jags Rohmer."

"That's right," Dan replied. "I was wondering if I might have a word with you. It's actually about Jags."

She hesitated. She seemed to be pondering the question or perhaps was uncertain whether to grant him an audience without consulting her appointment book.

"You what…?"

"I'd like to ask you about Jags Rohmer," he repeated, louder this time.

"Jags? Yes, of course."

She waved him in impatiently. He followed and caught the disapproving look she gave her reflection in the mirror. What did she see: the downturned mouth and greying hair? Time and drugs had taken their toll, but she was still handsome despite the stark cheekbones, despite whatever inner turmoil she'd endured, and the eyes that had seen more than she'd intended. *This pill makes you stronger, this pill makes you sad …* She was beautiful, yet it gave her no consolation. *Too many memories*, Dan thought. The drugs hadn't dulled her past enough for her to appreciate what she still had, as opposed to what had been left behind.

She retreated to a kitchen that hadn't been remodelled in years. A shelf of tin boxes, with cups and saucers running the length of one wall. Small ceramic figurines danced above them. Dan suspected they hadn't been dusted for some time. Some would have called it cozy, charming. He called it cluttered, claustrophobic.

"Would you like coffee? Tea?"

She laughed when she saw his expression.

"Despite whatever impression you may have formed of me, I don't drink in the daytime." So demure. "I could offer you something stronger, if you prefer. I didn't think police officers drank while on duty."

"I'm not ..." he began then stopped. "Tea's fine."

"I'll put the kettle on," she said, turning.

"No rush," he said.

She turned back to him. "I'm sorry?"

He smiled. "I said there's no rush."

"Good. We'll have a nice chat then."

She went into a pantry. He heard her clanking around. When she returned, she set a teapot on the table. She plucked the kettle from the stove and brought it over, pouring carefully, as though she didn't trust her hands to be steady. She passed him a cup and looked up expectantly.

"You said you were having difficulty with Jags?"

"Not exactly," he said. "I just wondered if you might shed any light on what sort of a man he is."

She smiled. "Jags Rohmer is a man who is extremely hard to get to know. A very private man. Does that answer your question?"

Dan picked up his cup and sipped. "Would you say he's a trustworthy man?"

She looked slightly taken aback. "Goodness! If you're asking me such questions, I would say you need to get better acquainted with your boss."

"Yes, perhaps."

She scrutinized him. "What exactly are you wanting to know?"

Dan hesitated.

"Please, be frank," she said. "That's why we're here, isn't it?"

"You were his lover, weren't you?"

"Yes. It's no secret." She shrugged. "There were so many …"

Dan wondered if she meant rock stars for whom she had spread her legs or lovers in general.

"I'm trying to find out if certain things about him are true. Certain allegations about his sexual nature."

She gave him an appraising stare then looked away. Something seemed to hold her attention outside the window for a moment. Then she turned back to him. "Are you asking me if Jags Rohmer is gay? Because I can assure you that wasn't the case when I knew him."

"When was that?"

"Oh, well," she said, waving a hand in the air. Brushing aside decades, not just years. "We go back a ways. A few years, at least. How far back is hard to say." She gave him a flinty look. "I'm not as young as I look."

"Then that makes you just a little bit past thirty," he said.

"Flatterer." She laughed. "Not that I mind, of course. I'm not one of those women too modest to accept a compliment."

Or too honest to lie, Dan thought.

She took a silver case from her pocket and flashed a cigarette at him. He was surprised by how large her hands were, the fingers arthritic and swollen. Almost like a man's hands. He shook his head.

"No, thanks."

She glanced down at the coffee table. "Do you mind?"

Dan took his cue. He picked up the lighter, a monstrous pink granite piece that might have passed for a souvenir in an era of oversized cars with gigantic fins. He flicked it, leaning forward to let her catch the flame much the way he'd seen her do with her son. She inhaled and sat back, comfortable in her kingdom of memories and bric-a-brac that strangled the room like weeds.

"Now where were we?" she said, like some femme fatale waiting to pounce.

"Jags Rohmer."

"Yes." Her eyes flashed with pleasure. "My, that was a while ago. I remember the first time I saw Jags. He wasn't famous yet. He was performing at the Nuts and Bolts Club on Victoria Street. I was just a teenager, a mere child really. And Jags was just starting to become known. I remember he had a hit song back then. It was on the radio. Every time you turned it on you would hear that song. Something about blue skies and sunny days that lasted forever."

"'Summer in Mind.'"

"Yes, that was it. Good for you!" she exclaimed, as though they were teammates playing Trivial Pursuit. "He used to sing it for me. He could be quite charming company when he tried, you know."

"I got the impression your son liked him too."

She stared blankly at him, the eyes of a raccoon caught up a tree with no way back down. "Did my son tell you that?"

"More or less."

"Then perhaps you should ask him about Jags Rohmer," she said, gazing at him over a cloud of smoke. "I should hardly think he would remember Jags. He was very young at the time."

"He told me Jags was a religious man. He said you went to church together."

Her face showed disquiet, though she didn't contradict him. She took another drag, pulling her face into a grotesque mockery, a death's mask, as her skin tautened and her cheekbones showed the hollows beneath the flesh, spewing smoke like some charnel house beauty queen.

"That's a strange sort of memory. I don't know what to make of it."

"Would you say Jags was religious?"

"I really don't know what to say to that." She looked discomfited again. "I suppose everyone has something odd about them. I can't really see Jags as a religious person. He was very iconoclastic back then. He couldn't abide traditional values. But then again I didn't know everything about him."

Dan considered his next question carefully. "Were you aware of any extremes in his sexual nature?"

"Such as?"

"Do you know what the term 'gasper' refers to?"

Marilyn looked away for a moment. Dan thought she wasn't going to answer. Finally, she turned back to him. Her mouth had hardened into a thin line.

"You're referring to one of his later albums. Yes, I'm aware of the term and what it means. I never saw anything of that side of him. He was always very respectful to me." Her eyes narrowed. "Despite the times, we managed to be discreet about some things."

"Of course."

"Is there anything else?" she asked sharply.

Dan tried for an offhand smile before the next assault. "Would you say that Jags had a negative impact on your life? Is there anything you blame him for?"

Now she focused her gaze directly on him. "In what way 'negative'?" She blew a cloud of smoke at him. "Drugs, for instance? Is that what you came here to ask? Whether I'm a drug addict? And if so did Jags Rohmer get me started? Is that what you want to know?"

"I'm sorry if I ..."

She frowned and stubbed out her cigarette. "I don't think those are appropriate questions to be asking me about your employer."

Dan nodded. "I'm talking about a time long ago, in the past, when he might have been a different person than he is today."

"We were all different people in the past," she said emphatically. "You're still young. You have no idea what I'm talking about." She looked up at him. "For the record, I don't blame Jags Rohmer for anything. If you don't have any relevant questions for me, I think you should leave."

Dan stood. She followed him to the door. He held out his hand, expecting her to shake it and close the door behind him. Instead, she paused.

"Do you know, Mr. Sharp, what my son thinks of me?"

She watched him closely, a gambler waiting for the turn of a card that will make or break her. A flash of red or a streak of black. Breath held back, barely daring to hope. The longing was almost tangible.

"He seems to think very highly of you."

"Is that so?"

"I'm sure it is."

She shook her head. Not the right card after all. "I don't think it's true, for what it's worth."

"Why would he not think highly of you?"

She smiled ruefully, perhaps the first genuine expression he'd seen on her face since he arrived.

"I was a bad mother, Mr. Sharp. A very bad mother. I'm sure he blames me for a lot of things."

It was her refrain, Dan realized. She'd said as much already. Even her self-professed failures made her special, a cut above other mothers, famous or not: *No one has failed as spectacularly as I. No one could be so sad and miserable as I.*

Dan smiled. "It's what children do."

She contemplated this. "Perhaps."

"If it's any consolation, he's never said anything negative about you to me."

"Thank you," she said simply. "I appreciate that."

"Thank you for your time," Dan said.

"I'm sorry I couldn't be of help."

She looked relieved as he made his way out the door.

TWENTY-FIVE

Ladybug, Ladybug

Ordinarily, the fire on Symes Road would have been classified as a three-alarm blaze. The call that came in to emergency at 1:13 a.m. on Friday, September 12, should have resulted in a simple designation that would ensure a basic response unit of some twelve vehicles. Instead, it was classified as a "one-alarm probable." Meaning there might or might not be a fire.

The exact classification of a blaze is never a precise thing. Fire fighters will tell you it depends partly on location, with the number of alarms indicating the required level of response. Larger alarms mean a greater response. Once a fire is confirmed, additional units such as ladder trucks, ambulances, and even civilian cars for various officials may be dispatched. Each alarm "upgrade" could mean as many as four or more additional vehicles being sent.

Precise or not, contemporary classifications are a far cry from early fire fighting efforts, which relied on church bells and watchtowers to ring out the alarm. Once alerted, fire fighters would scan the horizon for smoke in an effort to locate the blaze. As the system progressed, it gained in sophistication. Bell ringing grew to utilize a system of codes indicating direction or even the precise district where a fire was occurring. In 1852, Boston became the first city to employ a telegraph alarm system, greatly speeding response time and increasing efficiency.

The accuracy of an alert is also tied to eyewitness description, though not always wisely. The first call to Fire Station 423 on Keele Street came from a handful of drunken teenagers stumbling from one party to another. Initially unable to agree on what they were seeing, they took cellphone photographs of the flames tickling the second floor windows and spurting through the roofline for nearly a quarter of an hour before deciding that it might in fact be an actual fire and not "some fucking awesome rave" replete with lights and strobes. Finally, after another minute spent arguing over whose cellphone to use, the call was made.

"Uh, yeah, we think there might be a fire?"

There was no wind that evening and it had rained earlier, so the event was at first sight less dramatic than it might have been had the wind spread it faster and more conspicuously. What was also not clear was that the entire inside of the building was already being consumed. Which was why the fire began jumping from roof to roof less than thirty minutes after it began.

The first engine arrived on the scene at 1:19 a.m., along with a quickly swelling crowd of young people, thanks to a series of cellular and text messages sent by the teenagers to their friends in anticipation of a little excitement prior to making the emergency call. The fire department arrived to discover a blaze spreading much faster than normal. It was the first indication an arsonist was at work.

There was no question of gaining entry into the building. The north wall began to collapse within minutes of the fire department's arrival. Additional fire fighting units were quickly dispatched and neighbouring stations roused to help in the battle. The delay in designating the fire as being serious was one of the complications that contributed to the extent of the damage. It was nearly 6:00 a.m. before the blaze was sufficiently under control and a suggestion to evacuate the vicinity no longer considered necessary. By then the warehouse and three neighbouring buildings had been destroyed.

By afternoon the following day, forensics investigators were able to conclude that at least one life had been lost. The body was so thoroughly incinerated that they were unable to make even a cursory guess as to the age or sex of the victim. A number of beer bottles and cans were subsequently found in the area where the fire was believed to have started, so the initial suspicion of a rave that got out of hand was still being considered. According to the property owners, the building had been unoccupied pending renovation. In the rush to get the premises ready, a low-cost decorating company was hired to strip and paint all the interior walls. Large quantities of paint strippers, thinners, and turpentine had been imported for the job, which was to have begun Monday, leaving the place filled with a considerable amount of incendiary material.

The question of insurance fraud was considered unlikely since the owners had been doing well with long-term rentals. The investigators leaned toward a decision of accidental combustion, partly as a result of numerous reports of teenage intruders partying on the grounds. Unknown to the public, and unreported in the press till many weeks later, a disagreement erupted between the members of the investigating committee on whether to classify the blaze as arson or accident. The death made it tricky, as this put the onus on the building's owners to prove that every precaution had been taken to prevent trespassers from entering the premises.

The possibility of an arsonist-at-large quickly spread fear in the surrounding neighbourhood, where several of the city's notorious garage fires had occurred earlier in the summer. The worry was that the arsonist had been using the garages for practice till he got his technique down, and was now en route to bigger and brighter things.

None of this would particularly have interested Dan, except for a midnight phone call from Germ suggesting the fire might be of importance to the Bélanger case. Once again Dan high-tailed it over to Germ's bunker.

"It was an alternate site," Germ explained. "We almost didn't set this one up. It was a last-minute thing. Velvet Blue decided it was worthwhile, so there you are. No one showed up on camera before, but two days ago Little Boy Blue entered the premises."

"Wait a minute! Are you telling me that Little Boy Blue was at that warehouse?"

"Dude, that's what I'm saying."

Dan thought back. Two days ago was when he had discovered Gaetan Bélanger at the abandoned retirement home. If Bélanger had wanted to find an alternate site to hide, he would have chosen his alter-ego to make an appearance. That way, if anyone saw him, it would be easy to back out with no one the wiser as to his true identity.

Germ showed Dan the tape. He watched as the boy in a cap and blazer approached with a knapsack on his back. It was Gaetan Bélanger. He was talking on a cellphone and looking over his shoulder. Then he simply turned the corner and went inside, disappearing from the screen.

"Do me a favour," Dan told him. "I want you to check all your cameras in the vicinity and see if you can find him on the same site the day of the fire. Then I want you to look for a police officer or anyone who even looks like a cop checking out the warehouse any time before that."

Germ gave him a look. "As long as you're not in a rush. That could be hours of recordings."

"Take your time. This needs to be done right."

Dan was in his car, traffic whizzing by. He got on the phone to Ed Burch.

"Another late-night call," Ed said. "Should I be worried?"

"Maybe."

"Well, I've been meaning to call you anyway."

"I beat you to it. Not with the best news, I'm afraid."

"Hit me."

Dan drew a breath. "Do you know about the fire at the empty warehouse south of St. Clair?"

"Possible arson, yeah, I've been hearing about it. Someone died, I heard."

"Yeah. Someone did."

Dan let the pause sink in.

Ed caught his tone. "Do you think you know who it was?"

"Maybe," Dan said. "I don't think we're going to like what we find out about the victim."

Ed's voice was cautious. "Are you thinking it might have something to do with Gaetan Bélanger?"

"It's my guess it does."

"Why?"

"Ask a leading question …"

He proceeded to tell Ed about his confrontation at the retirement home and the break-in at Germ's studio.

Ed took a deep breath. "You should have told me sooner, Daniel."

Dan heard the worry in his voice.

"Ed, it wasn't my break-in to report."

"I'm not talking about the break-in." There was an edge to his voice. "I don't like this. Argue what you will, this is a murder investigation. You had a duty to disclose what you know."

"I still don't know anything for sure."

"I'll let that go for now, but if you're right then this is another murder. You're getting in way too deep here. How can you even be sure that Pfeiffer was behind the break-in at your source's studio?"

"Again, there's no proof, Ed, but he was following me around and getting antsy about not having contact with my sources."

"But that still doesn't mean it was him."

"Not in itself. But consider that what Pfeiffer wanted was access to tapes showing the possible hideout of Gaetan Bélanger. Then consider that he destroyed the tapes. Two days later, a fatal fire breaks out in one of the locations targeted by the cameras set up courtesy of my source. To my mind, there's only one way that adds up. Pfeiffer has to be behind it."

Ed was thinking this one over. "You're right. There are too many coincidences there for me to swallow," he said at last.

"That's what I thought. Question is, what do we do about it now?"

Ed's voice was gloomy. "I'll have to call the chief about this. Sit tight. Chances are you're going to receive a call in the next couple of hours, if I can wake anybody up. I'll try to keep you out of this as much as I can, but I know they're not going to like it."

"Do what you can, Ed. I trust you."

"I hope you don't regret saying that, Danny."

When Dan arrived home he reluctantly woke Trevor. His boyfriend sat up and blinked at the light, elf-like, a boy awakened on Christmas morning.

Trevor's face fell as Dan explained what had been happening. "What can we expect?"

"At the very least I'm going to get a rap on the knuckles for withholding information."

"And at worst?"

Dan sighed. "Things could get difficult."

Trevor nodded. "Is this the point where you tell me to start worrying?"

"I doubt it will help," Dan said. "But this is the point where I would normally decide to have a very strong drink."

"I could probably use one, too. Do you think Ked would mind?"

"Not this time. Get dressed and meet me in the kitchen."

TWENTY-SIX

Three Blind Mice

DAN'S PHONE RANG a little past 4:00 a.m. It was Ed calling to tell him to be at police headquarters in an hour. When he finished the call, Dan saw Trevor watching him with worried eyes.

"Don't worry. Everything's all right."

"Should I come with you?"

"No point. I could be there a long time and I doubt they'd allow you in with me."

A thin drizzle began to pelt his car windows when he drove off. August's heat had given way to September's cool wet. This time, when he arrived Dan was ushered directly to the chief's office. The room was stark, austere — red trim, plain cabinetry — unlike the cushy showroom of the previous month. Inside were the chief, Detective Danes, and Ed Burch. Constable Pfeiffer, Dan noted, was absent. That was good news then. He assumed they wanted to hear Dan's accusations before confronting Pfeiffer.

A sober-looking chief of police glanced up mid-sentence. Danes indicated a seat for Dan on the far side of the table.

The chief turned to the recorder. "Please note that Mr. Daniel Sharp has joined us. The time is 5:21 a.m."

Dan watched the chief sift listlessly through a couple of files on the table before continuing.

"The body is that of a Caucasian male. Probable age range from sixteen to twenty-four. That's all we know for now, apart from certain physical evidence found at the scene indicating a possible identity …"

He paused and looked over at Detective Danes, a grim set to his face. "Anything?"

"We're trying to track down the dental records."

"Nothing on file with the Quebec police?" the chief asked. He wiped his eyes with his hand. He looked tired.

"No, sir. They wouldn't have his dental records," Danes offered reluctantly, as though unwilling to contradict his boss.

"Oh, of course. Excuse me, Karl. I'm not thinking straight."

The chief continued to look through his report. Time ticked by. Dan glanced across the table at Ed, whose eyes shifted to Dan and then away. Something wasn't adding up here. It took a lot for his ex-boss to be made uncomfortable by what went on around him.

The chief looked at Dan. His eyes took him in, assessed him quickly then retreated to his files. The Grim Reaper double-checking a certain date in his appointment book, rendered in a clear, hard script.

"Thank you for coming in, Dan. Ed called a few hours ago to update me on some of your activities in the past week. I understand you had some contact with the murder suspect Gaetan Bélanger."

"I can't say for sure that it was —"

The chief put up a hand and looked directly at him. "I want clear answers here. If you don't cooperate, I'm ready to charge you with obstructing justice at the very least, and maybe with aiding and abetting a homicide."

He paused to let this sink in.

Ed coughed. "Please just answer the chief's questions, Daniel."

Dan felt ambushed. Too late, he understood Ed's discomfort. "I was in touch with someone I believe may have been Gaetan Bélanger."

The chief looked up wearily. "When?"

"Wednesday evening, between five and six."

"From our point of view, it would have been helpful if you had come to us with this information earlier, but that isn't important now. What I'd like to know is what you were doing there."

"First off," Dan said, "I want to make clear that I came across Gaetan — if it was Gaetan — by accident."

The chief's eyes narrowed.

"I was searching for someone else, but I won't go into that now."

He described his confrontation with the teenage killer.

"Was this at the site of last night's fire?"

"No," Dan said. He gave the address of the retirement home.

The chief made a note and gave an order to send men over to the site.

"Clearly, I spooked him," Dan continued. "He'd be very unlikely to return there once his identity was blown."

"You couldn't know that for sure. You're guessing …"

"It was a likely conclusion, but yes, I guessed."

"And you think he ended up at" — the chief looked down to check his records — "at this other address, whatever it was."

"Thirty-two Symes Road, sir," Danes put in.

"Thirty-two Symes Road. Thank you, Karl." He looked at Dan again. "How did you know to look for him at this location?"

Dan shook his head. "I didn't know. As I said, I was looking for someone else."

"All right, all right." The chief shook his head impatiently. The colour in his cheeks said he was about to blow a fuse. "Whoever it was you were looking for …"

"My source had a CCTV set up there."

The chief's eyebrows crawled up his forehead like caterpillars. Just then a knock came at the door. A junior officer entered and handed the chief another file. He looked at it briefly and set it aside.

"Thank you, Constable."

"Sir."

The junior officer left.

Dan's impatience was getting the better of him. "What have you learned about the fire? It was arson, wasn't it?"

The chief shot an angry glance at him. "I realize we asked your assistance on this case, but I'm sure you understand there are things we can't reveal to you. Certain people we have under investigation, for instance."

"And others you're protecting for their co-operation."

The chief's face was a stone. Whatever target Dan's comment may have hit, he was too practised to give anything away.

"That's not at issue here."

Dan returned his stare. "It might be. One of my sources had an unwelcome visitor the night before last. That visitor wore a mask. He forced my source to divulge information about his camera set-ups."

A desk lamp reflected in the chief's glasses. An acetylene glare. Blankness had taken over his features.

"An unidentifiable intruder made your source divulge information relating to the case? Is that what you're saying? Information we asked for your assistance in obtaining, but which you refused to offer?"

Dan clenched his teeth. "He forced my source to show him footage of several derelict buildings, including the warehouse, in the days prior to the fire. My belief is that the intruder was a police officer. I think it was Pfeiffer. Whether or not he was acting under official orders during any of this is impossible to guess."

Ed looked stricken. "Daniel, do you realize what you're saying?"

"Of course I do, Ed. Someone got to my sources and now a fire kills a suspect in a murder investigation in a location pinpointed by my sources. But it's not me who should be telling you this. Why don't you ask Pfeiffer?"

The chief's face fell. "First of all, there is nothing to indicate that any murder suspect died in that fire." A dark hue glossed his features as he struggled to contain himself. "Second, you need to accept that I can tell you only so much. Suffice to say that finding a serial killer in the city has been my top priority. I invested my officers with the power to do whatever it took to capture Bélanger. I cannot and will not tell you exactly what that entailed, because it is none of your fucking business. In the meantime —"

"How else would someone have known where Bélanger was?" Dan interrupted.

A hand pounded the desktop. "Because we already had that address under investigation. Constable Pfeiffer informed me of his intentions to look into the matter personally."

Dan took a breath. Pfeiffer had been ahead of him all along. He knew he shouldn't be surprised.

"In the meantime," the chief continued, "I will look into your ridiculous allegations."

"I doubt you'll find anything." Dan glowered. The fact that Pfeiffer had already admitted to knowing Bélanger's new location didn't change the possibility that he'd set the fire. "Do you have any more questions for me? Or are you going to charge me with anything? Because if not, I have better things to do than listen to this whitewash."

The chief sucked air between his teeth. His face turned bright red.

Dan looked him straight in the face. "Why don't you get Pfeiffer in here? I'm sure he'll have a lot to say about this matter."

The chief swivelled his chair till he faced Dan. His eyes were the eyes of a sharpshooter. "Daniel, the reason Constable Pfeiffer isn't here is because he perished in that fire."

Dan felt the wind taken out of him.

The chief glared at him. He looked down at the file the junior officer had placed in front of him after Dan came in.

Dan stood. "I'm very sorry to hear that, but what was he doing there?"

The chief put a hand to his forehead. "I won't discuss the reasons for that with you."

Dan waited.

The chief nodded. "If you have anything else to add to this inquiry then you had better come out with it now. Otherwise, I am ordering you to stay as far away from this investigation as you can possibly get. Go to Cuba, if you need to. Go to the fucking moon. But if you meddle any further from this moment on, I will have you up on charges so fast it will make your head spin. On top of that, your sources will be subpoenaed and their files checked."

Dan waited, a lump in his throat.

"Furthermore, as for primary sources of information protected by this or any other police or secret service, I would advise you to stay well away and stop prying. You have no idea how deep this is or what you're trying to open up here."

"You're right, I don't," Dan blurted out. "That's why I keep asking questions and keep feeling more and more frustrated with the answers I don't get."

The chief shook his head. "Get him out of here."

He turned back to his files.

The console had been rebuilt, though it now held half as many screens as it had previously. All the cameras seemed to be operative.

"I need to cue this," Germ was saying. "Help yourself to coffee."

Dan walked into the kitchen and poured himself a cup before coming back out to where Germ was working intensely.

"Here — this is what I wanted you to see," Germ said.

Dan peered at the screen. He saw the outside of a building in the dead of night. Nothing moved. The views were as static as a camera pointed at outer space.

"I had to go through hours and hours of tape." Germ looked meaningfully at Dan. "Even at fast forward — and it can't be too fast or you might miss something — it still takes a hell of a long time to watch everything."

"I appreciate it, Germ."

Dan waited, wondering what he should be looking for. Then he saw it: a brief flash that lit up the top right-hand corner of the screen and died out again. After another minute, a glow took hold and grew steadily.

"That's the first shot of the fire. Let's go backwards from there."

He tapped in a few commands. A new file began spooling on the hard drive. After a few seconds, it began to play.

"Now watch this," Germ told him. "This is about an hour before the fire began."

Dan watched as a figure approached. He had on a blue blazer and cap. As he passed, he looked directly at the camera and flashed an indignant finger.

"He knew!" Dan said.

"The little fucker was on to us the whole time."

The figure disappeared and was not seen again.

"Now, look who arrives just before the fire."

A second figure approached the warehouse, a baseball cap pulled down over his forehead. From what Dan could make out, it was Constable Pfeiffer. He entered the building and did not return. They watched until they saw the spurt of flame that signalled the fire's beginning.

"So it's true. Pfeiffer was there. He must have been caught in the first explosion. But when did Bélanger leave?"

"It's on another camera. I've got him leaving by the back door. Same get-up, blazer and everything."

He sped the recording forward. A few minutes later, a group of kids stood and watched the flames without moving.

"I take it these were the kids who discovered the fire."

"Probably," Germ said.

Dan looked at the code on the bottom of the screen. "That works with the fire department report. The call was made a little past one o'clock. The time code places the start of the fire just before one. Do they go anywhere near the place?"

"Yeah, I wondered that too. But not that I can see." Germ paused.

"What is it?" Dan asked.

"There's something bothering me about this. Something that isn't right." He thought about it a moment then shook his head. "Maybe I just need to smoke a little more dope. It'll come to me."

"Okay, keep on it."

Germ ended the playback. "That's it for this tape. The camera was destroyed not long after."

Dan stood. "Good work," he said.

"Wait. There's something else." Germ pointed to another monitor.

He fiddled with the keys, snapped ENTER, and a website swirled onscreen. They were back on Bélanger's blog again. A skull-and-crossbones flashed across the screen. The entry had been dated the previous day, one day after the fire.

"What is it?" Dan asked.

Germ looked over. "Hold on, it's coming."

A handful of words flew across the screen and vanished. Dan's eyes flew open wide. "What did it say?"

"I got Velvet Blue to translate for me," Germ said. "It says, 'Another pig got roasted tonight.'"

Dan felt a chill. He sank back in his seat, wondering if the chief of police had read this yet. "Okay," he said at last.

The phone message was jarring. At first Dan couldn't make out if it was good news or bad. Donny was keyed up to the point where he sounded out of control. He hardly ever got that way, but lately he'd changed. Whatever he'd been through had put him in a state of mind Dan rarely encountered in him. *This is so unlike him*, Dan thought. Was there nothing fixed in the world?

He scrambled to piece together the disjointed narrative. There seemed to be some biblical reference to Noah and his ark and another one about freedom. Finally, he grasped that Lester had flooded the bathtub in his family home, letting it overflow and scramming when the fire department arrived.

At least he hadn't set fire to the house, Dan thought. He'd had enough incendiary incidents to last him a lifetime, but he was relieved to hear that Lester was safely back home and that Donny had not had to get involved.

At least one person had been rescued that day.

TWENTY-SEVEN

I'm All Ears

It was going on noon. Dan debated whether to stop at Wendy's or wait and eat at home. Wendy's seemed too much of a diversion. He flipped down the glove compartment that had never held a pair of gloves, or socks either, for that matter. It occasionally became the repository for chocolate bars, but in summer that would have proved a sad liability, tithing both the chocolate and the time required to clean up the oozing mess. But perhaps a lowly granola bar lay in wait. He searched. Sadly not, in this case. Forbearance would have to be the better part of valour. Besides, there were healthier things like apples at home.

Ralph trotted out to greet him then quietly returned to the kitchen, where he spent his days lying in the sunlight that dappled the thick backdoor rug. He was nearing senior citizen status and seemed to be taking his retirement prospects seriously.

The light blinked on the answer machine. Dan pressed PLAY and a quiet voice leapt out: "Greetings, Mr. Trevor James, this is Andy from the Tile Place in Markham." A pause ensued, as though Andy had lost his train of thought from information overload. *Well, Andy, I know how that feels*, Dan thought.

The voice revived. "Mr. James, sir, your special order is ready for pick-up at our Markham office." Another pause ensued. "If you need it delivered, sir, please let us know, but we won't be able to get it to you before Monday. Uh, sorry about that."

The call clicked off. There were no more messages. Dan called to let Andy know he'd be picking up the special order for Trevor James that afternoon, to what sounded like immense relief on Andy's part.

Dan thought about how little time he'd spent with Trevor lately. Was it a reflection on the direction their relationship was taking? If so, it was his own fault, Dan knew.

In the kitchen, a square brown envelope sat propped on the kitchen table, his name scrawled across the front. He looked it over. Something about it struck him as odd. He was already getting a bad feel. No reason, just bad.

He picked it up and turned it over. There was no address and no postage stamp. In which case, it would have been hand delivered through the slot in the door. The air seemed to buzz around his head. His hands shook as he opened it. A single piece of paper, folded once, fell onto the table. He recognized the pattern immediately. There were three of them. They didn't look like fallen leaves this time.

Dan sat and stared at the photograph. *This can't be happening*, he told himself, forcing the panic deep down inside himself.

He thought of the dried pig's ears Ked sometimes brought home for Ralph. They were meant as a reward. This wasn't a reward; it was a punishment. But for what? What had he done? How had this monstrosity got in here? He looked around the room, scanning for suspects. At that moment even the furniture looked ominous, the bookshelves seemed to harbour dark secrets.

"What the fuck are you trying to tell me?" he murmured.

He cocked his ears and listened to the rest of the house. No sound. He looked over at Ralph, who seemed to be enjoying the sun more than anything else in the world at that moment.

"All good, Ralphie? Everything okay here?"

The dog thumped his tail against the floor.

"I'll take that as a 'yes.'"

He could have used one of Germ's joints. Something to dull the immediacy of life right then. He thought how there seemed to be no fixed objects in his universe these days, only satellites and asteroids rolling around in deep space and threatening to fall back on earth, their orbits failing like everything else. He thought of Domingo's injunction against Little Boy Blue: *It's like he doesn't really exist*. But someone had to have delivered this to his door. Dan thought about his current state of affairs. He felt as though he'd been out of touch with things for far too long. Maybe it was time to re-enter Earth's atmosphere and burn himself up. He was like a man at a cosmic sideshow with the carny barkers yelling at him: *Step right up, friend! Pick a gravity field, any gravity field …*

Dan thought of the nearest next best thing. He grabbed the phone and dialled Trevor's number, wanting to hear his solid, reassuring voice. That was as close to a centre of gravity as he got these days.

"Just checking in," he said, when Trevor answered. His own voice sounded thick and tight. He tried for casual, trying to force himself to believe in normal, which at that moment seemed next to impossible.

"So everything went okay with the police this morning?" Trevor was saying.

"Oh, that. Sure!" Dan had nearly forgotten what had transpired in the past twelve hours. Everything had come down to a piece of paper sitting on his kitchen table. "Nothing to worry about. How are things with you? It feels like I haven't had a moment alone with you lately."

The conversation sounded so absurd he felt Trevor would suspect something for sure.

Trevor laughed. "I didn't think you'd noticed."

"I noticed. I'm sorry I've been so busy."

"I'm feeling a little more relaxed about things these days."

The deep tones sounded soothing to Dan's ears. If only he could believe the words. "That's good," he said.

"Actually," Trevor continued, "I'm glad you called. Kendra phoned earlier. She invited us for supper tonight. I told her I'd check with you first. She's such a sweetheart."

"Supper sounds good," Dan said, still striving for something to help cement him back into the everyday. His voice was dull, wooden. "What are your plans for the rest of the day?"

"I'll be here at the house."

No! Dan wanted to scream. *Don't come back here.* Then it dawned on him. The *other* house.

Trevor went right on, oblivious. "The cabinetry looks great. You'll have to come by and see it when you have a moment. We're fitting in the new bathtub this afternoon and tiling tomorrow. We're actually a bit ahead of schedule."

"That's terrific," Dan said. "In fact that's why I was calling." *Liar!* "There was a message about a special delivery from the Tile Place. They can't get it out till Monday. I said I'd pick it up for you."

"That would be very helpful. Thanks, Dan."

Dan paused. "Oh, yeah … just one other thing. Did you leave the envelope on the kitchen table?"

"Envelope?"

"Brown manila?"

"No. It must have been Ked."

Dan's heart lurched.

"Anything important?"

"Nothing that can't wait for later," Dan said. "Don't let me keep you. What time is supper tonight?"

"Supper's at six. Ked's got a game this afternoon. He said he'd meet us there. I've got a full day too. I'll probably go straight from here, if that's all right with you."

"No, that's great. See you then." He paused. "I love you."

"I love you, too, Dan. See you tonight."

The line clicked off.

Fear returned. In an effort to avoid its grasp, Dan turned and ran smack into the banister. He lost his balance, sliding to the ground and clutching his solar plexus.

The pain was intense. He pictured Darryl Hillary's ruined face staring down at him from the meat hook. *You won't get me*, Dan declared to the unseen Bélanger. *I have far too much to live for.*

Then reason crept in. This was a threat from a sixteen-year-old. A desperate sixteen-year-old, but still, he wasn't a madman with an Uzi prowling the corridors of a high school picking off his victims. Dan simply had to avoid dark corners, not let himself get caught in places where someone could aim a crossbow or come at him with a knife. The police would catch him eventually. How long could an invisible kid steer clear of them? Rogue planets rolled around in his head until they crashed into some imaginary force field. He'd get through this, one solar system at a time.

The afternoon sun was blistering red as he headed west. He was travelling north of the city, around the Tenth Line. To Dan, it was all foreign territory up there. Everything looked the same: trees, houses, open space. No defining landmarks in a place where everything replicated itself perfectly. The outer limits. Surely he was a city boy if ever there were one.

He found the Tile Place, went in, and asked for Andy. A well-groomed, muscular young man came out beaming with confidence. Dan had expected someone soft and inefficient, someone he was prepared to feel sorry for in advance. Not this demi-god. Maybe the boy was phobic about phones. *It takes all kinds*, he thought. You could never tell about voices on phones.

Trevor had picked a plain tile, matching it with an intricate border that offset the colours nicely. Of course he would have done, Trevor was an expert. Not that Dan cared about tiles right at that moment. He just needed to focus on the small details to get through this day.

He paid Andy, smiling like a satisfied customer. Next he stacked the boxes in his trunk and headed for the highway. If he acted normal then he might feel normal. If he could feel normal then all might be normal. Or not. Tonight, he reminded himself, he was having dinner with his male lover and the mother of his child, a woman he'd never really dated, let alone married. There was going to have to be a new normal before he could claim any part of it.

In the distance, fields gleamed with giant orange bubbles, pumpkins ripening in the autumn sun. They made him think of the nursery rhyme: *Peter, Peter, pumpkin eater* ... For other kids, it had been a simple tale embodying the absurdities of childhood in a ditty straight out of *Monty Python's Flying Circus* or Doctor Seuss. For Dan it had always held ugly, sinister connotations: misogyny, imprisonment, cannibalism. Why hadn't Peter been able to keep his wife? Maybe he was gay and couldn't be bothered to fake it. Still, why put her in a pumpkin shell? Or maybe Peter was like Jack Spratt and just wasn't attracted to his wife. Far better to put her in a pumpkin shell then.

But why cut off an ear?

He zoomed past the fields, well over the speed limit. Trying hard to forget. Trying to break the sound barrier and outstrip his life, leaving it all far behind him.

Candles flickered and sucked air when Dan opened the door, before settling back into place. He felt calmer just being there. Kendra came up to him, soft and flowing. He breathed in her scent as she kissed his cheek. Subtle, like cornflowers on a summer's evening. Hers was a beauty hard to claim or pin down. It was elusive, always in motion. Her eyes carried a rare intelligence. Had he been a straight man, Dan thought, he would have fallen for her, but he never could have married her. Not simply because her Muslim family would have forbidden it, which they would, but because he would always feel outclassed by her.

He put her in a pumpkin shell ...

Trevor lined up behind Kendra for a kiss as Ked came out of the kitchen to greet him. Maybe this was the new normal.

"Mom made lamb," he announced.

"Well, aren't you spoiled," Dan said with a wink at Kendra.

Ked gave him a look. "It was for you guys, not me."

"Actually, I made it for all of you," Kendra said. "You're all my special boys."

Dan glanced around at this tastefully modern home. There were a few reminders of her Syrian upbringing, but these were trimmings on the package. She had no problem breaking practices that didn't suit her needs. She dressed from the pages of *Vogue*, readily imbibed alcohol, and ate what she pleased. Her television was poised on the W Network at all times, even when she wasn't at home. Dating and sex were at her discretion. She would not be circumscribed by tradition.

Her one reservation, the one taboo she'd been unwilling to break, had been Kedrick. Kendra's family knew nothing of his existence. It would have caused a permanent rift, she claimed. Dan felt that keeping them ignorant amounted to the same thing. *It's like Ked doesn't exist*, he thought. Kendra visited Syria every other year, letting her family believe she was upholding Islamic practice. The charade seemed not to bother her at all. In fact, it meshed perfectly with her elfin personality.

She ushered them into the dining room. The table was set with hand-woven cloth, delicate china, and gleaming crystal. Dan seldom saw her domestic side, but he knew she had one when required. Her cooking was always top of the line. He joked that she could have had the best Middle Eastern restaurant in the city, if she'd wanted. But she was a businesswoman at heart and clearly wasn't ready to give up her career.

Dishes arrived from the kitchen, bringing the scent of stewed figs, dates, apricots, almonds. Dan sipped soda and looked around the table at his family. Nothing could be allowed to threaten this, he told himself. Everything was going to be fine.

He was momentarily distracted from his thoughts. Kendra was looking at him questioningly.

"Are you with us?" she asked.

"What? I'm sorry."

"You were in La-La Land again," Trevor told him.

Kendra smiled and shook her head. "I swear sometimes he doesn't hear a thing I say."

Dan looked at her laughing face. "Sorry. What did I miss?"

"I asked how work was going. How are you managing without your regular salary?"

"Oh, that." He shrugged. "It could be better."

"I'm afraid I haven't been much help," Trevor said.

"You are a big help," Dan insisted. He turned to Kendra. "He's doing all the work on the new house single-handed. Just having him in my life is reward enough. I don't know how I managed without him."

"Ah, so sweet," Kendra said.

She caught Dan's eye and nodded to the kitchen. He excused himself and followed her.

"You've really changed, Daniel. I've never seen you so sweet on anybody before."

"I know. Is it sickening?"

"Not at all. I think it's time you opened up your heart to someone. He's a wonderful guy, so good for you."

She handed him a dish. It was the prelude to something, he could tell.

"I don't know if Ked mentioned his date to you yet …"

"Date? No, nothing."

She smiled. "He will. He's a bit shy about it, so try not to make a big deal out of it when he does."

Dan made a face. "Are you saying I make a big deal out of things?"

"No!" She swatted him with a dishtowel. "I'm just warning you not to make any jokes." She giggled. "He doesn't want you to be disappointed that he's interested in girls."

"Oh, that. We talked about it before. I thought he knew I was fine with whatever he does."

"He does. Sort of." She shrugged. "He will be. You're the centre of his universe, Dan. He does everything to please you."

"I know. It's a bit hard trying to live up to the legend some days."

"Cut it out. I don't think a kid could have a better father, frankly."

Dan smiled "If it hadn't been for your brother …"

"I know, I know. You weren't exactly my type, either. But it was a happy accident."

They went back out to the dining room.

Supper proceeded apace. Eventually, Ked brought the subject around to his upcoming date. Dan listened to his plans for taking a young lady out to a movie the following evening.

"Any questions?" Ked asked when he'd finished, as though he'd just given a term report and was expecting to be grilled.

Dan's eyes darted to Kendra then back to his son. "Just one. How old is Elizabeth?"

Please let her not be too young, Dan prayed.

"She's, um, sixteen," Ked said quietly.

"Sixteen?" Dan repeated.

Ked nodded, looking apprehensive. "Is that all right?"

"An older woman," Dan said, relieved. "Yes, it's fine. It's terrific. I hope you enjoy yourself."

Ked gave him an awkward smile. "Thanks, Dad."

Dinner resumed. Dessert was brought out on trays, silver spoons handed out, cups and saucers extended. As much as he tried to shake it, Dan's working class upbringing was never far off, always under his skin in one form or another. Yet here he was, tonight, having this very cosmopolitan dinner at an elegant dining table, eating Middle Eastern food with his teenage son, the woman who had given birth to him but whom he had never married, and his male lover. It was so far away from anything he'd been raised to expect. At times it was hard to say what was real and what a dream.

He looked across at this disparate gathering of people who were so important to him. He was filled with a sudden joy at how his life had turned out. To have all this, and love too. At times, it seemed too much. He wouldn't allow himself to think that it might be taken away from him again. He wouldn't allow himself to think about an envelope left at his front door with a threatening image of severed ears.

For a moment it seemed as though all would go well, that everything was going to be fine. It was, if not quite normal, then at least sane.

TWENTY-EIGHT

Stepping Out with My Baby

DAN STILL HADN'T MENTIONED the photograph to Trevor. He knew it wouldn't be fair to keep it to himself forever, but the Saturday night dinner had been just the thing to make him feel his life was more or less safe and secure. He clung to the fiction. Still, he knew he couldn't afford to forget the threat that had been delivered to his home.

On thinking it over, he decided to tell Ed. Predictably, Ed counselled full disclosure to the chief. Reluctantly, Dan agreed. To his surprise, the chief asked if he wanted protection. The threat was so nebulous Dan was inclined to turn him down, but agreed to having an officer in a patrol car on the street over the next few days for Ked and Trevor's sake. His man would be there that night, the chief told him.

Dan's nerves were on edge, but he managed to pass a pleasant afternoon with Trevor. It was their first uninterrupted day together since his return. Trevor had received news that morning: he'd already had an offer on his villa in BC. They made plans to celebrate later in the week. A fun evening out, perhaps Easy & The Fifth, one of Dan's favourite restaurants for when he craved a bit of conspicuous consumption. In the meantime, they spent the hours lounging and reading newspapers, legs intertwined on the sofa. A shopping trip completed the day's events.

After supper, Trevor excused himself to phone his real estate agent. The conversation sounded as though it might go on for some time. Dan looked over at Ralph, who leapt up, sensing opportunity. Dan put his leash on and they stepped outside.

In his excitement, Ralph lunged down the steps. Back in Dan's drinking days, the dog would have managed to get him off balance, enraging him. Dan kept him in check now, letting Ralph guide him around the neighbourhood. Ralph still surged forward as if they were on a treasure hunt, but Dan maintained his command. He looked, but did not see the patrol car yet.

They passed a number of down-at-heel watering holes Dan had frequented in his single days. They held no appeal for him now, so far in his past as to have belonged to another person. Cinderella before her glass slippers came on the scene.

Ralph's stride quickened along Queen Street East. With the return of the cooler weather, his energy had picked up. He seemed to enjoy his nightly walks more now.

"*Is you is or is you ain't my baby?*" Dan sang playfully under his breath, feeling more than a trifle goofy. He wondered where the hell that little ditty had sprung from, which overworked synapse had released it right then.

Passing a florist's window, he saw a disembodied face staring back, an alien self he didn't recognize. It seemed like an apparition in a horror film intended to get a rise out of the auditorium, empty but for a man and his dog walking along an abandoned street. Dan moved his arm and the reflection moved with it. The ghost within, always showing up when we least expect it.

At the next corner, he caught the headline. Bélanger had made the news again: *Martyred Cop is Killer's Fourth Victim*. Dan leaned down to read, caught Pfeiffer's name, then stood up, not wanting to read any further.

He steered Ralph toward home. He didn't want Trevor to find out. Not just yet. Dan would have to make sure the news was turned off till they went to sleep. He needed to find a way to bring up the photograph without spooking him, but that seemed a fruitless exercise. Anything further that happened would fuel Trevor's fears.

His mind drifted back to the previous night's dinner. Something was playing out at the back of his mind. Something Kendra had said was trying to catch his attention, like a spark in a windstorm. It was too distant, not near enough to grab onto. He couldn't recall it, whatever it was.

They'd just turned onto Brooklyn Avenue when Dan felt the stirrings of fear. He stopped and looked around. The street was noticeably darker than the rest, but that wasn't it. Ralph gazed at him curiously. Dan listened, but heard nothing unusual. Cars whizzing past on the pavement; the wind blowing in the branches above. Still, something was telling him to be wary. *Watch out*, it said.

"Do you feel it, Ralphie? Is something odd happening?"

His cell beeped. The display showed a call from Germ. He'd check his messages when he got home. For now, the hair was standing up on his neck like a werewolf with a full moon eclipse coming on.

They continued up the street, with Dan throwing occasional glances over his shoulder. Nothing stirred. Nothing moved. Paranoia was striking a home run all by itself. At the intersection, he stopped and looked back. He had a clear view of the entire block. Nothing.

By the time they returned Dan was sweating. Still no patrol car. Let off the leash, Ralph bounded for his water dish. Dan looked for Trevor. No sign. Ked should have been back by now, too. The house was silent. It was odd.

Just then he heard splashing above. He slipped up the stairs and peeked around the bathroom door. Dan peeled off his clothes and slid into the shower. Trevor grinned at him through the steam like a gremlin.

Making love in water was one of Dan's few kinks, but one not so odd as to label him damaged. He felt free to indulge. They had just begun to kiss, erections jammed together against their thighs, when they heard Ralph making a fuss downstairs.

"Must be Ked," Dan said, cocking an ear to listen through the running stream.

The barking continued. If it had been Ked, Ralph would have settled down as soon as he stepped in the door. But Ralph seemed to think it urgent, whatever it was.

"It's probably just a raccoon," Trevor said. "He'll stop in a moment."

He didn't. In fact, his racket grew louder. Dan shook his head. "I'd better go look."

He towelled himself off briskly and threw on a robe. Ralph's uproar continued even after he'd reached the bottom landing. Maybe the officer on patrol had been told to introduce himself.

"This better be good, Ralphie," Dan said, heading for the door.

At first, nothing registered. Ralph stood, hackles raised, staring out at the backyard. Then it hit him. Flashing lights, the revolving strobes of an emergency vehicle. What was it doing in his backyard?

What he saw didn't make sense at first. It wasn't an emergency vehicle. It was his garage engulfed in silent, eerie flames. Inside the house, there was no corresponding soundtrack, nothing to tell him the fire was real. He started to open the doors then checked himself.

Somewhere out there was a killer waiting for him to show himself.

"Is everything all right?" Trevor called from upstairs.

Footsteps pounded on the stairs. Trevor came up behind him, dripping and tying his sash. He looked out at the blaze.

"Oh, no," he said softly.

Ten minutes earlier all had been peaceful. Now the living room was awash in reflected flames.

Dan lunged for the drapes, yanking them across. "Keep out of sight," he commanded. "There could be someone outside with a gun."

He put in the 911 call under Trevor's watchful eyes.

"Shouldn't we do something to stop it?" Trevor asked.

Dan shook his head. "We're safer in here."

"What's happening, Dan? This is crazy. Who would be out there with a gun?"

Dan went around to the kitchen and peered through the window. A figure stood in the driveway staring at the flames. For a moment, Dan thought it was Little Boy Blue. Then he caught the profile, the longish hair.

It was his son.

"No!"

He yanked open the doors and called out. Ked turned to him.

"Stay inside!" Dan told Trevor.

He dashed down the steps, looking around crazily in an attempt to see whoever might be taking aim at him or Ked.

"Ked!" he yelled again. "Get down!"

His son looked at him as though he were deranged. Dan tackled him and brought him to the ground just as a siren screamed in the distance.

"Keep your head down!" he yelled, trying to cover his son's body with his own.

They lay there in a confused pile, getting up only after the police car stopped right beside them in the driveway. An officer herded them both into the vehicle, closing the door and reassuring them they were safe.

"Dad…?"

"Where were you?" Dan demanded. "What the hell were you doing?"

Ked looked at him in confusion. "Dad, I'm sorry …"

Dan felt tears stinging his cheeks. He reached out and put an arm around his son. "I was worried."

"What happened to the garage?"

Dan waited to catch his breath before continuing. "Someone set it on fire. I don't know who." He took another breath. "Where were you? Why were you out so late?"

"I told you …" Ked began.

"Told me what?" Dan felt himself getting riled again. "You never said you'd be home late. I didn't know what to think."

Ked huffed. "Dad, I told you yesterday at dinner. I was going out with Elizabeth tonight. We went to a movie."

Dan smacked his forehead. The date Ked had told him about.

His son was watching him intently. "Dad, I think you're cracking up or something. It's like you don't listen to me."

Dan shifted a mop of hair from his son's forehead. "You're right. I listen, but I don't hear you. You did tell me about your date. I'm sorry."

The officer was on the radio, giving an update on the situation. Dan remembered the call from Germ. He checked his cell: *Mayday, dude! You're not going to believe what I found. Can you come over tonight? It's urgent.*

He checked the time: just before ten. He sent back a reply: *Be there by midnight.*

The officer turned and took Dan's statement before allowing him to go back into his house.

"I would advise for your safety and peace of mind not to stay here tonight, sir," he advised. "Have you got a place to go?"

"Yes." Dan nodded. "We've got a place to go."

They went back inside together. Trevor offered him a glass of whiskey and ice. Dan took it gratefully then phoned Kendra and made arrangements for Ked and Trevor to come over.

Ked shot him a look. "What about you? Where will you go?"

"I'll drive you and Trevor over to your Mom's. I have to go somewhere, but I'll be back tonight."

Ked's dark eyes looked at him accusingly. "Where are you going?"

"I'll be fine. Go up and pack whatever you need. Make it for a few days, all right?"

Ked grabbed his arm. The grip was surprisingly strong. "Dad? Please don't get killed."

"It's all right. I promise not to get hurt or killed or anything."

Ked went up to pack. Dan walked across to the window and stared out at the darkened street. Somewhere out there, the Bogey Man lay in wait.

"When I saw it I couldn't believe it. I said to myself, something isn't right here. But it took me a while to piece it all together."

This was the new Germ talking. Dan had never seen him so animated. Maybe he'd run out of his supply of weed and the real Germ — nervous, gritty, and talking at hyperspeed — had emerged

"Whoa, whoa," Dan said. "Slow down a bit. What are we talking about?"

"Sequence of events, man. We're talking about the sequence of events. Remember I told you something was out of sorts with the video?"

"Yes."

"Well, it wasn't just one tape. I played the two tapes back to back and I finally figured out what it was."

Dan waited and watched as he scrolled through the footage.

"We had two cameras on this site, one in the back as well as the one in the front."

Dan nodded. "Yeah, I remember."

"So there's this, which you saw yesterday ..."

Dan watched the clip of Little Boy Blue arriving and flashing his finger at the screen.

"That was an hour before," Germ said. "Now here's the other camera."

He scrolled through a second clip. They watched as the same figure emerged from the back of the building and stood in the shadows then left the frame. Germ let the footage keep rolling.

"What am I looking for?" Dan asked.

"It's coming."

They waited. Eventually, they saw it: the spurt of flame that signalled the start of the fire.

Dan sat back. "I'm confused."

"I was too."

"Oh," Dan said, things finally dawning on him.

"I told you you weren't going to like it."

Dan put a hand to his forehead, trying to accept what he'd just seen. "How does this work? A boy arrives by the front door then leaves again by the back door ..."

"Long before the fire starts."

"If no one was there then who killed Pfeiffer?"

"Exactly, dude!"

"So there were two of them after all?"

Germ nodded. "Had to be. It's truly creepy and just the sort of thing you'd expect in a really nasty horror film. They knew about the front door camera, but they didn't see the one at the back door."

Dan thought of the empty room in the retirement home, the hair products lining the bathroom sink, the towel, the French science fiction reading matter. The camera hidden inside the home. There were two of them, always switching disguises, each similar enough to the other to fool a security camera.

It's like he just disappears into thin air, Domingo had said.

No one can be nowhere, Dan reminded himself.

His mind was jolted back to what Kendra had said at dinner the night before, the phrase that had been jarring his memory, trying to get through to him: *I swear sometimes he doesn't hear a thing I say*. And what Ked had reiterated: *It's like you don't listen to me*. Only this time it was coming through loud and clear.

Little Boy Blue, come blow your horn.

He pulled out his phone and dialled. An answer service informed him that the caller he wanted was unavailable, but that he could press one to leave a message.

"I got the photograph," he said. "No more fires, okay? I know what you want. I'll deliver it when you give me the name I want."

He swung around and faced Germ.

"Now we wait," he said.

It was nearly morning by the time a name showed up on Gaetan Bélanger's blog. It meant nothing to Dan. He suspected it would mean nothing to anyone else.

TWENTY-NINE

Who Killed Cock Robin?

Dan was poking through the closet, pulling out clothes on hangers and holding them at arm's length as though he were considering buying them. Only nothing was in his size.

His search was quite tidy, all things considered. If he'd really been with the police and had a search warrant, as he'd claimed when he arrived at the door waving a Rogers cable TV bill without letting her look at it, then it would have been very different: books tossed from the shelves, clothes strewn across the floor, plants uprooted and the dirt spread around. Maybe even a few pillows sliced up for good measure, feathers floating in the air. If he failed to find what he wanted.

"What are you looking for?" she demanded. Her face registered shock and outrage. If she could still feel then maybe she wasn't that far gone yet.

"There was a fire. You may have heard about it on the news."

She turned a blank stare at him. It was like it hadn't touched her at all. Whatever she was on, it barely left her a mind to think and respond with. He thought for a moment she was going to ask him what "news" he was speaking of. He was tired of her spaced-out addict routine, tired of her "bad mother" excuses. Instead, she nodded.

He turned his attention back to the room. For all intents, it was a typical teenager's room. Posters on the walls, an old-fashioned wooden dresser, shelves with model airplanes, spare linen stacked on top. Bright shadows hiding dark things.

He felt her watching him.

"I heard about the fire. What has that got to do with what you're doing here at this ungodly hour? You said on the phone you had something to show me, otherwise I would never have let you in."

Dan took a breath. He'd waited till eight before phoning, and even that had taken all his patience. It was going to be hard to continue with this conversation. "I do have something to show you," he said. "Just give me a moment."

He found what he was looking for, yanked it from the hanger and laid it on the bed. "This was his?"

Knowing that it was.

"Yes. Everything in the room was his. I already told you that. I haven't changed anything since he left."

He went over to the shelf. It held a few athletic trophies, a handful of photos in frames. There was a silence as he fingered one photograph in particular.

He turned to her. "Do you mind if we have a drink first?"

He saw the corners of her mouth turn up slightly. "Yes, of course. In the kitchen."

He waited till her back was turned then he pocketed the photograph. With the frame, it barely fit inside his jacket.

They were sitting in the kitchen. Morning sunlight slanted through the blinds and lit up the room with a burnished glow. This was fall light, still rich and radiant, but no longer the full light of summer that seemed to burst open over everything it touched. A rich and possessive light, like the love of a mother for a child.

"I'm sorry for your loss, if I didn't say so earlier."

She was staring at him.

"Yes," she said in a dreamy tone. "They called yesterday. It was a shock. They told me they found his gun at the fire."

In fact, Dan thought, she looked anything but shocked. Placid, resigned. But not shocked. He wondered how long he'd have to play this cat-and-mouse game with her.

"Did he ever marry?"

She seemed to be struggling with the question, as if she had to make a special effort to retrieve the memory from some long lost corner of her mind.

"No." She shrugged. "Well, yes, briefly. But it didn't last."

"No," Dan said. "These things never do."

He watched her fingers curl around the edge of her glass. Arthritic and swollen. Manlike. She'd poured good whiskey. He was thankful for that, at least.

"Any children?"

She gave him a blank look.

"Did he have any children?"

She shook her head. "There was a little boy. He was stillborn."

Stillborn. Dan counted back. He couldn't possibly be old enough, in any case. No matter. He was pretty sure he already knew what he needed to know. It was so obvious, he couldn't see how he'd missed it.

"I'm still curious about his interest in Jags Rohmer," Dan said, leading her here and there, wondering how long till she told him the rest.

"You may be right in thinking my son had an obsession with Jags. I know I certainly did."

Past tense on both counts. He had to give her credit for playing the game well.

She was smiling, looking back in time. Being totally candid for once. The drugs, the alcohol, and maybe the importance of the situation conspired to make her let down her guard. Who knew how long it had been since she'd been completely candid about anything?

He'd looked her up on the Internet. The IMDb site for actors and directors listed her credits. If the information was to be believed, she was fifty-nine. Not so old, but it placed her in her mid-thirties when she'd had her son. Her film career had spanned a mere five years, before she'd married. Her fame was brief, apart from one long-lived flame that everyone seemed to remember. It hadn't been hard to figure out how old she was when she met Jags Rohmer.

"You weren't really from Jags' world, were you? He was from a rough and seedy counterculture, while you were well brought up, I think. A real lady."

A smiled crept over her face, the memory playing itself out.

"Yes, I was a lady. It's how I was raised. My family was quite well off. When I met Jags and entered his world, I had no idea how to behave. You have no idea what it was like to go from my world to his."

"Is that why your son blamed Jags for your addiction?"

"Did he?" She looked off now, trying to piece together the fragments of her past. "That may be true. Yes, I can see why he may have thought that."

Dan waited for her to go on. The smile had left her now. Her playful expression collapsed.

"I know I didn't blame him. I … I don't think I did, anyway." She turned to him, wanting his understanding. "You had to know the times. They were different then."

"That's what Jags said."

Her face lit up. "Did he? Yes, of course. We did such extreme things. It seemed natural to us then."

Dan waited.

She laughed again. "How could you blame someone like that?"

"That's just what I was wondering. How could anyone blame Jags Rohmer?" He shook his head, as though perplexed. "Do you know?"

Fear edged her eyes. She was fighting remarkably hard. A Herculean effort. *Impressive*, Dan thought, *even if it was just an actor's trick*. Who could say what was real and what not when your brain and your sense of morality were so fogged by drugs?

"Did you ever leave Jags with your son unattended for any length of time?"

She shook her head impatiently. “No. Never. He wasn’t even born when I knew Jags.”

Dan stared at her. She understood what she’d told him. She stood shakily.

“I think …”

“So they never actually met?”

She gripped the back of her chair and shook her head. The word came as a whisper: “No.”

She brushed her hair from her face. He waited and watched. Her expressions came and went with such rapidity. How could you ever know a woman like that?

“Does the name Gaetan Bélanger mean anything to you?”

She appeared to be trying to recollect something, gathering the thoughts from some other time. Finally, she shook her head. “No. Nothing.”

He mentioned the other name, the one posted on the website several hours earlier. Again, she shook her head. He believed her. It probably wasn’t even real.

He slid his hand inside his jacket and pulled out the photograph he’d picked up in the other room, laying it on its back. Three figures filled the frame. The first was a boy in a blue blazer: Little Boy Blue, looking at most a few years younger than he appeared today. It was remarkable. The second was a man in a police uniform. An arm lay around the boy’s shoulder. His resemblance to Constable Pfeiffer was impossible to deny. The third figure was the man who had recently become the chief of police.

Dan nodded toward the picture.

“Recognize them?”

"Of course. Why wouldn't I?" Fear clouded her handsome features. "Where did you get this?"

Dan interrupted, pointing to the boy and the man with his arm around his shoulder. "Would I be correct in thinking them father and son?"

She looked confused for a moment. Then her eyes closed. She turned her face away.

"Yes."

Her voice was dusky. The leading lady steeling herself for the dénouement, the explosive finale.

"And this man?" Dan asked, pointing to the other.

"He was … a friend of the family."

"Did he know what was going on?"

"Not at first."

Her hands were trembling. Dan waited. He didn't dare move, didn't dare breathe till it was over. You can make yourself believe almost anything, he knew.

"Some things are hard to accept, aren't they?" Dan asked. "I expect that there are some things you can't say to anybody. Not even to yourself."

She reached out and took his hand across the table. She wasn't acting now. "Then don't. Don't say it."

"It's simpler to make up the truth, isn't it? To create stories?"

Dan waited. She sobbed.

"It happened to him, too, didn't it?"

Would she be able to admit it? The eyes were withdrawn. Drugs may have been able to numb her senses, but they couldn't kill the memories.

Finally, she spoke. "Yes. It happened to him. It was my fault." The tears were falling. She looked up, focusing directly on him. Accusing the accuser. "That's what you wanted to hear, wasn't it?"

Dan nodded. "Will you come with me to the police station?" he asked.

Everything was arranged. Coffee cups sat on the table between them. All that remained was to call Jags. It would help smooth things over in case anyone was listening in, which Dan thought likely. In all probability, there would be more than one interested party waiting to hear what he was about to say.

He picked up on the first ring.

"Hey, Jags. It's Dan. Where are you?"

There was a hesitation. *It's okay, buddy*, Dan thought. *I wouldn't trust me either*.

Finally, Jags answered. "I'm at the penthouse," he said. "What did you find out? Did she tell you anything?"

Dan spoke clearly and slowly. "I'll tell you everything when we meet. I want you to meet me on the island. We need to have a little talk. Just you and me. What time works best for you?"

Jags took his time answering. He seemed to be thinking it over. *This is where it all fucks up*, Dan thought.

Then Jags spoke. "Around four o'clock should be okay. Have you got the key to my place, in case you get there first?"

"Yes, I have the key. I'll let myself in."

"Good. I'll see you there." A pause. "This better be worth it."

"It will be."

Jags hung up. Dan waited. Maybe he was just being paranoid, but you never knew. He thought he heard a very faint click on the line right before it went dead.

The island seemed to waver in the distance, that insubstantial bit of sand that had floated downstream and accumulated for hundreds of years. Did nothing stay put? Coils of mist eddied up from the dark water as he motored along the estuary between the islands, found an empty dock and leapt out. It was late enough in the season that he needn't worry about some angry cottager showing up and making a fuss. Even if they did, who cared?

Next to the dock, three children playing at being sailors in an old beached rowboat. Dan watched as they jumped in and out, pretending the sand was water and that they were drowning or swimming, whichever action seemed appropriate to their character. No one was content just being themselves these days.

He climbed up the bank, feeling the sand shift beneath his feet till he reached the sidewalk. He followed Dacotah Avenue till he came to Jags Rohmer's island retreat. It could be such a handy little place, he thought. Except for the inconvenience of getting over here and the isolation that made it a natural death trap.

He stood on the porch and looked around. All was quiet except for the drone of a plane coming in for a landing at the island airport. His cell rang. He put the phone to his ear and listened for a moment before pocketing it again. He let himself in with his key, leaving the door unlocked.

"Hello?" he called out. "It's Dan, Jags. Are you here?"

No response. *Good.*

He sat and waited. A clock ticked so loudly it began to get on his nerves. He felt jittery. So many things could go wrong. Timing was crucial. He knew they had the ferries covered. There were scanners in place on all the docks. If he came armed, they would know.

His nerves were getting the better of him. He went over to the bookshelves. He'd been too distracted to pay attention to them the last time he was here. Now he read with fascination: there were titles obscure and erudite. Here were first editions of Darwin and Freud, Dickens and Mann, political tracts that had spawned revolutions and scientific treatises that had cured previously incurable diseases. If Dan had walked into anyone else's home and found such a collection, he'd have thought it a put-on, that they'd been purchased along with the house rather than collected. But not Jags Rohmer.

Here was the source of Jags' impressive lyric-writing skills, his erudition and the range of subjects he tackled. A title caught his eye. Dan reached up to grasp a leather spine on the top shelf. It was a seventeenth-century tract on sexual psychosis, with chapters on every supposed sexual deviance, fetish, and the various sexualities once classified as "insanities."

"*The sexually insane may number in the thousands,*" Dan read. "*They are everywhere around us and are adept at hiding their unnatural urges from even the most highly trained professional. They may be hiding among your colleagues, or*" — shock and awe — "*even hidden within your own family ...*"

He turned the page on a diagram of a tall, thin man in evening dress staring at a fit young man in working garb like a mongoose studying a cobra. The irresistible will of perversion.

"*They may be known by various names: inverts, sodomists, homosexualists, paedophiles ...*"

The book was a fetishist's wet dream, an orgy of foreplay. *All that repression needed an outlet*, Dan reasoned. He placed it back on the shelf and pulled out another volume.

He'd been there half an hour when footsteps approached, crossed the porch, and entered the cottage by the front door.

Dan's phone rang again, giving him a jolt. He looked around the corner and held up a warning finger.

"Sharp."

He listened for a moment, a frown forming on his face. He hung up without a word and turned back to the new arrival.

"There's no sign of him on any of the ferries. He may have come by water taxi. We'll just have to wait."

He looked out at the mist-covered lawn, the darkness gathering under the trees.

"Will he be safe...?"

Dan shrugged.

"They promised not to shoot him."

"Oh, god, I hope not. He's all I've got left."

Dan gestured to a sofa. "Have a seat," he said.

The clock ticked menacingly. They tried not to look at one another. Dan kept his eyes peeled for an approach across the lawn. That was the way he'd come, he felt sure. He would assume there was no need to hide or slip in through the trees on either side of the cottage. Dan had promised to deliver what he wanted.

A floorboard creaked somewhere upstairs.

No. Was it possible?

They waited, but not for long. The legs appeared first, followed by the blue blazer. Dan held his breath as the figure he knew as Little Boy Blue appeared before them. Holding a crossbow cocked and ready.

For a moment, his sense of reality failed. *Rule Number Nine: The villain is never who you think it is.*

Dan felt a hand grip his own.

He's not dead, he thought, as the figure descended one step at a time.

But of course, he wasn't dead. It was Gaetan Bélanger who was dead, no matter what the papers reported about the martyrdom of a heroic police officer, the gun found beneath the badly burned body. No matter what anyone believed, it was Bélanger who'd died that night, or maybe even the day before, while Little Boy Blue had escaped via the back door, giving him just enough time to return as Constable Pfeiffer and start the fire himself, waiting till the camera feed died before slipping away unseen.

Somehow Pfeiffer had fooled them all again. He'd gotten here first. Maybe he'd been here since the night before, waiting for Jags to arrive.

They watched as a hand reached up and brushed the girlish nose, almost knocking the school cap from his head. The transformation was remarkable. Clean-shaven, with his hair combed down over his forehead, you might have mistaken him for his fourteen-year-old self, the boy in the photograph. The same boy, a decade earlier, standing with his father on one of a handful of supervised visits. Anyone else might have accepted the make-believe that this was just a schoolboy come out for a bit of truancy, casing a rock star's home while he was out. Only this was a man, not a boy.

Pfeiffer looked from one to the other of them. Rage consumed his features. He glared at Dan. "You shouldn't have done this."

"Pierre …" his mother said.

"Shut up!"

He swung the crossbow around. One arrow. Whose heart would it pierce? Whose red, red breast?

They sat there, unmoving. No one seemed to know what to do. The cellphone startled all of them. Dan feared for a moment that Pfeiffer's finger might slip accidentally. He looked to him for a sign.

"Go ahead," Pfeiffer said. "They're expecting you to answer. Just be very careful what you say."

Dan raised the phone slowly to his ear. "Sharp."

He listened for a while, not taking his eyes off Pfeiffer. "No sign yet. I'll keep my eyes open for him."

He closed the cellphone and set it back on the table.

Pfeiffer grinned. "They still don't know I'm here, do they?"

Dan shook his head. "No. You fooled them completely."

"They set up metal detectors on the ferry docks. I heard them talking about it on the phones. But I didn't bring a gun. They didn't even notice me when I walked past them."

Marilyn was nearing some sort of breaking point. She couldn't keep silent any more. "Pierre …"

He swung the arrow in her direction. "What do you want?"

"I … I'm so sorry, darling."

He sneered. "Really? Really, Mummy?"

She nodded.

"It's a bit late, but why are you sorry?"

"Oh, sweetheart. This has nothing to do with Jags Rohmer."

"Yes it does. You remember what he did. I'm going to kill him."

She shook her head. "It wasn't him."

"You're lying."

"It wasn't Jags."

"But I remember. I remember waking up in bed with the two of you. I remember what he did to me. Time after time. Coming at me. How he always insisted on going to church together afterward. How we always had to take the host because" — here his voice changed, taunting — "because he said we were sinners."

Marilyn choked back the tears. "It wasn't him. I know I told you it was him, but it wasn't."

"It was *him!*"

"Sweetheart, you never even met Jags."

The eyes were crazed, the expression contorted. "You're lying again!"

She shook her head. "No, I'm telling the truth."

"You crack whore. You wouldn't know the truth if it raped you."

Dan felt her tremble.

"She's telling the truth," Dan said.

Pfeiffer whirled on him. "You shut up!"

Marilyn pushed a strand of hair behind her ear. Dan saw the tiny hearing aid curled over the left ear. Her vanity. He wondered how long she'd had it. Maybe for years. He recalled their conversation at the house, how she'd struggled to hear him, not wanting to ask him to repeat himself. It wasn't what the killer wanted silenced, after all, but what hadn't been heard: all the cries for help. *It's like you don't listen to me.* His son's words, echoing Kendra's the night before.

The hair fell back in place. That was all. He didn't think about it again.

"It wasn't Jags," Marilyn said insistently.

"Stop saying that," Pfeiffer commanded.

"I never wanted you to know," she said. "I never wanted you to face the truth. It wasn't Jags. I'm telling the truth now. You never even met him."

Dan put his hand over hers, squeezing hard, willing her not to say it.

"It was your fa …"

The arrow struck as the word was still forming in her mouth. The force of it threw her slight figure back against the cushions.

Dan heard the gasp, the whine as Death seized the opportunity. He saw it in her eyes, wild and backsliding, as her body recognized its predicament. She shuddered once and the breath left her. It was over in less than a minute, though to Dan it seemed to take hours while the clock ticked on and on.

THIRTY

Baa Baa Black Sheep

The days thinned and blew dry again till they felt reminiscent of a true Canadian autumn. Everyone welcomed the coolness, none more so than Dan. Colours swirled in the air as the leaves changed, the world dissolving in primary hues, becoming a Tom Thompson painting for the briefest of moments. A week later they were gone, leaving a barren landscape, the circus having fled town for yet another year, the clowns and acrobats and jugglers put away with the tigers and elephants. Duty done.

Two significant birthdays were celebrated back-to-back. Ked turned fifteen and grew one step closer to manhood. The previous day, Lester turned sixteen, making him legally responsible for choosing his place of residence. Applications were pending to make Donny his legal guardian.

"They wouldn't even call me Lester," he griped of his mother and stepfather during his recent incarceration. "I told them I'm not Richard anymore. Why couldn't they understand that?"

Dan laughed softly. "How does it feel to be home?"

Lester shook his head. "Why did I ever leave?"

"Story of the world," Dan told him. "One day you'll figure it out."

He'd enrolled in a local high school, to everyone's relief. For all intents and purposes, it was as though he'd suddenly resurfaced from nowhere. *Except that no one can be nowhere*, Dan reminded himself.

They were outside on the balcony. Trevor tippled a Scotch on his knee, while Donny tilted a cigarette at the sky. Dan looked back inside the condo, where Ked and Lester hovered over a laptop on the kitchen counter. Lester's jeans were settled well down around his hips, exposing a good deal of his underwear-encased buttocks.

"Do you approve of that kind of dress?" Dan asked.

"Approve?" Donny repeated, exhaling a wreath of smoke. "No, but this is how all the other kids dress and I refuse to become a censorial parent, even step-parent. I draw the line at naked flesh in public, however."

They turned to each other and laughed.

"How quickly we grow old," Donny said.

"Amen to that," Dan agreed.

They both looked off for a moment. Ked's voice reached them from inside.

"Don't go away again, okay?" he told Lester. "You're the closest thing to a brother I have."

"I'm not going anywhere for a very long time," Lester told him. "No worries, bro."

Dan smiled. “Weren’t you concerned about being questioned for harbouring a minor?” he asked.

Donny, permanently wreathed in calm again, blew a considered exhalation of smoke and shrugged.

“Not really. His ID says he’s eighteen.”

Dan laughed then grew serious again. “So what do you think about getting him to help with the case?”

Donny frowned, the only outward sign of inner perturbation. “I don’t like it, but I’ll let you ask him. If he says no, then you have to back off. He’s out of all that now and doesn’t want to be reminded of it.”

“Agreed,” Dan said.

Donny shook his head. “A former police officer, huh?”

Dan nodded. He thought of his recent conversation with Ed Burch. Pfeiffer’s father had been the chief’s best friend when they joined the force together, and later became his right-hand man. But the branch divided, one going up the light side while the other chose the dark.

“I gather deals were made that allowed him to disappear with dignity rather than spend his life in jail,” Ed told Dan.

“Unfortunately, it didn’t stop him from doing his dirty deeds.”

“Bad cops are nothing new,” Ed said. “There are two kinds of people attracted to the uniform. The first come in as idealists. Some of them actually want to change the world.” He shrugged. “Ideals seldom last, however. Sometimes they get tempered by a more realistic outlook with time and experience. Others become soured. It’s too bad, but it happens. You see them all the time, burning with rage underneath the surface. Rogue officers. Unpleasant. Unpredictable.”

"I've met plenty of those."

"Then there are the other kind who come to the force looking for trouble. They want power and demand respect without necessarily earning it. We try to weed them out in training. Still, what it comes down to is the nature of the beast. Is it black-hearted or just weak-willed? The first type will always be trouble. The second can surprise you. You can appeal to their better natures. Let them know they can help others if they try."

Dan nodded.

"But in my experience, a rogue officer will always be a rogue officer."

"Which were you?"

"I was an idealist who hit the wall early and decided that I had joined for the wrong reasons. So I quit. Simple as that."

"Meaning you operate on principles."

Ed smiled. "Thank you for that."

It had been a telling conversation.

Dan stood side by side with Donny now, staring out across the city. His new home lay somewhere just this side of the river. He'd stopped by again the other night, placing his hand against the brick, trying to envisage a future there. The images wouldn't come. Maybe Domingo was wrong after all. The future was impossible to conjure, nothing there to scry. Time was immutable. It formed one second at a time, the present sloughing off the skin of the past. How could you read into something that didn't exist yet?

Still, he had to give her credit: she'd been right about Jags and the light that went off and on. Self-extinction. Auto-asphyxiation. That was something, at least. And then there was Little Boy Blue, who disappeared into thin air. *It's like he doesn't really exist*, she said. Perhaps he hadn't really existed for years, not since his childhood was stolen from him.

Dan had read the stats. He knew what happened to abused kids. Suicide was common; others became drug addicts or alcoholics. Others lost all interest in life, a form of non-existence that must have seemed preferable to what they had.

He looked over at Donny.

"They say there are three things necessary for sexual abuse to occur: opportunity, power, and secrecy. He had all three. First of all, he was the boy's father. On top of that, he had friends in high places. If it wasn't for Ed Burch, this would have gotten nowhere. It was the chief of police who finally agreed to name him. Unofficially, of course. It was the main reason young Pfeiffer got away with so much — the chief felt he owed him because of his father. He still can't be charged with offences that occurred before the date he was granted clemency. That can't happen."

Donny nodded sagely. "I understand." He pondered this for a second. "Just how big is this investigation going to get? Politicians, celebrities … who's next, royalty?"

"Hush your mouth," Dan told him.

When the question was put to him, and he was assured that the man who abused him would be put away for a long time, Lester agreed to identify him. The clothes he'd been wearing the night he was raped were bundled in a locker in a friend's basement. If they were still there, as he believed, forensics would be able to find physical evidence linking the man to the crime.

"Does this make me a snitch?" Lester asked Dan as they walked up the steps of the police headquarters together.

"Guess you could say that."

"Good. It's my turn to make *him* feel bad."

"Keep your mind on justice rather than revenge," Dan told him. "This is about making things right for you and making sure it doesn't happen to others."

Lester considered this. "Uncle Dan, how come you're so smart?"

Dan was glad it wasn't going to be a live identification parade, even through one-way glass. He waited, a prayer hovering on his lips as Lester looked over the photographs laid out on the desk before him. Despite Donny's trepidation about letting the boy face his past, they both knew it needed to be done. In the year Lester had spent with Donny, he'd grown from a grasping, devious adolescent into a young man with a sense of self-worth. Dan was fairly sure this wasn't going to hurt him. Rather, he suspected it would help Lester walk away from whatever hold the past had over him. Hadn't he been smart enough to realize that any chance of having a normal life with his mother was impossible as long as she stayed with the monster she had married? He might take a while getting there, Dan felt, but he knew which way the wind was blowing. No, Lester was going to help put away the man who had raped him, once and for all. And the world would be better for it.

They watched him flick over a page then glance back at it. With a look of gratification, he put his finger to the bottom of the page. It looked like an older version of Constable Pfeiffer, the father who had left his family when his son was still a baby.

"That's him."

"Are you sure?" asked the female detective.

"I am sure," Lester said, without a hint of emotion. He looked up at her and nodded.

Germ alerted Dan to the updated blog on Gaetan Bélanger's website. While Pfeiffer had added occasional contributions to the site under Bélanger's name, including his own death notice, the real Gaetan had prepped his final entry to be automatically released.

In it, he outlined his plan to kill Little Boy Blue and then himself. The taunting tone was gone. There was a sense of finality to the words.

> When you read this, I will be dead. It's time to end this torture. I am going to kill the person I thought was a friend, and then I am going to kill myself. I tried hard to avoid him, but he found me. I don't know how he did.
>
> What Father Thierry did to me was wrong, but what was done to him was worse. I don't believe in love. I don't believe in forgiveness. But I did not kill him. It was Pierre. I am going to kill Pierre then I am going to kill myself.

He wrote briefly about his tortured life, about being sent from one home to another before finally feeling he'd found a place to belong when he became an altar boy at the church where Father Thierry worked. Sadly, the feeling didn't last. It was a typical Lost Boy story, one Dan related to. After the sexual abuse, the boy grew up hating his life and everyone who tried to befriend him.

"I know I don't really have any friends," Gaetan wrote. "And I don't think I feel anything any more, but I still like Pierre, despite what he did."

Sadly, the one person he'd trusted turned out to be his worst enemy. He probably hadn't once been allowed to choose his own fate in his short life, Dan reflected.

Domingo was beside him while he read the entry. They were discussing their own pasts, how they'd both suffered through their familial relationships.

"Yet we grew up to be decent human beings," Domingo said. She looked Dan in the eye. "We were lucky, of course. We still have the capacity to love and trust."

Dan nodded.

"Even though we like to joke about our early sexual proclivities, I sometimes wonder if those urges were because of the people we missed out on building relationships with."

"How so?"

"My father left home when I was young. My mother didn't want me, so I found someone who did. I just wonder if your urge to have sex with older men as a teenager was some way of making up for your father's drinking, for his abandoning you emotionally."

Dan shrugged. "You may be right. To tell you the truth, I don't worry about it now. I like who I am."

She looked at him. "Good. That's important. You and I are survivors. We know who we are and what matters to us. What matters is today, not yesterday."

"It's the Gaetan Bélangers of the world we have to worry about," Dan agreed. "I just wish …"

She waited. "What, honey?"

Dan drew a breath. "I just wish he would have talked to me that day. Maybe I could have said something to change his mind. Are there people who are past help? Too far gone for hope?"

Domingo shrugged. "No one can be nowhere."

EPILOGUE:

Unhappy Endings

JAGS DROPPED BY. He wore a linen suit and casual slacks. White cotton. Deliberately disobeying the fall fashion injunctive: no whites after Labour Day. Perhaps he thought the seasons stood still for him too.

Dan listened as he explained how he wanted to take him on permanently. Thanks to the interest stirred by his book, Jags had a new recording contract in the works. That meant studio time and eventually a tour. It could be worldwide if the response was big enough.

"But what would I do for you?" Dan asked. "You don't need me to keep you safe any more."

"Maybe I just like having you around. I still need someone to tell me what's what."

Dan leaned back in his chair, thought briefly of touring with a rock band, backstage passes, visas, vetting the press. "It's not for me," he said.

Jags reacted predictably, offering him more money.

"Nah," Dan said. "Besides, I don't like feeling that I can be bought. I'm still a puritan about some things. A little struggle is good for the soul. Money can't buy happiness."

"No, but it can get you a really nice Porsche Carrera."

Dan waited.

"I'll tell you a secret," Jags said. "I'm sick of my life, Dan. I just don't know what else to be."

"Why not go away for a while? Somewhere they don't know who you are."

"Hey! There's no such place. I'll break your bones if you say there is."

Dan laughed.

"You know what they say: tough guys don't dance. I ain't moving anywhere. Besides, I have to finish the recording. I've got at least one more great one inside me. I can feel it."

"I hope that gives you reason to stay sober," Dan said. "If you do, you could be back on top in no time."

Jags snorted. "Yeah, for a year or two. You know what these entertainment industry assholes are like. When you're up they offer you the moon, but when you're down they can't remember your name or whether you ever existed."

"I don't see you being that low on the totem pole."

"Don't fool yourself. It's money we're talking about, not fame or artistic reputation. If I can't make someone a buck, I'm as good as dead."

They hadn't really discussed the events of the previous few weeks. Dan thought they weren't going to when Jags suddenly mentioned Pfeiffer.

"It was that thing about making him take the host that really got me, you know? I can't say I've never been inside a church, but I can guarantee you I've never taken the host with anybody. I'm a devout Jew, for god's sakes."

Dan thought for a moment. "That's not what your book said."

Jags laughed. "Of course not. You think my rock-and-roll readers want to hear I'm a man of spirit?"

"So that story about growing up in smalltown Ontario wasn't true?"

"I was born on a kibbutz in Israel. Both my parents lived and died there. I have no family in Canada. The only part of my past I still have is a picture of them at their wedding."

Dan pondered this. "Maybe you should tell the truth next time. That's far more colourful than saying you were raised in a middle-class home in Belleville."

"Colour I don't need at this point in my life."

The house was finished. Dan stood by the window in the newly completed sunroom. The place was amazingly still and quiet. It almost seemed like a dream home. But then that was what it was intended to be.

Two coffee mugs sat on the table. Dan's was empty, Trevor's half-full. They'd been up all night. Dan felt the fatigue.

He glanced at Trevor over the horizon of the tabletop, as though it represented the border of a possible but unimagined world, something beyond the ordinary, everyday world that confined and defined. He felt as if he were standing at the edge of the sea, trying to imagine what lay over the horizon, away from this place where everything ended.

He'd sent Ked off to his mother's again. Weekends were convenient for serious discussions like this. Ked would be heartbroken, he knew. There was nothing he could do about that. It was his own heart he should have been guarding.

Dan shook his head. "I'm not trying to make you feel guilty, if that's what you think."

Trevor's brow furrowed. "I'd never think you would resort to emotional blackmail." He paused. "I just wish you'd give it a chance. Live here for a while and see how it feels."

"This was supposed to be our home. I can't live here without you."

"You could try it for a while."

Dan looked down the length of the house then back at Trevor. He shrugged. "My heart won't be in it. Besides, I can't afford the mortgage. I just realized I'm not cut out to be anybody's bodyguard. I've got to go back to my routine of finding deadbeat dads and other scum."

"You'll make money. You're good at what you do."

Dan looked off again. "I know."

Trevor searched for the words that would inevitably cut the cord between them. "I don't want to be the one to drag everyone down. You and Ked have a great life here in the city. It suits you both far more than you know."

"We could live apart. I'd fly out to see you on the weekends."

Trevor smiled sadly. "I can't have you part-time, Dan. I couldn't do that. And it wouldn't solve anything. I don't belong here. You have to let me go."

Dan saw it now, how Trevor was like a caged bird beating its wings against the bars, trying to remain tranquil, but all the while terrified and wanting to be free.

"I need to go back to my forest, my trees. Joe's ashes."

"When?"

"Soon. But if you want me to leave right away —"

"I wouldn't dream of it."

Trevor inclined his head. "It's got to be soon. No use dragging it out. This will be hard on both of us. Not to mention Ked. Your son and I have grown very fond of one another."

"Ked's pretty adaptable. And I'll get along. The one I worry about is Ralph. He doesn't understand these things."

He thought back to his meeting with Domingo at the restaurant, how she'd squeezed his hands and looked into his eyes. *You don't need me to tell you*, she'd said. *You already know how it will go*. Was it pathetic or amazing to think that he had known all along and still denied it? He'd been too dependent on the dream, the illusion that he and Trevor had a chance at making it work. Because he saw now they never had. Not really. Not because the love wasn't real or the need couldn't bind them together, but because other currents held sway. Some seed planted in both of them had been destined to sprout at this moment and drive them apart. Not the love that conquers, but the fear that divides. Dan felt all the security and serenity he'd been nurturing over the past year ebbing away. It would never return.

"In any case, the market is pretty good right now. My agent said she won't have trouble selling a 'beautiful, newly renovated home in fabulous, trendy Corktown.' I'll make sure you get some of the proceeds, of course."

Trevor shook his head. "I won't take a cent from you."

"But I want you to have it."

"I can't take it."

"You could always give it away to the animal rescue shelter."

Trevor smiled. "You can do that, if you like. I won't take your money."

Dan watched him, wondering what he'd miss most: the gentle smile, the eyes that crinkled softly around the edges, or the deep, confident voice that hid so many fears and insecurities.

"So that's it then? Is there nothing I can say to make you change your mind?"

"I wish there was. I'm just too fragile to fit into your life. You won't be content till you've solved everyone's problems and put everything in its place. I would just worry us all to death and end up making you hate me. I'll still worry about you, for that matter. I'm sorry."

Dan shook his head. "Don't be sorry. It had to happen, sooner or later. Better to happen before any more damage is done."

"Yes."

Rule Number Ten: The hero can never go home again.

Silence took hold for a moment.

This is it, Dan thought. The ending. Finality. Everything stops here, like the last notes of a composer of genius squeezing out a few more drops of greatness on his deathbed, but one who has revealed himself mortal after all. He walked over to the table, cautious, not trusting things around him to remain intact, including the table and chairs. He sat and reality asserted itself, the laws of physics resuming their normal functioning, barely noticed by anyone. He looked over at Trevor, who somehow had never looked more beautiful, so glowingly right, despite the early hour and their mutual fatigue.

Dan recalled the first time they slept together, in Trevor's villa on his island sanctuary. He remembered the shape of those early tentative feelings: hesitant and wistful. It had felt as though something was beginning to fill in what had till then only been an outline. Miraculously, of course, because he hadn't known it was only an outline, like a cartoon figure breathed into life, or a kiss that awakens the sleeping lover, rising to meet the future with optimism; not knowing it had already eluded them, that it already lay in ruins behind them like the shape of what could never be.

A shadow fell across the table, dividing it into dark and light, as though everything was once again retreating to a mere outline. *The elusive mystery of life*, Dan thought. *We walk away from the edge, no longer daring to look at what might have been*. He sensed that he would carry this moment with him wherever he went, into every love affair, never finding what he was looking for: a life that does not grow old, a love that does not grow cold.

No one is dying here, he told himself. *Life will continue.*

Perhaps that was the problem. He would stay here, in Toronto, and Trevor would return to his island. They would live apart, each knowing the other existed elsewhere, at the same time, but out of reach. Only just. He saw himself walking down a tree-lined street one day years from now, his feet scuffing the leaves and imagining for a moment that he was not alone, that Trevor was there beside him. Maybe he would recall a bit of conversation, speak a few words until he remembered and stopped himself before carrying on with a shrug.

"More coffee?" Dan asked.

Trevor looked over at him. "Sure. I'm going to need it."

Dan picked up his cup and started to pour. Something stopped him. He looked out the window at his new backyard. Daylight was beginning to show at the edge of the sky. Here was one more day to get through, he thought. It sounded like a simple enough task, but then there would be all the others to follow after that.

It was time to start thinking about what he was going to do with them.

ACKNOWLEDGEMENTS

Thanks to Mark Round and Lyn Nottingham for patiently explaining to me the elusive whys and wherefores of police protocol and then some. I also extend my gratitude to the kind folks at Dundurn who make me smile and give me reason to write, as well as to David Tronetti for being a good and careful listener. Cheers to David Bowie for the late-night vibes that kept me going.